EDGE OF REALITY

A NOVEL
BY ANDREI LIVADNY

*Thank you FOR your support
and inspiration!
They mean so much to me,
Andrei Livadny.*

PHANTOM SERVER
BOOK# 1

MAGIC DOME BOOKS

Edge of Reality
Phantom Server, Book # 1
Second Edition
Published by Magic Dome Books, 2017
Copyright © A. Livadny 2015
Cover Art © V. Manyukhin 2015
English translation © Irene Woodhead & Neil P. Mayhew 2015
All Rights Reserved
ISBN: 978-80-88231-06-6

Table of Contents:

PROLOGUE

DARKNESS HUNG LOW, VEINED with crimson, growing and swelling like an abscess. From time to time it spewed clouds of ashen discharge, rapid and greedy, that melted rocks and evaporated the cracked earth, then dissipated into a toxic gray haze.

The hill towered over a spine-chilling sea of statues.

The mist disgorged the petrified figures of warriors. Steel had crumbled to rust. Silver and mithril glistened defiantly.

The scarce reddish light seeped through the eternal fog, forming bloody droplets in the curves of my armor. It trickled snake-like down my sword blade, shaping a runic script on the moon silver.

The castle's ruins rose on top of the hill. Ramparts circled the slopes. A barely discernible ash-buried road led to the castle's main gates that were formed by two monolith ledges of limestone. Once snow-white, they now looked dull and ghostly, tinged with red. Above the gate towers' liquid outlines, the donjon loomed through the toxic fog.

I stopped, glancing over the statues' faces.

My heart was empty and cold. I must have known some of the petrified warriors in the past, but I couldn't remember any of them anymore. Where were those happy days when excitement ravaged my thoughts, its waves running up and down my spine, pushing me into the thick of events?

The ash reared up, its swirls encircling me, transforming into the figures of dark guards. Their eyes were ablaze with gloom.

They charged at me from every direction all at once. Playing solo, I performed a well-practiced combo, stripping the most brazen ones of their hits. The Sky Shield ballooned out, causing a dozen Curses of Stone and some weaker debuffs to dissolve into a fountain of pure flames as my Paladin's unique abilities transformed them into a cleansing wall of return fire.

The moon blade quivered, impatient to join the battle, but the monsters had already crumbled to dust. My level was way above their league.

I'd been trying to delay this moment for as long as I possibly could. The last quest castle. The last tiny blank space on the now completed map of the game's enormous world. Another reality I'd traveled far and wide.

I took another step. More ashen twisters flared up, disgorging the blurred outlines of new attackers, but...

Boring. Even my new sensation-enhancing device didn't help me much with its ability to experience things beyond the usual human range of feeling. My perception had been enriched with unique gameplay phenomena: I could feel energies coursing down my armor, the very fabric of Creation flowing in these veins of the level-430 Paladin that I now was.

My path led toward the donjon. There I would take out an artifact I'd found long ago and lay it onto the cracked altar. The crimson abscess of the sky would finally break, sunrays bursting through the parting thunderclouds. The disappointed screams of the dark guards being cast out into the gloomy depths of the virtual world would be replaced with a pure crystal chime. The castle's walls would shake themselves free from cinders and the bubbled molten crust as its majestic buildings would once again rise from the dust of oblivion.

The light would take me in — to no avail.

The game developers had nothing left to reward me with. Not one of them would consider creating a new patch for a single player, opening new mind-blowing locations or introducing new quests unachievable for all the other gamers.

I had made too much progress. Now I had to leave. To seek new experiences in the vast expanses of the Net — something yet unknown and unexplored. But was this at all feasible?

It had to be. It was purely a question of luck. And a lot of it. No matter how clever the game designers and script writers believed themselves to be, I didn't think they could offer anything truly new to my seasoned eye.

* * *

STILL, THE WORLD OF THE CRYSTAL SPHERE offered me one last surprise, rekindling a weak spark of interest within me.

Higher up the hill, the earth groaned open. Lumps

of dry clay showered my armor, revealing a dim crevice.

I shifted my gaze, pointing the cursor to this new object. Surprisingly, the interface remained dead, offering none of the expected information. Three of the dark guards aborted their attack and swung round, scaling the rockslide and diving into the gaping opening.

Excuse me? Who could have possibly taken my top place on the local NPCs' aggro lists?

I scanned through logs looking for a missed debuff that could have possibly reduced my stats, but found none. Everything seemed to be fine.

The next moment the depth of the crevice exploded in a series of rhythmical flashes of light. I could hear the earth grumble as the dark guards screamed their disappointment, dying.

I'd never believed in guesswork. Mechanically I renewed the Sky Shield when I saw a player, barely alive, crawl out of the narrow crevice. An unfamiliar avatar. His weird gear resembled an overall covered in engine oil. His face was engraved with a complex silver tattoo distorting his features. An artifact lurked within his right eye socket — it must have been Dwarven craftwork, judging by the machinelike twitching of the wires that framed the transparent crystal. The stranger sported a thick collar — a *slave's* collar — complete with the remaining few links of a chain.

He struggled some more, forcing himself out, but lost his hold and rolled weakly down the slope. He tried to scramble to his feet but collapsed, convulsing, his fingers clawing the ash.

The interface remained unresponsive. It simply

failed to identify the player.

I didn't think long. The Healing Hand, no doubt about it, then the Breaking of Shackles. Wouldn't *you* be interested to find out who he was?

The former ability, capable of healing all friendly and neutral players, sent fountains of sparks into the air, showering the poor bastard. To no avail. Either he had indecent amounts of hits or he was super immune to magic.

The earth crumbled yet again, spewing out three new characters. Just over three foot tall, squat and broad-shouldered, they were clad head to toe in an armor the likes of which I'd never seen before. It was made of an unknown glossy black metal which seemed to surge with high-tension energy. Their helmets immediately caught your eye: one couldn't see their eyes at all behind the thick opaque visors made of something that looked like tinted glass.

Immediately the dark casters that guarded the castle gates aggroed them, launching a torrent of spells. First, curses of Stone, Paralysis, Strangulation, Crushing; then the skies joined in, white-hot meteors searing through the heavy clouds and bombarding the hill, exploding into cascades of fire.

The three "gnomes" didn't look impressed in the slightest.

Finally, my interface kicked back in, sporting their life bars. *Full* life bars! The space below was hatched gray. Zero mana! It wasn't restoring, either! Their names were shown as sequences of unreadable symbols — definitely a bug — followed by something even curiouser:

Race: Unknown

Level: 500+

While I was trying to fathom the meager stats, the "gnomes" (how else was I supposed to call them?) promptly distributed the targets. One of them hurried toward the slave; another one headed for me. The third one turned to face the castle gates and raised his staff that rather resembled some futuristic firearm, gunning the casters down with a long burst that reduced them to dust.

The gaming mechanics were bursting at the seams. The interface icons blinked. The strangers' levels dropped to 400+. It was as if the game engine had reevaluated them, adapting their levels to the Crystal Sphere.

This was a bit better. I went for the nearest "gnome", assaulting him with my signature combo. The moon blade ripped through the gnome's armor, sinking deep into his flesh.

He wheezed, squirting bubbling green blood everywhere. His legs gave way beneath him. Dropping to his knees, he instinctively raised his hands, clutching his severed throat. A human player, definitely. Reflexes don't lie. NPCs had a totally different body language.

The second one was forced to leave the slave alone. He leveled his gun and gave me a burst of it.

My life bar shrank to thirty percent. It was a good job I always had scrolls ready in quick access slots. Old habits die hard.

The Healing Hand!

I darted up the slope, a golden cloud of healing

sparks following in my wake, and performed a level-300 combo. My sword struggled to slice the armor that seemed to cling to it. I had barely had time to complete my move.

By then, the crevice was crusting over. It was disappearing!

The third gnome began a hasty retreat, expertly ducking for cover as he ran. I cast Weakness over him. No good. Magic wasn't working.

He disappeared from sight. More gunfire flashes came from amid the ruins. My recent apathy faded into nothing, replaced by intense interest. The castle was already enveloped in the swirls of ashen discharge as more dark guards hurried from everywhere trying to attack the gnome. Pointless: he'd chosen an excellent position, mowing down his enemies from afar.

He's mine.

My hands closed around the scroll. My stare locked onto the target. The seal crumbled in my hands. A teleport popped open. Runes glistened on the moon blade. Another combo!

This time my sword struggled with his black armor streaming with energy. The combo failed, my enemy's life shrinking by only one-third. Sturdy little bastard!

The gnome changed his grip of the weapon. Holding it like a club, he went for me. All the NPCs in the location were happily aggroing us, the ashen swirls around us obscuring the dim light of day.

I had to act fast.

Paladin's Fury performed with a moonsilver blade was a killer argument in any combat.

Bouncing off the rocks, his severed head still in the tinted helmet rolled down the slope, splashing green blood that hissed and bubbled in the air. About a hundred dark guards sprinted toward us in excitement, closing their circle.

I glared around me. Another seal crunched under my fingers. Another teleport popped open. From further up the slope came the disappointed wail of many voices that echoed behind the jagged walls of the castle's ruins.

* * *

CATCHING MY BREATH, I CROUCHED next to the freed slave, peering at the complex silver script of his unusual tattoo.

You can't surprise a player of my experience. Still, this time they'd done it. The gaming interface was still in a coma — so I had to strain my memory, rummaging through all the worlds I'd ever been to.

They didn't mean it!

The stranger's features were distorted by a web of sophisticated wiring. His slave's collar sparked defiantly, betraying its high tech nature.

The remaining two gnomes were now bleeding to death, slaughtered by me. Their avatars, so obviously not of this world, were fading, disappearing. No, I had nothing against game developers flexing their imagination muscles, but you shouldn't forget that their efforts were restricted by the given game's conventions.

They simply couldn't allow a botch like that — neither as an insider joke nor for any experimental purpose. Cyborgs stuffed with implants, in a world of sword and sorcery — one that had won over users exactly by the purity of its fantasy content?

What could have happened then? A hacking attack?

I watched the tunnel between the two worlds contract. The crevice was shrinking, its outline blurring. Finally it turned into a fiery dot, flared up and disappeared, leaving behind only the sound of small rocks crumbling down the slope.

I had about a couple of minutes until the NPCs respawned. I glanced over at the cyborg-like monsters. What if they were NPCs too? Would they come back to life? Would this world's engine accept them?

Remembering my dangerously shrinking life bar, I decided not to push my luck. This definitely was an extraordinary event. I glanced over the screenshots I'd made earlier. They confirmed my initial suspicions: better safe than sorry. Picking the slave up under his armpits, I dragged his body further down the hill, leaving a good thirty paces between us and those squat implant-stuffed bastards.

He groaned weakly.

"Hey? You okay?" I peered into his face. This time the virtual cursor helpfully highlighted the crouching figure.

????? Level 18. Mechanic.

The "Mechanic's" life continued to dwindle, losing its last hits. I tried to heal him. No way. The red bar kept shrinking slowly but surely.

Immune to magic. What a shame.

His eyes opened. The mangled lips twitched in pain. His hoarse whisper scorched the air. Blood bubbled up through his lips, preventing me from hearing him well.

"The Phantom... Server..."

"Say it again?"

He struggled to focus, blood gurgling in his throat, then wheezed,

"The Phantom... Server... find it..."

For a second, I remained speechless. A quest from a different world?

Curiosity sparked within me. What if this was meant for me? An exclusive quest, a secret location? A gift from the developers attempting to keep the interest of one particular player?

I hurried to open the quest list.

As if. No new entries there.

"?????" was losing his last hits. I made one more attempt to heal him. I had this one-off ability allowing you to restore a thousand life points. But the spell's aura bled through his body and impotently ran down the slope, radiating glowing golden circles.

Dead.

Once again ash swirled in the air. I was forced to jump to my feet, accepting the challenge.

It took me about thirty seconds to smoke the nearest guards.

I turned around. The slave was gone. So were the strange monsters. They had disappeared to respawn somewhere else, leaving nothing behind but the gasping whisper echoing in my mind,

The Phantom Server... Find it...

CHAPTER ONE

LOGOUT

I WAS SLUMPED in a sagging old chair.
Toxic industrial haze wove patterns behind my studio's window. The green light of the airtightness indicator glowed reassuringly.

Welcome to technosphere. Unlike the cyber world, here any equipment failure could result in some very nasty consequences. No amount of buffs could help you here.

It took me several minutes to come round. For the last six months, the virtual capsule with its massage rollers and life support modules had been serving me as a clothes dump. Why, might you ask?

I'll tell you. By then, I had abandoned the relative safety of a virtual capsule in exchange for new experiences unknown to me before. Now I didn't need the holographic screens with their poor version of cyberspace; I didn't need the capsule's impact membranes poking my ribs. I always carried the virtual world around with me. A small implant had been fixed behind my ear like an earpiece, hugging my temple and part of my cheekbone, sinking millions of its nano needles into my skin.

Its flesh-colored plastic concealed unknown quantities of chips, all forming a complex neural system connected to my personal nanocomp bracelet. That was all it took. The future of the gaming industry.

A product of the highest-end technologies, this neuroimplant processed gaming sequences in its artificial neural network which in turn formed series of impulses it then sent directly to the brain. The neural network was learning constantly, generating new sensations, even those totally alien to the real world.

Risky, you might say?

I wouldn't argue on this one. But I didn't care, anyway. A man who's long sunk to the depths of cyberspace has more dangerous things to worry about, each of them capable of sentencing him to a long and agonizing death.

Like boredom, for one.

You can't fight boredom. To me, living in the real world is unbearable. It's gray and poor. And don't even try to convince me otherwise. I'd made my choice and burned my bridges. The virtual capsule had been great — until a certain moment when my mind had learned to tell truth from fiction. I wanted to live there, in these worlds of infinite possibilities, but every day had been worse than the one before it. The 3D space kept losing its depth. My eye had learned to see through illusions. All I could see was the shell of my high tech prison. I struggled with depression, losing my mind, as I realized that there was no way the virtual world could ever replace the real one. Which was why I'd agreed to this experiment. It had brought thrills back into the game, offering lots of new opportunities previously unavailable to me.

I scrambled off the chair and shuffled my feet into the kitchen to feed my precious biological body.

The little icons before my eyes didn't disappear. The artificial neural network couldn't be switched off — it just changed interfaces, closing or opening certain options. Glancing at the clock, I dialed the delivery service for my late dinner. A couple of minutes later, the hydraulic elevator hissed. A capacious cylinder rolled out into the receiver tray. I picked it up and sat at the table, pulling the sides off and ripping open the seam along the middle. The wrapper unfolded, becoming a placemat laden with everything one could need. Food, drinks, each in its own airtight container. Healthy and nutritious, but most importantly, convenient. No need to go anywhere.

I had two meals a day and slept in the virtual capsule. So practical and familiar. So safe.

A mental disorder? Absolutely. I am the first to admit it. Still, I wouldn't change anything.

I'd received my first holographic nanocomp for my twelfth birthday. Since then, the real world had gradually faded into insignificance. I was increasingly reluctant to come back from the game. Had it been down to me, I'd never have come back at all. But unfortunately, our technologies still weren't up to much. This neuroimplant I had was the first sign of things to come.

I was thirty-nine. Single, well-off, commitment free. How I earned my living... I'll tell you about that later.

I ate unhurriedly as I skimmed through my mail and PM box, deleting most messages with a swipe of my eyes.

Having discovered nothing of interest, I opened the search engine and entered *Phantom Server*.

I had to admit it had piqued my interest. The rest, as experience had taught me, was purely a question of application.

No results found matching your search criteria.

The incoming call icon flashed insistently. It was from the developers of my unique wetware. Vultures. They had to have their daily report on the dot.

Okay, okay. A promise is a promise. My eyesight clouded, blurring out of focus, while the artificial neural network scanned my mind, uploading some of the more memorable neurograms.

A test model, yeah right. The implant's developers promised that the finished version would perfectly comply with the Privacy Law. Somehow I didn't believe them.

Having finished with my daily report, I rose and walked over to the window, feeding the wrapper with its unfinished dinner into the macerator on my way. I just wasn't hungry.

No results found, they said? I stared at a city enveloped in a cloak of emissions. The urban landscape served as an abstract backdrop to the more and more search reports that flashed before my eyes. No results found.

Could whatever had happened simply have been

my imagination playing up?

No way. Impossible. It wasn't for nothing I'd uploaded my daily report. Had they found the slightest malfunction in the implant, they'd have already been on my case by now, telling me to switch on the dedicated communication channel, then "sit comfortably and try not to think about anything".

What were they waiting for, then? Hadn't they noticed the sudden surge of emotional activity in my logs?

Anxiety was growing within me. I could definitely smell a rat there somewhere.

Should I leave it as it was? Should I maybe take a shower and go to bed? Then first thing tomorrow morning I could start looking for a new game world that could become my life's purpose for the next few years.

Still, the spark of awakened curiosity began to burn me from inside — the anxiety within me growing, inexplicable. What if everything that had happened was the neurocybertechs' setup?

Admittedly, I hated feeling like a half-dead mouse at the mercy of a fat cheeky cat. It always gave me the desire to strike back.

The Phantom Server.

The name sat like a thorn in my memory.

Never mind. I'd had this implant for about a year and had a decent idea of how it worked. I'd also come up with a couple of backup scenarios in case someone tried to use me as a guinea pig.

I'm relaxed. I'm perfectly happy. I have no disturbing thoughts. I peeled off my clothes and headed for the shower.

The neural network was safely sealed within its

plastic casing. Water couldn't damage it anyway, but the developers apparently wanted to minimize any risks considering the device's cost. So I'd long noticed that the mnemonic interface shut down every time I took a shower. I also knew about the micro slot in the machine's lower part. Currently it was empty, but I'd already found out, by very careful trial and error, that it was perfectly adapted for a 1Tb memory card. A couple of them I kept at home just in case, filled with pre-recorded neurograms of deep sleep.

I picked the slot's lid with my nail and pushed the card into its groove without locking it. It wasn't yet time. I turned the water off, toweled myself dry and jumped into the capsule, leaving the lid open. I set it to repose mode and moved my body around, making myself comfortable. Like, I was fast asleep.

After a few minutes I touched the implant, pushing the card in until it clicked. I'd done it many times before. Predictably, the icons of the internal interface faded.

I waited some more, just to be on the safe side, then slid out online. Reality disappeared. I closed my eyes and entered a very rare login I virtually never used.

The chat room was crap: empty and boring. I entered a code phrase. The PM window flashed, the cursor blinking inquiringly.

The Crystal Sphere. Agrion. The Tavern.

OK.

My message had been accepted.

* * *

THE TAVERN WAS NOISY AND PACKED with players. There, no one could tell me from a newb. I walked in humbly, looking for an empty table at the back.

"Hi," a rather scruffy goblin took a place next to me. I looked at his hands. The sign was correct. I showed him mine.

We spoke quietly without attracting any attention.

"So you finally decided to make a few bucks? It's been a while. How's it going?"

"Fine."

The scruffy goblin was in fact my first online employer, no less. We went back quite a while, doing business together — for whatever good it had done us.

By the age of fifteen (by then I had already sunk in cyberspace, devouring various gaming worlds indiscriminately regardless of their genre) I'd realized that the best and most interesting bits lay beyond the average teenager's financial and age restrictions.

Well, parental control chips were easily hacked by amateur experts the same age as myself. This problem could be easily fixed — unlike the financial one. I'd long given up on my studies and even managed to get a student loan, immediately splurging it and unable to keep up with the compound interest. I could sense I was walking a tightrope; no — running a tightrope, keeping my balance purely out of habit.

I played passionately and without mercy. I didn't have time to level my chars properly. The way things were going, I was looking at a career as a low-level PK — a Player Killer — as I kept clutching at straws in the naïve belief that the loot from the killed players would allow me to stay in the game for just a little longer, trading it in for in-game currencies.

Which was when, as luck would have it, I'd met Arbido. I'd never known his real name — nor had I even tried to find it out. He, however, had a complete real-life rundown on me.

Our first meeting had been brief and in many respects unpleasant (for me at least) but, as I later found out, very productive.

He promised to pay off my loan and sort out my school innuendos. Naturally, he couldn't upload any knowledge to my head but at least he seriously promised to improve my grades and make sure no one pestered me in the future.

What did he want in return? My gaming skills. My yet undeveloped talent that I'd been wasting so uselessly. Actually, he wasn't interested in my talents at first. My initial jobs were quite primitive. Have you ever heard of a dedicated driver? You haven't? That's funny. The idea is, you are granted access to a client's gaming account. Then you get all sorts of tasks, from completing certain quests that the client either can't or won't do himself — or even leveling his char. Some of the tasks can be rather mind-numbing, like ore crafting or collecting certain ingredients. But once you become acquainted with a particular world, learning its secrets and tricks, it takes you less and less time to complete your tasks.

That's how I'd started earning online. Working as a char driver was only the beginning. Soon they began entrusting me with more complex — and dirtier — jobs.

Gradually I started learning the lay of the land. I would register a character in some popular game world, level it up, then sell it through Arbido. Or use it myself. I was accepting orders for artifacts or unique armor you just couldn't buy — because they were dropped by particular mobs.

If you'd like to know more about it, it's no secret. An Internet search will provide you with a long list of these and similar paid services.

Arbido had a rather solid business. He had thousands of players working for him in most popular games. He was very correct, too: ripping off a client just wasn't worth risking his reputation. Recently I'd worked for him on a few VIP orders even though I didn't need the money any more. I was quite capable of earning my own way now. The game had taught me that.

The goblin's familiar squint landed on me. "I've been following your progress," he said. "This is a young world. Completely virgin. Should we bleed it dry?"

I shook my head.

Arbido raised a quizzical eyebrow. "Don't you think you're taking the game too seriously? You need to shed this Paladin role once in a while," he said with fatherly concern in his voice. "Very well now, what is it? My time is money, you know that. How many Easter eggs have you found?"

He never wasted himself on little things. What he needed was gold mines and mithril fields. Oh yes, I knew of a few, plus a few more locations that were off limits to average players. They would only be open after a couple of years. But me, I did know how to arrange a premature global event that included mass raids on the unexplored territories. I was the one with the portal keys.

"I've come to you as a client," I said.

He frowned, trying to imagine me as a customer. "Spit it out."

"I need an account at Phantom Server," I said matter-of-factly, not even questioning the doability of my request.

He immediately knew what I meant. The search engines didn't, but he did! His stare became decidedly prickly.

"Don't you think you're getting too big for your boots?" he grumbled. "What's wrong with this one?"

"Boring."

"Then you should create an alt character. Try some other ways of leveling him. This world has potential. You're not bored, if you ask me. You're just plain lazy."

I cast a surprised glance at him. He'd never been known to reject a client.

"Just say you can't do it," I shamelessly upped the ante.

"It's a shady project," he shook his head. "A closed world stuck in the alpha testing stage."

He frowned, probably realizing he'd said too much. "Are you fishing?" his practiced stare halted at my temple. Naturally, my current avatar had nothing there at all, no signs of a neuroimplant whatsoever, but you couldn't keep a cat in a bag for too long. I hadn't told him anything. He must have found out via his own channels. He was one influential motherfucker.

I gulped. "No, it's a clean game. I wanna try. I'll pay you."

"You idiot," he answered ungrudgingly as he thought about something. "Didn't you hear me? They're alpha testing it. It's a closed shop. No paying members. If they didn't invite you, it means you're not good enough. No idea what at. You can knock at their door, no problem. They might even let you in. But then it gets weird."

"Please explain."

"Please pay. If you're so smart it's gonna cost you."

"How much?"

A six-digit sum appeared in the interface window. It wasn't in any of the in-game currencies, either. Arbido was playing it big and proper. At the time, it didn't even occur to me that he might be trying to protect me from any potential problems.

Greedy bastard. He knows I don't have that kind of money.

"How about a swap?" I offered a solution.

"For what?" his stare was cold.

So I made a counter-proposition. A list of all the yet undiscovered — and unmapped — unique locations plus some artifacts from my own little stocks.

"Not enough."

"Are you raving mad?"

What was wrong with me today? I just couldn't control myself. I hadn't even noticed the moment when the spark of initial interest had transformed itself into a little bonfire of still unclear but already pressing desires. I felt like the last needer but I could do nothing about it.

"As you wish," he shrugged and stood up, about to leave.

"No, wait," I threw in the closed locations and the portal keys.

He sat back down, reproach in his stare. "Aren't you gonna regret that?"

"Regret what?" I flashed him a stubborn fearless

smile trying to suppress the ever-growing anxiety. "Happy with the price now?"

"Yeah. Now look. This is how it works," he got straight to the point. "This is a new-generation game, the game of the future," as he spoke, the information I'd just swapped was changing hands. "How long since you've had the implant?'

"About a year."

"They've been testing the Phantom Server for five years now. They only accept veteran players. They want single loners — those who have no family or friends in real life."

"What's the catch?"

"Not many of them come back. They log in and that's the last you hear of them. I do know that all of them had these same neural network implants installed first. Just like yours. Also, there're rumors, of course. About worlds being breached. Virtually all games have had incidents of those. All sorts of weird creatures crawling out of the woodwork. According to my information, they're all from the Phantom Server. But there is no direct evidence. The admins make sure they cover up all trace."

I listened, piecing the information together.

The first game based on direct neurosensory contact? That was breathtaking. Every ounce of adventure spirit within me cheered at the news. I'd already had the opportunity to experience one side of this new technology. Admittedly, I was impressed. What could be waiting for me there if every object in that world was interacting with the neural network?

Surely Arbido simply was unable to grasp it all. But I, I could see it clearly: the only reason those players hadn't come back was because they didn't want to!

My craving for a new adrenaline fix had got out of control, bundling reason into the farthest corner of my mind. As long as my brain was dominated by my selfish urge, it blanked out any suspicions the old man could offer.

"You don't think they might have died there, do you?" he snapped, ripping the wings off my hopeful dream.

"Why would they?"

"These things are dangerous," Arbido glanced at my right temple again. "They cause brains to pack up."

"Know of any cases?"

"No, I don't. But I have reasons to believe it. Trust me."

"You can stuff your reasons-"

"So you've made up your mind, then?" he asked with a bitter smirk.

"Yes, I have! You can't talk me out of it."

"Well, suit yourself. Go back home. And wait."

"I'm gonna stay here a bit. I need to auction a set of armor."

"Leave it to me. And all your other accounts, you need to either sell them or rent them out to me."

"Depends on the price."

"Have I ever had you over?"

"Very well. I can do that. You can keep the money for the time being."

"Why?"

"You never know. I might need some cash injections, whatever."

He didn't say anything, just sat there all grim and gloomy as if I was already dead.

"So is it a deal?"

Arbido nodded.

Moments later, his avatar disappeared.

Logout

NIGHT HAD SWALLOWED THE REAL WORLD. I was pacing the room, stopping and staring out of the window trying to while away the anxious hours of waiting.

You think I'm an addict? A nutcase? Take a look out the window.

The stepped silhouettes of the megablocks pierce the clouds. Smog envelops the wind-pervaded city stretching half the continent. The buildings' blank walls are prudishly covered with eerie holograms; rivers of lights flow between them, disappearing into the clouds of all-pervasive emissions. The city gasps, struggling for breath, still alive and full of energy — but in all honesty, it's been hopelessly dead for a long time.

Only the *serves* can survive outside the sealed house units. It's their planet now. The only place for me and billions of others that still guarantees some semblance of sanity is cyberspace.

When I was young I used to think it was infinite. But with time I started to understand that most virtual worlds are just copies of each other. What used to take your breath away — the world, the gameplay — had long faded. My disenchanted mind demanded new experiences, but where was I supposed to take them if I'd done it all already hundreds of times in a hundred different ways?

Leaving the boring predictable cyberspace and going back to the miserable real life was especially unbearable. Many of you can relate. It's driving you mad, the glimmer of unknown new experiences tearing your mind apart.

The game of the future! Alpha testing, so what! I wanted so badly to give in to this new neuronet-technology world.

No incoming messages.

Waiting was unbearable. But this agonizing anticipation felt too good. A selfish cocktail of craving and adrenaline.

At three in the morning, the interface blinked.

I opened the message.

A web link. A user's name. A password.

I shivered uncontrollably as the capsule whirred its start-up gears. Why did it take it so long!

I climbed inside. The life support sensors clung to my skin.

Warning! You're entering a restricted area.

I entered the user's name and password.

Neuronet connection activated. Neuroimplant connected.

I closed my eyes, collapsing into the void.

PHANTOM SERVER
LOGIN

I WAS SHAKING.

I couldn't think straight. Never had my introduction to a new game world been accompanied by such a bunch of weird and painful sensations.

I couldn't see a thing. I tried to move but I didn't feel my body. My temples throbbed with a fading pain.

All the interface icons were gray.

A painful tingling sensation pervaded my muscles. My unfocused mind barely registered some of the vague shadows that slid past. A whimpering, similar to a child's crying, filled my brain.

I wheezed, ripping my lungs with the effort.

I was lying on something hard and covered in frost. That's all I could tell at that moment. The air was cold and depleted of oxygen.

Messages flashed before my mind's eye.

Mind expander: not installed
Metabolic corrector: not installed
Reflex enhancer: not installed
Semantic processor: not installed
Alternative start conditions met.
Alternative start initialized.

By then I had half-caught my breath and was now courageously waiting for all the opening fanfare. You know what I mean, a full-dimensional visual masterpiece.

The pain returned in a flash. I failed to suppress a shriek. A hot breathing burned my cheek, forcing me to open my eyes. Their first "visual effect" was incredible. Some ugly creature the size of a monkey was trying to bite through my weird gear, its fat neck ring preventing the monster from sinking its teeth into my throat.

Instinctively I struggled with the failing muscles, trying to whack it nice and hard. The creature leapt back and disappeared into the darkness, crying like a little child.

That was spooky.

I couldn't believe their authenticity levels. I could still feel the creature's hot greedy breath on my cheek. Adrenaline was clouding my gaze crimson. Shivers ran over me; I was well and truly feverish.

Slowly the interface icons lit up one by one, coming to life.

Immediately I opened the logs and checked the entry,

A Kicker, a 15-level Xenomorph, has attempted to bite your throat.

Your aggressive reaction has scared the Kicker who runs away.

Yeah, right, I thought struggling to sit up. This had to be a newb location by definition. Why level 15 NPCs? Why the alternative start? Where was my character generation menu? Where were all the talent trees and available skill points? Where... where, in fact, was I?

It was cold. I was freezing in the heart of some wintry void. The floor was smooth — definitely not earth or stone. Was it some kind of artificial installation?

Messages started flashing before my mind's eye.

New quest alert! Alone.
Explore the location. Try to find at least one human being.

New quest alert! The Sleep of Reason.

In order to gain access to the character development panel, you need to find and install a mind expander.

New quest alert! It's Your Problem.
In order to survive, you need to find and install a metabolic corrector.

New quest alert! The Price of Freedom.
In order to be able to move between locations, you need to find and install a reflex enhancer.

New quest alert! I Can Hear Them.
In order to understand the language of Xenomorphs, you need to find and install a semantic processor.

Epic quest unblocked: Phantom Server.
In order to unblock new skill tree branches and activate the global story, you need to find out who created the world around you.

I opened the character generation menu.

Zander. Level 1. Human

A human body outline, gray slots, weird armor.
I studied the prompt.

A light armored suit. No integrated weapons. Contains five slots for dedicated cyber modules. Not airtight without a helmet. The environment sensor reports 10% oxygen content. Toxic contaminants content: 20%.
Effect: you are struggling to breathe. Every minute without protection deprives you of health and life. In

order to survive, you need to install a metabolic corrector or find a helmet.

I heard more whimpering and whining that now sounded more like hysterical laughter. It seemed to be coming from all directions.

I burst out coughing. They were right: breathing was a struggle. The location swam before my eyes. I saw double.

You have received a dose of toxins.

What were they thinking of! I scrambled to my feet and struggled to focus, looking around.

Judging by the echoing sounds, the location was huge. I couldn't see its walls. The floor was covered in ice. No idea which way to go: the place was sinking in this hostile, arctic, toxic haze.

For the first time in years I felt lost. This was like none of the game worlds I'd ever been to. On one hand, my curiosity grew with every heartbeat. It had been a very long while since I'd experienced anything like this: a half-forgotten intoxicating feeling of an invalid leaving his bed for the first time, greedily taking in all the revived sensations.

In the twilight depths of my mind, Experience was holding a whispered counsel with Caution, making it clear: this was one hell of a world. They call it an alternative start? I'd very nearly had my throat torn out!

I had to think fast. My every breath stripped me of hits. I needed to find the helmet.

Question: where did they want me to find it? I activated the quest and switched over to the map. No direction markers. The location was swimming in the mist of war. It looked as if the difficulty levels of the alternative start were all maxed out. Specially for some hardcore lovers.

The first impressions made it clear: it looked as if I was stuck here for quite a while. Firstly, I had to find my respawn point. Normally they're situated in safe locations where the sheer amount of neutral characters saves the newbs from immediate mortal danger.

Doubtful. This Price of Freedom quest worried me a bit. In the absence of their mysterious Reflex Enhancer I could resurrect right here. Somehow I didn't think I could change my bind point. I had a funny feeling that this "alternative start" had been introduced for a reason...

I cast another look around me, trying to inhale as little as possible. The game designers must have been away on holiday when this particular level had been introduced. The emosphere made your blood curdle. The far-off whimpering and wailing really worked on your nerves, and the cold drove you to frustration. There was also no stage setting worth mentioning.

Occasionally the floor echoed with distinct vibrations, easily recognizable as someone's heavy gait.

Never mind. I've seen worse than this. Guided by the sounds, I tried to choose a safe direction.

The icy sheets of mist clung to my shuddering body. The laughter and the whimpering seemed to distance somewhat. My heart fluttered in my chest, my breathing refusing to obey me. The life bar had already begun to shrink before I'd even met a single target!

A few minutes later I noticed an enormous mound of small sharp-edged bits of debris. Was it a rockfall? I turned and staggered toward it. The toxic fog thickened, acquiring a greenish hue. Every breath I took resulted in acute pain. Those neuroimplants were quick learners. So I wanted authenticity? There it was, the whole nine yards of it.

I doubled up in a paroxysm of coughing. Everything was swimming before my eyes.

I swung round to a rustling sound, just in time to glimpse some squat silhouettes through the haze. Mechanically I picked up one of the angular stones, not even noticing that I'd cut myself. I had no gloves. The unknown creatures disappeared from sight, replaced by a message,

You've received critical damage!

Since when? No one had even approached me yet! I stared at the piece of rock I still clutched in my hand. It was glowing — dimly and unevenly. A barely noticeable glow. I focused on the item.

Radioactive ore. Effect: radiation sickness. Any intervention is currently impossible. In order to neutralize the deadly exposure, you need to find a metabolic corrector.

Suddenly I became quite disillusioned with both the gameplay and this particular scenario. My life bar kept shrinking rapidly. My legs were shaking. I retched violently and collapsed to the floor, convulsing.

The brief agony ended in paralysis. The spasms

stopped. Darkness encroached on me, devouring my mind.

At the last moment my vision sharpened; I could see a ruptured domed ceiling overhead. My gaze penetrated the haze, making out the futuristic outline of a spaceship. It had rammed the ceiling and was forever stuck in the framework. The rockslide that had just become my ignominious and agonizing undoing was the ore that had poured out of its holds.

RESPAWN

THE HEAVY STEPS SHOOK THE FLOOR.

The toxic haze; the ground covered in a thick layer of ice; the whining noises in the dark. Been there. My fists clenched. Instinctively I waited for the monsters to attack, feeling angry, lost and deceived. Talk about a stupid death. What an embarrassment for someone with my twenty-five years of gaming experience.

What on earth was going on? The developers' main objective is to ease new players into the game, permitting them to embrace their new reality. Not alienate them! I could imagine the newbs' reaction to this kind of alternative start. They'd just slam the Logout button, end of story.

Lying on the icy floor made me shiver. I scrambled to my feet.

I felt like crap. I hadn't exactly lost interest but was dangerously close to doing so. Couldn't they give me a chance to do some leveling for a change? After the top bucks I'd paid them?

My anger kept mounting.

I hadn't yet pressed the Logout button out of

principle, even though I had every reason to believe the location glitched big time. The game was still in alpha testing, after all. Trying to stay cool, I sent a technical support ticket describing all the problems I'd encountered.

No reply. The whimpering and the laughter were growing closer, approaching from three different directions.

I could make out a squat ugly shape in the haze. Barely visible, the creature was running on all fours.

A Kicker. Xenomorph. Level 15.

Time to move my respawn point. Wish I knew how to do it though. I had no suitable skills nor artifacts. The interface had no relevant options at all.

My anger mounted some more. *Calm down,* I told myself. I needed to disconnect, then try to login again. I could see no other way. Trying to fight three level-15 mobs was an exercise in futility. I just hoped that the alternative start was a glitch. Next time I'd find myself in a normal location.

LOGOUT

SLOWLY I CAME ROUND. My apartment was warm but I was still shuddering from the rheumy cold that had permeated my bones.

My throat felt raw from the toxic fumes. One might think I'd really inhaled them. Wretched implant! High authenticity levels were all good and well but there had to be certain limits!

I gulped down some water without leaving the

capsule.

Okay. Let's try it again.

I entered the address. The familiar message popped up.

Warning! You're entering a restricted area. You must have arrived at this page by mistake.

LOGIN

THE TOXIC HAZE STIRRED.

I held my breath. Hearing the scampering sounds of approaching footsteps, I swung round. Too late. One of the monsters had already taken a powerful leap. The creature rammed my chest. A paw rose to claw me, sending fireworks of pain as it slit my head open.

Blood gushed onto the floor. I collapsed, unable to stay on my feet. The creature sprang back.

Grrrgrrr. The hunching silhouettes circled me in the dark, closer and closer.

I crawled back. The depth and intensity of feeling were mind-boggling. Everything I'd experienced before was just a shadow of what I was feeling now. Blood gushed into my eyes — I could taste it, my hastened breathing tearing up my lungs, defying all gaming stereotypes.

Their authenticity levels were going through the roof. I was gasping, struggling for breath. Blood-curdling instincts escaped my subconscious, breaking the age-old ice of boredom. I was driven by one need alone. I had to survive, whatever the price.

Grrrgrrr, a shadow rushed out of the gloom.

Instinctively I threw up my left arm to protect myself. Sharp teeth sank through the armor into my flesh, mauling the muscle. Pain pierced me from shoulder to tail bone. Everything went dark. A hoarse scream escaped my throat. Two other xenomorphs met my insane glare, apparently unsure about assaulting me. They recoiled as if they'd been burned and began circling me at a distance, whimpering hysterically.

Wheezing, I grabbed the monster by the scruff of its neck with my right hand and forced the creature off me, seeing its hateful furrowed face. Its eyes glared greedily, its teeth hurriedly munching on a piece of *my* flesh.

The room swam again. Deluded with pain, I rammed the creature's head against the floor in a fit of uncontrolled fury. Again. Again. And again. The gargling sounds, the crunching of bones breaking — I watched it all through some crimson daze, unable to stop.

You've received a new level!

The message sobered me like a slap in the face.

My fingers slackened. I looked around, but the two other xenomorphs had disappeared somewhere. Their mocking hair-raising laughter had stopped. Silence hung in the air. The new message contorted before my eyes.

You've received a new level!
Congratulations! You've received a unique human ability: Berserk. In case of your fighting unarmed with less than 5% Health, you'll be able to ignore the

enemy's defenses, dealing only critical damage.

The sight of you terrifies your enemy. They flee, unable to attack you.

I slid down onto the bloodied floor. Some of the ice had melted, forming little red puddles. I kept shuddering. Then I began to retch. I couldn't help it. I was convulsing in revulsion. A hum in my blocked ears replaced the piercing silence.

My left arm hung listlessly. I didn't feel it.

The life bar was barely glowing. The pain wouldn't subside. My injuries bled. So this was your game reality of the future?

* * *

THE BERSERK STILL SEEMED TO BE working. I could neither see nor think straight in the all-consuming agony.

I had nothing to staunch the bleeding with. I didn't have a single shred of fabric with which to make a tourniquet.

My stare stopped at the xenomorph I'd just torn apart.

Loot was loot. Even though my stomach protested fiercely. The entire gameplay seemed to defy convention. Take this Kicker, for instance. What kind of monster was that? A regular monkey with slightly more dangerous teeth and claws. And how about the emotional backdrop? What was so terrifying about it? I'd seen much worse mobs and spookier locations where your teeth literally chattered with horror. And what was this? An empty space fitted with some toxins and a handful of monkeys. Child's play, you'd say: I was getting a bit jumpy, that's all.

And you'd be right, of course. Only the problem was, I couldn't move my hand. I watched blood, hot and sticky, dripping from my fingers. Each breath stripped me of some hits but also made me feel physically sick. You wanna try?

My inner opponents promptly shut up, demoralized.

I crouched next to the xenomorph and turned him over. Did you enjoy your breakfast, you bastard?

His face was a mess of blood and gore. His skull had cracked. His teeth were gone.

So how was I supposed to search him? I could agree to lots of things but this was pure trash. What kind of developers did they think they were? He had no gear, for crissakes! All he had was his own skin covered with matted hair. Did they want me to cut his belly open?

Squeamishly (I'd never thought I was squeamish before) I touched the monster's belly. Ah! That was clever! He had a pouch there. Just like a kangaroo.

I pulled out some incomprehensible clot of slime. I weighed it in my hand, studying it, trying to focus.

A symbiont. Under normal conditions, strips you of 100 pt. Life. Offers a one-off restoration of 1000 pt. Life if you're wounded. Metabolically compatible with the Kickers, Dargians and the Haash. Its effect on human metabolism is unknown due to the fact that it has never been tested on humans.

I sensed the familiar weak spark of curiosity. I wasn't going to consume something as disgusting as that, of course. I didn't even know how I was supposed to install the wretched thing.

The lump then stirred, stretching out a semblance of a tentacle — it must have sensed blood.

Better safe than sorry, I thought as I stashed my loot away into one of my gear pockets while looking around, listening intently. What was that saying I'd heard — *You can never be too paranoid?* I couldn't agree more.

It looked like I didn't have to fear another respawn soon. The blood had already caked. The pain abated. I still struggled for breath but my life bar was gradually restoring. I couldn't fight to say the least, so I had to be cautious and act quickly before the scared xenomorphs returned.

Only then did the thought strike me: what did I even know about the Phantom Server?

Nothing, apparently, not to mention whatever meager experience I'd already had. Judging by the quests I'd received, this was some kind of technogenic world. No wonder I'd seen that spaceship or whatever it was. The very name xenomorph, too, suited the theme.

So where was I supposed to be?

Well, that I had to find out, didn't I? The obviously artificial smooth flooring could mean anything. The toxins? Likewise. I had to explore the location. As I'd already found out, the choice of direction was vital. The thicker the haze, the more toxic it was. The green glow was also pretty clear: I had to avoid it, at least until I got myself some decent gear.

I didn't even notice when this Berserk thing had worn off.

Yes, it looked like my life bar had grown a bit. Five percent or so. I tried to make a furious face to scare off any imaginary NPCs, but winced. The gaping wound that stretched from my chin to the crown of my head smarted immediately.

Never mind. I looked scary enough as I did. I couldn't see myself in the mirror and it was probably for the better.

The haze seemed thinner in one particular direction. So that's where I headed toward the unknown.

* * *

THIS TIME I'D CHOSEN the right direction. The haze thinned out quickly. I could breathe easier. Then I started coming across some weird objects.

Unfortunately, they did little to change my opinion of the designers' skill and attention to detail. Various molten structures suggested that this place had witnessed some incredibly high temperatures.

I tried to explore a few of the items. I'd stop and focus, touching a surface that looked like glass strewn with air bubbles. Pointless. The interface wasn't working. I had a funny feeling that the developers didn't really know what it was they had erected here or how we were supposed to use it.

You think it absurd?

But did you ever have to test a shamelessly raw product? I had. And I'd had the same feeling as I did here: lots of empty locations with markers that were supposed to represent most gaming objects. Utterly boring. Vast spaces where you could walk for miles without encountering anything of note.

Wait. The interface seemed to work, finally.

Now if I concentrated hard I could see the blurred, shimmering outlines of the items lurking inside the molten overhangs. I couldn't make out any details, though.

But it had to be something truly valuable.

The vitrified surface had cracked in places. I began exploring a few of these weak spots, wincing as I tapped them with a clenched fist. I didn't try too hard. My life was restoring slowly. Their regeneration rates were crap. It had been ten minutes since I'd fought the xenomorph but my every movement still hurt.

Whatever had they hidden in there? I was dying to find out. My decades of gaming experience screamed that this was some long-abandoned site. Possibly, I was the first person to have ever made it here. The items could turn out to be priceless — unique, the only ones of their kind.

There you have it. I was already drooling over it. Leaving all this booty behind was worse than nonchalance — it was a crime. Especially in my situation when I had no chance to do some proper farming.

So what did they have inside?

At that moment I sensed an unpleasant nagging feeling, as if I were a bug being watched. As if someone was deciding whether to squash me or leave me be.

I stopped and looked around but saw nothing unusual. The same darkness as everywhere else, studded with the flowing outlines of vitrified mounds.

But the objects that were inside them, I could see them much clearer now! The nagging feeling had left me, replaced by a message,

You cannot fully explore the concealed items without a mind expander.

You need to install a mind-expanding implant or purchase a mobile scanner. You can also destroy the obstacle with a suitable tool of your choice. Chances of damaging the item: 90%.

Oh well. I heaved a sigh. Those implants again. Where was I supposed to get them?

Never mind. I could always come back. I switched over to the location map. Aha. This was where I'd found the radioactive ore. And this was where I was now. I added a placemark. I absolutely had to come back at the first opportunity and do my bit of archeology.

In the meantime, my life bar had grown to thirty percent. More messages kept flashing, reporting available skill points, but at the moment I had nothing to spend them on. All of my char's talent branches were still closed.

The Admins never replied to my ticket.

* * *

I SLOWLY LIMPED TOWARD a yellowish glow I'd noticed from afar. I'd been in the game for an hour already. So far, my initial impressions had been mixed.

The terrain gradually changed. The annoying toxic haze was now gone. The enormous ceiling had become lower while the molten objects had become more diverse. Here they were taller, repeating the shape of some of the unidentified devices, forming chimeric figures, columns and arches leading me from one room to the next. There were more sources of light here. Some of those weird shapes glowed weakly, too. Now the damage to them seemed superficial; soon it was gone completely.

I had already realized that I was walking away from the epicenter of some ancient disaster. Subconsciously I expected the normal gaming process to start any minute now: the low-level NPCs would arrive, putting everything back into place.

As I took a closer look at the massive devices surrounding me, I noticed that most had been reduced to mere skeletons. Someone had done a good job ripping out everything that was still salvageable or usable. Exactly. It made the artifacts still concealed within the molten shapes all the more valuable.

If I could only find a suitable tool, go back and try to break into the vitrified mounds...

Deep in thought, I missed the new danger entirely. The floor became steeper and caved in, forming an enormous impact crater that sneered at me with its stumps of broken concrete beams and fractured construction steel. Bunches of cables snaked everywhere. I slipped and lost my balance, tumbling over, cutting myself on the sharp edges of the metallic debris.

I somehow managed to grasp onto some eroded pipe or other and clung to it, casting cautious looks below.

It was a good fifty-foot fall, no less. A yellow light seeped through an ugly gaping hole below framed with some gleaming metal. The crater was deep, almost vertical at its center. As I grabbed at the dangerously squeaking bits of crumbling ancient pipework, I looked around, taking in the opening panorama. The crater's steep sides were littered with mummified remains. Everywhere you turned, you could see bits of unknown creatures stuck between the warped pipes and the snaking cables. I noticed several steel lines disappear inside a hole at the bottom and some sort of jury-rigged welded grating that had apparently been added after the crater had appeared.

My eyes were getting used to the dim yellowish light, allowing me to see new details. Apparently this was a regularly used route and a place of many a desperate combat. Only a few of the bodies impaled on the protruding bits of construction steel looked like victims of an accidental fall.

A sudden bout of vertigo made me cling to the crumbling pipes.

You're deprived of oxygen! -2 pt. to Strength, Stamina, Agility and Perception. You can't survive much longer without a metabolic implant!

I know, I know.

I froze trying to sit out the bout of sickness — which in fact had saved me some much more serious problems.

Long shadows rushed below. A muted screeching sound crept through the rarefied air as about a dozen skinny sinewy creatures hove into view underneath and shinnied up the grating. They had no clothes on, only the familiar slave collars.

I focused on one of them. This time the interface reported without delay,

A Haash. Sentient Xenomorph. Level 17. Pilot. Current status: Prisoner.

Sentient they may be, but their frame gave me

cause for serious concern. The Haash were over eight foot tall, skinny but incredibly strong, with a reptilian-shaped skull. Their arms were long, ending in four-digit hands with strong multi-phalanxed fingers.

I froze studying them, pretending I was part of the surrounding scenery, as more shadows appeared below and began scaling the grates. This time they were stocky armor-clad warriors.

Again I focused, but much to my disappointment received no information whatsoever.

Without a mind expander, you cannot identify an opponent in a pressure suit. Find and install the implant in order to read the stats of your opponent's armor and weapons.

Well, that remained to be seen. The squat "gnomes" definitely looked familiar.

I kept watching. The Haash creatures had already scrambled up and disappeared from view.

The gnomes climbed noisily albeit with equal ease. The hum of their micromotors and the clatter of steel reached far even through the rarefied air.

A raid! This was a raid!

I counted about fifty squat figures in total. They were followed by some truly weird creatures: a separate group of what looked like jellyfish hovering in the air.

The Guides, the interface reported.

Chills ran up my spine — purely mentally, of course, considering I was dripping with sweat trying to stay inconspicuous.

The Guides definitely seemed to be the ones in control of the raid. I squinted till my eyes hurt, following their unhurried travel. Their jelly-like bodies permeated with some gristly cartilage substance were generously stuffed with various cyber modules. This became especially clear when one of the creatures brushed against a sharp metal fragment. I expected it to rip the thing open. As if! A force field flashed open. Molten metal splashed everywhere. The creature's translucent body filled with a visible grid of what looked like white-hot wire — the power fibers connecting the multitude of implants into one integrated system.

Dangerous things.

A couple of dozen heavily loaded Haash followed up the rear. Despite all their power and stamina, they staggered under the sheer weight of the huge cratefuls of equipment, struggling to climb up the grating.

I decided to check the information I'd received earlier. Locking my stare onto the last Haash in the group, I read,

A Haash. Sentient Xenomorph. Level 21. Pilot. Current status: Prisoner.

You can set a Prisoner free by destroying the collar's control module. Doing this will affect your reputation. Not all Humans will appreciate your helping a Xenomorph escape. This will affect your reputation among certain human groups depending on the levels of xenophobia they practice.

Finally some good news! I'd already started to think

this was a game for some rather sick individuals. Then again, why not? Lots of people play for goblins, orcs and other mythical creatures — so why not xenomorphs?

While I was thus thinking, the Haash group in the rear had already climbed out of the crater and disappeared from sight.

I breathed a sigh of relief, then asked myself: now where could this raid be heading? They're not after my unique items by any chance, are they?

Stop it, I told myself. *No need to be greedy.* I'd already done well for my level 2. I took a closer look at the crater's almost vertical walls with their mummified bodies pinned to the mauled metal. This was my chance to find something worth my while. I needed to get some gear and weapons before I even thought of pushing my luck further by going down the crater.

* * *

I DECIDED TO LEAVE the grating well alone and start from the opposite side of the crater.

My first impression proved to be wrong. This wasn't a crater — not technically, anyway. I'd no idea what could have caused a huge hole like this to appear nor why would its walls, initially quite shallow, had suddenly grown so steep.

Forcing my way through the chaos of misshapen metal wasn't easy. In actual fact, the structure's walls resembled a layer cake conceived by someone far removed from the culinary profession.

Imagine strong sheets of unknown metal interlaced with compact layers of various technogenic filling, such as pipelines of various diameter, power ducts (which I'd initially mistaken for reinforced steel), unidentified devices and narrow service tunnels.

I counted five such layers in total, their contents partially gutted, broken and molten. Their mechanical guts hung out, interwoven, forming an unstable and dangerous support.

I took my time climbing over. Every now and again the seemingly reliable objects betrayed my expectations, collapsing or dissolving into a treacherously loud avalanche of rubble. If I lost my grip, I'd fall to my death. My respawn point was located in the worst possible place. Considering the raid that was heading in that direction, I had better not take any chances.

I froze every time the debris came crashing down, but no one had arrived to check out the suspicious noises. Gradually I got a handle on it and threw caution to the wind. I advanced faster now.

The unusual — I'd say, excessive — authenticity levels kept reminding me of themselves. The palms of my hands were now covered in blisters. Every muscle in my body ached. Any reckless movement made my heart miss a beat.

I couldn't help it. My neuroimplant seemed to have a life of its own. It got completely out of hand, playing with my instincts and reflexes. Apparently it wanted me to know what it really felt like, doing aerobatics fifty feet up.

Whew. I made it. A five-foot pipe led deep into the floor's mysterious depths. I crawled inside it and lay there restoring my breath, my muscles sore and shaky from the unusual exercise.

Once I caught my breath, I rolled over onto my

side. A yellowed skull grinned back at me, pieces of flesh still sticking to the bone. A "gnome". Let's see what you have for me, buddy.

His pressure helmet lay some distance away. I reached out and picked it up to study it.

Not my size, definitely. The catches didn't fit, either. I focused to read,

Cargonite helmet. Part of the Cargonite armor suit. Equipped with an integrated combat scanning system. Typical of the Dargian civilization and worn by Dargian pilots, raiders and scouts. Effect: +1 to Armor. The device in the slot is a slave collar controller. The device is damaged and not in working order.

You can improve or alter the helmet to fit your own size. In order to do this, you will need a molecular converter (you will have to provide the blueprints of the desired alterations). Alternatively, you may have it done by a master craftsman in possession of the Alien Technologies Expert ability and Repairs and Science skills. Skill points required: 70.

They didn't want much, did they? I turned the helmet over in my hands and found the slot they'd mentioned. When I tried to prize the damaged device out, the following message appeared,

Skill required to remove the module: Repairs. Points required: 25.

They did like to complicate things. I put the helmet away into my generous hundred-slot inventory. The weight was a problem though. Considering the low gravity, I could carry a hundred and fifty pounds. I had no idea how it was going to affect my speed and agility, but I had my doubts. How was I going to climb down those flimsy gratings if my weight had doubled?

So he was a Dargian, then. The gnome's mummified body stuck to the pipe. I turned him over, disregarding the sickening crunching sound. One of his arms came off. Further inspection brought another discovery and yet more disappointment. His Cargonite armor didn't fit my body type, and I only managed to rip a couple of implants out of his body. Their stats were reduced to three question marks and a reminder that I needed to level up Science.

Thanks for the tip. The implants — the cyborgizing modules — weighed next to nothing, so I took them along.

The discovery I'd meant was the weapon.

It looked like a submachine gun. The entire length of the barrel was bulging with the casings of electromagnetic accelerators. The stock housed battery slots. That much was clear. But how about actually using it?

This time I was in luck.

IMP34, the interface reported. *Suitable for use by all humanoid-type creatures. Weapon class: pulse. Bullet propulsion is produced by battery-powered accelerators.*

The two indicators of the micro nuclear batteries glowed yellow. All the mechanical parts seemed to work. The rate of fire slider and the stiff firing button looked simple and well-conceived.

I couldn't help myself. I just had to try it. I had to find out how it worked, didn't I?

The result was impressive. It was a good job I'd had enough sense to point it at an old crate fifty feet away. The single shot sounded woolly. The impact produced a burst of flame as the bullet evaporated the timeworn metal, leaving behind a fire-polished hole the size of a fist.

The blast wave shuddered through the air. I ducked inside the pipe and lay low, waiting for all of the location's NPCs to come running and make a quick job of me. I changed the clip and braced myself.

I kept waiting. The pulse in my temple clocked up the seconds.

In the last hour, I'd been indecently lucky. No one came.

I'd tested my weapon. Things were looking up.

I SCRAMBLED FURTHER ON but encountered nothing extraordinary. Most bodies proved to belong to the Haash and the Dargians. They'd had one hell of a fight here. The traces of combat were everywhere: molten gaps in the metal, impact craters of energy weapons; in places, whole sections of utility lines had been cut cleanly as if with a knife.

The Haash's gear was way too large for me. Shame. Too much weight with nothing to show for it. I expanded the map and added all the details I could, marking down every item I'd found in order to come back. If only I could find a vendor trading in armor and high tech devices. I picked up two more types of pulse weapons: something that looked like a handgun and an analogue of a 12-millimeter sniper's rifle. This particular Haash had fought to the last. I counted about a dozen and a half dead Dargians around his position. Hit by his large-caliber, their armor was only good for the scrap heap.

I was seriously tired. It was time to log out and give myself a break, but I knew from experience that leaving a char in a place like this even for a short while was asking for trouble. A couple of times I glimpsed the xenomorphs' stooped outlines almost out of my field of vision. I didn't get the chance to have a better look but I took the point.

Better safe than sorry. I had to find a safe place before taking a break.

As I collected the loot, I moved closer to the grating. There, I'd have to decide whether to go down or climb up.

Going down was risky but promising. Climbing up probably wasn't a good idea. All I could find there was more xenomorphs, toxins and radiation, with the added danger of walking into the raid. Alternatively, I could find a pipe or a service tunnel and climb deep into it, barricading myself in.

Was I the only smart one here?

During my next stop, I took a good look around. The damaged lines seemed to be occasionally releasing bursts of toxins that immediately faded, dissolving into the air. Exactly my point. Why wouldn't xenomorphs use these pipes as ready-made holes to live in?

The low oxygen content didn't make my life any easier, triggering regular bouts of vertigo and nausea.

That's sorted, then. I had to go down.

* * *

CASTING CAUTIOUS LOOKS AROUND, I was approaching the makeshift steel grating, or the "bridge", as I mentally baptized it, when I had an impossible, incredible stroke of luck.

My eye chanced on something familiar. I peered at it. That's right. Something gleamed a blurred purple amid the heaps of debris, the hue identical to that of my own armor.

Without a second thought, I climbed the short distance up, grabbing at the sagging bunches of cables at the risk of falling to my death as my arms were already shaking with exhaustion.

A mouth of a rather narrow tunnel opened up in front of me. A small platform hung in front of it, apparently made with whatever had come in handy. On top of the platform was a hideout. The glow I'd noticed was produced by a glove.

A human? I pulled a rusty sheet of steel away. Behind it was indeed a hiding place.

I crouched, shaking my head. Whoever had made this was a hardcore type. He hadn't been interested in small scale, but had lain here in waiting for some big game. A large-caliber sniper's rifle, quality gear, prearranged escape routes — and still he hadn't made it. He was literally chopped down by laser beams. His armor hadn't helped him much. For some reason, I immediately thought about the jellyfish "Guides". I had a funny feeling they were the only ones capable of making such a job of a human body. Besides, the laser beams seemed to have hit him directly from above.

I still couldn't understand lots of things. Take me,

for instance. Having received deadly doses of both radiation and toxic gases, I had respawned wearing full gear. Why were these bodies slowly decaying here then, armor, weapons and all? Or was he an NPC?

Lots of questions, no answers.

His armor looked very similar to mine. I threw caution to the wind and began collecting the trophies. It took me a minute to work out the jammed fixtures of his helmet. Finally I was able to remove it — and I looked away.

Sick motherfuckers! I felt my jaw lock. It was the first time in my life that picking up loot made me feel like a grave robber.

A human skull stared back at me with its sunken eye sockets framed with long matted blond hair.

A girl?

I lay the skull gently next to the body. I wanted to turn around and leave but stopped myself just in time.

Arbido had been right. The three years I'd spent playing a paladin had seriously affected my head. This wasn't the Crystal Sphere anymore. And I wasn't the level 430 top player.

Trying not to look at the skull, I crouched and picked up the helmet.

Not a trace of human flesh inside. The discovery made me feel better. Apparently, these bodies didn't belong to dead players. Could they be part of the gory interior design?

I put the helmet on. The locks clicked shut. The neck ring rotated close. The dull milky visor began to clear. I glimpsed a brief sequence of incomprehensible system messages. With a hiss, the row of lights lining the helmet's rim flickered and went out.

You're not suffering from oxygen deficiency anymore, the interface reported breezily, then immediately threw cold water over my excitement, *Warning! The battery charge of the life support system is dangerously low!*

Well, this I could probably manage. I had already begun to find my way around this new world. I picked up a damaged rifle and studied its stock. Predictably, I found two micro nuclear batteries still intact in their slots. I replaced my old ones with these.

The power lights changed their mode to a dull green.

Excellent.

I didn't have any qualms about getting myself a pair of gloves. The blisters on my hands had by then long burst. I avoided looking at my bleeding hands nor did I have to: the pain wouldn't let me forget about the damage done.

Once I finished putting my new gear on, I received a message,

You have collected a full set of light pressure gear.

I studied the bonuses it offered. Apparently, now I could resist the toxic haze, low levels of oxygen and even spend up to two hours in a vacuum. That's what the charge still left in the batteries was going to last: two hours. I also discovered ten empty slots for additional equipment.

The helmet only had one option — which had to be extremely expensive considering its purpose. It was a set of electronic sights complete with a self-adapting system of enemy vulnerability analysis and a ballistic calculator which computed all environmental factors such as gravity, atmospheric density, wind direction and force. Absolutely indispensable for extreme long-range sniper missions.

Actually, I could use it too, couldn't I? Why not? Now I could finally hunt a few xenomorphs if I wanted to. I could do a bit of leveling, if the ammo and remaining charge in the batteries allowed.

The idea was good, with the exception of a few cons. My talent branches were still blocked. I could still grow in levels, of course, simply accumulating the new available skill and ability points. Choosing specialization, however, required some quality thinking to make sure I didn't repent at my leisure later on in the game. At the moment, I didn't have enough information about the Phantom Server world to be able to make this kind of decision.

But plain leveling wasn't going to do me much good, either. Game rules dictated that my opponents grew in levels, too. Fighting them on bare hits alone wasn't an option.

Some predicament. Should I go hunting or should I continue gathering intel, searching for the apparently so indispensable implants?

As I pondered over this, the pain in my hands was replaced with a prickling sensation. My character's cartoonish outline in the tiny status window had turned green.

Yeah, right. Was this world geared toward technology alone?

I removed my left glove and studied the palm of my hand. Just as I'd thought. Not a trace of the injuries I'd received. Imagine the regeneration rate! Having said that, the life support bar had shrunk considerably. There's no such thing as a free lunch — or a free miracle. Everything has its price.

The hunt would have to wait. I needed to stock up on batteries and other supplies before everything else.

My gaze chanced upon a mummy's withered hand. *The creature must have been a quest NPC,* I thought noticing a dull metallic glow.

A ring?

Exactly. I carefully removed it, trying to study it, but no amount of focusing helped me this time. More question marks were all I could see.

Okay. I had to start playing at some point, after all.

I slid the plain ring onto my own finger and very nearly screamed with pain.

The metal was melting! I tried to pull the morphing ring off my finger, but I could just as well pull my own finger off. My vision blurred, a sudden numbness touching the back of my head. My legs gave way under me. I slumped down, trying not to faint, and lifted my left hand, overcoming the ever-growing pain.

The liquid metal had run, forming what now looked like a signet ring made of quicksilver. Its surface turned into a diamond-shaped blob which began growing a multitude of stalks very much like the microscopic pins of my own neuroimplant. I broke into a cold sweat, watching them expand. Then they began filtering through my skin.

I suppressed a scream, gnashing my teeth, wriggling with pain and horror. To hell with such authenticity!

Grinding my teeth, I wheezed, sweat dripping to the floor. Tears welled in my eyes.

My left hand throbbed from wrist to fingertips. A

net of blood vessels appeared under the pallid skin, fiery red as if they transported liquid plasma and not blood.

I balanced on the edge of consciousness, forcing myself to stay aware. No idea why, considering the agony was dreadful. You'd think I'd have been happy to zone out for a couple of minutes — but no, I stayed awake even though the torture seemed to never end.

An intense aura enveloped my hand and flared up, dripping sparks. Then it went out.

My ears rang. In the crimson darkness a new message flashed before my eyes,

New quest alert! Alien Mind.
Availability: only Humans
You have found and absorbed a techno artifact of the Founders era. Find four more in order to put together a complete module.
Reward: Unknown.

That's when it finally clicked.

I turned my head slowly and looked at the remains of the blonde girl. Her skull grinned ungainly, staring at me in silent sympathy as if foreseeing my own fate.

I remembered Arbido's warning.

No. I couldn't believe that this girl was a dead player.

I had to come back to this question at some other point in time.

* * *

THE REMAINING DESCENT WENT without any new surprises.

The armor was comfortable, leaving plenty of space for movement. I used my new sniper system to study the way ahead but it didn't detect any traps or enemies lying in wait.

I slung the gun over my back and slid down the cable. Had it not been for the gloves, it would have stripped my skin to the bone.

I landed in a rather small room flooded with a dull yellowish light. No furniture, no equipment — I only noticed the gaping holes where some sort of mountings had been ripped out of the walls. Through a rather human-size doorway I caught a glimpse of a bending corridor.

The only way was straight on.

Honestly, I wasn't a big fan of technogenic post-ap worlds but I was left with no choice. Besides, they kept continuously rekindling my interest, adding a liberal dose of cheap thrills.

The silence was dull and muffled. Mechanically I glanced at my left hand. The pain was long gone and so was the numbness. I was dying to remove the glove but I stopped myself just in time. The moment wasn't quite right.

The short arching corridor took me to a large low-ceilinged hall. Here, the air was very rare. The sound of my footsteps died on the noise-reducing flooring that felt spongy and springy underfoot.

I looked around. The place resembled a large looted warehouse. Everywhere I looked I could see broken containers — oblong with rounded corners. Lots of sectionalized bulkheads hindered my advance. The shelving spaces within them fit the murky-green containers perfectly.

I proceeded slowly and carefully, casting an

occasional glance on the map. The gun in my hands had offered little security so far. I knew from experience that until I had tested it in battle, the two of us wouldn't be inclined to trust each other.

Nothing special was as yet happening, and still tension was growing inside me, a mind-chilling premonition ringing like a taut string.

Another bend. Another sectionalized bulkhead. This time the containers weren't broken but just lay there in a heap. I tried to prize one open. No way. Not a sign of a lock or any other access device.

Yet another bend. I could see the outline of the room clearly on the map. Beyond it, everything was dark. Was it a dead end?

There was one way to find out.

I stepped out, bracing myself for whatever might come next. I expected anything.

But not this.

This was beyond all expectation.

I slowed down, unthinking, oblivious to everything around me, not even noticing that the containers behind my back had begun to glow with the same coursing of static. Then their tops fell apart into segments which began to open like mechanical flowers.

But I hadn't seen it yet. This understanding would come later. Now my gaze was slowly sinking into the Void.

An entire wall of the large room was in fact an enormous observation blister. Beyond it, billions of bright stars clustered generously in space.

I was smitten. Slowly I approached the window, amazed at the clarity and the thinness of the material that separated me from the vacuum and its eternal cold. More pulses of energy shimmered across its surface.

A force field?

All the questions crowding my mind had faded away, losing their importance. Countless more details came into view. I could see a large ledge one level below, its ribbed surface arching toward the stars. Its compartments were shaped rather like launch pads — some were empty while others offered a glimpse of spaceships ready to take off. Judging by their size, they must have been airspace hybrids.

Two planets glowed at a distance. One was yellowish brown surrounded by several rings; the other a light bluish gray blotched by swirling clouds.

I began to shiver. A multitude of tiny sparks could be seen moving on the foreground of the magnificent constellations. Immediately my helmet reacted to my mental state, enlarging the sparks and bringing them closer one by one, switching between potential targets.

Enormous space stations floated in the dark. A plethora of cargo craft and warships scurried between them.

Before I could get a good look at them, the helmet switched to other objects. Several clusters of some technogenic Leviathans drifted through space, their outlines dark and menacing, their hulls gaping with past impacts. I was looking at the aftermath of a space battle between some ancient Titans!

My heart sank in awe. The sheer scope of it dwarfed you, teasing your imagination. All this knowledge to pursue! Would one life be enough to explore every corner of this stellar system? And what if there were even more of them here? I focused on one particular spark of a spaceship orbiting the grayish-blue planet until it zoomed in to a reasonable size, descending, actually entering the planet's atmosphere!

Yeah, right. Did they mean you could land on a planet here?

That could expand the already-impressive world to the size of infinity. And that was only what I could see and grasp now. By the fact that the stars were stationary I concluded that the space station I was currently on didn't rotate, which must have left scores of unknown objects hidden from view. I could only guess about the true scope of this world.

The scintillating shock of this sudden change of scenery began to release me. I wasn't yet trying to process what I'd just seen but I was already celebrating all the new opportunities multiplied by the new gameplay's doubtless authenticity.

A suspicious noise distracted me from the scene. I swung round, instinctively raising my weapon but having no chance to shoot first. Lightning-bolt discharges hit me from every direction at once.

For a split second, the armor had withstood their pressure. Then my muscles froze solid.

You've been paralyzed!

Several mechanical creatures were approaching me. They looked like spheres a couple of feet in diameter, with lots of sensors. Their ribbed tentacle-like manipulators writhed around freely.

Dargian combat drones, my interface offered helpfully.

Another lightning bolt hit me. Everything went

dark.

* * *

I CAME ROUND IN A DARK PERSONNEL module, cramped and dirty, divided slapdashly into tiny little cells.

My armor was gone and so was my gun. I was dressed in some crumpled oversized gray clothes. On my neck was a slave collar.

I could barely see and I definitely couldn't think straight.

Through the thick gloom I glimpsed a few Haash-like shapes. One huddled on the floor in the cell next to mine; another clenched the bars of one opposite, piercing me with his glare; the third one was crouching, whining and rocking from side to side.

That was me done here. Enough for today! All I could feel was a mind-numbing exhaustion bordering on indifference. Never before had I ever been so depleted both physically and morally.

Should I just sit there cursing myself for being so gullible? What was the point? I definitely hadn't been the first one who'd frozen open-mouthed at the observation window, dumbfounded, exposing his back to the conveniently arriving drones.

A noob trap.

Very well. So I'd lost my gun and my gear. They hadn't killed me on the spot which meant they intended to use me. For the time being, my avatar wasn't risking much — meaning, things were unlikely to get worse.

That was settled, then. Time to log out. I needed a break and a bite to eat, as well as some quality sleep and time to think my options over.

I pressed the virtual button. Nothing happened. Instead, a message popped up,

Your current status: Prisoner. According to the Terms and Conditions you accepted by signing, you cannot exit the testing mode while being imprisoned. We strongly recommend you activate the in-mode by sending a remote command to your capsule. If you are unable to do so personally, send a message to our technical support team to visit your current physical location.

They were too much! All my apathy was gone in a flash.

I hadn't signed any terms or conditions! I hadn't even seen them!

I cut myself short.

Arbido. The bastard! He'd signed it electronically in my name, hadn't he? How else was he supposed to register a Phantom Server account for me?

I pressed the logout button again.

New quest alert! A Prison Break.

Find a way to escape from your current imprisonment. In order to do that, we strongly recommend you activate the in-mode. If you are unable to do so personally...

With a swipe of my eyes, I got rid of the message and crouched on the floor.

The Haash opposite was still staring at me.

Whatever.

I fell deep in thought, none of it particularly rosy. The moment I was out of here, Arbido could kiss his reputation goodbye. Then again, what was the point of him risking it for the dubious pleasure of setting me up? No. I wasn't buying it. He couldn't not have read the TAC before signing it. Not with his experience. Something smelled very badly here.

This logout ban should have sent alarm bells ringing. Then again, he *had* warned me — or at least hinted at it. So what had he been playing at? Had he hoped I'd become a mindless chunk of flesh wound with cables? And what were my prospects like now? A lifelong coma in the tender care of miscellaneous life support systems?

After a while, the door clanged open. One of the "gnomes" walked in, accompanied by two drones. The lights went on automatically. The Haash stepped back into their cells trying to stay as far from the passage between them as possible.

Still brooding, I studied the gnome. Disgusting. There was nothing human about him. A pushed-in nose, a pair of nasty beady eyes. A long face, an enormous toad-like mouth. Instead of hair, his head was covered with warts. What a heinous creature.

I focused on him.

A Dargian. Sentient Xenomorph. Level 22. Slave Driver.

He had tons of hits — at least five hundred — plus two purple bars and an orange one. Let's presume that the purple ones signified the two drones' status. Where did that leave the orange one? A particular skill? An energy supply?

Pointless trying to second-guess it. I was going to find it out sooner or later, anyway.

I just couldn't work out what had prompted them to come up with such crippling imprisonment terms?

There was a catch there somewhere, I just knew it. I also knew that getting to the bottom of the logout ban wasn't going to be easy. Still, I would do it.

In the meantime, the Dargian stopped in front of my cell.

I didn't avoid his stare. I had nothing to lose. Somehow I doubted they'd changed my respawn point. But still I didn't want to find out.

He grinned, as if reading my thoughts, and pointed at the Haash. On his signal, the drones bent their ribbed tentacles and peppered the prisoner with pulse charges.

Blood and pieces of flesh flew everywhere. Then I noticed the air shimmering green to my right.

A respawn.

The Haash winced with pain, growling under his breath. Point taken. They made it perfectly clear that my death would be equally painful and ignominious, followed by my immediate reinstatement as a slave.

Lesson learned. I put this particular Sentient Xenomorph on my personal KOS list. For those not in the know, KOS stands for Kill on Sight.

He grinned again. The magnetic locks clicked. The door of my cell slid aside.

I lunged forward, aiming for his throat. My collar self-constricted, strangling me. The ever-watchful drones rewarded me with two paralyzing charges.

I didn't lose consciousness. I hurt, fury clenching at my throat harder than the collar itself. All pointless.

The Dargian entered my cell and lifted me in the air. He laid me on the floor and unbuttoned the top of my clothes.

I tried to struggle free but failed. My muscles were lax and unmoving. For a few moments, the gnome watched me. Finally, satisfied with my helpless state, he produced a narrow box made of black plastic and touched a sensor button on it.

A servomotor hissed gently. A bluish glow escaped the inside of the box. Five identical devices in their respective nests radiated an intense light, each reaching out with thread-like charges of energy that probed the air around them blindly, as if groping for a... a victim.

The Dargian gave me a dirty look. His gaze focused. His fat fingers touched my right upper arm, squeezing an invisible pressure point. Pain surged through me.

Anatomy had never been my forte. He, however, seemed to know what he was doing, feeling for a large nerve center. He found one and wheezed, reaching for his box, then reconsidered. His gaze focused again, studying me. His short fat fingers reached for my throat.

Cold sweat erupted on my forehead. I was immobilized and utterly helpless while he grunted with contentment, feeling the vertebrae at the base of my skull.

No, he was wrong again. His beady eyes grew harsh. The Dargian was getting nervous, apparently unable to find the problem. I can't have been the first human prisoner they'd had here, but now things seemed to have gotten out of hand. Something wasn't working right for him.

My paralysis seemed to be wearing off. I tried not to show it but the gnome's keen eye immediately noticed my cheek twitch.

More paralyzing charges tore at my mind, plunging me into a brief but welcome slumber. Then reality returned, drenched in pain and fear. The neuroimplant flooded my brain with an entire range of painful feelings available for all those billions of credits invested in its development.

The objects and actions around me came back into focus.

The Dargian leaned over me, panting heavily. In one open hand he held a glowing ball of thread-like energies. In the other he clenched some sort of surgical tool. The Haash craned their necks, watching the scene in silent tension. I thought I noticed a glint of sympathy in one's stare. That was the thing that finally did my head in.

Suddenly I knew. Arbido had been right. This was a place of no return. First the neuroimplant turned the game into reality; then the developers' sick mercenary imagination joined in, wishing to evaluate, at these early testing stages, the adaptivity threshold of the human mind, creating neurogram databases and trying to determine the authenticity level at which the game's world would turn into a virtual tomb.

I assure you it's very scary when you suddenly realize that the monster coming for you is *real*. That the rusty iron hook that he uses to strike sparks on the wall could soon tear your flesh apart. This is when the game ceases to exist. At these authenticity levels, the brain just can't tell the truth from fiction. One blow followed by going into pain shock could result, instead of a respawn, in a very real dead body. No amount of the "in-mode" could help here.

All this flashed through my mind as some sort of intuitive epiphany.

So all those dead bodies in full gear I'd believed to be part of the scenery were in fact dead players?

No. It didn't sum up. I refused to believe it!

The black box in his hands jolted.

A wound gaped in my upper arm, reeking of burned flesh. There was no blood: the laser discharge had seared the blood vessels closed. The Dargian bent down, grinning. The ball of crackling electric charge slid off his hand right into the wound.

It doesn't hurt!

My eyes popped out.

It doesn't hurt! It's a game! It can't hurt!

My mind shut down mercifully.

* * *

I SURVIVED BUT IT TOOK ME some time to recover.

I had no idea how much time had passed. The wound on my arm had closed, leaving an unpleasant tingling sensation under the skin like the crawling of a tiny mechanical bug.

The icon of a new system message kept flashing. I opened it.

I Can Hear Them: quest completed!

You have successfully implanted a semantic processor module. Now you can understand the language of the Xenomorphs!

+1 bonus to Intellect

+2 bonus to Perception

You've reached the next level! You have new Talent

and Characteristic points available!

I was surprised to discover a letter from the Admins. Had they finally replied to my ticket?

Oh no. This was much more serious:

We inform you of the following actions we have undertaken:

1. A support group has been dispatched to the address you provided.

2. The capsule has been serviced, including the activation of the in-mode and replacement of life support cartridges.

3. We have studied the existing neurograms in order to optimize the neuroimplant's functionality. Feedback levels have been lowered seven percent. Thank you for your cooperation.

Scumbags.

Then again, what was the point in spouting bile now? It had been my decision from the start.

I chose not to argue with myself. Instead, I checked my inventory. All my possessions were still there: the Dargian carbonite helmet, a full set of human pressurizers and three types of weapons.

The slots in my gear worked too. The only thing missing was the fact that all the batteries were dead, armor as well as weapons. Without them, my gear was little more than a heap of technojunk.

I activated the Prison Break quest but found no prompts. It was swim or drown.

What was the deal with my new abilities?

I looked around me. Indeed, my perception seemed to have upped a notch. I could see much better in the dark.

It was time to try this semantic thing. I looked around me, searching for the Haash who'd looked at me with sympathy, and tried to strike up a friendship.

"Hi. How did you end up here?" I asked the first thing that came to mind.

He paused, casting a sideways glance at the fellow prisoners. Then he nodded.

The mnemonic inbox blinked its icon. Mind boggles. Were we going to converse telepathically? My interface had no virtual keyboard: the advent of the neuroimplants had rendered them obsolete.

Are you a Human?

I crouched, leaning my back against the cold wall, and closed my eyes. *Nice to meet you.*

It felt weird. My very first attempt to use the mnemonic chat. Forming phrases in my mind wasn't easy. *My name's Zander.*

I'd already noticed that characters had no nicknames here but I'd explained this away by the fact that I'd so far only met NPCs.

Apparently, I'd been wrong.

I was speaking to another player!

My... name's... Charon.

I opened my eyes and tried to focus. That's right. I could see nicknames now. Did that mean that I couldn't identify the players properly without this semantic thingy of theirs?

I hurried to check my KOS list.

That's right. The char's information had grown. The Dargian slave driver's nickname was Rash.

Charon? Have you been here long?

Two full orbits, he answered promptly but obscurely.

Two what?

Two complete circles of the station around the star.

You mean two years? I couldn't conceal my astonishment. Were the developers raving mad? Two years? The skin on the back of my head tingled, growing taut. I gulped, trying to calm down. *Have you tried to escape?*

Impossible, the Haash answered darkly.

Well, that remained to be seen.

What's the problem? I struggled to pose clear-cut questions. I needed information badly. Personally, I wasn't going to stay here long.

Rash is strong. You can't remove the collar. It will strangle you. The drones will paralyze you, Charon listed the problems one by one. *We have nowhere to run,* he added after a pause. *This station has suffered a lot of damage. It's not easy to survive here.*

How about the other stations? And the planet?

They won't let us in. And the planet belongs to the Dargians. It's their world.

I felt curious. *Where are you from, then?*

I'm from another star system, he answered calmly.

I paused, thinking. I didn't want to play father confessor to the guy just to find out why he'd chosen a xenomorph as his char. The gaming worlds had their own etiquette. He'd tell me himself when he was ready. If he didn't, then I'd just have to consider him a xenomorph.

Very well. I opened the inventory and checked my helmet's stats. The broken device was still there. Rash was going to regret his oversight.

I addressed Charon again, *Are you a pilot?*

Yes.

Excellent. Time to try out more complex message

options. I wasn't sure if I could do it but surely it couldn't be more difficult than sending an MMS?

I closed my eyes trying to recreate the view out of the observation window just before the drones had attacked me. The view of the station's docking facilities.

The Haash followed this mental picture with interest. This kind of communication sent shivers down my spine. Still, I was getting used to it.

You know what it is?

That's Yrob! despair was rapidly draining from his voice.

Which is?

One of our ships. We arrived at this system, he faltered, *in a big ship. We wanted to study the Founders' stations. The Dargians attacked us. They destroyed the mothership. Our group broke away and landed here. Then they captured us.*

I see. What do they want from you? How do they use you?

They want to use our knowledge. To study our ships.

And none of you has ever broken down and told them anything? After two years?

We have. We showed them. After torture. But they can't fly them. They don't know how to. These are our ships. They're not easy, he faltered again, searching for the right word, *not easy to customize. Lots of things will have to be changed.*

Are they flightworthy?

There's nowhere to fly to.

How about the station next to this one? Who controls it?

Humans. Your race.

Are they a problem? I remembered the warning message about potential repercussions of my mixing with "xenomorphs".

They'll kill us.

How do you know?

We divided into two flights during the attack. My group headed here. The other went to the other station. The humans took them prisoner. Then they killed them.

It's been two years. Lots of things have changed since, I assured him even though I didn't know much. One problem at a time. At the moment, the Haash were my only chance of getting out of here. It wasn't that I was trying to take advantage of Charon. But I knew that in order to survive, a gaming world was obliged to have a well-developed economy. If the Dargians owned the planet and the humans were in possession of the station, they were bound to engage in intensive trade with each other. Which lowered xenophobia levels by definition. This I knew from experience.

We can't escape.

They had broken Charon's spirit well, hadn't they?

We can still try! I, on the contrary, was filled with resolve, my mind replaying various options, going through the details of my daring plan.

We can't.

Why? You don't even know what I want to say!

We don't have enough ships. Only three are still functional. And we are many, he sent me a mental image. At least fifty Haash prisoners!

We can escape together, the two of us, I came up with a solution.

A long pause hung in the air as he mulled over my words, exchanging a whispered word with other prisoners.

If I escape, the Dargians will kill them.

Not necessarily, I expected him to say something like that, so I'd come up with a suitable response. *All they need to say is that it was all your idea. That they're happy to serve their masters. Trust me, it'll work. In fact, you can just blame everything on me!*

Will you help us? the Haash sidled over to their bars, hope and mistrust in their eyes.

I felt uncomfortable. What could I promise them with my laughable level 3? Still, I couldn't even consider this torturous imprisonment for much longer. So I answered confidently,

I will! You've been suffering here for two years already. Do you think you can take it for a little bit longer?

They nodded.

No sooner than I gave them this questionable promise, a message popped up,

New quest alert! The Ties that Bind.

Help the Haash escape from the station. Deadline: 50 days.

Reward: doubtful, unknown. Your relationship with the Humans may deteriorate considerably.

I paused, thinking. It was no good trying to get out of here without a pilot and a ship.

Whatever. Once the Logout button was back on, I'd have plenty of time to think it over.

I pressed *Accept*.

CHAPTER TWO

PHANTOM SERVER
LOGIN

CHARON AND I IMMEDIATELY SET about plotting
our escape. Although my experience was limited
to gaming, it suggested that we shouldn't drag it out.

The distance between the bars was enough to
squeeze my Dargian helmet through it. I "discarded" it
from my inventory. It worked. Charon picked it up
without a problem.

"Why?" he studied the helmet. His unusual stunted
speech patterns drove me to distraction sometimes.

"Do you have someone with tech skills maxed out?"
I asked.

My question hung in the air. Somehow I didn't
think they understood me. Which was weird: how
simple was it? Then again, two years spent in
confinement must have been rough. Their mental
state must have suffered a terrible blow.

"I mean I need a *good* tech."

Now they nodded their understanding. The helmet began changing hands until it ended up in the cell of someone called Danezerath. Some name. He had probably joined late in the game when all the nice nicknames had already been taken so he'd just entered a random combination or used the name generator. Happens to the best of us.

"Danny," I adapted his name to my liking. It sounded ridiculously out of synch with his Haash appearance but he didn't protest. "Have a look at the device in the slot. You think you can take it out?"

He easily removed the broken module and began studying it.

"I need to have it repaired," I defined the problem. The Haash can be terribly slow on the uptake. Still, I didn't want to rush them. The impossibility to log out could turn anyone into an emotional wreck. We may say that we don't really need the real world, but it's extremely important to know that you can quit the game at any moment and never come back again. I had no idea what I'd feel after two years spent in limbo.

Danezerath sat down on the floor and began taking the device apart in skilled practiced motions.

Charon glanced at me, hope and doubt in his stare. I tried to get as much information out of him as I could. "Why did they implant me with the semantic processor?"

He answered promptly without even thinking, "They do it to everybody. The Dargians love bossing everyone around. They go mad when you don't understand them. The top decks are dangerous. Quick information exchange equals survival."

"What do they want on the top decks?"

"They look for the Founders' devices. As well as ore, power supplies and ancient machines."

"Why?"

"The Dargians are restoring a large ancient ship. Once they finish doing it, a war will start."

"With humans?"

"No. The Dargians will eliminate them. They aim to take over their planet."

"Does it mean slave drivers are outlaws?"

He nodded. "Their own world treats them as criminals."

"And humans? How do humans treat them?"

Charon cringed. I didn't like the expression on his face.

"Humans are bad," his voice changed, allowing a few angry hissing notes. "They're all for themselves. Against everybody else."

Most likely, the station I hoped to get to was controlled by gamers' clans. No idea yet why they were so aggressive toward xenomorphs. I'd better start thinking how not to end up caught between the gears of their war machine.

After some pondering, I thought I'd come up with a suitable solution. I didn't say anything to Charon though, not yet. He wasn't going to like it.

In the meantime, Danezerath had already put the device back together. Now he was shuffling from foot to foot nearby, casting occasional glances my way.

"And? Cut the crap," my rude tone didn't seem to offend him at all. "Report!"

"I've fixed it."

So! That was impressive. "Let's test it, then. Can you switch off my collar?"

"I can't," he looked down guiltily. "I need a power supply."

"Okay then, you can stash it somewhere."

I turned to Charon. "We'll need micro nuclear batteries. Seven or eight. Think you can get hold of them?"

He gave it some thought and nodded, "Half-charged, yes. We'll have to work now. The overseer will come soon. I'll try to get a few batteries. Can you tell me how you want us to escape?"

"That's my problem," I wasn't quite prepared to lay my trump card on the table. Watching the Haash and their behavior, I could clearly see that the majority of them were broken. They had accepted their situation and were obviously scared of the Dargians. Entrusting my secret to them would be rather stupid. I couldn't do that.

The arrival of the slave driver saved me from more questions. He wore a full space suit. Silently he unlocked the cages and left.

The Haash began suiting up. I followed their example, then walked out into the corridor where about a dozen drones were overseeing the procedure. Silently the Dargian began distributing the micro nuclear batteries: one each. I clicked it into the slot. Thirty percent charge. Not a lot.

The communication system clicked on.

"Move it!" a command crackled.

I experienced an unnatural surge of energy. I was buzzing, my perception sharpened. My hatred for the Dargians was still there but it sort of withdrew, peering spitefully from behind a barricade of common sense. I couldn't afford doing anything stupid now. So I trailed along obediently without raising my head, my gaze shuffling through the interface icons looking for the option I needed. There it was. The map hadn't been blocked. Excellent. I hadn't had the chance to explore the location, so now the thin line of our route lay through the omnipresent expanse of the mist of war.

We headed for the deck below. I marked down a vertical shaft that looked very much like an obsolete gravity elevator. We began climbing down using the manhole steps. About halfway down I noticed the shimmer of a force field. That was worrying. Now it was barely visible, letting the Haash through with just a hint of a spark, but if the place was put on full alert, it would shut our route down. We had to prepare for the worst.

I cast a few inconspicuous glances around. The shaft's walls sported a few semi-spherical blobs. Emitters, most likely. Once we were back, I'd have to ask the Haash about them.

We'd left the force field behind. The sensors on the rim of my visor changed their color. We were floating in a vacuum.

The experience was unusual. Awkwardly I tried to move, feeling nausea rise up to my throat. Was this zero gravity?

My sense of balance was confused. Unwillingly I let go of the step. I was floating. I waved my hands around me, trying to get hold of something. I hit the wall and bounced back. The Haash descended with a practiced ease. The slave driver was already below, looking at me. It must have been fun watching a newb like myself.

I allowed the Dargian a generous eyeful. Let him think I was useless. In fact, the nausea had subsided quickly as my old skills had kicked in. Ten years previously, I'd spent some quality game time in a space station simulator. The job was a pain: solving all sorts of technical problems while floating in mid-air, but at least now it had done me a good turn.

I bounced all the way down the elevator shaft and floated out, spreading my arms wide as I enjoyed the sensation of flight while trying to suppress an instinctive bout of fear. Awkwardly I hit the ledge of a structure overhead and ricocheted up, helplessly drifting away into the void.

I was scared, of course, but the risk was worth it. From above, I could see the external launch pad and could make all the screenshots I needed to study them at leisure.

The Dargian looked worried. I didn't think he'd be disciplined for the loss of a prisoner. I'd respawn in my cell anyway. But the delay caused by my freefall could cost him. The Haash stopped moving, watching me drift away. They stood comfortably and confidently thanks to a special substance that covered the soles of their space boots.

A few drones took off after me. They caught up with me quickly, their snaking manipulators hitching me under the arms and towing me back.

The Dargian was furious but he couldn't punch me. The communication system crackled again.

"Remember: only place your foot on an even surface!" he instructed me. "Can you feel it lock?"

I nodded. Both my feet felt glued to the surface. "How can I walk, then?"

"You slide," he quipped. Another delay will mean three deaths in your cell."

Okay. I got it. I broke my footing with the surface

and slid off, then stopped abruptly, lodging my foot firmly on it. This worked. Now the other foot...

Unlike me, the Haash proceeded quickly. They seemed to be used to this kind of space walk. I lagged considerably behind but at least I was trying. Soon I got the hang of it, moving my feet rather well. One of the drones followed me closely.

I didn't have a chance to enjoy the beauty of space. Only occasionally during our short breaks did I get a chance to take instant pics, seeing as no one could have caught me doing so.

The Haash were already far ahead. I was amazed at their agility and coordination. In front of us lay some sort of wall of heaped-up debris. The Haash took it in their stride, moving in well calculated leaps from one support to the next. Wish I could learn to do the same, otherwise I could jeopardize our entire escape plan. It would be no good me crawling like a crab when there was a chase hot on our heels.

Suddenly the collar constricted, strangling me. The slave driver appeared from around the bend. He looked furious.

I spread my arms wide, gesturing my willingness to do my best.

I couldn't see the Dargian's face. The visor of his helmet was opaque. No idea how he was seeing everything around him. He probably had a screen on the inside of the helmet — either that or he was in possession of some unique ability.

I couldn't breathe. I started wheezing.

He came close to me and mumbled something bitterly. Suddenly a new device appeared in my armor's slot.

The collar released its grip slightly.

"Watch where you're going!"

The meaning of it wasn't quite clear. Still, I obeyed. I found a small flat platform halfway through the destroyed area. Suddenly the thin broken line of my path became visible in my projection visor. Mechanically my brain processed the information, sending my legs moving on their own accord, reaching my destination in a series of leaps.

Wow.

That was breathtaking. While both the drone and the slave driver approached, I studied the surprise gift.

The Movement Coordinator. Produced by Haash technology. Suitable for use by all humanoid species. Define your destination, then allow the system to calculate the optimal effort necessary.

This was awesome.

I just hoped the Dargian didn't claim it back on our return. This was a most useful thing. Without it, moving along the station's deformed hull would be murder.

I hurried to catch up with the rest. Today I was an obedient and helpful prisoner, ready to do anything they told me to.

The ridge of mangled metal ended abruptly, revealing an enormous open space.

I froze unwittingly. Here, the station's hull wasn't damaged. But that wasn't what had puzzled me so. In the middle of a vast platform, clutching at its launching towers, sat a gigantic spaceship.

Some damage it had taken! My eye slid along its soft outlines, noticing a multitude of gaping holes and other damage. The Haash were already busy working in several groups. Some of them were removing the warped diamond-shaped armor plates, others were checking the utility lines while yet more of them were bringing new armor segments, installing them into the restored mountings.

A piercing light flashed nearby. Some Dargians were working there: you couldn't confuse their squat figures for anyone else. Armed with plasma torches, they were cutting out more diamond-shape plates.

I began descending, using every opportunity to take some panoramic screenshots.

The first impression was quite mind-blowing. The ship was rather big, about three hundred feet in diameter. But when I remembered the veritable Leviathans drifting nearby, I began to realize how tiny this ship was compared to them.

Whatever made the Haash think the Dargian slave drivers could use it to attack and even invade their planet?

We'll see.

* * *

THAT DAY I HAD TO WORK long and hard.

As it turned out, the station did have its own gravity. I hadn't noticed at first that my freefall jumps, controlled by the movement coordinator, did have a certain trajectory. But the moment I was ordered to help bring in the armor plates, I sensed the artificial gravity straight away. As the Haash explained to me, its source was located somewhere in the station's unexplored bowels.

Lugging the multi-ton parts proved hard. I was struggling; by the end I could barely move my feet. The Haash were taking it much better: they were both stronger and used to this kind of work.

One of the drones followed me everywhere. I studied it inconspicuously. Why would Dargians use prisoners for the job if they could use machines instead? Surely drones could do the work more efficiently and with better precision?

I didn't get a chance to get close to the ship.

By evening, I had plenty of questions to ask the Haash. But once back in the crumpled darkness of my cell, I was too exhausted to talk.

I couldn't keep my eyes open. I was neither hungry nor thirsty, the capsule's life support module providing my mortal body with everything it might need. But sleep, that was something I had to get for myself.

* * *

I DIDN'T HAVE THE CHANCE to sleep properly. My mnemonic interface beeped insistently, another person's mind waves forcing their way through all the filters, rendering me awash with anxiety.

What is it?

Ten micro nuclear batteries, Charon reported. *Each thirty percent full. Is that enough?*

The Haash didn't seem to sleep at all. Were they made of steel?

I shook myself out of my slumber. Time to get working. I looked through the screenshots I'd made earlier, forwarding some to Charon. You could clearly see the fighter craft in their docking pods. There were seven of them. There, the makeshift "path" forked, the crudely welded sheets of metal laid right on top of the ravaged upper structures.

I wanted to know why we'd had to move on the outside of the station. Why such an awkward and dangerous route? Couldn't we get to the launch pad and the ancient ship via internal tunnels?

Charon answered willingly. Apparently, the Dargians had only managed to reclaim about a dozen sections for themselves. The rest was still part of the Founders' ancient technosphere. Most adjacent corridors were blocked with security devices that respawned in under eight *Seggs*. Charon's use of some weird time and distance measurements made it hard for us to understand each other. He had really grown into his gaming character's role!

What a shame for him, I pondered. He must have been a normal kid who'd decided to make a quick buck by participating in this alpha testing thing, and what now? Was his mind deformed irreversibly?

The thought made me cold and empty inside. Compared to him, I'd been lucky. My neuroimplant had been a much more advanced model; besides, I had adapted to the direct neurosensory contact while playing in much more forgiving worlds.

The thought didn't sound like fun. Now I didn't have the slightest doubt that the whole "closed alpha testing" thing was only an excuse to have a trial run of the new device. I'd have loved to know how many players had arrived here with the first wave and if any of them were still alive.

This theory could also explain the existence of the "alternative start". Understandably, the test operators wanted to milk the subjects of their experiment for anything they were worth. And the developers were interested primarily in the character's behavior in various emergency situations. They didn't care about his or her reaction to the comfortable process of mundane leveling.

If this is not clear enough, let me explain. Here we were watching the future of gaming in the making. By the time of the revolutionary game's release, they had had to bring the risks of players' death or insanity down to acceptable figures. The developers had to amass a wealth of statistics, create numerous neurogram databases and optimize feedback, all in order to allow the consumer to experience incredible new sensations without the risk of ending up in the morgue or a mental asylum.

My conclusions weren't happy to say the least. Surviving here (literally) wasn't going to be easy. I'd have to accept the rules of the game and act ruthlessly but cautiously if I didn't want to become a new stage prop to decorate their scenery. Take Charon, for instance. Let's presume he'd escape — and then what? Would his mind, distorted by the implant's continuous use, be able to come back to real life?

Most likely, he'd be appalled. By then, his physical body would have been in the in-mode for years. But that wasn't the worst thing about it. He really thought he was a Haash! He was now a true xenomorph, both in his actions and his train of thought. Exactly. I never envied the players who'd been tempted by the exotic abilities of alien races. I was pretty sure that all of them had a special version of the neuroimplant installed, one that contained additional neural chains that gradually, bit by bit, distorted their mindsets.

Why did I think so? Well, once you grasped the essence of what was going on, adding details to it was easy. Watching thc Dargians would be enough. How much of human nature had *they* preserved?

I could be utterly wrong, of course. Each and every "sentient xenomorph" could be just an AI module complete with its own mindset and even identity.

I couldn't really judge, not yet. As far as I knew, no one had ever created a fully functional artificial intellect.

So if you thought I could think of nothing but gaming you might be in for a surprise. In this technological era, self-education is constant and natural. My job added to it, too. Earlier I'd mentioned the space station simulator. A more boring gameplay you can't even begin to imagine. With one catch: completing their quests demanded real knowledge. These kinds of educational games have their place and their niche, sometimes becoming the first step in a professional career.

Corporation recruiters call it dredging. They closely watch these simulators as the easiest way to discover grains of talent amid tons of online fool's gold.

What had I been doing there? Working. I'd been busting my hump like a dog to add a touch of glitter to some dumb rich numbnuts to make them look like real talent.

Enough of that.

I was in the game. The bets couldn't be higher. They'd thrown down the gauntlet and I'd accepted the challenge.

That was it. I'd said it, never to repeat it again. I might not like it but it was true: someone somewhere read and analyzed all of my neurograms.

* * *

THE HAASH WERE PATIENTLY WAITING.

I studied the screenshots, planning our escape. I kept forwarding some of the pics to Charon, with questions,

"There's a force field here. How can we get past it?"

He furrowed his forehead. "We must shoot. At the emitters. To create an explosion. Decompression."

"Are there any emergency bulkheads there?"

He nodded, marking it down on the scheme. We went on exchanging brief messages.

You think the bulkheads could stop the pursuit?

They would slow it down. Not for long. We'll have to run fast. The Dargians will send out the drones.

The fighter's cockpit, will it hold two people?

You'll have to stand and hold on tight. I will fly it. It won't be long but unpleasant. Lots of Gs when maneuvering. Not enough battery power for the G-force absorbers.

I'll survive.

Hundreds of questions were crowding my head. So many things I wanted to know! Like, who were the Founders? I had to remind myself to stay focused. This wasn't the right time.

"Danny? Have you checked the controller?"

The darkness stirred. Danezerath stood up, stooping. The low ceiling didn't allow the Haash to stand up properly. For some reason, he also tried to squeeze his head through the bars but failed and sniffed angrily, reaching out his long sinewy arms. I made out his open hand and a small device in it. His long many-phalanxed fingers were shaking. What had made him so nervous? Was he afraid?

Then I understood. Charon had mentioned decompression. I'd never experienced it before so I could only speak academically. The prisoners, however, must have been familiar with it already.

"How possible is it that the bulkheads won't work?" I asked.

"They're old," Charon answered curtly.

Of course. They all were facing death, followed by respawning and dying again. And no one knew how long it would last. I could see fear in the Haash's eyes as they awaited a chain of inevitable suffering. They would die and resurrect incessantly in their crumpled cells until the Dargians restored the atmosphere.

I had the feeling that the ugly gnomes weren't going to be in a hurry.

As I pondered over it all, the stooping figures of the Haash were passing to each other both the repaired device and the helmet that had held it. Good idea. No point in leaving evidence behind, giving the Dargians an excuse for further repression. Their cover story would be that I'd done everything on my own. I had forced Charon to join me at gunpoint because I needed a pilot.

I'd promised them I'd be back but how sure was I I'd be able to keep my word?

I tried to dismiss the thought. Here, it was every man for himself. Not that it helped much.

They passed me the repaired device and the helmet which I dumped into the inventory. Then I tried to put the device into a slot in my gear. It worked.

Their hands sprang into motion again. Now I also had a handful of micro nuclear batteries. Seven. The remaining three Charon wanted to use himself. Not much, an hour of autonomy at the most. I clicked two of them into the submachine gun and another one into the handgun. I had to give the heavy sniper's rifle a miss this time. The remaining four were going to power the spacesuit.

All set.

I began removing my gear. The Haash watched me in surprise.

"When do we start?" Charon's voice tensed up. He couldn't understand the point of my actions — and had every reason to be suspicious.

"Wait up a bit."

"Rash is strong. Put your gear back on."

"No," I walked over to the bars. "Can you reach?"

Charon hunched his shoulders. He slowly tilted his massive head, covered in rough skin spotted in places with rudimentary scales, and opened his large mouth, gasping hotly, "Why?"

I deactivated his collar and handed him the gun. "Now hit me," I commanded. "Just make sure I have about twenty percent life left."

"Human, I don't understand..."

"Do it, I tell you! And you — all of you — I want you to yell and stomp your feet."

Charon didn't look too sure.

"Trust me!"

I could see desperation in his eyes. No idea what he must have been feeling at that moment.

The Haash began to tap their feet. A perceptible vibration rolled across the floor, filled with a vague but passionate rhythm. As if the wave of their pent-up fury had suddenly burst out, making the bulkheads shudder.

A second passed, and another, and...

Charon growled and punched me. His sharp claws ripped the skin on my chest, spilling blood.

Again... again... again...

The vibrating rhythm quickened. The door clanged. The drones were the first to burst into the room, rotating in apparent confusion. Their target finders just couldn't prioritize properly in the chaos that reigned here. Then they focused on Charon splattered with my blood, recognizing him as the aggressor.

One of the Haash stepped in, taking on the drones' paralyzing charges. Two squat figures appeared in the doorway.

I focused on their name tags.

"Rash, you scumbag! Come over here!" I could barely wheeze but he'd heard me. He wasn't afraid, feeling himself the master of the situation. He waved the drones away and headed for my cell, enjoying the sight of the Haash being strangled by their collars. Charon played along and collapsed, clutching at his throat.

The door of my cell screeched aside.

Rash entered it confidently, his beady eyes glowing with blood lust. My miserable state only excited him.

He punched me sharply and expertly. My heart missed a beat, my life bar shrinking to four percent.

Berserk!

A crimson haze clouded my eyes. I lunged forward. A punch. A bone snapped broken. Another punch. The drones didn't interfere: they had been ordered not to. Anger and confusion glowed in Rash's stare. He stayed on his two feet, his life only fifty percent down, but I didn't stop and kept hitting him, not letting him regain control.

You've received a new level!

The other Dargian backed off, about to leg it. One of the Haash grabbed at his boot, gasping. It was Danezerath. His neck muscles bulged and turned crimson. Hold on, Danny!

I kicked the other slaver, stripping him of half his hits. I kept kicking like someone possessed, but it didn't take long: Rash's assistant was only level 10.

Now I had to concentrate. Berserk was still working, not allowing me to think straight, my reflexes impatient to make a quick job of the drones.

I reached into my inventory. Full gear on.

Life support kicked in immediately. The alarm hadn't been raised: not for something as mundane as prisoners yelling and screaming in their cells.

My life bar grew considerably as the murderous frenzy released my brain. Nasty ability, no doubt about that.

I quickly checked Rash's pockets. Aha. Another collar controller. Shame it was built into his armor so I couldn't take it out. But where were the cell keys?

Only then did it dawn on me that they could be accessed via the mnemonic interface. I tore his gear off him, glimpsing some complicated devices in its slots. I'd have to sort through them later.

I purposefully didn't touch the drones. They must have been filming everything. This way no one would have any doubts that I was the only culprit.

I raised the submachine gun and shot the lock off of Charon's cell. Now — go!

In two short bursts, I gunned the drones down. They rattled to the floor, sparking and spewing smoke.

Charon was already standing next to me, armed and wearing full pressure gear.

"Run!"

Dozens of eyes followed us to the door, glistening with hope. Was the human going to betray them?

How would you know, poor bastards?

THE CORRIDOR WAS EMPTY. Most of the Dargians were away on a raid. Besides, you couldn't surprise anyone here with a bit of noise. As far as I understood, Rash had made a habit of torturing the prisoners. Everyone was used to his nightly visits to the prisoners' quarters, accompanied by screams and even shooting.

We ran in silence.

My gear systems had almost restored my life back to full, but the charge in the batteries was rapidly going down.

The next bend revealed a patrol drone. I shot it down before it had the chance to alert the rest, but the explosion echoed through the corridor. They'd know!

But now we were practically there. A small walkthrough module held a guards' post. Beyond lay the shaft of the gravity elevator protected by the force field.

Charon and I stormed the guards' room simultaneously. The two Dargians hadn't expected a breakout. And still the alarm must have gone off as I could see the channels switching fast on their holographic monitors. On one of them, a couple of dozen squat figures came running out of their rooms.

We'd done it nice and neatly. Now for the shaft!

A lot in my escape plan depended on our luck. The force field emitters were located on our side, which was logical. The Dargians feared attack from outside. But now they would probably learn from their mistake and install additional force emitters on the inside.

The stomping of many feet was already echoing through the corridors.

Suddenly Charon took over from me. "Hold on!" he stepped forward and raised his weapon. Grabbing at the rungs of the service ladder, he began shooting down the shaft.

I dropped to the floor, bracing my legs against some sort of vertical stand and grabbing at a thick sturdy pipe lining the floor.

A jet of flame escaped the shaft and was immediately extinguished by a roaring blast of air.

Explosive decompression is a terrible thing, trust me. The air rushed into the gap like a tornado. I glimpsed various objects rushing past — bodies and pieces of equipment.

Still, the localized disaster only lasted a mere ten or fifteen seconds. The roar of the air died away as the atmosphere thinned out.

The light flickered and went out. The emergency bulkheads hadn't worked, after all. Whoever hadn't been wearing spacesuits was about to respawn now. I just hoped it didn't apply to the drones. Logically, they had to be inanimate objects.

I held on for dear life until Charon touched my shoulder. "We can go."

He was full of gloomy determination.

* * *

BOTH OUR BRAZEN ESCAPE AND the decompression had proved a complete surprise to the Dargians. They had allowed themselves to become lax.

We climbed down quickly but cautiously. The air torrent had ravaged the shaft, pulling out many of the steps. Soon we noticed a whirling cloud of tiny ice crystals, flakes of oxygen, low-density gas and various debris.

I switched on the movement coordinator, my gaze choosing a spot further on the station's surface. Then I kicked myself off the lower edge of the destroyed elevator shaft and floated amid the fire-polished structures.

My heart froze in my chest. At any moment, I could collide with a piece of debris (there was plenty of it around), decompressing my suit and changing the direction of a well-calculated jump.

The Haash's lanky figure moved parallel to mine. Together we crossed the murky area affected by the decompression. The stars were pale behind the gaseous haze. We did everything in absolute silence.

Something blew up.

I pressed both my feet hard onto the smooth surface. One foot slipped and lost grip. Forcing myself not to thrash around in panic, I managed to grab onto a nearby hull structure.

The Haash looked back, anxious. So did I. From the small platform where we both stood we could see the elevator's gaping exit, ravaged by the ancient disaster. From here, it looked like the ragged end of a pipe surrounded by deformed armor plates. No idea what had happened there in the past.

"Did you see anything?" I whispered.

Silently Charon raised his hand, pointing.

To our right I could see a fire-polished gap in the hull from which several drones appeared — five in total. They must have used some alternate routes and were now scanning the area. I had stupidly hoped that no one would notice our escape, too busy looking into whatever had caused the decompression and how better to repair its consequences.

The drones were followed by two Dargians who scrambled out onto the station's hull.

My sniper's sights reacted immediately. An additional window opened. The figures came into focus, zooming in. They were clad in low-quality, well-used spacesuits. Even their visors were different, allowing me to see the gnomes' angry faces.

Rash and his assistant. I'd removed his gear, hadn't I? He should still be there, dying and resurrecting in a series of agonizing respawns.

As if! Either they had somehow managed to get out of the prison module or they had their own respawn point somewhere in the area.

I had to remember that.

The worst thing was, he'd second-guessed our intentions.

I could see his plan. The drones took up position amid the mangled technogenic ruins. Both Dargians were armed. Charon and I didn't speak: I was sure they monitored our frequencies. And mnemonic messaging took too much concentration to the exclusion of everything else. At the moment, that was out of the question.

We exchanged gestures, struggling to understand

each other. Charon was anxious. I entirely shared his concern. The Dargians made no attempt to chase after us. Why?

Rash was a clever little bastard. He was armed with something rather bulky. It didn't resemble a handheld rocket launcher. Unfortunately, I'd had neither the time nor opportunity to find out what kind of weapons they used here, but I had a very bad feeling about it. He was aiming his weird weapon. I followed its direction, realizing that both the Dargians and the drones controlled all the access routes to the launch pad.

Did they hope to intercept us? Or were they prepared to sacrifice the Haash fighter by shooting it down?

While we lingered there, a new group of pursuers appeared from the elevator shaft. Our situation was getting desperate. We seemed to be cornered from both sides. Our hideout wasn't safe enough; besides, it was located below the slave drivers' positions.

We had to act immediately, but how? Should we open fire? They would see us and kill us straight away. Should we run for the ships? They would gun us down in their own sweet time.

I touched Charon's shoulder, attracting his attention. I pointed at the still-swirling cloud of decompression blowout that was drifting toward the launch pad.

The Haash seemed to have understood me. He nodded.

"Go!" I gestured, encouraging him to move his backside.

He didn't lose time. Immediately he began the dangerous descent deep into the gas cloud, using it as a cover to get to the fighter. I just couldn't see any other options.

The Dargians hadn't been idle, either. Our pursuers (I counted nine of them) had broken into two groups. Four stayed by the elevator while the rest fanned out, moving in graceful leaps trying to scan the biggest area possible.

Having taken in the situation, I realized I had to divert them by drawing fire to myself. I climbed still higher. The low gravity allowed for a risky maneuver. Using the movement coordinator, I kicked off and floated along the half-molten paneling of the hull structure. Immediately I began shaking. This was an adrenaline thrill unlike anything I'd experienced before. The scene unfolded in complete silence. One wrong movement, and my silhouette would float away from the station, becoming a perfect target, even though somehow I doubted the Dargians would open fire. They'd love to see me suffocate, then respawn in my cramped cell of the prison module.

I had no idea of the purpose of the tall spire I was approaching, but once I reached its splayed top, I noticed large oblong openings in its upper section. I grabbed at the edge of one of them, forcing my body inside.

They hadn't seen me!

I cast a quick look around. Nothing special, just a chaotic mess of misshaped equipment amid abundant traces of high temperatures and decompression.

The room had a dome-like ceiling, with panoramic windows lining the wall below. I checked the thickness of the armor. Not bad. I had to anchor myself somehow without losing the ability to move freely. I noticed a few long severed cables and tried to pull one out. It budged enough. Now I had a safety tether of about fifteen feet long, supple enough to tie it around my waste and attach the other end to a seemingly sturdy spar of the room's skeletal frame.

I cautiously approached one of the oblong openings. Idle thoughts crowded my head. Wonder if this used to be a control tower?

I looked out.

Now I was the one controlling the high ground. I could observe the gaping hole harboring Rash, his assistant and the five drones. I reached into my inventory for the heavy sniper's rifle, sacrificing two of the spacesuit's batteries for the purpose. The life support system indicator immediately shrank into the red zone. Still, I had no choice. I shoved the submachine gun into a quick access slot. Charon had my handgun.

His fate was still unknown. I couldn't see his lanky figure anywhere. He'd disappeared into the darkness.

Would he shaft me or not? We weren't yet clear on the subject of trust. I knew negligibly little about the xenomorphs. Their semantics were a mystery to me. How was I supposed to know what they meant by honesty? I wasn't even sure they had a word for it.

I cast an anxious look around. Whatever happened to the pursuit group? The lighting was poor to say the least. The system's star was too far away: a bright spark amid billions of smaller cold ones littering the void. The station reflected the brown twilight shimmer of the gas giant, casting profound sharp shadows all around. The light that reflected from the ragged relief of the destroyed equipment made the station look like a gigantic camo net. If an enemy was hiding there in the dark, there was no way you could detect him without a scanner.

Rash had everything covered. Had I not known the location of his group, I could have walked right past it without even noticing. Same with our group of pursuers: once they'd disappeared from sight, you could only guess what had happened to them — until the moment they decided to declare themselves.

I realized full well that I wasn't going to last long. Charon was my only hope.

The setting was eerily weird: the chaos of metallic debris, soundless and timeless. The subsystem indicators nervously blinked an occasional red light. The sound of my breathing ripped through the silence. Beads of sweat covered my forehead under the helmet but I couldn't wipe them off.

Welcome to freakin' space.

I searched the area for Rash. He was the dangerous one. The target recognition sights in my helmet's slot worked like a dream. They zoomed in on the slowly moving details of the mangled technogenic relief outside. Suddenly a Dargian silhouette pulsated on the screen as the target finder managed to localize Rash's figure in the surrounding background.

I squeezed the trigger.

I expected the powerful surge of a recoil — which was why I'd secured myself with a rope — but the weapon proved to be compensated. The recoil was negligible while the hull of the station exploded in a ball of flames. Where the Dargian had stood only a moment ago, a small cloud of plasma hung over a white-hot impact crater.

Now they saw me. Five drones opened responsive fire. In dead silence, the floor, the walls and the domed ceiling shuddered from the impacts. Rays of light illuminated the room. The firing angle didn't allow the combat machines to hit their target but they were gaining ground quickly, their charges passing through the windows, crushing the mauled equipment inside.

I lay on the floor, protected by my thick armor. The vacuum around me seemed to be whirling in a blizzard of debris. In the flashing of the incoming rounds, a crimson haze of incandescent gas rapidly filled the room.

I slid the rifle back into the slot and pulled out the submachine gun. I just hoped that the drones' mode of thinking was predictable enough. If they couldn't breach the hull, they had to break inside.

The fire died out. I watched the crimson haze seep away, enveloping the ancient structure. The drones' cameras couldn't see much. Doubtful they'd be able to tell my exact location.

I waited.

I couldn't stick my neck out. This world obeyed the real-life laws of physics. In the absence of gravity, you couldn't run from one hidey hole to the next, shooting at those "stupid pieces of junk".

And they weren't in a hurry to provoke me. They circled outside, scanning the area. I felt as if I'd lose my patience any moment. I kept seeing spots of reddish light amid the swirls of gas, reflected from their spherical bodies. My cheeks were twitching with the urge to shoot.

Too early, I kept telling myself. *Let them try to get inside first.*

* * *

UNFORTUNATELY, INSTEAD OF THE drones an assault group turned up.

The robots stayed outside. Suddenly the oblong widows were swarming with Dargians.

I gunned two of them down. A long scream froze in my earphones as the shot breached the armor of one of my erstwhile attackers. Mind you, I couldn't tell whether he was screaming with pain or with fear. The others took cover.

This was when I knew: this was it. This was the end of me. I stood with my back to a blind wall, cornered between some towering equipment. I'd been caught in my own trap. All I could do now was fight back to the full extent of my strength, skill and ammo.

The whole structure was vibrating even though no one was shooting. The Dargians lay low as if they suddenly had more important things to do.

Charon?

There was an explosion outside. Lasers sliced across the gloom. Another flash; then an enormous shadow slid past, taking the shape of a fighter craft.

Charon was one hell of a pilot. His attack on the drones was swift, graceful and deadly. You'd think the enormous ship would be hard to maneuver but in fact, it was remarkably responsive. Before I could come to my senses, the Haash had already disposed of his enemies, leveled off his machine, pointed it at the domed structure and had begun moving sideways around it, masterfully using the attitude thrusters. The ship's sleek predatory outline slid from one window to the next, illuminated by the short flashes of laser charges.

The Dargians lost it. Those who were still alive fled

their cover, but I didn't give them half a chance and smoked at least three of them. Charon did away with the rest.

The communication system clicked on. "Jump inside, quick!"

The ship turned its back to the window, killed its speed and stopped its drift dead. A hatch opened, protected by the iridescent glow of a force field.

"Wait!" I hurried to collect the loot while ripping gear off the Dargians' bodies, pulling out whatever implants I noticed indiscriminately.

Soon I was floating toward the lock. Had it not been for the zero Gs, I'd have been deep in overload by now.

The inside of the fighter glowed with the subdued flickering lights of many machines and holographic screens. A massive chair with a high back towered in the middle of the cockpit, resting on the foundation of gravity absorbers and surrounded by clusters of control consoles.

Charon's lanky hands clutched the controls: two complicated devices that rose from somewhere below, wound with servodrives and equipped with a multitude of firing buttons.

The hatch closed shut behind my back.

Charon craned his neck and twisted his head at an impossible angle to steal a glance at me. "*Haaram utaashgort!*"

I didn't understand a word but grasped at the back of his seat. The semantic processor stalled, trying to interpret the phrase apparently addressed to me. Smoothly the ship turned round and began gaining speed very slowly, heading for the far-off glimmer of the station.

Alone: Quest failed!
A Prison Break: Quest completed!
You've received a new level!

* * *

WE WEREN'T TALKING.

Charon was in his element. The ship obeyed him eagerly, filling the many screens with data.

The most I could understand peeking over his shoulder was the search radar screen. It showed all objects around us within a sphere with our ship as its center. Every marker sported lines of symbols in an unknown language.

Finally the semantic processor jumped back to life, unfolding a long sheet of fine print before my inner vision.

So this was the meaning of the two words he'd said? Can't be. The wretched thing mush have glitched.

I started reading.

It turned out to be a modest list of my merits. According to the Haash, I was a monster of virtue. It felt embarrassing and funny and also a little bit sad. They probably stuck to the age-old philosophy that you couldn't do good without using your fists — preferably heavy ones, too.

Apparently, I had spilled my blood for the sake of other creatures.

I had ripped apart two heavily armed *enemies* — the word which, according to the semantic processor, played a very special role in the Haash language.

According to them, there are opponents and there are *enemies*. You could make peace with the former, living happily ever after. But not with the latter.

I had broken the shackles.

I had shown them the way to freedom.

I had willingly drawn the *enemy*'s fire to myself, allowing Charon to flee.

And finally, I had (again) killed the *Enemy*. In this particular context the capitalized word was supposed to signify Rash.

I had a funny feeling that most of the text was the semantic processor's very own conjecture. Had Charon known that my exploits had been driven exclusively by my desire to escape captivity, he'd have been quite upset.

Still, I wasn't going to be the one to disappoint him. Especially because, once I'd finished reading, another message popped up,

You've received a unique ability: Friend of the Haash.

Bonus: every time you fight alongside the Haash, you will receive +1 to all characteristics.

That was great but the timing couldn't have been worse. I wondered if I could hide this information from prying eyes. At the moment, we were heading for the station which wasn't known for its inhabitants' friendly feelings toward all xenomorphs.

As it turned out, I could indeed hide it. I only wished I could say the same about Charon. Somehow I didn't think they were going to offer him a warm welcome.

Actually, I'd already come up with a solution to this

problem but I had no idea how Charon would react to my suggestion. He might just change his rosy opinion of me.

In the meantime, the station had grown to the size of a bright pea.

Ships were swarming around. I didn't think I could classify or even describe them, so various were they in their design principles. I had the impression that most of them had been put together by hand using various standard modules and sporting a certain degree of uniqueness and creativity.

We were given a wide berth, everyone apparently wary of a Haash fighter.

Soon the station filled the entire front of the spherical observation blister. It was a pumpkin-shaped spheroid, its monolith hull bristling with a technoscape of outer structures — mainly space defense systems and vacuum docks; I also saw two large ships in the hangars and a cluster of launch pads that looked like bits of honeycomb.

The center of the structure bulged with round openings at regular intervals. They looked very much like tunnel exits, currently shut with diaphragm hatches.

I had to cut my observations short as the communication system clicked on,

"Attention unidentified ship. You're about to enter the space of the Independent Station Argus. Identify yourself or change your course. Failing to do so will force us to open fire."

Seeing as Charon preserved a gloomy silence, I took the initiative and tuned into the channel. "Argus, what is the required identification procedure?"

"You must report your login over a protected

channel."

"Charon? Kill the speed, will you?"

Gracefully the ship slowed down. I'd be lying if I said it felt good, but at least I didn't have to scrape myself off the wall.

I buried myself in the help pages trying to work out how to open this protected channel of theirs. Finally I asked Charon to help. For a few seconds he pondered over it, then nodded and flipped a few switches on one of the consoles.

I sent them my login.

Apparently, that wasn't all.

"You're not on our pilot list," the voice stated politely. "You can't fly a ship. Do you have a pilot? Would you be so kind as to identify him?"

Back to the help pages. Just as I suspected, there was only one way around it.

I offered the slave collar to Charon. He stared at it with understandable disgust, then looked up at me. "Why, Human?"

"I'm a friend. Trust me. It's only for a short while."

His eyes filled with fury replaced by agonizing amazement.

"Charon, we can't do it any other way," I tried to explain the situation to him. "I'll set you free at the first opportunity, I promise!"

No idea whether he believed me or not. Still, he took the collar from me and clicked it shut on himself, his fingers shaking.

I switched on the collar controller in the relaxed mode which meant that he had to stay within sixty feet from me.

"This is only a trick," I tried to impress upon him while uploading new information through the channel, *The pilot is my property. I intend to declare him as "personal possessions".*

Unexpectedly enough, they green-flagged us. The return message contained docking pad coordinates and a reminder that I had two hours to pay for the docking space.

* * *

THE SHIP CLANGED AND VIBRATED. Then the whining of the servomotors was replaced by a hissing sound as the craft entered the outer docking pad. The service mechanisms latched on to our long-suffering traveler, turning it around and locking it into place with its stern facing the station.

"Won't we burn the outer hull on takeoff?" I tried to break the awkward silence. Charon hunched moodily in his pilot's seat.

"*Nowr*," he answered curtly in his language, pointing at two symmetrical V-shaped ribbed structures. They must have been the launching boosters. There were lots of things there whose purpose I could only guess at.

Diaphragm hatches opened in the sides of the docking pad, revealing bundles of cables and pipes that reached out to our ship, connecting themselves to the on-board systems. Could it be a power feed?

Charon still hadn't said a word. And I was restless. In a moment, they were going to open the lock, letting us into an incredible new world. A world of limitless opportunities. I so wanted to believe it.

More system messages flashed in the foreground of

reality as the station's interface desperately tried to connect to my neuroimplant. Same old story: I needed to have a mind expander installed.

In the meantime, the sealing process was complete. The force field separating the docking pad from outer space had thickened. I watched through the viewing ports as hundreds of jets of murky white liquid sprayed the ship. I could only guess at the purpose of this, but chose not to ask questions.

"Come on, then!" I said.

Slowly Charon unbuckled and rose. I could see he really didn't want to leave the ship. Here he felt relatively safe, but I just couldn't afford this scenario. At the moment, he was my property, period. My leaving the ship alone could raise quite a few unpleasant questions.

The hatch opened, revealing a sealed sleeve between the station's hull and our ship. Having passed it, we found ourselves in a tiny chamber where we were showered with more of the murky liquid. Was it some kind of disinfectant?

More clanging and vibrating followed as the massive hatch retracted slowly, then rose.

I was the first to walk out. My first impressions were mixed. I'd imagined an enormous hangar bustling with activity. Instead, I was looking at an empty A-shaped corridor, dimly lit and rather dirty. Reinforcement ribs protruded at equal intervals from its walls. Darkness lurked in the service niches between them amid bundles of pipes and cables. The niches must have been cased in plastic which at some point had been ripped off, leaving bare fixtures on the walls.

As I took in the scene, two seedy types stepped

from the shadows. Both were burly, dressed in identical dark-grey uniforms, their assault vests equipped with various-sized pockets stuffed with tools.

The Mechanics Clan, a message popped up helpfully.

I must have been the reason they were there.

My gut feeling proved right. The two exuded confidence as they sneered at me. Little wonder. Both were level fifty and, judging by their behavior, this was their stomping ground.

"Hey you, *shnoob*. How about you pay for the docking?"

The word sounded offensive but I'd look into that later. Apparently, this wasn't the first time they were doing it. There was no one around. I hadn't noticed any surveillance cameras or defense turrets that could serve as makeshift law enforcement facilities.

"I have two hours to pay, don't I?" I said firmly just to show them I was familiar with the rules.

"We accept loot," one of them grinned. "On the spot."

"Thanks," I said as neutrally as I could. "I'll sort it out."

A punchup was the last thing I needed. But I knew this type. They weren't the kind who would leave you alone.

The other mechanic immediately moved on to threats. "And what if I accidentally confuse the cables as I service your rust bucket? Imagine how much you'll have to pay to get it fixed."

"I didn't order any servicing."

"It's compulsory," the first goon guffawed.

Reaching for my gun wasn't worth it. I needed them

to attack me first. That would justify my right to protect myself in any court.

"You can try," I sneered back which puzzled them a lot. "Or you can use your brain for a change. How could I come across this kind of ship?" I meaningfully played with the activation key that Charon had given me. It resembled a fancy key ring. "Think."

At that moment, Charon exited the dock. He looked sad — which to an uninformed onlooker must have appeared rageful. A dull growl was escaping his half-open sharp-toothed mouth. He stood up, revealing his slave collar to the dumbfounded mechanics, and froze expectantly in a well-practiced high guard.

Both men backed off. Apparently Charon wasn't the first Haash at the station.

So they got the answer to their questions, after all. A level-five noob who owned his own fighter with a xenomorph pilot simply had to be some millionaire daddy's son. They didn't know any other alternatives.

My first impression of the station wasn't rosy. The two mechanics seemed to be racking their brains searching for a way to fold their encounter without losing face. I was happy to oblige them.

"Where's the nearest gravity elevator?"

"Depends where you wanna go."

"Just want to get rid of the loot and have a bit of fun. And buy some implants, maybe, provided they're authentic. I don't need no fakes."

"Shaft seven, then three hundred feet down the corridor."

"Thanks," I calmly turned my back on them knowing they weren't going to do anything stupid anymore. Apart from Charon covering my back they must have realized the repercussions of upsetting anyone of my apparent caliber. So far, this particular incident was over, but I had to keep my eyes peeled.

If the truth were known, I was on my last legs. And still I couldn't yet afford to take a break. My initial resolve to slam the Logout button at the first opportunity had already lost its manic urgency. I had to have a look around, get rid of the loot, pay for the docking and find a place to stay, even if for one night. Then we'd see.

Thus thinking, I stopped by the elevator doors.

* * *

OUR TRANSFER BETWEEN THE STATION levels proved fast and unpleasant. The moment we stepped into the shimmering energy torrent, its invisible force lifted us and swirled us away. Personally, I felt like a twig caught in rapids. I froze inside as the shaft's walls turned into stripes of light. Several times the tunnel turned smoothly, changing direction, before we were finally nudged out onto a small platform enclosed by a low railing.

I barely stood on my feet. The momentum made me take a few more steps until I clenched the railing.

My vertigo soon subsided. Every now and then I could hear the popping sound and feel cold air rush over me as new people appeared out of nowhere and headed toward the wide staircase leading down.

Charon and I stepped aside.

Argus. The Market Deck, my interface informed me.

The hall was enormous. I couldn't even see its opposite walls lost in a far-off haze. The round arrivals' platform encircled a clutch of twenty elevators. Below lay an entire city of squat one-story houses, wide streets dividing them into blocks.

I cast a wary glance around. This wasn't how I'd imagined a space station's living quarters. The opening panorama was weird to say the least. My helmet's sniper sights system reacted to my confused state immediately, transforming the nearest buildings to show me how the city had been built. Red ink traced the original jagged remains of walls. All that the first settlers had seen at the station was ruins. They had cleared away the debris and cut away everything they didn't need, turning the tunnels into streets and building those squat houses in place of the once-destroyed personnel modules.

The place could use a bit of light. The enormous vaulted ceiling that had appeared as a result of an ancient technogenic disaster was lost in a vaporous haze that formed about sixty feet up, condensing in places into a cloud-like mist. A few remaining pieces of the framework reached up asymmetrically here and there.

Everything was new to me, everything piqued my curiosity. I could see a few *serves* as their cyber bodies scampered across the roofs and shinnied up the columns, servicing life support systems and fixing various bits, judging by the far-off flashing of welding torches.

The Market Deck was packed with people. It didn't look as if this bustle ever stopped here. The Haash and I were attracting quite a few unkind sideways glances, suspicious and hostile.

I noticed quite a few androids among the crowd. After having watched them for a while, I realized that they performed some kind of police function. They were armed; some of them guarded shop entrances while others patrolled the busy streets.

While I was thus gawking around, drones came from everywhere and surrounded us, flashing holographic advertisement that offered all sorts of services.

We'll move your respawn point to the Founders' Square! Safe resurrection for just 1000 credits!

Neurus Corporation: the best choice in implants! Affordable quality!

Exobiological symbionts from Xenus Corporation will boost your abilities and contribute some unique skills to your current configuration! All return customers get 50% off their third order.

Pimp your Ship! The Technologists clan offers a complete customization of your spacecraft with the use of the Founders' original blueprints. Modern quality through ancient technologies!

The Pilots clan invites all ship owners to join their raids on deserted stations. Excellent loot and the possibility of fast skill leveling.

Myrus&Myrus will buy scrap cargonite, quantity no object.

The Engineers clan will purchase any of the Founders' devices or their original blueprints.

Go exo! We offer a wide choice of alien metabolites!

Normally this kind of aggressive marketing drove me up the wall. But being surrounded by it now, after everything I'd just gone through, felt like a breath of fresh air.

I looked up at the direction signs. Founders Square was situated in the very center of the enormous hall. Still, it had to wait. My first port of call was clear: I had to find the nearest Myrus&Myrus scrap yard.

And there it was. You just couldn't miss the large double *M*. I motioned Charon to follow me.

We walked down the wide staircase, attracting more unfriendly attention from onlookers.

Apparently, cargonite was all the rage here. Most players were wearing light armor as an alternative to everyday clothes. The entire Market Deck looked like an enormous Eastern-style bazaar with its multitude of interesting offers and potential opportunities. Still, I had more important things to take care of first. I had to find money to move my respawn point and pay for the docking space.

TWO ANDROIDS GUARDED THE entrance to Myrus&Myrus. They looked only marginally humanoid. Their armor plates gleamed purple, their build a rough semblance of our own. Their weapons were integrated. Although my meager abilities didn't allow me to scan them, I was more than sure these guys could be quite dangerous in combat. The androids stood a head above the human players. They had no faces, only tinted front plates flickering with scanner lights deep inside.

They paid no attention to us whatsoever.

Before entering, I asked Charon, "Do you think you can extract devices from Dargian armor?"

"It depends on the type," he answered and froze, focusing on his inventory where I'd moved nine of the trophy gear kits.

Soon he handed me the modules he'd managed to extract. Five in total. Not many. Shame but at the moment, I couldn't do much about it. Time was working against us. I'd saved Rash's armor till later. I needed some time to look into it first.

Now we had to hurry. We only had one hour left to pay for the docking space, and I didn't even know how much it was going to cost me. I had no access to the station's network (due to the fact that I didn't have their so-called mind expander installed) and in its absence, I started to feel a bit uneasy. While not explicitly aggressive, other players didn't seem particularly friendly, either. They cast hostile glances at Charon and curious ones at myself, their interest immediately replaced by confusion.

I could imagine that rumors of our ship would soon spread. I didn't at all like the reaction of the two mechanics we'd met by the docking pad. It was pretty clear that the craft was expensive enough. Many would want to lay they hands on it. I would have to either sell it or stick to my cover story which would demand some serious cash injection, primarily to be able to level my char up fast. Which meant I absolutely had to log out and have a few words with Arbido. We had a few things to discuss.

I walked into the Myrus&Myrus.

The shop's façade was impressive enough. The inside though was rather plain. The place resembled a hangar. About a dozen drones floated under the high ceiling.

I headed for a small office counter which looked like a child's toy amid all the mountains of scrap metal.

A disgusting-looking dealer stood behind the curved counter. I had no idea where my subconscious mind had borrowed suitable words and images from, but the first impression was depressing. I had no doubt that the owner of this loathsome, bloated, obese avatar had serious mental problems.

I focused on him.

Ingmud. Human. Level 37. Vendor.

This was another specialization typical of any game world. Having said that, normally the role of vendors was reserved to NPCs. More often than not they were also quest characters, too.

"Excuse me, sir," I humbly tried to attract his attention while thinking that I hadn't yet been given the chance to create my own unique character. What would *I* see if I looked in the mirror?

The thought made me uncomfortable. My interface tabs only showed a symbolic human outline. What kind of appearance had Arbido chosen for me? Or maybe he hadn't bothered doing it at all but had simply clicked the randomizer?

"Well?" the vendor gave me a rather dismissive glance. "The scale's in the corner," he mumbled. "Just dump everything you've got on it."

I didn't like his suggestion at all. "You'd better have

a look at it first," I said, trying to stay calm and polite.

"What's so special about it?"

"These are integrated devices," I tried to sound as if I knew their potential value.

"Not interested," the vendor waved the offer away. "We only accept scrap cargonite. You need to see the Technologists or Engineers about any devices."

"Still, I'd like you to have a look," I insisted.

"Very well, then," he sighed as if doing me a favor. His eyes glinted, though.

Without saying a word, I showed him the cargonite armor kits.

One of his eyebrows rose. He can't not have noticed the bullet dents and the laser scars on the armor. "So where did you steal it from?" he cast me a sceptic glance.

"I won it in honest combat."

"I'll give you ten percent over the scrap price," he drilled me with his stare. "On one condition."

"Which is?"

"I'll need the logs of the fight."

I shook my head.

"Ten percent off, then," he gave me a nasty smile.

"Why?"

"For the risk of trading in stolen goods."

I was a lousy profiteer. Who'd asked me to open my mouth even? I should have gone straight for the scales as he'd told me.

I did have the logs, of course. But showing it here would be a very stupid thing to do. At the moment, I didn't want anyone to know about my fight with the slave drivers. The information about their base and the ship they were restoring could prove much more valuable than the cargonite itself.

"Okay, then," I motioned Charon to dump everything onto the scales. I had no time to look for another vendor.

"Will you sell me your Haash?" the shop owner suddenly asked me.

"No."

"Think again. I'll give you fifty thousand."

"He's not for sale."

Charon had already loaded all the scrap onto the platform that floated a couple of feet above the ground. It sank slightly. The vendor made some brief mental calculations.

"Five hundred credits."

I sent a mnemonic message to Charon, *Can you read the weight?*

"Six hundred-" he paused as if he'd never encountered the word *pound* before.

I glanced over the price list exhibited on the transparent holographic clipboard. Eleven credits a pound!

"Charon, pick it all up. We're going."

The vendor rose in his chair, "Wait a second, young man! It's probably the scales playing up. Wretched piece of junk!"

Greed glinted in his eyes. I wouldn't have been surprised if integrated devices cost ten times the price of scrap cargonite. And it wasn't scrap I was selling him, either. "I don't think so."

We walked out into the street. It felt like a breath of fresh air after the shop's dark atmosphere. I took another look around. This time I didn't rush it.

The Armory.

Yes. Exactly what we needed.

We hurried across the street and entered the shop.

It was small, crammed with holographic models of their wares. They were really spoiled for choice here.

I hadn't noticed the vendor amid all the paraphernalia of weapons and armor. A young fair-haired man proffered me his hand.

"Serge," he said, casting a cautious glance at the Haash.

"Zander," I answered his handshake. "Don't worry. Charon doesn't attack anyone."

"What can I offer you, Zander? Are you interested in weapons or in gear? We have direct contacts with the Technologists. Some of the items are mind-blowing."

"I'll keep that in mind when I need to buy something. Now I just want to offer you some of my loot. Some gear kits and pulse guns. I can't extract the devices though. Haven't been in the game long enough."

"Where did you get it from?"

These questions began to annoy me. Normally, vendors don't give a shit where you got your loot from. Then again, I knew nothing about the local customs yet, so I decided to stick to my story.

"Thing is, I bought this account from someone," I said nonchalantly. "I arrived at the station in my ship an hour ago. And all the gear was already in the inventory."

Serge wasn't as stuck up his own backside as the last vendor. At least he seemed to accept my fake confession. "So how about I have a look at it?" he chuckled.

I motioned Charon to unload the gear onto the counter.

Serge scanned it meticulously. Then he made some

mental calculations. "How about three grand in total?"

"Cash."

He shook his head. "I don't work with cash. Too much hassle."

"I don't have access to the station's network yet. I didn't get a chance to get any implants."

"Not a problem," he pointed at a payment terminal. "Just log into it and I'll transfer you the money."

"What kind of cash do you use here, then?" I asked, curious.

"Microchips," he answered willingly.

"What's so valuable about them?"

"You don't mean you haven't even read the FAQ?"

"Nope."

"Microchips are everywhere. They make the base of any cyber system. There are some fakes around but there're not difficult to tell, all you need to do is test them in a dedicated slot."

"And what if someone pays me, say, a thousand of them? How much time will it take to test them all?"

He chuckled at my naïve question. "A thousand chips is a lot. I don't think you'll come across anything like that in the foreseeable future. The maximum an experienced leveled-up pilot can expect is ten to fifteen chips for a really risky mission. Normally it's about enough to upgrade one of the ship's systems. There are also neurochips but they're sold at the rate of one to a hundred. There it gets more difficult. You absolutely have to test them but you'll need special equipment to do so."

"How much does a neurochip cost, then?"

"A blank one is five hundred credits. A pre-recorded one, depends. And those with the Founders' software may go for tens of thousands."

"I see. Listen, I still need to pay for the docking space. Can I do it from here?"

He nodded. "I should install some implants pretty quick if I were you," he added. "You can't really function without them. Even the most basic ones. Or you risk being forever stuck at the shnoob stage. No one will want to deal with you. They'll charge you more for the docking and offer less for your loot. You really have to look sharp here," he opened some kind of list. "Was it an inner or outer docking pad?"

"What's the difference?" I didn't even need to pretend, I honestly didn't know.

"The outer docking pads are the cheapest," he seemed eager to teach me the ropes. "Think for yourself: about a third of all defense systems still aren't functioning. So who's gonna meet the intruder in case of an attack? Evidently it's the pilots docked on the outside. They're the first to reach their ships and go into combat. They have no choice. But if you're safely docked inside, that's a totally different ball game. Then it's up to you whether you join in or not. Most likely, they'll offer you a one-off station defense contract."

"I see. No, I'm docked outside," I sighed. "How much do they charge per twenty-four hours?"

"A hundred credits. For free, basically. I'm going to pay it from your account in a moment. How much do you plan to afford?"

"Three days, maybe? Then we'll see."

"Make it a week. First because there's a discount. Second, because if you do install some implants, you might land in a clinic for five days at least."

"Agreed. Is the station attacked often, then?"

He shrugged at the question. "Virtually every day.

Nothing serious, really. Between all those Dargians, Wearongs, Kamresh and the Outlaws, there are plenty of takers. Normally, the Pilots clan handles them no problem. But if your docking pad happens within the attack cone, anything can happen. If you don't make it there in time or you don't launch or you fail to engage, they can easily seize your ship. Especially the Outlaws. They have some top hackers there. They'll take your ship and you won't even notice."

This didn't sound too optimistic. "I see. How much does an inner docking space cost?"

"Five hundred credits."

"A bit pricey."

"But safe."

"Who are the Outlaws, then?"

He cringed. "Humans. A bunch of scumbags. Some have problems with the law. Others have dodgy implants. A lot are said to be on *exo*," I sensed a badly concealed fear in his voice. "They have their own bases within the asteroid belt."

"Are there many major attacks?" I tried to milk him for as much information as I could.

"Depends. Last week the crafters got it pretty bad. A month ago some Dargians and Wearongs landed in the deserted sectors trying to get to the oil. And," he lowered his voice, "they say there's been a few recent sightings of Phantom Raiders."

"Who the hell are they?"

"Phantoms," Serge answered meaningfully. "The word says it all. They appear out of nowhere. Some say they arrive from another star system. Even though the Technologists and the Engineers swear that a warp drive just can't be built."

"Where do they come from, then?"

He shrugged. "No one knows. We've never managed to get hold of any. When critted, their ships either disappear or they self-destruct. Depends on your luck."

"What's the difference?"

"You'll know it when you see it. If a Raider disappears, that's one thing. You're scored a win and subsequently get paid. Because the logs are still there, you see. But if they self-destruct, that's a totally different story. That's annihilation. If you happen anywhere near it, just pray to the Founders that your force shields hold. The clans will pay any money for a fragment of the Phantom Raiders' ships."

"How much will they pay for a whole one?"

Again he gave me this patronizing, unsettled smile. "That's science fiction," he scooped up my Dargian gear. "No one has ever seized a Phantom. One thing you need to remember: if a general alert is sounded, get up and run for your ship. If a pilot fails to show up, they will confiscate the ship and throw the pilot out of the station. Through the airlock without a spacesuit. To a respawn purgatory in a vacuum."

"Is it so bad?"

"Where the Phantoms are concerned, yes. We can't survive otherwise," he pressed a few buttons. "All done. The docking space is paid for a week, you've got twenty-three hundred on your account. Come back when you want a gear change."

"I will."

* * *

CHARON AND I WALKED out of the shop.

My next port of call: having my respawn point moved.

I kept meeting hostile stares. I hadn't yet met a single xenomorph which I found quite worrying. The passersby glared at Charon with undisguised hatred, followed by looks of surprised disdain directed at me. I hadn't yet worked out the reasons for such animosity but it would probably be better for us to finish whatever else we had to do quickly and find a place to stay. I needed to look into Wiki — the dated word I used out of habit when referring to gaming encyclopedias.

Founders Square didn't impress me much. It was vast and empty. We paused next to it, noticing a cordon of androids. The impassive steel robots stood watch over the respawning process. From time to time, the square echoed with a popping sound as a flash of green light released a newly respawned player. Generally, all of them looked pissed and confused, having just suffered a virtual death.

I could tell by their gear that most of the survivors were pilots. We lingered behind the cordon, watching. I noticed a few mechanics appear amid the incessant flashes of green. Judging by the few brief phrases they exchanged, it had been some sort of repair gone awry. A few shady individuals must have been the victim of some gang war or other. Then the square flooded with armed people in full armored suits — I could hear snippets of their conversation about mopping up the station's deserted levels and "those raid-wiping idiots".

Aha. They had counted on abundant loot but got a kick in the balls instead. Happens to the best of us. Still, as I studied their weapons and gear, I couldn't help asking myself what kind of mobs had to be lurking in the station's deserted bowels.

All of that was quite an eye-opener, but it was time for us to leave. Personally, I could barely stand straight from exhaustion.

I cast a look around, searching for the offer we needed. I didn't have to look long. At the entrance to the nearest shop, more drones glowed with their aggressive advertisement, pestering the passersby.

I was wary of more questions and technical problems, but the shop owner — definitely an NPC — just kept nodding with a happy smile. No, he didn't need to know where my old respawn point was. He could transfer it to Founders Square for a thousand credits regardless of its current location. The Haash wasn't a problem, either. He was a player like all of us so technically, he was entitled to one, too.

I shelled out two grand. Despite having made a big hole in my budget, it was definitely worth it.

I asked the vendor about any potential places to stay and received some very detailed directions. Apparently, the entire perimeter of the Market Deck was lined with living modules. In whichever direction we went, we could still get there.

The whole respawn point transfer procedure seemed a bit iffy to me. The vendor rubbed some silvery goo into Charon's and my forearms and reported happily, "All done!"

"What's this, then?" I studied an oblong silver spot just above my wrist.

"That's a marker," the vendor informed me. "Effective within range of up to ten light seconds from the station. Anything further than that is your responsibility."

I imagined the scenario: me and my ship, millions of miles away from my new respawn point. In case of trouble, I'd find myself back here at Founders Square, but what was going to become of the ship?

I asked the vendor about it. He shrugged. "Normally, pilots fly either in groups or at least in twos. So there's always somebody to tow your ship back to the station or at least to keep an eye on it."

"And if that's not the case?"

"We don't cover spacecraft. You might need to talk to some of the technologists about that. They might know of a solution. Or," he lowered his voice and leaned across the counter toward me, "try and find one of the Outlaws' bases in the asteroid belt. There're rumors they've cracked the Phantom Raiders' mystery. Because we don't get very many of the Outlaws' downed ships."

"Oh really?"

"Oh really what?" he said nonchalantly. "Have I just told you something?" the vendor gave me a barely noticeable wink. "In any case, Sir, I would be quite interested in buying some rare equipment. So if you find anything, I'll be very happy to consider it. Trust me you won't regret it."

New quest alert! Immortal Hardware!

Find any of the Outlaws' bases and try to find out more about the ancient technology they recently discovered.

* * *

"COME ON, CHARON. Time to go."

Enough for one day. I was already fed up with

today's dose of adventure. I could barely stand on my feet. I still wasn't hungry or thirsty, but Charon was already ogling a vending machine offering food tubes. To me, they looked utterly gross but I was surprised that he could be hungry at all.

"Fancy some?"

He nodded energetically, his eyes glowing with excitement.

He was a mystery to me. I walked over to the machine and bought a few tubes of my choice for him.

He swallowed them whole right there, wrappers and all. The nearest androids swung round to the distinct chattering sound of his teeth, but immediately lost interest, noticing his slave collar.

It was better he didn't remove it at all. Which made the freedom I'd promised him rather questionable. Charon didn't protest, though. He followed me meekly and obediently, showing no return aggression to anyone around.

I immediately thought about the earlier docking incident with the two mechanics. He'd behaved totally different then.

I remembered seeing him in the ship's cockpit: a free pilot, proud and confident. Apparently, the Haash possessed some enviable acting skills.

Then again, maybe he'd taken my clever little ploy seriously. If so, he'd probably accepted his fate thinking that I'd simply betrayed him.

Never mind. We'd talk it all over once we got to the hotel.

"Come on now," I pulled his hand, motioning him to follow me into the nearest street. It led from the central square away to the enormous hall's perimeter.

There we discovered lots of oblong hatches that

lined the hall's walls, with a holographic sign next to each. I checked them and shook my head. Capsule hotels weren't for the likes of us.

We spent some time looking for suitable lodgings. Finally, we'd chosen *Gardean's Living Blocks* — or so the ethereal advertisement claimed.

The hatch creaked slightly as I opened it. Charon had to stoop as he entered, otherwise his head would have hit the doorway.

Another long corridor lined with identical oblong doors. A lamp cast a cozy light from the reception at the far end of the passage. Noticing the Haash, the owner rose, reaching for his weapon.

I sensed Charon's hot breath on the crown of my head. "Keep out of it," I warned him just in case.

Then I walked confidently up to the counter. Charon breathed in fits behind me, sensing a threat and ready to charge.

I warned him once again, then smiled to the owner. "How much do you charge a night, Sir?"

"Twenty credits."

"I thought it said ten by the entrance?"

"You can be thankful I'm letting you in at all," his cheek twitched. He eyed the Haash. "Doing your bit of exo harvesting?"

I shrugged, making it clear it was none of his business. "Agreed. Here's a hundred," I noticed a payment terminal and hurried to transfer the money. In return he offered me a smirk and an electronic key.

The living block was warm and clean. A soft porous carpeting covered the floor. The five-sided room was small, a bit like a honeycomb: a basic hygiene unit in a corner and a folding bed along the wall opposite the station network terminal.

The massive hatch shuddered shut. Two new icons appeared before my mental eye: *Open* and *Block from inside.*

Naturally, I chose the latter.

It took me a few moments to work out the collar controller. Then I removed the deactivated collar from Charon's neck. Finally!

He cricked his neck, mistrustful.

"Didn't I tell you it was only a trick?"

He stared into my eyes long and hard. Gradually his gaze softened as understanding grew within.

"I know it can't have been easy for you. I'm afraid you'll have to grin and bear it for a tiny bit longer until I can think of a way to legalize you here at the station. But now at least you can log out. Do you understand? You do have somewhere to go back to, don't you?"

He didn't answer.

Very well. I was more than sure he knew what I meant. Then it was up to him. Personally, I was logging out. I needed some quality sleep, a meal and a shower. Followed by the next point on my agenda: having a heart-to-heart with Arbido.

"That's it," I pulled the bed down, lay on top of it and closed my eyes. "But whatever happens, Charon — promise me not to leave the room!"

The logout button glowed green, calling my name.

I pressed it.

Chapter Three

Logout

I WAS BACK!

Gradually my eyesight began to focus. My body was numb. I could make out a convex translucent surface in front of my face and the blurred outline of my room behind it.

Back to reality.

Only now could I pluck up enough courage to admit: I'd been so scared to lose this thin bond between the physical and made-up worlds which I'd been so eager to break before my introduction to Phantom Server.

The grass is always greener, as they say.

My muscles felt quite fit. I wouldn't say I was wide awake and bursting with energy — my eyes felt dry and tired — but even this initial awakening surprisingly felt like good news.

The fact is, it's not real life itself that matters. It's

- Phantom Server Book One -

knowing that you can come back at any time — the sheer freedom of choice. Apparently, once you are stripped of that choice, things aren't so funny anymore. Especially when you are stuck in a totally unknown world.

I had lots of things to do. No time to go to bed yet. I touched the glowing rune of an icon. Air hissed. The translucent lid began to rise.

My implant reacted predictably. *The in-mode is off.*

I grasped at the sides of the capsule and sat up, then scrambled out and headed for the shower. I needed to freshen myself up.

My head was going round a bit but I knew it would soon pass. Standing under the hot jets, I tried to depressurize. The Phantom Server had left a lasting imprint on my mind. I studied my forearm — no sight of any implants. I wiped myself dry and put some clean clothes on, then walked over to the front door. No sign of a break-in. The in-mode technicians were no dodgy customers. They'd got a proper entry clearance. I had this lock with special tracking software: it didn't prevent a break-in but it did signal an intrusion. This time there'd been none: their so-called "technical support team" had used a copy of my own electronic key complete with my biometric data. Just like a medical response team!

Now I had three potential courses of action.

1. I could cancel the contract and send the neuroimplant back to the developers.

2. I could keep the implant but never go back to continue the alpha testing of the Phantom Server.

3. Alternatively, I could stay in the game.

I sat at the table, ordered a breakfast and began thinking. I wasn't sure about the right choice yet.

Each of the three had its own pros and cons, but do you know what actually worried me?

You will never believe it. The Haash prisoners' fate.

Was I finally losing it? In game as in real life, it was every man for himself, wasn't it? No one had overrun this simple rule yet. It's true that I had always tended to join the forces of Light whenever I played a game. Then again, this Light also came with certain strings attached. Most likely — if I had to be brutally honest with myself — I was simply attracted by their design and all the potential abilities. But I'd never been a clan player. Sometimes, yes, depending on a particular assignment or out of dire necessity: then I could indeed work as part of a team but it never attracted me as such. It was a choice that must have initially been formed by the nature of my work for Arbido. Then I'd simply got used to it. I must have realized that any voluntary responsibility for other people's lives was a moral burden I could live without. Also, I hated obeying various statuses and charts. Freedom and adventure were my religion, unconcerned and commitment-free.

The thought of Arbido grated on my nerves.

First thing we had to do was to talk. I needed my money back as well as some information. Then I'd decide what to do next.

I NEVER FOUND ARBIDO. But I didn't push too hard, either. I created a new account in the Crystal Sphere for a bit of nostalgic leveling. I made level 5 and sold some penny loot. The game's rather boring opening offered a player plenty of motivation to seek any easy side routes — but no such luck.

No one offered me any shady services.

Very well. I did the same in another game world where I knew Arbido had a long and established history.

Not an online manager in sight. Not one of his old contacts still around.

I went as far as to buy a new microchip and change my nano comp's IP address. I knew from experience that any potential client always left in his wake what I'd call the "matching customer to product" trail. All of their online searches and their entire browsing history were meticulously recorded and analyzed in order to ensure that everyone could find exactly what he wanted.

Now this worried me quite a bit. Arbido seemed to have disappeared off my radars — and so had my money.

I wasn't in the brightest of moods when I finally logged out. Only when I glanced at the clock did I realize I'd been deprived of sleep for over twenty-four hours.

Our — my and Charon's — escape from slavery followed by our trip to the station and everything it implied had taken almost ten hours in actual time. In total, I'd spent a whopping two days in the Phantom Server.

Time to catch a few Zs. It never pays to take important decisions while unable to think straight. I switched on each and every security device, climbed back into the capsule, sealed it and activated the in-mode.

* * *

THE FOLLOWING DAY brought no relief. Arbido seemed to have vanished into thin air. I spent a couple of hours in the Crystal Sphere just watching other players and following the newsfeed.

Nothing new there. Not one of the artifacts I'd handed over to him had resurfaced in the local network. All the other agents known to me were offline.

I was bored out of my mind. The neuroimplant was working at maybe ten percent of its true capacity. Now I knew exactly how it could make me feel.

I wondered about Charon. What would he be doing now?

I walked over to the window and stood there staring at the city enveloped in industrial haze.

Arbido could wait, my gut feeling told me. He must simply be lying low. It had happened before during some major Net police raids.

So what was I waiting for, then? My Phantom Server account had been paid for. I had lots of things to do there.

A thin voice of reason tried to talk me out of it, reminding me of all the dangers these new neuronet technologies could harbor. But the thought had only challenged me. I was now itching to go back.

Surely I'd be able to raise some money to have those implants installed. And I wasn't going to let them catch me so stupidly the next time. I was desperate to get back now. The miserable cityscape behind my window annoyed and frustrated me. I knew myself well enough. I wouldn't be able to wait for much longer.

I turned round and looked at the open capsule.

Yes. That was it. I was going back.

The thought alone allowed me to breathe easier.

* * *

LOGIN

I OPENED MY EYES. i was lying on a narrow folding bed.

A strange spicy smell hovered in the air. Not unpleasant — just alien. Wary. I sat up and looked around me.

Charon lay sprawled out by the door. He didn't move.

I stood up and tried to shake him awake. Pointless. I listened to his breathing: it was level. Was he asleep? Or had he logged out too?

I'd no idea what happened to a logged-out player's avatar in this particular world. Normally, it should just disappear. But the Phantom Server seemed to be living by its own rules. Nothing would surprise me.

Charon's face was calm and peaceful. His skin, however, was covered with droplets of some substance which produced the smell that had alarmed me earlier.

I tried to shake him awake again — to no avail. I struggled to drag his limp body into a far corner and concentrated.

What was I supposed to do with him now? If Charon had logged out, then why was his avatar's heart still beating? Why was his skin warm, why was he breathing? That wasn't right.

I had no one to turn to for advice. All I could do was sit there and wait until he came round.

I left the Haash alone and slumped into a chair opposite the network terminal. I wanted to look into the local market.

First things first. I had to research this implant thing and, more importantly, find some money for the surgery.

The station network was crammed full of offers but admittedly dodgy ones. I didn't need a cottage job, that's for sure. Not one of the tempting affordable offers contained any clear-cut explanations. I opened one at random.

I'll install a basic mind expander for as little as 1000 credits. Ask for Claus the mnemotech at the 7th market block.

How cool was that? As if I'd allow some cowboy brain surgeon to mess with my head! What kind of expanders were they? Where had he gotten them from? Had he looted them off something or someone or just bought a second-hand one?

No, thanks. Anything but that.

It's not that I was too choosy — just wary of any potential problems. Such cyborgization of an avatar was going to seriously affect the character itself. This wasn't a mediocre sword or a suit of armor which you could keep for a while, hoping one day to swap it for something really good.

So I kept looking into it, searching for any criteria.

A mind expander is a neuronet module responsible for the reception and processing of incoming data from any implants or gear sensors. It exists in three basic models:

SynapsX. Receives data from gear sensors only. Its advantages: low cerebral overload parameters (needs 4 pt. Intellect, 4 pt. Willpower, 3 pt. Learning Skills) and low price. Downsides: your perception range will depend on the gear you wear. Any gear sensor damage will render the implant useless. Recommended for mercenaries, low-rank mechanics, small-craft pilots, crafters and artifact hunters.

Not for me, probably. I shifted in the hard chair, trying to get comfortable. What's the point in wearing a mind-expanding implant which demands the donning of expensive gimmick-packed gear?

So I went on reading,

Synaps2. Works exclusively with implants. Its advantages: average cerebral overload parameters (needs 5 pt. Intellect, 5 pt. Willpower, 5 pt. Learning Skills) and the possibility of linking it up with a one-off choice of three sealed cyber modules (which are implanted simultaneously with the mind expander). Downsides: once chosen, this configuration cannot be altered or upgraded. Recommended for all-round pilots, owners of cargo craft and mid-rank mechanics.

This looked interesting. Having said that, I hadn't decided on my specialization yet. I didn't want to risk choosing the wrong cyber modules.

Well, what did they have next?

SynapsZ Universal. Five slots are implanted into

your skull, capable of housing multi-task cyber modules. Its downsides: high cerebral overload parameters (needs 7 pt. Intellect, 7 pt. Willpower and 7 pt. Learning Skills) and high price. Its advantages: the possibility of flexible module configuration depending on the task at hand and the ability to manually replace modules in slots. Recommended for scientists, technologists, mnemotechs, exobiologists and raid leaders as well as large spacecraft and squadron commanders.

The mind boggles. That was it, yes. But the price was going through the roof.

Never mind. One day we'd make it. The first few steps are never easy. One thing was for sure: I should take my time choosing the right implants. In the meantime, I could do very well on peripherals.

A sharp screeching noise attracted my attention.

I turned round, staring at Charon. He still lay on the floor with his eyes closed, but his right arm twitched, convulsing, clawing the bulkhead.

Whatever was happening to him? I stood up and warily approached him. Was it some involuntary reflex? If he'd indeed logged out, his avatar couldn't possibly have any!

Charon's hand twitched and clenched into a fist. Once again I tried to shake him awake. He didn't respond.

* * *

I RETURNED TO THE TERMINAL and continued studying the network.

The metabolic corrector and reflex enhancer were more or less clear. The former was basically a microscopic biochemical factory. It pumped your blood through, cleansing it from anything toxic and enriching it with various beneficial (or so they thought) substances and formulas. The implant drew heavily on your body resources but it also came with its own supply of metabolite cartridges. In order to refill them, special sockets were implanted under your skin; the formulas themselves were produced locally available in disposable tube syringes.

This was getting interesting.

The reflex enhancer consisted of nanites capable of forming artificial neural tissue inside the body. It was implanted by injecting special nanomachine colonies which then developed into a supplementary neural impulse transmission system. Working together with the mind expander, the nanites ensured knee-jerk reactions especially vital for pilots who had to implement their combat decisions swiftly and efficiently.

Oh well.

The easy way wasn't an option. A hasty and cheap decision could become a dead end. It was pretty obvious I had to opt for the best. Still, the best prices flickered an exorbitant amount of zeros.

What if I was trying to overcomplicate it?

I checked the information once again, then asked myself the question: where had they come from to begin with, these implants? And why did xenomorphs also seem to have them?

The answer wasn't hard to find.

Apparently, all the current technologies were based on the discoveries of the so-called Founders. This was the name given to the mysterious civilization that had built both these stations and the enormous spaceships I'd glimpsed drifting through space.

I stopped reading and cast a glance over at Charon. Still unconscious. I then tried to ponder over what I'd just learned.

Normally I never tried to purposefully look into any backstory of game worlds. I knew only too well that all the information I would need would be offered to a player at the right moment in the game in an impressive and well-measured manner. The Phantom Server didn't seem to be so simple. The memory of my alternative start was a prime example of the mess I'd found myself in instead of a colorful full-dimensional introduction demo.

I stood up and paced the room, then took a swig of water and went back to the terminal.

I was buzzing with too many questions. I knew instinctively that my survival depended on my finding all the answers. Here, no one was going to offer me a helpful prompt when the going got critical.

I SPENT THE NEXT FEW HOURS studying the Phantom Server world.

I had pieced together some shreds of unrelated information about the Founders, their history and technology, that I'd amassed from various sources. This was the impression I finally got:

The only thing known for sure was that the Founders weren't humanoid. We could only speculate about the location of their home star system. Without a shadow of a doubt, the creatures had attained some incredible development before they had been finally confronted with what must have seem like an unsurmountable problem: the light barrier.

This had been quite an interesting plot twist on the part of the scriptwriters. Normally, all game worlds solved this problem simply by introducing the idea of hyperspace and the so-called warp drives. So easy — and so utterly unscientific. This way you simply *jumped* to whatever star system you fancied, be it hundreds of light years away.

I kept reading.

The Founders had apparently discovered hyperspace too. After studying it, they'd arrived at the conclusion that it allowed you to transmit any structured signal, complexity no object — but not a material body.

It's well known that a civilization locked within its own solar system is doomed. The Founders must have realized this too — which was why they'd come up with a rather unique solution to the problem. They had built automated interstellar ships and sent them on their never-ending subluminal journey. Traveling from one star system to the next, these robotic explorers studied planets looking for available resources, then used them to build automated stations equipped with special biological reconstruction chambers and instant interstellar communication systems.

So gradually they'd developed their own intergalactic network. The Founders had forbidden their robotized ships to mine for resources on already-inhabited planets, leaving them to explore asteroid belts and barren worlds in order to build more automated ships equipped with biological reconstruction chambers. It enabled the Founders to travel to stars by transmitting the neural matrices of their identities to any station of their choice. And once they lost interest in any particular star system, they simply traveled on.

All this had happened millions of years ago. The Founders' expansion had left countless artifacts behind — all the abandoned stations, planet and asteroid bases, mines and shipyards — and their broken interstellar network. Whatever had happened to its creators, whatever had caused the destruction of most of their technogenic facilities, remained a mystery.

Whew.

It had taken me quite some time to puzzle this picture together out of various bits of fragmentary evidence.

Phantom Server: quest completed!
A new global plot activated!
You've received a new level!
You've received a new level!
New quest available: Phantom Server 1. The Mystery of Hyperspace.

Find one of the interstellar network installations and try to work out whether it's still functional. Does the network's central server, known as Phantom Server, still exist? Is it true that it used to control and coordinate all of the Founders' AI ships and stations?

Two new levels! This wasn't bad at all. I'd had no

idea that my humble attempt at research would be rewarded so generously.

The plot definitely thickened.

* * *

WHILE I WAS AT IT, I decided to spend a bit more time looking into the current state of affairs.

This time I had to sieve through tons of information trying to separate grains of truth from all sorts of rumors and fiction.

So. This star system only consisted of two planets.

The planet Darg was similar to Earth in many respects. I'd already met some of its inhabitants so I'm not going to dwell on them for the time being.

The planet Wearong was a brown gas giant inhabited by creatures which were probably best described as some sort of squid. I studied pictures of them, curious. They looked fragile but were in fact highly dangerous, having evolved in a high-pressure, low-temperature environment amid fierce air currents and toxic methane clouds. Which was why Mother Nature had equipped the Wearongs with a sealed shell capable of withstanding a broad range of extreme elements, including vacuum.

The Wearongs lived in the upper atmosphere levels and used organic jet propulsion to move around. Their bodies produced electricity which they used for both attack and defense. The screenshots available with articles showed enormous almost lightning-like discharges that the Wearongs used to shoot down Dargian spaceships.

The third civilization — the Kamresh — had originated and evolved on the gas giant's satellite. Judging by the images, the Kamresh possessed an exoskeleton which made them extremely resistant. They looked very much like our mole crickets and lived deep inside rock labyrinths that riddled their little planetoid.

Now it was time to turn to the Dargians.

They were the main local opposing force.

Their development was quite interesting. I downloaded one of the videos taken from Darg. You wouldn't believe it but one of the Founders' stations had drifted over to the planet's orbit. On the picture it looked like an enormous sullen moon taking up a good one-third of the sky. Add to this the station's two automatically activated orbital power elevators: two shafts of phantom energy sliding along the planet's surface, sucking in anyone who dared to enter its glow and beaming them up on board this enormous technogenic artifact.

My throat rasped. I took another swig of water and went on reading.

No wonder the Dargians had developed the cult of the Heavenly Guardian. While technically still living in the Dark Ages, they had gained access to board a rather well-preserved station of an incredibly advanced civilization. Imagine the impact it had had on their own progress?

The Technologists clan tended to believe that at the time, some of the ancient AI modules on board the station had still been functioning. Upon reaching maturity, each Dargian was supposed to enter the "phantom light". Some were killed by it while others received precious gifts from the Heavenly Guardian, like implants (I'd already known from experience what this felt like) and an incredible wealth of knowledge, while yet others died of radiation sickness. All this had lasted for hundreds of years.

This had allowed the Dargians to learn about the nature of the Universe. Over time, they had managed to restore a dozen of the Founders' large ships and discovered nine more stations — all this purely thanks to the technologies they'd adapted. They hadn't invented anything themselves, but they had enslaved the two other civilizations. They cybergized both the Wearongs and the Kamresh, using these sturdy alien creatures to work at the most dangerous and remote locations in deep space.

Today, the Dargians' science was a grotesque mix of borrowed knowledge and medieval mysticism. Their view of the universe was bigoted and aggressive, and their society was a divisive feudal system. With all this, they had become apt space travelers and decent technicians capable of using ancient devices.

There you go. Three alien civilizations against a still-inexperienced gaming community.

I rose and walked around the room, stretching my numb legs. I'd love to know how humans had gotten into the local picture.

I SAT BACK AT THE TERMINAL. Seeing as I'd already started, I might just as well do everything at once.

According to the Phantom Server's official story book, the First Colonial Fleet — headed by cruisers from the Neurus Corporation — had arrived in the Darg System five years ago after a long and enduring journey at subluminal speeds.

Humans had no idea of the Founders or their civilization. Thirty spacecraft and ten cryogenic platforms carrying hibernated astronauts had left the Solar system in search of a planet with a suitable living environment.

The fate of the First Colonial Fleet had been tragic. The Dargians had attacked it as soon as it had entered the system's space. A large-scale battle had lasted seventy-two hours. Only a few Earth craft had survived it: a badly damaged Titan — the corporation's flagship — two freighters, one cryogenic platform and lots of rescue capsules.

The Dargian fleet had suffered some irreversible losses as well, including all their large craft. Still, that couldn't have changed anything. Tens of thousands of human colonists had been killed. The survivors had been forced to seek shelter on one of the Founders' stations nearby.

The flagship had held out for two more days, covering the retreat of the rescue capsules and the damaged freighters. After that, the Wearongs (whom the Dargians used as some sort of living aerospace fighter craft) had destroyed the ship's defense equipment, allowing Kamresh assault groups to board the helplessly drifting ship.

Judging by the story, the flagship, radiation-ridden and mauled by the reactor collapse, was still drifting through space amid the debris.

The surviving colonists had boarded the station. The space battle had abated, proving to be only the beginning of a streak of hardships that followed.

In the five years that had passed since then, the players' community had managed to reclaim and restore three decks of the mammoth structure which had received the name of *Argus*. They had partially restored its defense systems and repaired certain segments of the infrastructure and docking facilities.

According to the Technologists clan, we'd only scratched the surface of studying the Founders' legacy. One or two percent at most. Around us lay a virgin land awaiting exploration: tens if not hundreds of thousands of locations complete with mind-boggling technologies and mysterious artifacts waiting for their pioneers.

The Dargians had lost control of their star system's space. Their remote settlements had been destroyed during the Kamresh and Wearongs' mutiny. Both now acted as separate forces.

And finally, the Outlaws.

According to human survivors living on Argus, the Outlaws were traitors, criminals and renegades. But if the story book were to be believed, they were mainly the survivors of a damaged cryogenic platform that had drifted away toward the asteroid belt, allowing the crew to take shelter in the ancient mines and capture the Dargians' mining bases.

The Outlaws believed that the Corporation had abandoned them. They didn't recognize the Argus' authorities and refused to abide by their laws, guided only by their own convictions and survival needs.

This time my sieving through this wealth of information hadn't brought me any more levels. And still it had been quite an insightful and — hopefully — useful read.

Gradually the Phantom Server was taking over my

mind, sinking me into its depths. One thing I knew for sure: this world was about to become my environment for the years to come, at least.

* * *

WHEN I FINALLY COULDN'T READ any more, I decided to stretch my legs and go for a walk. I needed to study the lay of the land and see if I could do some farming and leveling up somewhere. I had to earn my living. There was no way around it.

The thought of selling the ship — which was formally my property — bothered me. This deal could solve a lot of problems, allowing me to start leveling my char properly and promptly. Still, there was also an alternative route I had so far not wanted to dismiss. Charon was an excellent pilot. If only he came back into the game, together we could do a lot. True he'd still be obliged to wear his slave collar while at the station, pretending he was my "property". I could see now why the local population hated xenomorphs. They were still smarting from the death of the colonial fleet and the conquest of the station which humans had had to wrestle from the xenomorphs one deck at a time, losing countless lives.

I had two hundred credits left on my account.

I walked along the wall skirting the market blocks, my eye searching for any low-level players in the crowd. But the rare passersby looked too important and standoffish — not the type who'd bother answering a newb's questions.

Never mind. I'd work it out myself.

I needed to get some life support cartridges for my armored suit as well as a few micro nuclear batteries. They were pricey. I might end up spending my last pennies on them. Still, the first stage of the game was always the most difficult.

I soon came across a shop I needed.

A Wide Choice of Exo and Consumables.

I walked in. The inside of the shop was gloomy and dimly lit. Not a single hologram in sight. Its walls were lined with shelves displaying glass jars with symbionts floating in a yellowish liquid. A separate stand held copies of life support cartridges.

With a hiss of compressed air, a door opened. A vendor shuffled toward the counter and leaned against it, looking up at me. He didn't look well: stooping, almost doubled up, with sunken eyes and flabby cheeks. "How can I help you?"

"I need some life support cartridges."

"You don't need any exo, do you?"

"I might. Not now, though."

He glanced at my gear. "The batteries are fifty credits. The cartridges a hundred each."

Too expensive. Without saying a word, I turned round, about to walk out.

"Wait up," the vendor called out.

Reluctantly I returned.

"I have an offer for you. I'll give you everything you need," he lay a pack of compatible cartridges on the counter and added eight brand new batteries.

Naturally, it got me curious. "What is it?"

"I need a special exo ingredient."

Was it a standard newb quest? *Go to the forest and*

kill a hundred rabbits, you won't regret it?

I hated doing this sort of thing. Still, I wasn't in the position to choose.

I raised a quizzical eyebrow. The vendor didn't look like an NPC. Besides, standard quests never offered this sort of upfront reward.

"I need to make myself some medication. I just can't go on without it," the vendor wasn't complaining — he was simply stating the obvious. "But it's not easy to get the right ingredients."

"Why?"

"The Dargian fever can only be treated with Dargian metabolites. But we have no one from their planet here. Unfortunately."

"So what do you use, then?"

"The snakes. Or so we call them. They come originally from Darg. There's only one place on Argus where they live. But it's very dangerous. Think you can do it? I'll pay you a thousand credits on top of the cartridges and batteries."

Hope gleamed in his eyes. "Oh, one other thing," he added. "Take this," he produced a tiny device and lay it on the counter. "I can see you've got no implants yet. This is an external connection module. It automatically finds the nearest network terminal."

"How dangerous is it?"

"There's radiation. And toxins. And the snakes," he said. "Most importantly, don't go too far from the elevator shaft once you've climbed out of it. Just lay in wait there somewhere. There're tons of them around," he added by way of encouragement.

"How many of them d'you need?"

"Five if they're small. If they're large ones, three would do it. But basically, the more the merrier."

I'd already had some experience with both toxins and radiation. I could probably do it. It wasn't the worst of offers, if you think about it. "All right, then. Which way is it?"

"You need to find a disused elevator shaft that's marked *Gehenna*. You need to climb it until you get to the next deck."

"Agreed," I scooped up the cartridges, the batteries and the network module. "I'll be back soon."

* * *

I WALKED OUT OF THE SHOP and headed in the direction of the gravity elevators. My gear glowed with emerald lights: my brand-new batteries gave me all the power I needed.

Soon the gloomy haze parted, revealing the familiar outline of the elevator platform that Charon and I had used the previous day.

I had left empty-handed. Most of my stuff was back in the hotel, even the Dargian armor.

I stopped by the platform, reading the signs. Three holographic blocks glowed brightly, pointing at their respective shafts,

To Corporations Deck
To Clan Sector
To docking pads

The gravity elevator block comprised twenty shafts circling a massive center column. Most of them didn't work; these were marked with various danger signs.

Others sported flamboyant graffiti.

Farm, hardcore. Levels 15 to 30, one said.

The next one glowed with a predatory cartoon of a long-toothed smilie winking at me, *Noobs are welcome!*

I walked on.

Techno Graveyard. Next to it on the wall someone had painted a *serve*: a futuristic machine wound with wires and hung with weapons — quite powerful ones, judging by the four laser beams nuking the heavily armored figure of some hapless adventure seeker.

This had to be an interesting location.

The next two shafts were out of service, marked with radioactive danger signs.

The next graffiti: a saber-toothed amoeba reaching out its tentacles. *Exo: nature lovers are welcome.*

No, thanks. Definitely not my style.

I circled the shafts, stopping by the one marked with a sign faded with time,

Gehenna

"Looking for a place to snuff it?" a voice said behind me.

I turned round slowly. A blonde girl stood by the shaft leading to the docking pads. What would she want with me?

Liori. Level 53. Pilot. The Mercenaries Clan, a prompt popped up.

A bundle of nerves, that's what she looked like. Her stare, faded with fatigue, now betrayed a spark of interest: sharp, studying and just a tad surprised. I tensed up, trying to work out what could be wrong with me. Without the Haash, my mediocre gear and the absence of implants tagged me as a regular noob, a nondescript detail of the local landscape. Why did she stop? Or was she so pissed first thing in the morning she was looking for someone to take it out on?

She was cute. And dangerous. This was my knee-jerk first impression — uncomfortable to the point of being revolting, as if my intuition was trying to tell me to steer clear of her.

Never mind. We'll battle on.

She needs a good night's sleep, a thought flashed through my mind. I didn't look away. She'd have to wait a long time for that.

"Got some farming to do," I answered curtly. A normal newb's reaction.

She raised an eyebrow, her gaze alighting on my hand. The pupils of her eyes contracted: she was scanning. Suddenly I knew.

The ring.

My fingers started itching. She sighed and averted her gaze as if she'd mistaken me for someone else. Then she pointed at one of the out-of-service shafts marked with the radioactive danger signs. "You'd better try this one. Gehenna isn't the best choice for a newb. Just trust me.'

"How about the radiation?" I knew that my gear wasn't a hundred percent safe.

"Don't try to survive, as simple as that," the girl said in all seriousness.

She turned round and walked away.

* * *

NATURALLY, I HADN'T TAKEN Liori's warning into consideration. I'd already accepted the quest and the advance payment. The vendor was now awaiting his snakes. Besides, the thousand credits he'd promised was nothing to sniff at.

The vertical shaft of the gravity elevator dissolved in the darkness. My new sharpened perception, assisted by the helmet's built-in sniper sights and the movement coordinator I'd got from the Dargian slave driver, allowed me to make out a service duct buried in the wall. It was still lined with occasional step irons in places but I could see that it was going to be a tough ascent. The environment control sensors pinged, changing color; the radioactive contamination bar quivered and began filling, stopping well in the yellow zone.

My hand was tingling as if Liori's stare had disturbed the mysterious artifact dissolved in my flesh.

I made a mental note to look up any of the Founders' rarer devices and began climbing.

Thirty steps later, my arms and legs were shaking with exhaustion. I decided to take a break and climbed into the service duct, doubling up awkwardly inside. My hand throbbed with heat.

I pulled the glove off. Nothing. No glow nor any other visual effects that would point at the artifact's functioning.

What did it actually do? What was its purpose?

Much to my surprise, I still had connection to the station network. The little thingy I'd received from the vendor seemed to work. I hate wasting time in a game so I decided to put the moment's rest to good use. While my avatar was resting before his next ascent, I buried myself in Wiki. I found no mention of my mysterious artifact ring but discovered the description of the allegedly Haash-made movement coordinator.

As I read, a chill ran up my spine,

The use of all Dargian devices demands the obligatory installation of a mind expander.

But that was something I didn't have!

I looked around me. I could clearly see the green markers glowing in the dark, pinpointing the available steps within my reach according to the current gravity readings. The vendor's device seemed to be working, projecting its data directly into my brain and not onto the helmet's visor.

Indeed, a lot had changed in my perception, adding details I'd never noticed before. As an example, if you focused on a wall long enough, you could see in front of it some shimmering threads of unknown nature.

I only had two implants: the semantic processor courtesy of the Dargians and the mysterious ring that had dissolved under my skin.

I really needed help from a good mnemotech to work it all out.

Oh great. I'd barely begun to find my way around this new world and it was already time to get an appointment with a professional. As in, *excuse me, sir, but could you please tell me what I accidentally implanted myself with?* No wonder I was pissed. Then again, you never know, maybe this little ring only offered positive effects.

I remembered Liori's stare, distrustful and sharp.

She'd definitely sensed something but couldn't tell quite what it was. I absolutely had to look into this ring and its properties to find out how it affected my body and abilities and, most importantly in my current situation, how much it cost. I didn't look forward to losing my hand in some dark alley — and that was a very possible scenario, considering the station population was a bunch of ruthless thugs.

Never mind. I had to keep going. If all I wanted to do was meditate, I'd have better stayed at home.

* * *

IT TOOK ME ABOUT THIRTY MORE minutes to get to the next deck. I scrambled out of the shaft and lay there for a while, unable to move. Was I now supposed to go to the gym every day to live up to their authenticity levels? I lay there gasping for breath, all my muscles aching, my heart pumping overtime.

I caught my breath and checked my weapons. The elevator exit platform was raised over the floor's level and was cluttered with the debris from the damaged ceiling. Here the air was rare, gravity about 0.7. A reddish gloom enveloped the place. The debris hindered my field of vision but I did notice the low ceiling entangled within a rustling web of damaged cables.

The debris towered over me, forming a natural maze which wouldn't be easy to exit. I wasn't in a hurry, anyway. With my new life support cartridges, full batteries and only 30% more radioactivity I felt rather confident.

My feet constantly sank in some unpleasantly crunchy substance. I peered at it. Those were definitely organic remains even though not human: tiny skeletons of unusual shape, their spines forming sine waves or curving into spirals. I didn't see any limbs. Could these be the snakes?

I noticed more graffiti covering the debris.

Syd, have reached Sector 3. To go further is madness.

Guys, your respawn points will be reset automatically! The chat is dead! Do NOT try to reach the center!

Gothix, RIP man.

If you're under lvl 30, stay where you are!

Mechanically I stopped and read an unfinished sign written in a shaky hand,

The power unit has blown up. The raid's been wiped. The respawn point is at the center-

A chill ran up my spine. There was no one around. It looked as if the deck had been deserted for quite a while.

I moved cautiously until finally I'd left the higher debris behind. Now I could see better. The edges of the platform were littered with smaller pieces of collapsed ceiling structures. I darted to take cover behind them.

Gingerly I looked out. Ragged bulkheads gaped around like broken teeth. Virtually all of the modules, hangars and tunnels that used to comprise the deck had been destroyed, their walls reduced to chipped stumps barely reaching the ceiling. A crimson light was seeping from above through the gaps in the powerful roofing. Shadows lurked in the distance. The deformed molten beams arched overhead, hung with manipulators that looked like long human arms wound with bunches of cables.

The oblong bodies of spaceships rose amid the ruins (can't think of a better word to describe them).

A few flashes of light broke the crimson gloom. I heard another popping sound and noticed a barely visible pale green gleam. A respawn?

Another alternative start point? The thought froze my brain. The station network was unavailable. The radiation levels were not too high yet but the signs on the walls made me doubt that the thousand credits I'd just paid were enough to get me out of trouble.

A sudden power surge blinded me. My defense system kicked in, darkening the visor. The radioactivity ☢ bar went through the roof while the biological hazard symbol ☣ went out as if the area around me was now sterilized.

I heard a desperate shriek of pain, followed by the pattering of feet nearby.

I couldn't see a thing without the implants. Having saved me from losing my sight, the visor remained dark, so all I could do was wait.

Radiation warning! Your radiation exposure is 10% lethal.

Gradually the visor began to clear. I cast a tense glance around but it didn't look as if there was anyone here.

I gulped, swallowing thick saliva, and glanced at the sensors. Yeah, this was radiation exposure all right. My gear's defenses weren't up to these kinds of levels. I had to shift my backside instead of staying put.

I had to admit the setting was quite spooky. The metallic structures were glowing weakly from radiation exposure. Hot air currents swayed the manipulators, their cable insulation smoldering. The spaceships' oblong outlines showed through the gloom. They were calling my name, playing on my heart's more adventurous strings.

No. I wasn't going to leave empty-handed. Had I climbed all the way up here for nothing? Besides, it was time I started to find my bearings.

I sensed a movement and took aim, reading the far-off marker barely seen in the dark:

A Dargian python. Xenomorph. Level 13.

While I was reading it, the creature promptly disappeared amid the tangled mess of deformed beams.

I had to find a good position in order to smoke them from a distance. By no means should I allow them anywhere near. My current level wasn't yet up to a hand-to-hand with this sort of mobs.

The platform wasn't the best place to take aim from. It left at least three hundred feet between me and the monsters' lair, the visibility being seriously impaired by the gloom. Where the bulkheads had collapsed overhead about thirty feet from the floor, the intersections of beams above them formed natural islets. I could see some Dargian pythons slither between them, curling around some deformed grating-like structures.

I made a mental note of my route. I had to climb off the platform and cover about a hundred and fifty feet of debris before I found myself next to the destroyed hangars. I could see a spaceship's hull gleam softly in one of them. From there I could shoot a few snakes — and take a closer look at the ship, too.

I temporarily got rid of the sniper's rifle, putting it away into the inventory. Submachine gun in hand, I placed the handgun in the quick access slot. I was all set.

I could see the location's layout quite well from above so I made a few screenshots which were automatically integrated into the map. Quickly I climbed down, seeing the renewed data show in the interface window. Now I started to understand. The spaceships weren't here for nothing.

The wide collapsed tunnel was in fact a magnetic transport hub connected to a large outside docking area. The whole deck must have been part of it. Did that mean that it had once served to maintain spaceships?

The main tunnel branched out into smaller ones. The sheer scope of the entire structure was mind-boggling. At least my mind had nothing to compare it with. This segment of the station had to be at least a mile long.

Oh no, I wasn't going to walk that far. Not this time, at least.

The tunnel had long collapsed, its gaping U-shaped ribs offering good visibility. I mapped down the remains of three of the hangars. The closest of them housed the spaceship I'd noticed. Relatively small, the ship was shaped like an elongated horseshoe with the tear-shaped nodule of the cockpit in the middle.

Getting there proved difficult. The tunnel's enormous U-shaped ribs formed a sheer obstacle course. Had it not been for the debris compressed between them, I might have had to climb each rib up and then down again in order to get to the next one.

I kept looking around, listening intently. So far I'd noticed nothing particularly dangerous. As I grew accustomed to the gloomy setting, I asked myself in ever-growing alarm: what could have caused the death of the earlier groups?

The answer came out of nowhere. I noticed two fiery dots in the air about seven feet high. I dropped down, ducking behind a massive steel frame. A powerful surge of energy flashed overhead.

My visor darkened. When I was finally able to see again, the place was enveloped in yellow smoke and the stench of smoldering organic matter. The radiation meter was going off the scale. The metal around me was glowing red, scarred and molten.

Radiation warning! Your radiation exposure is 45% lethal.

Only now did I understand the meaning of Liori's warning.

Don't try to survive.

That was the best and most realistic advice she could have possibly given me. I could see my course of action perfectly well now. I had to get a few snakes promptly and then do whatever it took, kill myself with my own hands if necessary, just to get a respawn. Trying to brave radiation sickness wasn't a good idea. The sheer agony of it just wasn't worth the effort.

* * *

ACTUALLY, I SOON SAW that there were plenty of creatures around to take care of my agonizing death.

I had barely cleared the radioactive plume when a laser flashed from out of the hall's dark depths. Molten metal spewed everywhere. A decrepit chunk of bulkhead creaked and began to list.

I hadn't been hit but the droplets of molten metal hissing around had attracted the attention of the Dargian pythons. Their vision must have been infrared-based; they obviously had lived here long enough to know that such laser charges meant there might be food available.

Seven of them left their lair at once. I watched the long, lithe, muscular monsters slither between the intertwined beams, sending their bodies in powerful leaps from one bundle of cables to the next, then curling around them and freezing, swinging, without taking their eyes off me.

It was too late to run or hide. I whipped the submachine gun up and took aim, pressing my back against the steel frame. Three of the snakes went for me at once. How's that for an adrenaline rush? I hit one in mid-air, cutting it in half. The second one dodged to one side. The ricocheting sparks spattered the air. The third one curled up and froze, swaying before his final deadly leap but I beat him to it. A desperate burst of fire reduced him to a cloud of bloody mist, slapping his wet flesh all over the debris.

Where were the others?

I couldn't see them. Were they lying in wait? I was slightly feverish with tension.

Out of the darkness, a laser strobed. More molten metal showered me as the laser charges impacted diagonally downward. Chunks of red-hot construction steel and pieces of Dargian python kept falling at my feet.

I'd no idea who it was shooting. I just grabbed the snakes and stuffed them down my inventory slots.

Now back to the elevator. Apparently, I wasn't meant to get to the mysterious spaceships today. Another charge flashed nearby. My radiation meter went off the scale.

The danger warning was going crazy.

The darkness parted, revealing several drones of unknown design. My target recognition system highlighted their shapes, outlining their vulnerable spots. Their ancient hulls looked decrepit, riddled with holes.

Radiation warning! Your radiation exposure is 65% lethal.

I could deal with it. I had plenty of time to get out.

Or so I thought.

The air around me *squirmed* with movement. The heaped debris crawled with hundreds of radiation-mutated creatures scrambling out of their lairs.

A Dargian attacked me first. *Level 30, Pilot*, I read mechanically and recoiled trying to avoid his blow but stumbled. Falling, I pulled the trigger.

The impact threw him back like a bloodied rag doll. This sentient xenomorph barely had enough Health to last him a couple of hits.

A Wearong was the next to arrive on the scene. Paying no heed to me, it began tossing debris out of its way with its muscular boneless tentacles. Then it withdrew into the safety of its shell, rose into the air and headed for the drones.

I jumped up. The situation was now completely out of my control. The location had proven lethal. More Kamresh were now crawling out of their holes, their appearance both revolting and terrifying. I'd seen their images before but reality proved by far the more disgusting. Their numerous wounds seeped slime. I could tell by the miserable remains of their gear and leftover devices that they'd come here driven by their pursuit of loot and xp only to become prisoners of the wretched ruins. Time after time they died, killed by the mobs, radiation and the mysterious energy surges while the game engine kept bringing them back to life, destroying their minds and gradually turning them into these ravenous insatiable creatures devoid of identity and driven by instinct alone.

All this flashed through my mind in a tangle of disjointed thoughts.

My health bar had already sagged quite a bit with all the radiation I'd received. All escape routes had been cut off. The time was probably right to follow up on Liori's advice but by then, my mind had gone into shock as the Kamresh jumped onto the Dargian's body and began tearing it apart, gulping down pieces of flesh.

As I checked their stats, I realized that probably a respawn wasn't such a good option. All of them were marked as players which meant that in the case of my death, my avatar would have to stay here for another ten minutes — which, if the Phantom Server Wiki was to be believed, allowed the players to exercise their right to collect loot.

The game engine knew no exceptions. It didn't care that these creatures had long since lost their minds and identities.

They would devour my body and vandalize my gear, destroying the ingredients I'd obtained so painstakingly. Then I'd find myself back at Founders Square — unarmed and destitute.

No way.

An explosion blasted overhead. The drones proved worthy of the location. The Wearong hadn't lasted a minute against them. A piece of his legendary impervious shell tumbled to the floor next to me, splattering everything around with a kind of gooey jelly.

Finally, the target recognition system identified the drones. Their elliptical bodies and weapons configuration (one ranging pulse gun and two lasers in their armor's side mounts) betrayed their origins from the Founders era.

I pinned the nearest Kamresh down with a short burst from my gun and darted toward the ruins. I simply had no other option.

A couple of xenomorphs chased after me while the rest went for each other, fighting over the loot.

* * *

I RAN DESPERATELY, climbing the piled debris with only one thought in mind: to find a good firing position. I'd already cleared the skeletal structure of the destroyed transport hub and ran out onto a relatively flat platform not far from the hangars.

I cast a hurried glance around, noticing two intact bulkheads and a fragment of the ceiling: all that was left of a living module. Debris barricaded the approaches to it. Just what I needed.

I darted toward it.

Now that I had steel walls covering my back, I didn't have to fear an attack from the rear. I raised my gun and took aim.

The Kamresh were near. Those were some dangerous beasts, swift and revolting. Their natural armor was light brown with small darkish spots, their front legs ending in jagged pincers that could easily nip through steel bars. Their mandibles looked impressive, too. I'd seen them rip the Dargian apart, gear and all.

Whatever I did, I shouldn't let them get close.

I fired in short bursts, aiming at the face of one of them. A glittering aura enveloped him, then disappeared. Pieces of his shell flew everywhere. A hellish scream hung in the air.

A second one came for me. I put ten rounds through him but they failed to stop him. The same glittering aura lit up and went out again. With a powerful sweep of his arm, he brushed away the debris I was hiding in. The creature's enormous pincer barely missed my head. I recoiled just in time.

No idea how it might have ended had it not been for

the drones. They'd already finished off the remaining xenomorphs and turned to us, attracted by the firing.

I'd jolted my shoulder as I fell but immediately jumped back to my feet. The nearest Kamresh was obstructing my field of vision. His gigantic mandibles screeched, dropping viscous saliva. A shot, a flare, another shot... all pointless. He had one hell of a power shield.

I glimpsed the blurred outlines of some ancient mechanisms which approached from all directions, attacking us.

The nearest Kamresh was sliced and diced before he knew it. He collapsed over me, pinning me down with his body. Then everything dissolved in a thunderous cacophony as yet more blasts rose in a wall of fire, tearing apart one of the bulkheads.

I froze in disbelief that I was still alive. I could hear red-hot fragments of metal clanging on the floor. The Kamresh' stinking body, sliced by the laser charges, towered on top of me.

I didn't see the drones any more. The air was thick with smoke. An outline of some technological artifact pulsated in front of my mental eye: this Kamresh wore some kind of an ammo belt with lots of diamond-shaped pouches. I pulled it off his dead body and shoved it down my inventory. I had no time to look into it. All I cared about at the moment was getting back safe.

* * *

THE MOBS WERE LINGERING in the back. They'd split into groups controlling the elevator access.

The hull of the nearest airspace fighter gleamed within the hangar nearby. It looked brand new, seemingly defying time and circumstance as it rose amid desolation.

How could I resist the temptation?

Radiation warning! Your radiation exposure is 70% lethal.

I dashed toward the hangar in short bursts between any cover I could find. Who knows when I might get another chance to come back here? Now the unique relic ship was within arm's reach!

The hangar was empty and spacious, its floor littered with broken plastic. Several network consoles and repair terminals towered up — I knew what they were because I'd seen them in the Wiki already and all the information I read online was automatically uploaded to my account. Excellent system, by the way.

Some of the objects lying amid the debris were highlighted automatically — but unfortunately, all of them were beyond repair. Then again, I didn't allow any of them to distract me. Any part of the ancient ship that the current gravity reading would allow me to carry was worth risking my life to get.

You won't believe my disappointment. As I got closer, I discovered that all of the ship's hatches gaped open, darkness lurking behind them. A bad premonition grew stronger with my every step. The craft lay on its belly. Fearlessly I climbed inside, finding myself within its hollow, echoing hull. Not a single device in sight!

As if on cue, fatigue and nausea overtook me. I cast another look around, fighting off disappointment, but there was nothing valuable here apart from the cargonite hull itself. Shame I didn't have anything with me to nibble a few bits off!

I crouched, catching my breath, and cast another glance at the Kamresh's weird belt. I turned it over in my hands this way and that, noticing a few micro nuclear battery slots, but chose not to experiment and shoved it back down my inventory.

I mustered up some strength and climbed up the ship's wall using a few of my gear's devices, skidding through a narrow hatchway into the cockpit. Here too everything had been stripped out. The cockpit's thick armored walls were studded with holes of various shapes and sizes which must have held control panels and navigational devices.

I peered out through one of the holes. The drones still hovered nearby. There was little chance of getting past them unnoticed.

My life bar glowed orange. The target recognition system kicked in, zooming in on the outlines of the ancient cyber modules and highlighting the abundant damage to their bodies.

Should I risk it? Why not? This way I could at least make another level. I wasn't going to get out of here anyway. My radiation exposure approached lethal levels.

Overcoming the growing nausea, I changed my weapon and crouched next to a vertical gunslit.

My hands were shaking. My dry mouth tasted foul. I didn't want to use the expensive life support cartridges. Pointless. I might not be able to destroy all ten of the drones but at least I'd shoot down a few.

A daring leveling plan started to form in my head. What if I tried to find the docking area outside this deck and moor Charon's ship there? That might be interesting. I'd have to give it some thought.

I took careful aim and gently squeezed the trigger.

A flash. A shimmering golden aura enveloped me. The drone went down in a cloud of smoke as a message popped up before my eyes,

You've dealt critical damage!
You've received a new level!

I bet! Excitement surged over me, wiping away the weakness.

Another flash.

Missed! The bastard was still alive, but his laser guns were gone in a hail of fire. I took aim again. Got him!

Now the Founders' machines noticed me and hurried toward the hangar, firing back.

The spaceship's hull reverberated with all the hits. I had barely shrunk back from my impromptu gunslit when several laser charges went right through it and sliced through the cockpit, leaving red-hot traces on the wall opposite.

This cargonite was amazingly sturdy stuff. Those charges would have gone right through any other alloy but this one was still holding. Risky thoughts began flashing through my head. I had to come back here with Charon — in his ship. I'd love to know if we'd be able to tow this empty shell away somewhere? What if we could use it to build a spaceship? And to analyze the alloy from which it was made?

I had barely changed my sniper's rifle to the submachine gun when the first drone barged into the cramped space of the cockpit. No way you could miss there. Impulsively I showered it with long bursts of fire until you couldn't see the drone through the incessant flashes. I too was in trouble though: on hitting cargonite, bullets turned into clots of plasma. The cockpit filled with incandescent gas. The gun stopped working.

That was it. Nothing could save me from a respawn now.

Or so I thought. My gear began melting, triggering the armor's security.

Shield belt: equipped!
Micro nuclear batteries: equipped!

The haze around me cleared, filling with fresh air within the radius of an arm's length from me as if I'd suddenly found myself at the center of a large iridescent soap bubble.

A power shield?

I remembered a similar aura that had protected the Kamresh.

How cool was that?

The drones didn't seem in a hurry to attack. The incandescent gas was being rapidly sucked out of the cockpit into the rest of the ship. I heard resonating clashes as if the Founders' machines had suddenly lost their sense of direction and were now thrashing about, hitting the walls.

You've received a new level!

You've received an ability: Robot Technician. You've destroyed five of the Founders' cyber mechanisms without dying once. From now on, the damage you deal to any machines using firearms will increase 5%.

I heard more clashing sounds followed by an explosion. The drones were indeed old. The incandescent gas that had formed as a result of my desperate firing had gotten inside them, damaging their control circuits.

You've received a new level!

You've received an ability: Robot Technician II! You've destroyed ten of the Founders' cyber mechanisms without dying once. From now on, the damage you deal to any machines using firearms will increase 10%.

My life bar was hovering in the red zone. I could barely move: the radiation sickness hadn't gone anywhere, but I couldn't just let the Founders' machines lie around next door. I had to see what kind of loot they had for me.

On my command, needles sunk into my neck.

Stimulants and anti-radiation drugs administered.

My head cleared; the agonizing joint pain began to abate.

* * *

WHEN I FINALLY LEFT THE SPACESHIP, I had two microchips and five "cyber ingredients" stashed away in my inventory — loot from the slain enemy.

My power shield glimmered softly. Things were looking up. I was slightly feverish from the bumper dose of anti-radiation drugs and combat metabolites.

True, my success had had a lot to do with beginner's luck and adrenaline drive. Still you had to agree that this leveling scenario was much better than run-of-the-mill farming.

My life bar had grown a lot and was now staying at eighty percent.

My sensations were incredible. The Phantom Server world was sucking me in, consuming my mind. I knew too little about it yet but one thing I did know: I wasn't going to get bored here.

I cast a wary glance around. I had to go. I'd made three levels and found lots of techno artifacts including one unique device. Time to get going.

But I couldn't. Too many ideas crowded my head. I peered at the beams overhead repeating the branch-offs of the transport hub. It looked safe enough, rising high above the ruins of the hangars, above all the collapsed bulkheads and the docking pads.

Such a shame my submachine gun didn't work. I couldn't fix it here but I still had the handgun, plus the sniper's rifle and the power shield. Now that I'd killed all the drones, I had to try and climb up the beams. I had no idea of the mobs' respawn times but I might have another hour or two.

Yes, that was it: I had to climb high and make a few screenshots so that I could analyze them later and hopefully come up with some sort of strategy.

I cut my reverie short and dropped to my back as a laser charge impacted a few feet away from me, triggering my power shield.

Oh wow.

The air around me began to shimmer in ghostly sheets of light, glowing with radiation — but my gear sensors still hovered in the yellow zone.

I froze. It wasn't even my shield's prompt work but its adaptability that pleased me the most. I checked its settings. I was right: I could see several new options there.

I'd never seen these icons before. The semantic processor tried and failed to translate them. All it could come up with was, *A technological artifact. Circa the Founders' era. Language recognition requires installation of a dedicated database.*

Very well. Let's do it another way. I rose and reached out, immersing my hand into the shimmering glow.

The shield upped its shine but the sensors' readings stayed in the yellow zone. Excellent. I noticed two more option icons — or rather sliders. I focused on one, trying to move it. The shield began to billow out. Okay. So it could be maxed out to ten feet.

That was all well and good but the power consumption had grown respectively. Which wasn't so good after all. And how was I supposed to touch anything? What if I needed to pick something up?

This wasn't the best time to experiment but then again, the drones had done a good job of mopping the place up. It looked as if I was relatively safe for a short while at least.

The thought made me chuckle. Man can get used

to anything indeed. This place was death incarnate — and still...

Never mind. I had other things to do. What about that second icon?

Gingerly I moved the slider. The shield power control? Excellent. Just what I needed.

I began to gradually lower the power, keeping an eye on the life support readings. There! I seemed to have found the minimum levels of the shield's hazard-neutralizing properties.

My throat spasmed with nausea. The medication had slightly lowered the exposure dose. I wasn't going to die any more but I still felt like shit.

I went on studying the shield's properties. How was I supposed to touch things? I lowered power to the minimum and reached down, picking up a piece of debris. It worked! The item wasn't damaged by the shield.

And what if I tried to grab it? To imitate an assault attempt?

I made a rapid movement to try to grab a bent piece of metal. The shield ballooned up. The metal fragment glowed with heat.

Okay. I looked around, searching for the nearest scalable bulkhead and gingerly began climbing it.

THE POWER SHIELD SURPRISED ME once again by switching off automatically once danger levels had dropped.

That really scared me at first as I thought it must

have broken down or that maybe the batteries were already dead. But no — the moment I approached another radiation source, the shimmering aura enveloped me once again.

Knowing this was worth all the trouble. Now I had some idea of the artifact's unique properties.

In the meantime, the life support gave me a few more injections. By then, I'd already climbed up and was lying on top of a wide beam, looking around. Some distance away lay a huge transport junction, visible by the regular flashes of energy emissions.

I took a few screenshots, then used my sniper sights to zoom in on the ruins. My first impression had been correct: the deck was part of the ship's docking facilities. I counted nine ships: five definitely fighters while the four remaining larger ones must have been cargo craft. They probably contained cargonite worth millions.

Wait up, I told myself. *You can't be the only smart one around.* Now why wouldn't anyone have thought of getting in here via the outside docking area?

Gradually I moved forward, keeping my eyes fixed on the junction. I'd love to know what it was over there and what was causing those flaring emissions.

I was gasping for breath. All my muscles shook with fatigue. Ruins lay below. I looked up. Judging by the damage, the ceiling must at some point have been molten, then frozen in circular waves scarred in places by deep slicing cuts.

Whatever had happened here? A technological disaster?

My imagination offered scenes of a gigantic explosion that must have hit the ceiling leaving the circular marks behind.

That didn't sound good. I just hoped I didn't fall victim to another one of those.

Never mind. I decided to move slightly further on to get a better look of the junction and then call it a day.

After about a hundred and fifty feet I discovered a very convenient and secure platform formed by several beams. Here, radiation levels were considerably higher.

My sight-enhanced vision slid along the fire-polished walls noticing large faded letters,

No entry past this line... automatic respawn transfer... Respawn purgatory...
Okay. I got it.

Whoever it was, they'd marked down the spot beyond which your respawn point would be automatically changed.

Talking about which, where was that spot exactly? I seemed to have already made it dangerously close to the location's center.

Now I could see the junction clearly. Here the bulkheads were all but gone, reduced to short protruding stumps.

About a hundred feet further on lay a vast square with a jagged hole in the middle. This was where all the tunnels must have once met. Now however, there was little left. Even their massive U-shaped ribs were misshapen and molten, some of them turned into frozen pools of oxidized metal.

On the other side of the square I could see the gaping mouth of a tunnel — which must have led to the outside docking area.

I could make out some familiar shapes scattered amid the debris. I had to concentrate to think what they might be. Then I realized: these were crudely made modern-day spaceships, exactly like those I'd seen on our approach to the station.

Apparently, any attempt to loot some cargonite would end badly.

Who on earth had shot them down? I looked around me restlessly, then checked my rear. Had I missed something?

I peered at the ceiling and noticed a large gaping hole above me.

Around me lay a radiation-drenched wasteland. Had it not been for the power shield, I'd have died a wriggling, agonizing death long ago.

I had to turn back. I had absolutely nothing to gain here.

Too late.

A blinding light rose out of the depths of the jagged void below. I shrank into the beams. My visor darkened rapidly. A powerful flare roared out of the gap. The outer bubble of my power shield burst into flames. The ruins around the epicenter glowed red as it heated up. Not all of the energy surge had hit the ceiling: the gap overhead had deflected some of it, sending fiery tornadoes coursing around. I heard the sound of debris collapsing. And on top of all the visual effects, the location was instantly filled with invisible radiation.

You've received a lethal dose of radiation!

Dammit!

My micro nuclear batteries were nearly dead but the automatics kept replacing them with new ones.

The pain was like nothing I could describe. I very

nearly fainted. It felt as if my every nerve had turned into a live wire.

I tried to jump to my feet — no way. My body just wouldn't obey me.

I forced my head up. My vision blurred, then came back into focus as I received a new dose of metabolites.

Which was exactly what I didn't need. Hadn't she told me, *don't try to survive*? It'd only make things worse!

But it wasn't as if I could do anything about it. The wretched automatics had a mind of their own.

The pain didn't go but it had dulled somewhat. No, I wasn't going to push it any further. I reached for the handgun, my fingers shaking. These authenticity levels could drive anybody mad. I just didn't want to-

I froze, forgetting my suicide attempt.

About fifty feet away from me, amid scorched debris where the molten beams had merged with the deck, rose a column of emerald light. Another one. And yet another.

A respawn?

A Dargian appeared first. With a desperate yelp he darted off but had barely made a dozen paces. I wouldn't even speculate about radiation levels there.

A human followed. A male. He was a terrible sight, his gear all scorched. He too darted for cover and disappeared down a hole.

The third column of emerald light produced a goblin, of all things.

I froze, speechless. Mechanically I zoomed him in on him, noticing the familiar mark on his wrist.

Arbido? It couldn't be!

The goblin screamed in desperation. His green hide

was rapidly covering in crimson blisters. His eyes popped out, his swollen tongue suffocating him. His flimsy little legs gave under him. He collapsed and began thrashing about. Then he disappeared.

A respawn.

Once again the Dargian darted off. This time he made twenty paces or so.

A respawn.

The goblin reappeared in an emerald flash. I could clearly see his eyes filled with agony, devoid of hope. Immediately he collapsed, choking on his croaks, pointlessly trying to crawl away as his body erupted in bleeding ulcers, his flesh falling apart, baring the bones.

A respawn.

The man in the molten gear must have had extraordinary willpower. He didn't scream. He ran, his teeth clenched, knowing he was doomed and still trying to get as far from the epicenter as he could to avoid another torturous resurrection.

I glimpsed a faint name tag,

Jurgen. Level 43. Human. A Technologist

He must have had one hell of a metabolic implant, but without cartridges it was burning his own body's resources. His face was gaunt with sharp cheekbones and sunken eyes.

This time too he'd managed to hole up somewhere but I doubted it would help him much. I had no idea how often these surges of energy happened but it was pretty clear that anyone who happened to be around was doomed. What did that sign next to the entrance say — *Respawn purgatory?*

I broke out in a sticky cold sweat.

A flash.

Arbido. Sentient Xenomorph. Level 1.

All doubts were gone at this point. But how had he got here?

His blood-curdling scream froze in the hall's echoing silence. His eyes were bleeding. He had no chance.

All that stood between us was an invisible barrier and the faded sign at the entrance marking the trigger point of an automatic respawn transfer.

All that stood between us was his cynical arrogance, his greed and his hatred.

He'd set me up. He'd fleeced me to the bone, then sent me to a torturous death at the alternative start location.

They say revenge is sweet. And still my every nerve was burning with a renewed agony. I could see his death throes. They made me feel foul. I began to shake. Compassion was a strange feeling unfamiliar to me — but now it ripped through my brain like a razor.

A respawn. Him croaking again.

My hits were already down to 50%.

Before, I had only known two emotions — two extremes that framed my life flow.

Excitement. Boredom.

But the Phantom Server seemed to ravage your mind. It defied all convention. Goddamn authenticity.

My numb fingers wouldn't obey me, the emergency batteries refusing to click into their slots.

The life support system interface was ablaze with

data. I shot myself up with every metabolite and anti-radiation drug I had. My mind swam. My life bar jumped to 100%. Side effect warnings flashed before my eyes but I couldn't care less.

I stood up and ran down the listing molten beams.

I crossed the line.

Your respawn point has changed.

Ignoring the message, I jumped down on the other side of the collapsed bulkheads, maxed out the power shield radius and darted toward the emerald shimmer.

I reached the respawn point in a couple of leaps.

Flash.

Then another.

It just so happened that my shield had caught both of them. The Dargian was nowhere to be seen. Arbido and Jurgen stared at me uncomprehendingly, unsure why their pain was now gone.

"I've got a power shield! Get moving!" I tried to explain realizing I must have sounded rambling and confused. The goblin was shaking, awaiting the next dose of torture to come. Jurgen's eyes lit up with hope and understanding. He must have grasped at least the technical part of their rescue. Neither seemed to wonder about my motives — the moment wasn't right. My maxed-out shield was holding the radiation well but it wasn't going to last forever. The batteries had five to seven minutes at most.

"Which of us have you come to save?" Jurgen's eyes were filled with inhuman pain.

"Him!" I pointed at Arbido.

It all happened instinctively. I had no rescue plan

whatsoever, but the technologist didn't waste time thinking.

"Take him, then!" his commanding hand motioned at the goblin.

We had to move fast while staying within the power shield. If we made it to the elevators alive we had a decent chance of descending — and once we were back on the Market Deck, we could pay to have their respawn points moved.

The problem was, I had no money.

Jurgen seized the initiative from me. He'd long studied the area and knew exactly what needed to be done. He pointed at the nearest gaping hole. "Service tunnels!"

I gave him the handgun and lifted the goblin. His tiny shuddering body was weightless, his huge eyes welled with tears. Instinctively he clung to me, still incredulous at his survival.

* * *

FEVERISH, I DON'T REMEMBER MUCH of our return route.

The service tunnels ran the entire floor. They were hell incarnate. Their walls glowed with radiation. Each dark branch of them harbored creatures who'd long lost their identity in the mind-blowing sequence of respawns. Some were aggressive, others cowardly. Jurgen and I ran for dear life, him shooting, me trying to keep up without tripping.

Everything here was soaked in pain, hunger and fear: the triumph of primeval instincts. Not a single creature we'd met showed signs of intelligent behavior.

I quickly lost all sense of direction. I stopped counting paces, not even trying to understand where Jurgen was taking us. The stimulants had worn off, bringing back the pain which started to feed on my mind.

Jurgen could see the state I was in. He said nothing. He had very little ammo left. Now the power shield was the only thing that kept the monsters away. Seeing the shimmer surrounding us, they shrank back and let us through.

The tunnel took several sharp turns, always heading down.

I started to lag behind. Jurgen slowed up. His spirit was amazing, his strife for survival empowering me somewhat.

We seemed to have been running for eternity. The power shield began to fade. Were the batteries down already?

They weren't. The danger level indicators were turning green. But where was the elevator? I wasn't sure I'd survive another climb down.

Suddenly we found ourselves in a dead end. I stared at a bulkhead with its massive locked hatch.

I just couldn't believe it!

"What other weapons do you have?"

I couldn't think straight. Jurgen's voice barely reached me. I struggled to open the inventory and pulled out the sniper's rifle, dumping it onto the floor littered with debris.

He picked it up. "Stand back!"

He began shooting at the bulkhead, the firework of direct hits evaporating the metal a good two feet from the hatch. What was the point? Soon, however, something sparked within the resulting hole. A shortcut. The hatch jerked aside.

Jurgen climbed out first. I followed.

I'd never been here before. It was a small hall lined with fake building facades topped with holographic signs,

Technologists' Sector
Pilots' Sector
Mercenaries' Sector

I could see two more tunnels. They were also marked,

To Corporation Deck
To Market Deck

While I was looking around, Jurgen grabbed the hand of a tall pilot clad in force-field armor. They seemed to be arguing.

My life was dwindling. Seven percent left. Unable to stand, I slumped to the floor. That was it. That was the end of me. Welcome to respawn purgatory, you freakin' Samaritan.

High-level players kept walking past, slowing down to look at us.

I could sense hatred in their stares — although it wasn't addressed at me but at the goblin doubled up next to me.

He was a *Level 1 Xenomorph*, wasn't he? One kick in the butt would finish him off.

I forced myself out of my slumber and reached into my inventory, clicking the slave collar shut on my ex-employer's neck.

Jurgen came back, trying to explain something to me. Unable to procure a response, he tore the fire-polished glove off my hand and rubbed some silvery substance into my wrist, then did the same to Arbido.

I was virtually blind by then. My mind was shutting down.

Three percent life... two... one...

Darkness.

Respawn

THE EMERALD LIGHT ENVELOPED ME.

Death still held me, its doomed desperation freezing my avatar solid. But as I opened my eyes, I saw Founders' Square.

The goblin in a slave collar doubled up by my feet. Jurgen was nowhere to be seen.

CHAPTER FOUR

PHANTOM SERVER
LOGIN

I SAT UP, AWOKEN BY AN INSISTENT knocking at the door.

Our hotel module was dark. The Haash was still in a coma. The stench in the room was awful. I was parched. I stood up, nearly stumbling over Arbido who'd curled up on the floor by my bed, shuddering in his sleep.

Stepping over him, I staggered toward the wash basin and splashed some water on my face, then gulped some down. It tasted rusty.

I unblocked the door even though I didn't really want to see anyone.

Jurgen stepped in. He looked around, sniffing the air, but didn't say anything. He walked over to me and poked my shoulder with a fist. "We need to talk."

Why was he whispering? Was he afraid of waking

the goblin up? Or was he wary of the Haash?

We sat down at the folding table. All I could offer him was some water.

"How are you?" I had no idea what to talk to him about. What did he want from me? Had he come to say thank you?

"I'm all right," he looked me straight in the eye. "I owe you for my rescue," somehow he didn't sound particularly grateful. "Decided to pop by. Here. It's yours," he lay my handgun onto the table.

The goblin's ears pricked up. He wasn't asleep any more, just faking it.

I took the gun. It was fully loaded, its batteries fully charged. I knew this wasn't what Jurgen had come to see me for, though. So I just waited for him to go on.

"You've got problems, Zander."

I raised a surprised eyebrow. "How come?"

"Because of me," he admitted. "I'm not going to screw around. Gehenna is well-known. Whoever gets stuck in the respawn purgatory is never seen again. Lots of people used to die there at first. Now they all got smart. No one ever farms it anymore. Okay, maybe a few desperate idiots do, but they never stray away toward the center."

"How did *you* end up there, then?" my question sounded logical.

"Are you serious? You mean you don't know?"

"Not the slightest idea," I said, faking indifference even though I already had a funny feeling this Gehenna trip would cost me. "I've only been here for a couple of days. I've no implants nor xp, nothing. Just a noob."

"Yeah," he squinted unkindly. "A noob with a state-of-the-art Dargian fighter, a mysterious artifact and a menagerie of xenomorphs?"

I racked my brains for a suitable answer. Why was Jurgen so sure the ship was Dargian? Had Charon lied to me? Or was Jurgen's information incorrect? By the mysterious artifact he must have meant my funny little ring, no doubt about that.

"It just happened," I finally said, hoping to side-step the subject. It didn't work.

"The mechanics said you told them you'd just arrived from Earth," Jurgen's words lacked sense. "Then you sold the Dargian gear to the Armorers for peanuts. You know, don't you, that they extracted seventy thousand credits' worth of devices out of it?"

I turned pale. I'd known of course I was selling it off cheap, but not *that* cheap! "That's my business," it took all my willpower to conceal my fury. "What was it you said about Gehenna?"

"Whatever. As you say, it's your business. I just wanted to warn you: if you *are* an Outlaw, you'd better leave the station now. Don't push your luck."

"Beg your pardon!" now I was really furious. "What's that for gratitude? If you had your brains fried, it was none of my making! An Outlaw! How long did it take you to come up with that one? I can't even open my char's talent branches! Your wretched implants block my development!"

He listened, casting glances at my left hand. His eyes were cold and sharp. I didn't think he believed a word I'd said. But he'd apparently scanned the mysterious artifact because he tensed up and said through clenched teeth,

"Very well, Zander. You've got an hour to get to your ship and fuck off. One hour is all I can do to distract the local hounds... in appreciation for your rescuing me. If you don't, that's your problem. We have zero tolerance for xenomorph buddies."

"What made you think I'm an Outlaw?"

Again he glanced at my hand. "Who implanted you with an AI neuronet?"

"What neuronet?" I boiled inside, seething with fury. The wretched ring again! "I repeat, I really don't know what you're talking about! I don't give a shit about your turf wars! Understand? I'm not an Outlaw and I've never been one! I was set up! They made me take the alternative start!"

He frowned, apparently trying to see the problem from a different prospective. He blinked several times, as if accepting the idea that he was being told off by an ordinary newb.

I didn't give a shit what level he was! He could be level 1000 for all I cared!

I sensed the change in his attitude. "Let's set it straight, once and for all," I said. "I can prove my story. But you too will tell me the truth."

"Which truth?"

"How you ended up in respawn purgatory."

"All right, then!" he slammed his fist on the table. The goblin shrank. "If you're not an Outlaw, I'll tell you! If it's true that you didn't go to Gehenna just to save me hoping to win the Technologists' confidence!"

"I had no idea where I was going, don't you understand! I sure didn't go there to save *you*!"

"So why the fuck did you go to purgatory? You gonna tell me you didn't see the warning? That you can't read or something?"

"I went there to get *him*!" I pointed at the goblin. "I've had enough of this. I'm sending you my logs."

The beauty of log files is, they document everything

that happens in a game. Damage dealt, damage received, quests completed, locations visited and everything in between: all the levels, abilities, artifacts, all your gaming record in strict chronological order.

Battle logs and relevant screenshots can be used as direct proof of a player's claims.

Jurgen could fully appreciate my gesture. His stare clouded as he focused on the data he was receiving.

Soon he came out of his trance. "That's rough," he looked at me with respect. "But you've done really well for a newb. I owe you an apology. When I scanned your neuronet, I really thought you were an Outlaw. They're the only ones brave enough to install an alternative identity."

"A what?" I stood up. "What kind of identity?"

"One of the Founders' artificial intellects. Sit down, will you? I can see now you didn't mean to absorb it."

"Do you mean I'm now a host to an ancient AI?"

"Not all of it," he said. "What you host is only a fragment. But it explains a lot," he added.

"Like what?"

"The Founders' AIs are a combination of several neuronet modules," he explained expertly. "You need five of them to form the simplest AI," he sounded as if it was good news.

"I have one but it seems to work!"

"Exactly. That's because it's merged with your nervous system. It can't change you radically but it can add certain new abilities. Take your movement coordinator, for instance. Without a mind expander it's virtually useless. But judging by the logs, you seem to be using it, don't you?"

"I do."

Was this the Phantom Server's attempt to finish me off through anxiety?

"Relax," Jurgen repeated. "Nothing bad has happened yet. I used to know some Outlaws who had three of these module implants."

Well, if this was good news... My throat was dry again. I got up, gulped some rusty water from the tap, then came back to the table. "Is there a way to remove or at least neutralize it?"

"Not that I know of. We already tried. The Founders made sure their neuronet modules implant themselves into the host, then leave him when he dies. No good trying to get it out."

"Can I use it?"

He grinned. His opinion of me seemed to have upped a notch. "You might. The thing is, no one knows where or when it might happen. These artifacts are unpredictable. They can grant you control over some ancient system suites, unblock a sealed room or suggest a solution when you're stuck."

"What's the catch?"

He paused. "The catch is, if you find another one of these you won't resist the temptation to absorb it too. You'll honestly think it's your own decision. But it's really the Founders' neuronet that does the thinking for you. I've seen it happen before. So be warned."

"And what if I don't resist this... temptation?"

He gave a non-committal chuckle. This wasn't the answer I was looking for but apparently I couldn't expect more from him at the moment. Either he didn't know the answer or he didn't want to talk about it.

"Well, now," I said. "Your turn. How did you end up in respawn purgatory?"

He struggled with the answer. "It was an insider

job," he finally admitted. "We have our own laws here. They may be unwritten but they're tough, trust me. The Technologists clan was founded by five men. Two of them got mixed up with the Outlaws. Had they had their way, they would have gradually sold the whole station down the river on the sly. I discovered it all. I'm not going to give you the names, they won't mean anything to you. So basically, it all ended in a set of clan purges. They found those two and brought them to justice — but they did let them live which is a shame. How could they not? The pair of them were the clan's founder fathers. So they banned them from Argus and thought the question closed. But they thought too soon. The traitors had plenty of hangers-on left at the station. Technically speaking, I was captured by some Outlaws during their last raid. They threw me into purgatory. Only I know whose orders they acted upon. Lots of people aren't happy to see me back, trust me."

"Why are you at war with the Outlaws then? Aren't they human like ourselves?"

His face darkened. "There're humans and humans. This you should know. We're so few. The colonial fleet is defeated. Every deck of this station has been awash with blood. Argus is our home now, don't you understand? Divided, who are we? — We are a mindless mob. The xenomorphs would crush us and make us all wear slave collars. You've been their prisoner so you should know. And the Outlaws don't give a shit! They sell the Founders' technologies to the enemy!" crimson spots spread over his cheeks. "The Dargians don't have the guts to farm the Founders' artifacts themselves! They only survive thanks to the slaves and various *renegades*!" he spat out the last word. "So basically, Zander, it's like this: it's either them or us. No compromise is possible. Why do you think all the other stations are not explored yet?"

"I don't know. Why?"

"Because the moment a group ventures there, the Outlaws are already there waiting for them! Selling them into slavery and vending their artifacts and research results to the enemy!"

I didn't say anything. What could I say? I could understand the lay of the land perfectly well now. The Outlaws were to be avoided at all cost.

"Does that mean I have problems now?" I asked him. "Because of my rescuing you?"

"That remains to be seen!" he blurted out. "There're plenty of rotten hearts around, no doubt about that. Take the mercs — they keep themselves to themselves. They're accountable to no one. I'm pretty sure they work both for us and our foes. All the other clans and corporations are at each other's throats all the time. Listen, Zander," he gave me a crooked smile. "You've been honest with me so I want to repay you in kind. There'll be no problems. At least I'll do all I can to make sure you're safe."

This confession made me feel uneasy. In terms of gameplay, Jurgen was one of the top players. But he definitely had his realities mixed up. Or should I say, his mind had made a reality shift to the Phantom Server. I wouldn't be surprised if he'd even removed his Logout button: out of sight, out of mind.

"How long have you been here?"

He looked up in surprise. "Five years. I arrived here with the Colonial Fleet. I was a mechanic on board the Titan."

Aha. He must have been one of the first guinea pigs

who had to work with virtually untested implants. That could explain this weird reality shift in his mind.

"Your idiots in those colonial centers should have calibrated their machinery a long time ago!" he clenched a fist. "What's the point in sending you one by one and release you in the most unexpected places? I can't wait till they can finally employ warp drives! If they could send us a few fully manned spaceships, we'd sort this mess now and for all!"

"I'm pretty sure they're working on it," I just didn't want to argue with him. He'd had it bad as it was. After five years of using the implant, he wasn't likely to rejoice at my reminding him that this was only a game and that reality lay on the other side of it.

"Right," all of a sudden, he was in a hurry. "I've put you on my friend list. I'll be in touch. I'll sort it out with your ship. No one's gonna bother you with questions. If ever you decide to join the clan, I'll give you a recommendation. Having said that, you're more of the pilot type. It's up to you. And now sorry, I need to split."

He rose, about to leave.

"Jurgen? One more thing."

"What's that?"

I pointed at the Haash.

He frowned. "What's the problem?"

"He won't wake up. He's been like this for the last few days."

He shrugged. "That's fine. From what I heard, the Haash have this tendency to hibernate if they overexert themselves."

"D'you know how I can wake him up?"

He chuckled. "Well, you can go to the Exo sector, I suppose. Or just ask some vendor. There must be a metabolite that will do it."

"Will do, thanks."

"I'm off, then. Take care. Sorry, I really need to rush. Lots of things to do. Let me know if you have problems."

The door closed behind him.

I was left alone with my "menagerie" and tons of new information to digest.

* * *

THE GOBLIN DIDN'T MOVE. He curled up nice and snug. Like, he was fast asleep.

"Get up!"

Arbido startled.

"Get up, I say! I've had enough of your playing dead! Time to have words!"

He raised his head, looking bleakly at me. Someone must have tweaked his avatar: he was too gaunt and puny compared to the classical goblin build. Oh no. This time I'd be immune to his sob stories.

I pointed at the chair. "Now sit down and tell me everything. Don't play any games with me or you might regret it."

He touched his collar. Grunting, he staggered toward the chair and scrambled into it, hunching up so that only the top of his head showed above the table.

I folded the table to look at him, then waited.

He started shaking. His mouth contorted, his heavy gasps tearing through the silence. He didn't at all look like the shameless street-smart dealer I used to know.

What was he afraid of? My wrath? Doubtful. Not after the agonizing succession of deaths and respawns he'd just been through. Then again it depended on how exactly it had affected him. He might be scared witless of any kind of pain now.

He wasn't. His shaking subsided. He looked up at me from under his eyebrows and I could see the old expression in his eyes. Then it died away, his frail little frame shaking with renewed force.

"I can't," he finally managed.

"You can't what?"

"I can't speak," his voice kept breaking.

"Try it. If you put me in the picture, I might remove the collar. It's simple, really. The moment I remove the collar, the Logout button will go live again. You can fuck off back to the real world, on one condition. I need the truth. And I want my savings back."

He sank into a sullen silence. "Zander, I really can't."

"Why?"

"I don't remember!" his voice rose to a shriek. "There's nothing! Just the pain, death and more pain!" the chair under him began to vibrate with his shaking. "Zander, please... let me stay here for a while. I don't remember the last few days. Only the pain... I'll pay you back... I will, I promise... I can be useful..."

The old boy didn't make sense which only understandable, I suppose. A day or two in Gehenna would have driven anyone off their trolley. Still, I'd have loved to have known who'd fitted him with an implant and thrown him into purgatory. The way it looked, it was probably some turf war.

Possible. Arbido did business on a grand scale. There had to be quite a few people around wishing to take it over.

Memory loss, yeah right. He still remembered my money though. What was that supposed to mean? "So how can you be useful to me wearing this collar?"

Apparently, I had a heart. I actually felt sorry for him. I could clearly see that he didn't want to go back — but he was too afraid to admit it even to himself. What had they done to him? Didn't he understand that staying here wouldn't make it safer? He couldn't change his avatar. He was doomed to forever remain a xenomorph — and he might live to regret it.

After some thought, I decided to give him more time. He needed to get a break and find his bearings. I was different: I was already hooked on the Phantom Server with its adrenaline rush and the promise of a life as the adventure seeker I'd secretly believed myself to be. I'd long given up on real life. But Arbido wasn't cut out for this.

Or was he?

"Very well, then. You can stay here for a while," I just couldn't watch him shake for much longer. "Hungry?"

I expected him to forget his "poor goblin" mask by showing some interest. I was mistaken. Arbido wasn't pretending. He was still shaking violently and uncontrollably.

I seemed to attract some truly whacky partners. One of them had been in a coma for three days in a row while the other had gone all shaky and amnesiac. What was I supposed to do with them both?

* * *

ABOUT AN HOUR LATER I had finally sorted out my gear and decided to go out and do a few things.

Arbido hadn't said a word. He'd curled up in the far corner and was sitting there shaking and chattering his teeth.

"Are you cold?"

The room was warm though. The old boy had a nervous breakdown, that's all it was.

"Come here," I moved the chair to the network terminal and adjusted the seat. "Sit down."

He obeyed.

"Stop shivering for a second, will you?" I faked anger trying to shake him out of his shock. "If you plan to stay you'd better start by reading the Wiki or checking the markets!"

He shrank and nodded.

"Very well," I said. "I'm off. I have a quest to close."

The market deck was crowded. I took the familiar route. The shop vendor was idly twiddling his thumbs behind the counter.

Seeing me, he perked up. "Zander! I thought that you..."

"Dream on," I lay the chunks of Dargian pythons on the counter. "Good enough?"

"Of course! Look how fat they are!" he began weighing them. "You even cauterized the wounds with a laser! What an excellent thought! This way the blood gets clotted and you don't lose any! You're a born exobiologist, man!"

Okay, so I wasn't. I admittedly had only shot one of them — the Founders' drones had slaughtered the rest. But I didn't let him in on it.

"Fifteen hundred in total," he summed up.

I didn't object. I really needed the money. "Know a

place where I could get some Haash metabolites?"

He raised a puzzled stare. "Why?"

I shrugged off his question.

"You got to go to the exo sector."

"Thanks. How do I get there?"

"The first block to the right of the elevators."

I walked out and headed there, connecting to the network as I walked in the hope of finding out at least something about the Haash.

No one seemed to know that much though. The Haash seemed to have arrived out of nowhere. I found a mention of a battle between a Dargian cruiser and an unknown ship. The battle had taken place in Darg's orbit at quite a distance from the station. The Dargians had shot the intruder down. The ship had allegedly burned up on entering the planet's atmosphere. Twenty-four hours later, a group of unknown fighter craft had been sighted near Argos. At first they were mistaken for Phantom Raiders which set off a combined attack from all of the station's forces. The invaders were wiped out. Not a ship fragment was left over for examination. And afterwards, about a dozen creatures had respawned at the station's resurrection points. They called themselves the Haash.

Not a word was said about what had happened to them later.

The exo sector was nauseating with all the stench and the samples in shop windows. I'd done my fair share of alchemy in the past — you just couldn't avoid it in fantasy worlds — but the Phantom Server's authenticity levels seriously messed with one's head. Pardon me for saying so, but the sight of various organs floating in jars and the offers of *exococktails made to unique recipes while you wait* made my stomach churn.

I found a shop that looked slightly more respectable than most and walked in, looking around.

A pretty young girl greeted me, beaming with pleasure at seeing a customer. No surprise there. One glance at the price tags made one realize that every customer was literally worth his weight in gold.

Nayri. Human. Level 15. Exobiologist.

I got straight down to business, ignoring her inhuman charisma and beauty. Inhuman being the right word: the girl's neck sported tiny metal-clad sockets for exo injections. She wore them openly. The air around her was poignant with an amazing fragrance. I wouldn't be surprised if its biochemical formula was influencing me even as I spoke.

"I need a Haash metabolite."

"Made from a Haash," she clarified.

Why was I constantly cringing with disgust? I needed to get a grip. I, who used to drink various elixirs by the bucket without batting an eyelid!

The thought didn't help.

I clued her in. Nayri gave me an understanding nod. "It's true the Haash have this ability. They can survive the most extreme environment without the need for sleep and only a minimum of food. Then they fall into hibernation."

"How long does it last normally?"

"We don't know yet. We've had very little research material. But luckily, we still have some metabolites left over after some experiments we conducted two years back," she added cheerfully. "Those are some very special samples. Here, take a look at the price list."

I glanced at the numbers.

A metabolite capable of completely restoring Charon's depleted energy cost a hundred and thirty-two grand!

Nayri noticed my hesitation. "It works for humans as well, increasing strength ten times and allowing you to go without sleep for a month. People buy it for emergencies such as long-distance raids to the outskirts of the star system."

She paused. "You know what? I have a counterproposition for you. Why would you spend so much money on drugs for your Haash? We can buy him off you."

"Are you soliciting organ harvesting?"

Her mask of helpfulness faded, revealing contempt underneath. "You've only been here a few days. There're lots of things you don't understand yet. We'd have never survived had it not been for alien metabolites. These days we have life support systems in place, allowing people to make do without them. But it wasn't always like this."

"I need to think about it."

* * *

I CAME BACK to my hotel room an hour later. Things weren't looking good. I'd been offered ten grand for the five "cyber ingredients" I'd farmed. The two chips I'd decided not to part with yet. It would have probably been better to show them to Jurgen first. At least he'd be able to test them and advise me on the price.

If I wanted to survive, I had to get the implants. As Serge had so insightfully said, I'd be forever stuck at the shnoob stage. I had to bring Charon out of his coma somehow, too. So basically, everywhere you turned it was all about money. I couldn't see how I could earn enough by farming the station's ruins. It would take me all year to do that.

There was only one solution to all this. Sell the ship. I just couldn't see any other option.

The room was dark, its air thick with a sickly sweet smell. Arbido was still hunched behind his terminal. He wasn't shaking any more — in fact, he was so lost in the network he hadn't even acknowledged my arrival.

Whatever. I removed my gear and collapsed onto the bunk bed. Then I connected to the station network.

After all my escapades, I was level 10. It was decision-making time and I'd better take it seriously.

Once again I perused all the information regarding the implants and not only them. This time I also needed to know more about their character classes.

I ignored all the scientists, vendors, technologists, mechanics and engineers. This wasn't my thing.

Which left me with three specializations.

Two of which were the most dangerous but also the most lucrative: techno archeologist and xenobiologist. You could tell by their names that the former searched for the Founders' ancient technologies while the latter studied all sorts of alien beings.

The archeology bit was more or less clear. This stellar system had never been properly studied yet. Its outskirts (about thirty astronomical units from the station — that is, about three billion miles away) were jam-packed with all sorts of drifting junk: asteroids, clouds of gas and dust, various debris left of ancient disasters and most importantly, lots of artifacts of the

Founders' era. Getting there was a job and a half. I couldn't just jump onto my ship and do a quick run there and back, filling its holds with pricey techno artifacts. Its fuel tanks and life support system just wouldn't make it. It meant I had to call up an expedition or a raid complete with a mothership, a convoy and several recon stations, plus a few mining facilities which luckily could be set up anywhere, including dwarf planets, their satellites and even asteroids.

A lone player would never be able to pull it off. This was a niche reserved for clans and corporations. I did find a mention of a group of legendary pilots who raided the area in converted freighters backed-up by some very pricey drones — but this was more of an inspiring urban legend than fact.

The players who chose to specialize in archeology normally studied either the two nearest of the Founders' stations or the asteroid belt located two light minutes away from Argus — a very unhealthy practice considering the area was swarming with Outlaws.

The techno archeologists leveled four main skills: Piloting of Small Spacecraft, Repairs, Alien Technologies and Combat Skills. In other words, they were jacks of all trades and masters of none. They could pilot all kinds of ships, fix them when necessary, take over the enemy's defense systems, mop up the landing zones and defend themselves with weapons in their hands. They were capable of procuring technical artifacts but not of studying them.

The Exobiologists were a much tougher bunch. They leveled Piloting of Small and Medium Spacecraft,

Atmospheric Maneuvering, Science, Medicine, Exobiology and predictably, Combat Skills.

Compared to them, slave traders were cute. The Phantom Server version of exobiologists hunted xenomorphs and studied them, taking them apart and creating bio implants, symbionts and various drugs with both temporary and permanent characteristic bonuses.

This was one dirty job in all respects. When I tried to look into it further, I realized that although bio implants and symbiont creatures offered a number of unique abilities, they weren't crucial survival-wise. A good metabolic corrector and a wise choice of gear could protect you much better than any exo could.

The Pilots were the next on my list.

This was a dangerous profession surrounded by an aura of romantic valor — which however faded a lot once you browsed through the raid reports.

I had no idea that deep space exploration — as well as the humans' survival away from their home solar system — would obliterate their ethics and demand so much blood.

But I digress.

So, the Pilots. Undoubtedly with a capital P. They studied Piloting of Small and Medium Spacecraft as well as all types of Maneuvering and Repairs. Strength, Stamina and Agility all maxed out. If a player planned to make a career of it, he or she had to also level up Intellect and Willpower which allowed you to control groups of ships and study tactics, navigation and strategic planning.

Normally, pilots chose to disregard these vital characteristics. As a result, they either got stuck in their development or were forced to risk implanting extra symbionts and neural networks.

Apart from those above, there were plenty of little hybrid classes whose advantages were more than questionable. Badly configured and slow to level up, they made up, however, the bulk of the station's population. I understood of course how easy it was to overindulge once you started checking all those talent branches, but you still had to limit yourself somehow, for this was a shortcut to mediocrity.

So what should I choose?

Without a doubt, I wanted to be a pilot and a techno archeologist. I would like to go on long-range expeditions, discovering and collecting the Founders' artifacts.

Which meant that my current priorities were:

A SynapsZ mind expander, a Neurus Universal reflex enhancer and a top-of-the-range Xenus metabolic implant. I would also need some good armor and weapons, and also a Raptor-class ship. Unlike the fast Condors, this type of craft was equipped with powerful weapons and a capacious cargo hold which was crucial on long-range raids.

It looked like I knew what I needed now.

Next thing I had to check was my financial situation.

Arbido fidgeted in his chair, still busy online. I started counting.

The implants worked out to be about three hundred grand. A Raptor, half a million. Half-decent gear, a hundred grand. Plus Charon's metabolite. I hadn't decided what to do with Arbido yet.

All in all, I needed a million. Nothing more, nothing less.

I heaved a sigh. Apparently, I'd have to risk

auctioning the Haash ship. Its stats placed it somewhere in between a Condor and a Raptor. Which meant the starting price should be somewhere around four hundred grand. Plus a faint hope that the ship's rarity would spark a lot of interest amid top-level pilots.

"Zander," Arbido turned in his chair, shaking his head with disapproval. He scrambled down and pattered toward me. "Are you stupid or something?"

I slumped down, staring at him. "You've got a cheek! So you've come round, then?"

"Sorry," his face fell but immediately he looked back up at me. "Don't you understand you're walking on money? Why the fuck would you want to sell the ship?"

"Pardon me? Are you monitoring my searches?"

His face fell again. "I only want to help," he finally offered.

"Does that mean there's nothing wrong with your memory?"

"No, it doesn't! But you're about to make some stupid mistakes."

"I'm trying to find some ways to level my char! I need to get some implants! I need to bring Charon out of his coma! And-"

"Zand, just listen to me!" he begged.

"Go ahead, then. What's your big plan?"

Arbido's business hunches rarely proved wrong. Once he set his sights on a money-making opportunity, he'd go after it with a pitbull's tenacity.

"I heard you talk to Jurgen this morning."

"And? What's that got to do with it?"

"You're in possession of some unexplored alien technologies. Jurgen's mistaken about the ship's origins, isn't he? Isn't the ship Haash and not Dargian?"

"So what if it is?"

"How many subsystems does it have on board?"

I shrugged. "Search me."

"Have a look," Arbido walked back to the terminal, activated a backup holographic screen and transferred to it an offer posted by the Technologists clan.

We offer 100,000 credits for the right to study and copy any one of the yet unknown Founders' devices. The sample's integrity is guaranteed.

We offer 50,000 credits for the right to study and copy any one of the yet unknown alien devices. The sample's integrity is guaranteed.

My jaw dropped. Talk about business hunches. It hadn't taken him long to suss this one out, had it?

Now. I had to play it cool and think it over. How many subsystems would a fighter ship like this have on board? Had to be at least a hundred. What a shame I couldn't ask Charon.

I glanced at Arbido. "Well done."

"I told you I might be useful," he grumbled. "No one has studied the Haash fighter ships before. I suggest you contact Jurgen. I'm pretty sure he won't miss such an opportunity. He has to restore his authority now, and alien technologies are the most valued thing here. Jurgen will earn their gratitude and you, money and some quality implants. Promise you won't forget about me, will you?"

If the truth were known, I felt a bit lost among all

these prospects. "What is it you want, then?" I cast him a suspicious look.

"To begin with, I'd like a room of my own," he glanced at Charon. "And I'd like to get access to your logs."

"Why?"

"It's true that I really can't remember how I got here. So I'm not in a hurry to go back to real life. I don't think it's a good idea. So I'd like to stick around you. I won't be able to survive on my own."

"What have my logs got to do with it?"

"Didn't I tell you? You walk on money and you don't even notice it! Just think how much anyone would be prepared to pay for some information about an unexplored station? So please allow me to work for you. You won't regret it, I promise."

I stood up and began pacing the room. I had a funny feeling he hadn't told me everything.

"You'll have to wear the slave collar," I said.

"I know."

"The locals won't be less xenophobic."

"I don't even count on that. But with money you can live anywhere," he added cynically.

Yes, this was my old Arbido. "Very well, then. You may stay. Just remember I'll be keeping an eye on you. Understood?"

He heaved a sigh. "I should get on with it if I were you," he scrambled back into the chair in front of the terminal. "Get to Jurgen before his enemies do. That way you'll help him and will have something to show for it."

Okay. The advice was good. I went online and PM'd Jurgen.

It took him some time to answer. "What is it? Just

keep it short. What's the problem?"

"I have a proposal for you that you might find hard to refuse."

"What do you mean?"

"I mean alien technologies. For about two or three million in total. Are you interested?"

Arbido looked triumphant. Pleased as a pig in shit. He wasn't shaking any more.

"Wait up. I'm coming."

He didn't say much. Still, I was damn sure he was interested.

CHAPTER FIVE

PHANTOM SERVER
TEN DAYS LATER

I WAS A PILOT!

Jurgen had proved true to his word. The deal suggested by Arbido had worked fast. While I'd been recovering from progressive implantation, the Technologists had studied the Haash ship and even improved it. Now the pilot's antigravity seat could easily transform to accommodate a human body. They'd done the same to the navigational controls, adding another segment to the control columns which allowed them to fold, making them shorter.

The rest of the cockpit equipment was the same, apart from the addition of a new cyber module mounted behind the pilot's seat. I was the only person who could activate it with my own personal access code. This additional subsystem adapted the scanners' data to human perception.

In fact, this was nothing that a mind expander couldn't do. It had been Jurgen who'd insisted I invest in it. According to him, the first solo flights were also the most dangerous. The slightest delay in the data stream interpretation or a glitch in my mnemonic connection to the ship could prove fatal.

I just couldn't wait. According to the statistics, it took three to four months to turn a newb into a half-decent pilot but in my case, the process would be affected by some of the highest-end technologies.

The Founders' neuronet that had invaded my body had produced a sensation among researchers. Had it not been for Jurgen's putting his authoritative foot down, I'm sure they'd have vivisected me there and then. Luckily, we'd managed to come to a compromise. I agreed to participate in another dangerous experiment which offered the Technologists the opportunity to study my unique nervous system upgrade in action. In return, they offered to install me with the latest reflex enhancer type which hadn't yet been tested. Its main difference from the old ones was in that its nanites contained prerecorded neurograms of a pilot's typical reactions. That didn't make me an ace of course but endowed me with all the basic reflexes necessary to fly small craft. Whether I'd be able to use them, no one could tell yet. The Technologists were curious to see the results of this impromptu field trial. If my mind proved up to the pressure assimilating these new skills, it could become a revolution in neurocybernetics and mnemotechnics, shooting the clan to the top.

The risk was great but so were the prospects it offered.

Behind my back, the hatch slid shut. I activated

the seat adjustment memory and slid into it. My heart was fluttering. Immediately the metabolic implant kicked in, trying to curb my anxiety. But still the pressure of the moment was almost too great to bear.

The servomotors whined, transforming the controls. The armrests shifted closer; the joysticks shrank, the seat's back changed its rake angle. Feeders lashed around, snaking out of the seat's base, then bit into the helmet's sockets. Activation codes flashed before my eyes.

And then-

A surge of information flooded my brain, crushing it, sweeping my consciousness away like a twig.

I lost all sense of direction. The simulation training had been nothing like it. My vision blurred; a wave of heat rolled over my body. My perception shifted. The cockpit's outline distorted; then it thinned out and disappeared in the cosmic void.

I broke out in a freezing cold sweat.

I tried to find my bearings but immediately suffered a fierce bout of vertigo as if I were spun around at an inhuman speed. Suddenly I couldn't breathe. Instinctively I tried to jump up but my armored suit was already securely locked into the seat. I couldn't focus. Everything around me kept flashing past, blurring into streaks.

Enough!

My inner scream stopped the maddening spin. The streaks disappeared. I was enveloped by a gray mist. Then a convex wall began looming up out of the haze. What the hell was that?

Gradually I took in the details of a new technoscape. I could see the docking pads and structures next to them from a very different angle.

Was this data from the external sensors?

The ship and I, we were one in a cyber symbiosis. The ship's hull had become my skin.

The mind shift was shattering. The new sensations that a human being simply couldn't have were surging through my brain. A silent scream froze on my lips. I could feel the reactor's burning heat; I was awash with space radiation. It was happening too fast, way beyond human adaptivity levels. I was on the brink of insanity, losing my identity and purpose.

The informational pressure kept growing, surging through me, submerging me into the dark depths of a mind being reborn.

Then it receded.

The cockpit hoved back into view.

Thin holographic screens covered its walls and ceiling, forming my new digital environment. Their deceptive depths held the dark void of space, showing a corner of the station and the pea-sized distant planet.

Interface messages glowed over them, the screens crowded with icons I could move or activate simply by focusing on them.

The mind expander must have connected to my optic nerve, using it as the main data communication channel.

My heart beat slowly. The reactor glowed next to it. Breath in. Breath out. I could feel the joysticks' porous substance lumpy with trigger buttons, sensing the controls through the armored gloves as another edge of altered reality was opening up to my mind.

I sensed myself now human, now the ship. The two identities weren't in a hurry to merge.

Never mind. This was only the beginning.

* * *

THE SHIP WAS STILL DOCKED. I painstakingly studied the interface, sorting through the icons and shifting them in an easily accessible order even though I had no idea of their priority yet.

The hours of draining tension began to show some results. I had preserved my sanity. I was more or less comfortable now switching between the various perception modes. It felt so weird to sense the station's docking clamps holding on to you.

No one was rushing me or trying to intervene. I knew that the Technologists' top mnemotechs were busy now monitoring the process, adjusting certain details as I went, helping me inconspicuously. For them this was a wealth of priceless experience. The dawn of a new day.

Once again I'd found myself at the cutting edge of progress. The risks were enormous, but was I supposed to lag behind? Now I could understand why the Outlaws with their neural AIs were so superior to regular pilots. But this was nothing compared to what was yet to come. I'd already been warned that every impact hitting the ship would hurt me.

The ship would react to my instincts, the hybrid perception making us as one for the duration of the sortie.

I seemed to be all right. All the stress and anxiety was over. I was hungry as hell. Did that mean that the metabolic implant had already drained its own batteries trying to help me overcome the shock and was now syphoning energy from my own body?

I'd had enough for today, sure. Still I couldn't stop.

I needed to feel *it*.

"Argus? This is 2017. Request permission to launch."

There were loads of ships bustling around. Before I could commence accelerating, I needed their course data.

"2017, launch clearance granted. Commencing countdown. You have one intersecting course, a Stighawk freighter at azimuth 30, declination 18."

I could see it already. My mind had received and processed the data.

The power field began to fade. The air was pumped out of the docking pod. The power feed clamps reverberated, unlocking. Dozens of pipes and cables disconnected themselves from the hull. I could feel it!

"2017, prepare for launch."

The countdown neared zero. The electromagnetic catapult shot me into the void.

I just can't describe the entire scope and novelty of the feeling. The acceleration forced me into the seat as the station plunged out of view. The bright dot of the freighter on the intersecting course grew rapidly, gaining shape. Maneuvering thrusters, I dove deeper, flying at a five degree inclination regarding the ecliptic plane. We passed each other within a hair's breadth.

This was mind-blowing. I knew that my maneuver must have looked clumsy and amateurish but still it filled me with some ecstatic, boundless freedom. Everything I'd ever experienced before had faded into insignificance next to this, shrinking into bleak shadows in my memory.

The initial launch had given the ship enough momentum to continue on its way. Mentally I switched from one hemisphere to the other. Now I could see the station. I commenced the maneuver, watching the thrusters spew cloudy jets of gas from the starboard side. The stellar view shifted unhurriedly. Once I had the station in my crosshairs, I activated the compensating thruster.

I was going back!

This was way too slow and fluent for combat maneuvering. Then again, I hadn't got used to the ship yet. My perception came in jerks: too powerful one moment, too weak the next. I knew that the slightest twitch of my hands, the slightest pressure of my fingers could cause the course to change. I tried to steer it a little more to circumnavigate Argus and immediately went into a spin. In the split second that it took the autopilot to correct my mistake, my blood ran cold. Had I been maneuvering in the thick of a ship formation, or even worse, caught in the whirlwind of battle, the consequences would have been unimaginable.

Gingerly I leveled up the course. I was woefully unready for any close-range maneuvering.

I pulled myself together.

Sixty seconds since launch. I sent a docking request and located the landing beam. The station loomed back into view, the docking pad speeding toward me. My vision blurred.

Then reflexes kicked in.

I expertly manipulated the controls. The ship turned aft to the station. Thrusts began to pulsate. Acceleration forced me into the seat. Speed control. Thrust.

The station was within three hundred feet. Slowly the ship drifted toward the pad, banking slightly as it entered. I felt the magnetic dampers kick in. A dull thump. The ship vibrated as the clamps grappled it.

Ninety seconds since launch.

It felt like a lifetime, birth until death.

The tension wouldn't let go. The hair under my helmet were dripping with sweat. I was ecstatic.

I was in game. I was a pilot!

* * *

THE STATION'S LIVING QUARTERS were nothing like all those "hotel" rooms.

It was a fully restored and functional area adjacent to the Market Deck to house lone players unaffiliated to any of the clans, mainly pilots and well-to-do vendors.

My module consisted of a lounge with three doors. Now both Arbido and Charon had a room each to themselves.

Arbido had wangled a few screenshots of the Dargian station out of me plus a couple of logs. Now he was very secretive, spending all his time online preparing some sort of economic miracle.

I was still euphoric after my first sortie. The moment I removed my gear, I hurried over to see Charon.

He was gradually coming back to life. He was still very weak after we'd pulled him out of his hibernation with the metabolites I'd bought. He could barely move and couldn't think straight. Still, he reacted to my arrival by opening his eyes and turning his head.

"Zander..."

"Hi, man."

"I've been following your test run," he looked pleased with my success.

I perched on the bed next to him. "The ship is too

good for words."

He stared at me, cocking his head to one side and growling pensively without noticing it. "When are you going to keep your promise? We *are* going to liberate the Haash, aren't we?"

"Absolutely. But it might take a bit of time."

"Why?"

"You're too weak still. And I need to practice some more."

"I'm much better already!"

"Charon, we're going to set them all free, trust me. And we'll beat the crap out of the Dargians, I swear. But it's not going to be easy. We'll need to call up a raid. It'll take money. And a lot of it."

His eyes glistened unkindly. Holding onto the wall, he scrambled to his feet.

"Where do you think you're going? You have to stay in bed!"

"I'm going to talk to Arbido," Charon was definitely in a decisive mood. "He knows how to make money."

I didn't say anything. If he could befriend Arbido, that would be excellent. Besides, we really had to get the rest of the Haash out. That went without saying. But no matter how badly Charon wanted it, putting a raid together could take some time.

We had to think everything over and find some people we could trust. We wouldn't pull it off the two of us, even if we managed to buy another ship.

* * *

FOR TWO WEEKS ALREADY I'd been practicing combat maneuvers.

The Technologists clan kept receiving their data

from me. The implants worked without fail, growing more dependable with every passing day as they kept merging with my nervous and metabolic systems.

Today I was supposed to practice with five dummy drones. It had taken me a lot of arguing with Charon and consulting with the mechanics, but finally I'd had the weapons upgraded. Apart from the lasers, I had an anti-fighter turret and two EMPs. I'd had to order another battery pack and some ammo storage modules but in the end it was worth it. I'd already had the chance to fully appreciate kinetic weapons. In close-range combat against well-armored targets protected by power fields they were indispensable.

More experienced pilots cast funny looks my way. They didn't seem to agree. I could understand that: they had already become one with their ships, unwilling to introduce any changes. A newb always plays a smartass until his first sortie.

I wasn't listening to them, though. I just hoped that my fresh approach to the weapon layout might help us all survive at a later date.

Now the drone was banking this way and that, doing some complex aerobatics trying to throw me off its tail. A tiny, agile target. I had special training generators installed on all of my weapons to make sure I didn't destroy my targets. The drones were too expensive. Simulating the kill was more than enough.

I caught it in my sights as it completed yet another maneuver and unloaded my lasers into it. Four piercing beams made the target's power field shimmer. Normally this was a preparative measure aimed at bringing the shields down. Simple, really: no reactor in the world was capable of keeping shield batteries charged for the duration of a combat. The shields were obliged to lose power — and then, suffering constant pressure, they would deplete their charge and would momentarily go down.

I still remembered my experiments with my Shield Belt (I was never without it these days).

Let's see now. The drone in front of me was desperately banking this way and that. I fired brief preemptive bursts of my pulse guns.

Got him!

The missiles that would have normally evaporated with the fully-charged power field impact now went right through the weakened shield, white-hot, hitting the drone.

The target wasn't destroyed but it was seriously damaged. The impacts scorched the drone's hull and its sensors. Now its maneuverability was seriously limited as both aft and starboard thrusters were crippled. As a result, its very next maneuver sent the drone into a spin.

I stepped on it, shortening the distance and keeping the target within the attack cone. Two lasers kept hitting it non-stop until the shield dropped to 10%. A few more bursts of the pulse guns. Done him!

Combat duration: seven seconds?

This was unbelievable. Normally, a combat between two equal fighters lasted five minutes at least. First you had to remove the enemy's shields depriving him of power, then either chase the desperately fleeing target or catch the banking ship in your sights and then shoot it down. I wasn't in a hurry to make my logs public. I had a few things to analyze first. In a real-life combat it might have taken even less time. If its purpose is survival and not some grudge you have, you don't need to finish your enemy off. Just damaging his ship is enough, forcing him out of the picture, especially when there is a considerable disparity of power.

Most pilots weren't going to like it. This was no teamwork in any shape or form. They didn't like to let the damaged ships go, either. But at the moment, I was simply trying to suss out this new weapon setup and its potential. Just practicing some skills I might need in the future. I already knew enough about the Phantom Server to realize that whoever wanted to make it here had to think out of the box.

A sensation of danger swept over me before the aft sensors kicked in. Two drones were coming up my backside.

I banked, strafing out of their line of fire, and performed a pylon turn facing the enemy, my fighter preserving its momentum flying aft first.

I shot the first one down straight away in one powerful combined volley.

Its wingman was too close to its leader; it now had to swerve trying to avoid all the debris, thus giving me a few precious seconds extra.

It began to spin in an ever-widening spiral, heading "forward" in regards to the ecliptic. I chased after it.

I was getting better every time. I knew of course that a drone was a drone. I'd no idea how long I'd last confronted with a proper fighter pilot. But this was yet to come. I still had another couple of weeks to practice my reflexes and reaction, improving my pilot skills.

* * *

TWICE THE DRONE ESCAPED the attack cone. It had lured me about twenty thousand miles above the ecliptic plane before I finally shot it down.

Now I had to get the drone back. It wasn't going to be easy but this was a very useful skill for a fighter pilot. How else were you supposed to collect loot in outer space?

The Haash ships consisted of three modules. This diagram might give you some idea of how they looked:

)II(

The cockpit was located in the center of the craft. The two side sections carried two autonomous reactors and the weapon modules. After all the improvements I'd introduced to midships, it also held the pulse guns, their accelerators securely armored. The weapon modules didn't affect the ship's aerodynamics which allowed it to enter the atmosphere if necessary.

The small cargo holds were located at the back of the side sections, next to the tractor beam generators. My objective now was to grab the drone with the tractor beam, then switch off the power shield momentarily while opening one of the aft hatches.

This was something I hadn't quite mastered yet. I did everything by the book but it took me five to seven seconds to land the captured ship in the hold. You couldn't afford this kind of time in combat. They'd shoot me down before I knew it. I'd seen professional pilots do it: they just sped past their quarry, grabbing it with the beam and went on fighting, switching momentarily the aft power field emitters, showering the enemy with fire while stuffing their holds with loot.

I still had a lot to grow.

Six seconds.

Too long. I had to try to do it at full speed. The problem was, the Haash ship's power shield wasn't divided up. This was a serious drawback. I had to install more power field emitters to enable me to divide the defense between the two hemispheres so that I could redistribute the power when necessary.

I opened the holds and set the drones free.

I had another hour of practice left. This time I was going to practice attacking a large ship. I had two proton torpedoes slung on their mountings: it wasn't yet viable to install launching tubes. I didn't have guidance systems, either, but considering the sheer power of the proton charges they weren't strictly necessary.

The five drones linked up, docking onto each other.

A holographic image of a large military freighter lumbered onto the screens — very decently armed and equipped with ten-megawatt shields. Both the sensors and my own field of vision (which was spherical now with the implants I'd received) generated and registered the craft's signature.

My objective was to disable the shields using the first torpedo while driving the other one into the ship's engine compartment. The rest had to go according to plan. To assault an immobilized ship, you first had to nuke its space weapon defense systems.

I approached the target.

The torpedoes sitting in their mountings were real. But this time I was going to launch their holographic copies. It would be stupid wasting expensive ammo for training's sake.

The "freighter" had noticed me and activated its laser turrets while trying to maneuver out of my sights. While analyzing its trajectory, I locked on to it, simultaneously controlling the area around it.

My dedicated practice location was quite near to the station. And still I shouldn't forget that the Outlaws' territory was a mere twenty light seconds away. At any moment, real danger could come from that direction. Which was why even practice sorties always demanded a full load of ammo and a complete battery charge.

Most asteroids you couldn't even see: they merged with the darkness of space. Only occasionally could you notice tiny little sparks as the light of the system's star played with the blocks of ice.

The virtual "freighter" changed course sharply, trying to avoid the attack cone. I beat him to it. The proton torpedoes were ready for action. Everything was under control.

An alarm beeped. Staying on course, I quickly scanned my sphere of vision.

Some strange signatures had appeared in the asteroid belt area. The naked eye couldn't have spotted anything out of the ordinary but my mind was now short-wired to the ship's sensors, allowing me to notice even a barely visible shimmer.

The drones continued on their maneuver. I contacted them, ordering them to heave to. No more practice for me today. I was too curious.

I killed the speed and activated all the monitoring systems. I also switched on camo mode and maxed out the shields just in case.

Below me to my right floated the ancient starships, Leviathans of the universe or rather, only their enormous empty shells gaping with impact damage. The Dargians had long stripped them of anything that was worth salvaging. Argus crafters used to frequent them for a while cutting out whole sections of their cargonite armor, but the Outlaws' forays had quickly put an end to this practice.

A cluster of debris floated nearby — with the Titan, the corporation's flagship, at its center. Some distance away I could see the silent procession of the dead cryogenic platforms and remains of the colonial freighters. Hundreds of Dargian ships destroyed in the epic battle circled them, making an outer frame of this mammoth techno graveyard.

This area was an arena of regular skirmishes between the Outlaws and Argus pilots. About a year ago, the Engineers' clan had managed to unearth, amid all the debris, two relatively well-preserved Founders' frigates which were now being restored at the station.

The shimmering spots I'd noticed were getting brighter. What was going on? I changed the scanners' focus.

It was a gas and dust cloud.

Now where could it have come from? I downloaded all the data on this particular location. There was no record of it being there before.

The first thing that jumped to my mind was that it had probably been formed by the collision of two larger asteroids. In which case, why hadn't I noticed the impact itself? None of the instruments seemed to have registered it, either.

This was truly weird. It was as if a good dozen asteroids rich in metals had been suddenly dispersed, their atoms losing their bond with each other forming a cold nebula in a matter of seconds.

At least that's what the ship's sensors were trying to suggest. But I knew that in order to blow these gargantuan boulders to dust you needed indecent amounts of energy.

Had I just witnessed one of the Founders' yet unknown technologies being used by the Outlaws?

If so, what was its purpose?

Zander, get real. This is a game world. Its developers can make anything possible.

True. My initial anxiety subsided, replaced by acute curiosity.

In the meantime, the cloud began forming hundreds of swirling patterns as matter started clustering together. I watched, unable to take my eyes off its mysterious metamorphosis, when I started to realize: each of the hundreds of clusters was gaining shape and structure.

I focused on the one nearest to me. The skin on the back of my head began to prickle as I looked at the translucent opaque outline of a materializing spaceship.

A Phantom Raider?

Images from the promptly downloaded databases flashed before my eyes. I had no doubt left. This was a heavy Phantom Raider.

* * *

THERE WERE HUNDREDS OF THEM.

The ships materialized swiftly. Knowing the Raiders couldn't intercept the laser communications system, I quickly sent word down. I just hoped they wouldn't notice me. This prompt warning could save hundreds if not thousands of lives.

It looked like I was witness to some major global event in the making.

I felt uncomfortable. From what I'd heard, the most that the Argus pilots had ever had to deal with were about a dozen Raiders which was considered a large battle.

The swirls of materializing starships weren't opaque any longer. Two hundred and fifty heavy raiders exited the cloud all at once, accelerating in synch and falling into formation, docking together creating a complex spatial structure of twenty-five ships clustered together to shape a sphere with three long sickle-like "wings", each of them comprised of seventy-five Raiders.

Where were the Argus pilots, dammit? What was taking them so long?

The Phantom formation converged on the station and began rotating, each of the ships firing its heavy lasers.

The laser beams turned into a wall of fire that knew no obstacle along its path. The energy charges sank into the station's hull, striking up fires, then slid along, ripping through it, blowing up the outside fixtures, scorching the docking pads and slicing through cables and pipework, leaving nothing but fissures breathing fire in their wake.

The freighters en route to the docks began to scatter. Some even attempted to attack the slowly rotating Phantom formation but were immediately destroyed by return fire.

Instinctively grasping the enemy's potential, I shuddered realizing that the station was doomed. Nothing or nobody could delay its undoing. A few occasional and uncoordinated fighter launches would change nothing. Soon the station's hull would collapse, starting a chain reaction of decompression in all the outer layer of modules.

There was no way you could stop the Phantom Raiders. I'd only just started to integrate into this new world and now it was coming crashing down around my ears!

Why hadn't Argus heeded my warning? What had they been waiting for? I'd given the pilots plenty of time to get to their ships and-

Suddenly the station rotated faster. I glimpsed one of the ancient transport tunnels that both the Mechanics and Engineers had been toiling in all this time.

In all honesty, I couldn't understand why they would want to restore some useless service tunnels. The next moment, it all clicked into place.

The mouth of the restored magnetic hub pointed directly at the center of the Raiders' formation. Its ring accelerators, freshly renovated and modernized, gleamed intensely. The station's correction engines kicked in, stopping its rotation.

I would never have thought the Engineers would have turned a transport channel into a weapon!

The station shuddered, losing its orbit parameters. Five juggernaut steel slugs, each weighing hundreds

of tons, accelerated to an unthinkable speed, shooting out of the makeshift electromagnetic cannon and hitting the Raiders' formation head on.

The first impact destroyed their inner control sphere. The second and third ones grazed the sickle-shaped wings, plasmifying about thirty enemy ships. The remaining rounds overshot their target.

The enemy's laser beams faded. The spatial formation of the hundreds of ships was now falling apart. Some of the craft collided, filling space with clouds of debris. Not a single Phantom Raider had had the chance to self-destruct, so sudden and shattering was the station's response.

I WAS STILL IN SHOCK from these rapid developments when the station resumed its unhurried rotation, engaging its space defense systems.

Argus had withstood the first strike. I could still see cloudy jets of decompression everywhere but at least the station was in one piece. We'd repulsed the surprise attack. The surviving launching pads began flashing, propelling hundreds of fighters into space.

They shot down about a dozen of the nearest alien ships, disabled and disoriented, signaling the start of a massive space battle.

It wasn't a pretty sight. The enemy chose not to restore their formation; instead, they headed toward our Condors in ones and twos. Heavily armored, Phantom Raiders with their ten-megawatt shields were a force to be reckoned with.

A battle broke out. Laser beams strobed in all directions, criss-crossing, fading and blazing again.

Tracers of missiles punctuated the dark. A multitude of thrusters burned bright as the ships banked, circled and zigzagged through space, chasing down their targets. Power fields pulsed as many a ship erupted in blinding flames.

The two armadas passed through each other. Only two thirds of our pilots made it through the Phantom Raiders' loose ranks.

Immediately the battle disintegrated, breaking up into countless skirmishes swirling through space like wheels of fire. The station's guns began engaging section by section, firing volleys at separate targets while trying not to hit our own ships.

The Phantom Raiders were a cut about the station defenders. They were better armed and protected, and their maneuverability lay way beyond human endurance. Even when ducking our especially daring assaults, they still managed to fire their heavy lasers at a turret or a docking pad they'd barely glimpsed in their sights. They'd then bank avoiding a head-on, shaking off the pursuit in a series of intricate maneuvers amid the station's outer structures before resuming their attacking courses.

The battle lay below me. It took me ten seconds — fifteen at the most — to analyze the situation. I'm not joking. Between the mind expander, the metabolic implant and the Founders' neuronet I hosted, they must have unlocked a new height in my thinking and perception levels. Faced with an emergency, my brain seemed to work in a different way somehow. I might end up regretting it later but at the moment, I was able to instantly grasp and evaluate the entire picture.

The Phantom Raiders were trying to force their own tactics onto the station defenders, surreptitiously trying to get closer to the sections where defenses were already down. I could hear the station's yet undamaged guns fall silent as they had no targets left in their fields of fire. Tails of swirling debris marked the enemy's rapid progression. Our pilots in their Condors and Raptors must have realized that they were being pinned down to the station — but the enemy kept them engaged to make sure they couldn't do much.

The ball of fire kept shrinking, the ships' maneuvers growing briefer and faster. I watched as more and more human ships exploded, destroyed, in the chaos of decompression discharges which clouded the station's molten outer structures. I could see the whole picture — but the others couldn't. Each was too busy with his or her own target, the station's ragged outline hindering their fields of vision while the swirling wheel of fire was already upon the station.

The two ancient frigates restored by the Engineers' clan were still sitting in their hangars, crewless. The station's factions had failed to come to an agreement regarding their use so now they were useless — at the exact moment when they were needed the most.

I knew of course that alone I wouldn't last a minute against a Raider. Still, I couldn't remain a passive onlooker.

I accelerated, simultaneously sending commands to the drones while switching the mind expander to broadcast its data to the station network, sharing my vision of the situation with everyone else. I saw a Condor followed by a trail of incandescent gas from its damaged reactor's cooling system. The pilot persistently banked, trying to shake two Raiders off his tail. I caught one of them in my sights and appraised its signature. Its shields were barely glimmering at two megawatts at most.

My drones flew on either side and at my rear, forming false targets.

The distance between us kept steadily shrinking. I switched my four lasers to continuous fire mode and blazed away. The Raider's shields collapsed. Yes! Two tracers sank into its body just above the engines, at the exact spot marked by my target indicator as *vulnerable*. A ball of fire welled up straight ahead. I banked just in time to avoid all the debris while noticing the fiery gas trail again as the downed Condor was trying to hightail it away from the station. I fell in behind him, hurriedly scanning both hemispheres in search for the other Raider. Where was he now?

He's behind me! Closing in, shooting down two drones in the process.

I threw the ship sideways into a widening spiral. Predictable, I knew — but so did the Raider.

All the drones were downed. A scanning wave of radiation surged over my ship — I was in the crosshairs. It felt akin to skin tingling. I went into a hook turn. Too late.

The raider closed in. I could see the frontal slopes of the ship's armor, complete with its laser gun ports: the heavy one in the middle and six medium ones in sloping nacelles on both its sides. I fired everything I had. His ten-meg shield caved in but only slightly, swallowing up the damage. Too late to swerve out of its way.

A missile soared overhead, hitting the shield in a flash. Then another. The Raider's shield was now in the red zone. A third missile turned it into a ball of fire.

I swung round, forcing the engines into overdrive, maxing out the Gs as I tried to scramble as far away as I could from the Phantom Raider's possible self-destruction zone.

"2017, follow me," I heard as the Condor flew past, still followed by its fiery trail. The pilot must have stabilized the reactor if he thought he could rejoin the battle.

I scanned his number. Liori! The merc girl I'd met earlier!

I mirrored her maneuver. Now both of us were moving away from the station, restoring our shields and reloading our weapons. We then both turned round to face the battle.

They'd received my message. The surviving station defenders fought their way out from under fire and repeated our maneuver, moving away to allow the defense systems to do their job.

Shit. So few of us left. *90 ships*, the subsystems reported impassively.

The Raiders were a hundred and fifty. They split into several groups of different sizes most of whom had switched to assault mode, their heavy lasers ripping the station's armor open and wreaking havoc on their way, leaving nothing in their wake but mangled heaps of metal and clouds of decompression. All the others came straight for us all.

"Zander, keep right behind me," Liori's voice rang through my thoughts. "I'll disable the shields and get out, then he's all yours!"

"Got it!"

She attacked — seemingly head-on, strafing from side to side to duck the constant laser beams that barely grazed her shield. She was one hell of a pilot. I still had a lot of learning to do to be able to maneuver like that.

She slid past mere feet from the Raider. Both their shields billowed out, destroying each other. The Raider swung round, exposing its aft.

Fat tracers ripped through its armored hull, spewing fire. I banked away. The Raider sped up, maxing out its Gs.

In a blinding flash, it self-destructed.

I scanned both hemispheres.

The numbers of the station defenders kept dwindling. The battle continued with mixed success. We'd kicked the Raiders' ass good and proper but the station was a sorry sight. Enormous gaping holes were framed with sections of decks forced outside by internal explosions; mangled docking pads drifted in clouds of gas and ice crystals; debris floated everywhere you turned.

I found Liori and moved closer to her.

We couldn't change anything anymore. No amount of valor or piloting skill could make any difference. If it continued like this, the station would soon begin to fall apart.

We rejoined the battle. This time we chose a group of Raiders coveting one of the hangars. I still had the two proton torpedoes with remote controlled explosive devices, so we changed our tactics. I took the lead and fired both, then waited until they were a mere three hundred feet away from the Raiders. Then I sent a mentally activated command.

Two blindingly bright spheres of transparent blue scorched and seared the station's hull, deactivating the enemies' shields. Liori overtook me and shot down two of the enemy ships. The nearest pilots joined in the assault. Together we ripped the Raiders group apart. Only a few managed to flee the scene leaving their fiery trails of incandescent gas behind.

This wasn't victory yet, not by far. The remaining Raiders — about a hundred still — turned their attention away from the station in order to get rid of us first.

THE BATTLE ENDED UNEXPECTEDLY.

The Founders' frigate, fire-damaged but still functional, powered up its engines and exited its docking hangar.

My earphones vibrated with triumphant cheers. We watched as the other frigate left its berth. Messages flooded the network with the sensational news: apparently, the Pilots' clan had seized both ships. The Engineers were furious but we, we celebrated.

Beams of stationary lasers sliced through the dark. The frigates' plasma generators and heavy pulse guns fired in automatic mode. In a matter of minutes, the Phantom Raiders had lost half their force. The surviving ones left us well alone and charged onto the Founders' frigates.

Liori turned her Condor toward the nearest docking pad that still seemed intact. The gaps in her damaged hull streaked crimson.

"Get in, I'll cover you!"

"Thanks, Zander!"

My reactor went into overload. My ship's batteries were empty, the ammo stocks depleted. My emotions went into an overdrive. I couldn't even tell the number of Raiders I'd shot down — three for sure and possibly two more. I'd have to check the logs.

Molten scars were cooling down on my ship's hull. There were several air leaks — nothing important. Once I was back in dock, they'd quickly patch me up.

Liori docked. Her Condor disappeared in the haze of the power field.

Just about time I did the same. The two frigates, already much the worse for wear, were commencing a twin assault maneuver, accelerating in pursuit of a small group of Phantom Raiders that attempted to flee the scene.

End of story. The nearest docking pad was mine.

I turned around, glimpsing a few groups of small ships almost out of the scanner's range. Signatures: unidentified. They flashed past, disappearing in the direction of the station's uninhabited sectors which were crammed full of old breach holes, allowing anyone to get on board.

Outlaws?

In all honesty, I had more important things to do. I had to weave my way amid mangled steel beams, dead deformed ships and enormous chunks of the station's hull which rotated slowly past.

I struggled to steer the ship into the pad. Only now did I realize how this brief melee had drained me.

My hands were shaking. My state of fatigue was deafening. I was hungry as hell. It looked like both the reflex enhancer and metabolic corrector had simply burned me out.

I spent a few minutes just sitting there listening to all the messages, trying to piece together the whole picture. My mind refused to accept the scope of these latest developments.

I unbuckled and stood up, keeping the helmet on. I had no idea if there was any breathable air left inside.

I contacted Charon and Arbido. They were beside themselves with worry.

I had survived. I'd survived my first real melee!

At that, my emotions died on me. Fatigue enveloped my body. I could barely shift my feet. The corridor was airless. Luckily, the elevators still worked.

Wish I could say the same about the station. It was agonizing.

Everywhere you turned you saw fire and impact damage tinted by the crimson emergency lighting. The station was dying. Judging by the messages, a few Raiders had managed to flee, disappearing into the asteroid belt. The two Founders' frigates hijacked by the Pilots' clan weren't in a hurry to dock, taking up defensive positions some two light seconds away from the crippled station.

* * *

EVENTS KEPT UNFOLDING — rapidly, dramatically and irreversibly.

I finally made it to the personnel deck and cleared the airlock. They still had atmosphere in there, even though the lights kept flickering. I could sense frequent vibrations.

The room I was renting had its own airlock. It too seemed to be sealed — undamaged. We were safe for the time being. Still, my anxiety kept growing.

I entered the airlock and activated the emergency locking protocols.

The inner hatch slid aside. Charon's lanky figure

hurried toward me. He gave me a hug, peering through my visor.

"I'm fine," I slapped his shoulder. "I've made it back."

I collapsed into the massive chair which alone was capable of supporting the weight of my armor. Arbido shifted from one foot to the other nearby. He looked pale and anxious. I bet! The world was coming down about his ears and he didn't even have a spacesuit his size. How could we have known that something like this would even happen?

"Cool down, man. You can wear my old gear in the meantime. It's a bit big for you but that's the way it is. Charon, can you help him? You too will need to suit up."

The station was shattered by secondary explosions. It was in turmoil. Losses were mind-boggling. The Pilots clan had lost half their craft. Their authority was on the rise but their strength had been seriously depleted. The Top100 list kept updating: thirty-seven of the best pilots hadn't returned to base. Fifty more personalities of considerable weight and power had disappeared during decompression. Their fate was unknown.

The network was in chaos. There were no safe respawn points left. Founders Square was overtaken by vacuum, radiation and cosmic temperatures. Same applied to the whole of the Market Deck. The survivors feared new attacks, this time from the Dargians, Wearongs, the Kamresh and the Outlaws.

Everyone already blamed both the Mechanics and the Engineers for the chain of secondary explosions which continued to destroy the station. They in their turn didn't bother to qualify it with an answer, explaining it away by the age of the equipment.

The station's economy had collapsed. Groups of looters were sighted on the Market Deck. The corporations had called off their drones to protect their own property. This was new to me. Apparently, all law-enforcement mechanisms belonged to the corporations.

This had turned out to be an event and a half.

There was no water. The lighting panels were barely glowing. The air regenerators were still in working order but how long would their accumulators last?

I was at a loss. And angry. I tried to put myself into the Admins' and developers' shoes. Why would they need such a disaster? Had the players had the choice of ten stations protected by a squadron of NPC-flown craft, I could understand. But they'd just destroyed their entire game world! Had they decided to play God or something? Or had they destroyed the location the way a spoiled child crumples a failed drawing? Well, give us a chance, then! Offer us an alternative!

Somehow I didn't think that anyone would like a game dominated by other races dooming humans to a miserable existence. But it was certainly heading that way. The Mechanics and Engineers had to bring the situation under their control, or...

Arbido walked over to me. He still hadn't suited up. His eyes were popping out, his green skin blotched with gray: as goblins went, he was pale as a sheet. "Have you seen this?"

My interface flashed with a new incoming message.

I opened it, motioning Arbido to a chair. As in, *sit down and stop freaking out.*

This was an excerpt from the last Wiki update.

The World's History

... THE DESTRUCTION OF THE ARGUS STATION by Phantom Raiders caused humans to lose control over the Darg system. The last of the pioneers fell in desperate clashes with the enemy. There were no survivors. Most of them died; a few were taken prisoner and spent miserable years in captivity. Their further fate is unknown. The destroyed station fell into the hands of the Dargians who thus came into possession of all the research results conducted by the Corporations.

Still, the Xenomorphs' rule wasn't meant to last. A year before these tragic developments, the Engineers' Clan had managed to study and restore one of the Founders' hyperspace communication units. They used it to send detailed reports about the loss of the First Colonial Fleet to Earth. It's not clear whether their signal ever reached the Solar system. An answer never came.

The pioneers' death wasn't in vain. Their message that contained unique scientific information was indeed received, decoded and studied from every possible angle. By then, the situation on planet Earth had worsened. A large number of ecological and man-made disasters as well as climate catastrophes followed in quick succession. A new world war was brewing. In that situation, the new knowledge received from deep space granted humanity a chance of survival.

Independently from each other, the governments of the five inhabited continents took the decision to build new colonial fleets.

Two years after the death of Argus' last defenders,

enormous starships started leaving the Solar system one by one.

Eurasia was the first to venture into deep space, accompanied by a convoy of two hundred freighters and battleships.

So began the era of Exodus. As the new starships finished completion, humans began leaving the doomed planet Earth to head into the unknown, hoping to retrace the tracks of the First Colonial Fleet and solve the mysteries of the Founders. They wanted to understand the mechanism behind the Raiders' interstellar jumps and finally find the Phantom Server which would allow them to take over the ancient network and populate the Universe.

Holy shit! Talk about a global event!

"Where did you get this?" I glared at him, still not quite grasping the magnitude of the looming predicament.

"It's in the Wiki!"

"Bullshit! It must be somebody's sick joke!"

"This is an official update," Arbido said sullenly. "The patch has just been installed."

The station shuddered with a new impact. What had happened now? I scanned the newsfeed. That's it. The station's framework was crumbling under pressure. A new decompression had just occurred in the Corporations area. The number of casualties was still unknown.

The station was disintegrating. Prices for available spaceships skyrocketed. The depressing news was interspersed with offers,

Will pay any money for a safe respawn point.

"Right," I quickly replaced the life support

cartridges in my suit. "Any idea what's going on? Your version?"

He paused, sulking, then shrugged and began, "Don't you understand? The alpha testing is over. They don't need us anymore."

"It's over, so what?" I really couldn't see how this update could be bad news.

Judging by the available information, the beta testing phase was to start with the arrival of the Eurasia Colonial Fleet. A very logical move on the part of the developers. Whatever had happened here during the alpha testing phase would now be filed as the world's epic prehistory. The new players could visit Argus and see for themselves, witnessing their world's past with their own eyes.

The way I saw it, the arrival of Eurasia and its convoy could happen at any moment. In a game, time was relative. Decades of subluminal flight could take hours provided the developers had an update ready.

Both the fleet and the station would just appear at the assigned location, obeying the developers' will.

Arbido sniffed, his glare laced with desperation.

"What's there to worry about?" I tried to reason with him. "A new update, big deal! They're sending us a new station and a new colonial fleet. What's wrong with that? We'll have new safe respawn points and a new guaranteed protection. Trust me, they're going to "rescue" us all and greet us as the heroes of the First Colonial Fleet who'd held the fort until their arriv-"

"Where does it say that?" his voice rose to a scream. "Read it again, Zander! *There were no survivors!*"

"Stop it," I skimmed the page again and shrugged. "Okay, so we'll log out and log back in. Or create a new account, if it ever comes to that."

"Sorry, Zander. I know I owe you my life and all but your stupidity amazes me sometimes."

"Any proof?"

I was offended, of course. But the familiar tough tone in his voice made me swallow my pride and pay attention.

"When did you last check your Logout button?" he asked.

"It's been a while. I was too busy just lately," I opened the interface and stared at the dead, nameless gray button. "What the f-... Are they raving mad?"

He cracked a gloomy grin. "So now you believe me, don't you?"

I gulped. "How long since *your* logout button has been off?"

The station shuddered again, convulsing in the grip of another technogenic accident. Arbido's stare grew sharp.

"I never had one in the first place," he admitted.

At this point — no good me playing the hero in front of you — it started to sink in.

"Now we're little more than a bunch of comatose bodies wound with wires," he didn't even try to sugarcoat the news. "It's not the game that's the problem even. It's the way we connect to it. You've already worked out quite a lot, haven't you?"

I nodded. My mind raced trying to come up with a solution. The memory of the mummified avatars flashed through my mind. This time I didn't have to wonder what had happened to their players. They'd all died. The neuroimplant's effect had proved too much for them. I could say the same about the Haash and the few Dargians I'd met — about Jurgen who was absolutely sure he'd arrived here with the First Colonial Fleet! Most of the alpha testers were already dead; and those who'd survived had lost their memory under the influence of their neuroimplants, taking the place of NPCs. How about that vendor I'd met at Myrus? He was one sleazy motherfucker, perfectly believable, and why? Because he *was* real! Because his avatar was backed up by a deformed human identity!

So what was this, then? This game of the future that was supposed to awe everyone with its authenticity was based not on its unique engine, unforgettable settings and limitless possibilities, but on trapped human beings playing for NPCs?

"Right," I sprung up and began pacing the room. "Let's assume you're right. But why would they want to get rid of us, of all people?"

He screwed his face. "Well, as far as I'm concerned, it's all pretty clear. They're cleaning up after themselves. I provided them with players. I knew too much and guessed even more. And as for you, you didn't have enough time to lose your identity the way Jurgen did. We're still conscious, our memories untouched — which means we present a threat to their project. Nobody needs a scandal. No one wants an eyewitness to come out of the woodwork who can tell everyone exactly how this game was made and how many people had died while the developers fine-tuned their neuroimplants. The Raiders' attack was preplanned by the Admins. Can't you see the station is falling apart? There're no safe respawn points left! The logout doesn't work. We've been condemned!"

I paused, trying to take in what he'd just said. "You're too much, you," I chuckled nervously. "Don't you think you're overcomplicating things? If they wanted to get rid of us, all they had to do was switch off the in-mode. Easy!"

"They still need our neurograms," he snapped back, adding angrily, "The extreme neurograms of a chain of deaths, respawns and new deaths. How many players would they have needed to kill in order to collect the material they're about to get now by recording people's minds dying and respawning in a radioactive vacuum? Why kill us if they can first get all the data they need? It's not every day you lay your hands on the records of the suffering of souls in hell."

His every word cut me to the quick. I'd have loved to object, but I had nothing to say.

Still, I was trying to find a solution. "We've got to contact Jurgen. We need to explain everything to him. We might find a few modules that we can convert into a shelter. We might be able to hold out until the betas arrive."

"Pointless. The developers can read our neurograms, don't you understand? They know perfectly well who is dangerous to them and who isn't. Jurgen might survive, as an NPC. But you and I, they've written us off, man..."

"I have no intention of dying!" I felt fury rising within me. "No one's going to trick me into their respawn purgatory again!"

I checked the batteries charge. "What're you standing there for?" I yelled at Arbido. "Get Charon here now in full combat gear! Same applies to you!"

"But Zander-"

"Do it!"

I have to admit I went off the deep end. I just couldn't understand what had prevented the admins from exercising their power.

Was it that they couldn't — or they just didn't want to?

Were they sitting there sipping cold beer and smirking as they watched us?

My left hand tingled. Mechanically I pulled off the glove. My fingers were ablaze, enveloped in an aura. My skin had become parchment white, the maze of blood vessels aglow as if I had plasma running through my veins.

I refused to believe it. A game artifact couldn't protect me from anything. How could a piece of binary code deign to defend me?

What was going on, then?

A message popped up in my mental vision,

Neurogram transmission failure. Restoring communication. Neurogram transmission failure. Restoring communication. Neurogram transmission fa-

Was the AI inside me trying to strike back, blocking out the admins' control over me? If so, then how was it done?

I was shaking. So what was it, then? Was the artifact indeed based on an alien AI? Had it found a way to outsmart its developers? How had it done so, by improving part of the program code? Had it indeed managed to block the neurogram transmission, putting the game creators before the dilemma of either leaving me alone or turning off the in-mode?

I expected my breathing to cease, strangling me, but nothing of the kind happened.

* * *

THE STATION KEPT SHUDDERING. The bulkheads vibrated, the floor buckled underfoot.

The newsfeed brought an update: the Corporations Deck was completely decompressed.

My thoughts raced. What was it the Wiki update had said? The last station defenders had fallen long before the arrival of the colonial fleet? It meant that staying at the station was pointless.

I tried to come up with potential escape scenarios. This enormous world offered a countless number of unexplored locations. But first of all, I had to find a safe respawn point.

The station was by now vibrating non-stop, the bulkheads echoing with the impacts from minor but constant breakdowns.

A new system message popped up,

Neurogram transmission restored

My hand was still enveloped by a purple aura. Still, it looked like the AI had failed. But me, I wasn't going to give up so easily.

The door of the adjacent room opened. Clad in my old pressure suit, Arbido could barely walk, the oversized gear hindering his every movement. Charon followed, looking alarmed. He was holding two helmets, Arbido's and his own.

Arbido stopped, staring at my hand. Naturally, I'd forgotten to put the glove back on. Now he'd pester me with questions.

What we need is a safe respawn point, my thoughts returned to the problem at hand. *All the rest is superfluous.*

Arbido couldn't take his eyes off the glowing veins of the blood vessels that entwined my hand in their fiery web. I put the glove back on and cast him a meaningful glare to stop any potential questions.

"Put the helmets on," I said. "We're going to try to get to the elevators. Time to leg it, guys," I turned to the Haash. "Charon, I meant to ask you-"

The lock's internal hatch opened.

Liori?

I'd no idea what made her come here. How on earth had she managed to hack the coded lock?

She recognized me. Still, she didn't look too happy to see me. Surprise and displeasure flashed through her face.

"Which one of you is Arbido?" her voice rang with strain and exhaustion.

The goblin shrank back, probably trying to hide behind Charon but only betraying himself.

"No, wait!" I couldn't understand what was going on.

The girl wasn't listening. She grabbed Arbido's throat with one hand, lifting him effortlessly in the air, while whipping out his gun with the other. The muzzle pressed hard into the wrinkled skin between the goblin's eyes.

What a day. Everybody's nerves were playing up.

"The coordinates, now!" she demanded.

Arbido croaked something unintelligible.

I too had already whipped out my gun but I wasn't in a hurry to use it. I liked the girl. I glared warningly at Charon. "Which coordinates?"

She didn't bat an eyelid, but my PM box flashed with an incoming message. I opened it and stared at a screenshot: the station's outer hull illuminated in a dull brown light and the Founders' starship clinging to it with its docking ports. The ship was surrounded by the tiny figures of the Dargians, the drones and the Haash busy restoring this relic of ancient technology.

"Where did you get the pic from?" I asked her.

"A certain Arbido published it on the net! He auctioned it! Demanding *three million credits for the exact coordinates of a fully restored Founders' starship*," she quoted.

"Let go of him, please. He'd been pestering me for this picture so I was the one who gave it to him."

Her lips quivered. I thought she would dissolve in tears. Her fingers slackened, letting go of Arbido. He slumped to the floor.

Slowly the girl turned to me. Tears welled up in her eyes. Her face was ashen. "Do you know the coordinates? Zander, please help. Please."

Whatever had happened to her aggressive stance? The image of a cold-blooded mercenary girl had melted away and faded in my mind, giving way to a totally different person. I could see she was on edge, driven to the limit. I just couldn't understand why.

"Liori, why on earth would you want this old rust bucket? The ship is worth a lot, I agree, but it's seriously damaged. It's not flightworthy."

"That doesn't matter. Its life support system still works."

"I wouldn't know. I've never been inside it. I'm going to ask Charon about it in a minute. Take a seat. We'll work it out."

"The life support works!" she stared at me in some sort of delirious hope. "The Mercs clan was seriously considering the offer. They analyzed the screenshot.

When you study it through a set of filters, you can see the puffs of emissions being discharged."

Her voice was shaking. Tears streaked her face.

"Calm down, Liori. I know that Argus is about to fall apart and-"

"You know nothing!" She turned to the airlock and breathed out, "You can come in now."

If the truth were known, I expected to see a squad of mercenaries armed to the teeth. But — my heart skipped a beat — a shy group of children ventured into the room.

There were five of them. Three girls pale with fear and two boys, all about three or four years old. They flocked around Liori, casting wary glances at Charon.

"Oh," the youngest of them noticed the goblin who'd scrambled out of his restraining pressure suit and was trying to hide behind Charon's back. "He's so funny. Is he real?"

Do you still remember your childhood? It took me two heartbeats to remember mine. The happy carefree time when my mind was still free from the void of cyberspace. When I hadn't had to worry about the toxic haze outdoors. When I'd wake up every morning, untroubled and inexperienced, welcoming every new day.

All I had left from those days were a few faded fragmentary flashbacks but that was enough to knock the wind out of me.

For years I'd been trying to ride the wave and stay on top of progress in constant search for authenticity and finally, I'd made it.

Pain had become real pain. A game had become reality. I looked at Liori surrounded by the children — but I wasn't looking at a level 53 merc. All I could see was a pale tearful woman who stared at me in hope and desperation.

In moments like this, your mind snaps. "Arbido."

He peeked from behind Charon's back.

"I want you to take care of the children."

Once again the Founders' neuronet within me kicked in. Neurogram transmission failure messages flashed non-stop. This would force the admins to interfere, and I had no idea what they might do.

I motioned Liori aside for a talk. Arbido didn't seem to have heard my order. He stood there catatonic, black desperation in his stare. Charon saved the moment. Hunching up, he slumped to the floor and tilted his head to one side, assuming the perfectly harmless pose of a huge cuddly toy.

Liori and I stepped aside. "What are the children doing at the station?"

"It's a long story."

I wasn't going to take that for an answer.

"They were born here. Into the families of those who'd arrived with the first wave."

That wasn't true. No one could have actually been born here. There was a *real* child acting behind each one of those avatars.

"The logout button?" I asked, letting her know I knew what was going on.

She wiped away her tears. "They have nowhere to go back to."

"So they've been condemned just like all of us here?"

She nodded.

"We're gonna sort it out," but I wasn't good at comforting. The hair on the back of my neck stood on end. A lump blocked my chest. "The ship is crammed full of Dargians," I gulped and tried to speak dryly and to the point. "If we mop them all up, we'll get both the ship and a relatively safe respawn point. What do you think?"

I nodded at Arbido and at Charon surrounded by the children. "That's my whole army."

"I could pull in five more people," she spoke with a speck of hope. "Two are pilots. The other three are mercs. They're proven. They're good."

"Not enough. There are about a hundred Dargians there."

"We can call up a raid," she suggested.

I shook my head. "We can't afford to leak the existence of the ship. You understand, don't you? Everybody is losing their grip. This kind of intel will get you killed by your own kind. Let's do it this way. You go and find five pilots and at least fifteen mercs. Leave the children here. Charon will look after them. We'll also need two craft: an assault module and a personnel carrier. I'll take care of that."

I had to think fast. Lori cheered up a little. A new system message popped up in my view,

Neurogram transmission resumed.

Plot update alert! You've unblocked a unique plot line!

You have the following alternatives:

1. You can stay on board Argus. In case of your death, your safe logout is guaranteed.

2. You can activate the alternative plot line. In that case, you will remain in game and your logout will remain frozen.

Warning! Choosing option #2 will automatically qualify you as an Outlaw. The new pioneers arriving in

the Darg system on board Eurasia will regard you as a criminal.

My hand was still on fire. It looked like my mysterious artifact kept fighting against some attempt to block it.

A multitude of thoughts flashed through my mind. This "alternative plot line" offer was evidently the consequence of the neurogram transmission failure. It hadn't taken the admins long to come up with a compromise. I was sure they were itching to study this new problem. Once again I'd become a valuable commodity to them. And still they were sure that without the functioning Logout button we didn't present a threat to their project. We'd either be dead or completely out of our minds before the New Colonial Fleet and Eurasia made it here. And even if we weren't, who would listen to a bunch of Outlaws?

Charon was growling quietly. The kids weren't afraid of him one bit.

In moments like these, decisions take split seconds. *I don't need their "guaranteed logout".*

I was going to fight. For myself, for Liori, for the kids, for Charon and Arbido. I would know no mercy, fighting till the end whatever that may be.

My eyes searched for the right button.

Activate the alternative plot line.

The heat in my hand subsided.

* * *

I HAD NO TIME TO THINK. We had to act fast. The station was falling apart at the seams slowly but surely.

I took command. I hadn't told anyone about this "alternative plot line" yet.

"Liori, you'll find us some pilots and mercs. Choose only those you can trust. Arbido," I turned to the goblin, "I want you to find out where we can find children's size gear. Quick, while the station network is still online. Charon, you stay here. Don't let anyone in in our absence."

Charon nodded energetically. Gingerly he climbed to his feet and walked over to me, hope in his face. "Are we going to liberate my brothers?"

"Absolutely," I said without a shadow of a doubt. I really liked the Haash. Besides, they were the only ones who knew how to fly the ancient ship.

"We'll need some metabolites," he reminded me. "And food."

That was something I hadn't even thought of. That put an extra strain to our route. We'd have to check the Market Deck and the exo section.

"Got it. Ten sets of Dargian gear," Arbido had already scanned the shops' price lists. "The size is about right."

That changed our priorities. "Liori, you think you could work from here? Via the network?"

"Sure. I can use the mnemonic messaging."

"Then you're staying with the kids. Schedule RV with mercs at Launch Bay 7. Don't let them in on any of the details. Just promise them a safe respawn point. Think that'll be enough to keep them interested?"

"Quite. How about you?"

"Charon and I are going to get some supplies. We need metabolites and also life support cartridges for our suits. I might also try to get us a personnel carrier and an assault module. I think I have an idea."

She looked at me with respect. It was actually Charon who deserved praise. He'd been the one who'd suggested it. Imagine us leaving on a perilous journey through space without food or medication! We'd also need to stock up on batteries — and lots of other little things. A whole list of them, come to think of it.

"Charon, I want you to inject all the metabolites you have left. You'll have to work as a mule, I'm afraid. I won't be able to carry much on my own."

He obeyed without saying a word. The children stared at us with fearless interest. Unlike us, their young minds were still highly adaptable. Despite all the horrors of the last few hours, the only thing that upset them was that "uncle Charon" was leaving them on some business.

I gave them an encouraging smile even though I wasn't sure of anything yet. We had too much to do, and the station was still falling apart.

Liori's grateful gaze was full of unspoken anxiety. Once again she was a bundle of nerves, just like the first time we'd met.

We had to be off, then.

Charon and I walked out into the corridor, still sealed and breathable. Nevertheless, we clicked our helmets on, grabbed our guns and off we went on my preplanned route.

As we advanced toward the Market Deck, I tried to contact Jurgen. He didn't answer; then all of a sudden he PM'd me.

His combat chat was on.

That set alarm bells ringing. "Problems?"

They're here... to kill me... he couldn't control his ragged thoughts. Strange faces flashed amid his mnemonic images. His emotions were getting the better of him. Apparently, he knew his killers well.

"Think you can hold the fort for five minutes?"

If the airlock holds.

"We're on our way."

Another change of plan. I just hoped Jurgen could hang on until our arrival. He was a good guy. And now I really counted on his help. I couldn't even tell what was more important for us: his connections, his phenomenal willpower or that incredible spirit of his.

We were about to storm the Dargian station and fight to the death with at least a hundred Dargians. I tried not to even think about the Guides. We had no idea what they were, so we had to exterminate them on sight. We really needed support from some heavy guns if we wanted to take them on. We needed at least one assault module fully equipped with drones.

I hadn't even dreamt of getting Jurgen on my team but today it looked as if chance ruled the day.

The Technologists clan's section was completely decompressed, its massive armored doors smashed by powerful blasts. That's humanity for you. The moment their habitual world order had started creaking at the seams, it had all resurfaced: looting, robbing and violence. Some were busy stuffing their pockets while others hurried to take it out on their fellow clansmen, doing things they would never have dared to do under any other circumstances.

So basically, the station was in chaos. It was every

man for himself.

Charon and I ran along the endless corridor, disregarding the open doors of the looted warehouses, labs and test hangars.

The placemark pinpointing Jurgen's room was growing near. The Technologists' living quarters lay after the next tunnel intersection. I could see bursts of flashes: there, a battle was in full swing.

I held Charon back, motioning him to freeze.

The combination of the mind expander and the Founders' AI neuronet allowed me to connect to certain subsystems directly. I'd only discovered this ability of mine the day before, at the moment of the highest mental strain when I'd finally docked the ship and tried to assess the scale of damage done to the station by the Phantom Raiders' attack.

I had ended up with a headache from hell. But now the information was worth it. I connected my mind to the surveillance cameras that the Technologists had stuck on every corner.

The living tunnels were wide: the Technologists had completely overhauled this area of ancient communications. Every fifty feet the corridor widened into small neat landings with flower beds and doors leading to the clan members' personal modules. Now, of course, the plants were all dead. In fact, apart from the artificial gravity, all other life support systems in the sector were down.

Two electric cars blocked the tunnel next to Jurgen's room. Four mercs took cover behind this improvised barricade — ordinary soldiers, judging by their gear. Levels 15 to 20. I counted nine more standing by the room's outer hatch: one was cutting through the locks with a plasma torch while the rest stood with guns at the ready, casting wary glances around.

One of them wore some unusual gear, similar to what I'd seen on the Dargians. Its black cargonite surface too surged with flashes of energy, pointing at an activated personal power field.

I studied his marker. It's not that easy without direct visual contact. You had to really concentrate to see it through the camera. My strength was dwindling quickly. I was still new to this sort of mental exercise. The feeling was unpleasant — it felt as if your very nerves were burning out.

Jyrd. Level 50. Outlaw Elite.

He was bad news, I could feel it.

Yesterday I'd noticed a large group of enemy ships try to circumvent the station. I probably shouldn't have blamed it on regular players.

The Outlaws must have landed in the deserted sectors and used the commotion to penetrate unnoticed onto the inhabited decks. I wouldn't be surprised if they had instigated all the looting and rioting.

I really didn't like it. The power balance was definitely not in our favor. Still, we had to help Jurgen out.

Our position wasn't good, either. Unlike the enemy taking cover behind their cars, we were exposed. If we ran to attack them, they'd take us out in their own sweet time.

My gaze followed the tunnel's ceiling. The decompression had ripped the casing off, exposing the ribbed framework underneath. I could see the deep service niches housing cables and pipes. Everything was as it should be. I glanced at the beams: they were thick enough to hold my weight. Without switching the communication system on, I signed to Charon, trying to explain what I was about to do. He nodded tensely.

He seemed to have understood my plan. Now, the weapons. I changed the clip in my pulse gun and maxed out the rate of fire slider, setting it to *boosted power*. The sniper sights in my helmet were always on.

I activated the movement coordinator and decided on my route and firing position between the reinforcement ribs.

Go!

I'd never had to run on top of the wall before. I guess I wasn't very good at it — but still fast enough. I very nearly tumbled down halfway through but my metabolic corrector brought my panic under control in no time. My ears hummed. I anchored myself to the ceiling with the help of my gear's molecular suction pads and hung upside down in a discreet service niche.

I peeked out of my makeshift shelter.

Everything looked upside down. I aimed at the Outlaw. My mind expander was a great help. This was a weird firing position. Still, my body adjusted to it quickly thanks to all the practice flights. In outer space, the idea of "up" and "down" soon loses its meaning.

It was no harder than shooting down a drone while in a spin.

Charon kept glancing at me, awaiting my signal.

I nodded.

He darted forward and loosed off a few rounds, immediately ducking into the nearest tunnel and pulling sharply to one side.

His shots caused cascades of sparks to fly off one of the cars. One of the assassins went flying back. A huge hole gaped in his visor: Charon had managed to take one out.

I fired several brief bursts. My position was excellent. The field of fire was perfect. Besides, our enemies were still pretty clueless, focusing their attention on Charon's lanky figure. They couldn't see me!

Three of them went down. A few more scrambled back, apparently wounded, looking for somewhere to take cover. I put two bursts into the Outlaw. He only momentarily staggered in his massive armor that allowed him to stand steady on his feet. His powerful personal power shield had no problem absorbing the impacts, transforming my bullets into red-hot droplets of metal.

Charon had shrunk into the shadows, merging with the wall. Excellent. He was doing it by the book. I pressed my body to the ceiling as a burst of response fire ripped through the cables, slicing off sections of pipework. The whole structure vibrated. Chemicals gushed out of the damaged pipes, forming bubbling pools of acid on the floor and filling the air with toxic fumes.

Charon and I sprang into action on cue, the caustic haze our only ally. The bursts of the assassins' pulse guns were still hitting the ceiling when I dropped down and sprinted toward their impromptu barricade. Charon outran me, lithe and lethal, sliding along the wall instead of just charging blindly forward, covering the zone of fire in huge leaps. There was no way I could catch up with him. I stopped and opened fire, shooting at random simply to distract the enemy.

My belt's power shield could still take a punch but my battery charge plummeted into the red. I couldn't see jack shit. I moved in bounds, heading for the opposite wall and catching a few more rounds which pierced the shield and ricocheted off my armor, striking sparks and leaving deep dents in the metal.

I ran, giving it my all. The haze suddenly lifted, revealing the outline of the wrecked car. I flung myself over the hood and stumbled over a dead body. The time gap between a character's virtual death and his respawning serves to collect the loot from fallen enemies.

I ducked. A new burst of fire whizzed overhead. A black figure loomed out of the haze. The Outlaw charged at me like a tank, his pockmarked armor glowing weakly. His confident precise movements made it clear his gear had been mechanically enhanced.

I ducked to one side, sending a new burst of fire into his helmet. I breached his power shield but not the cargonite. The Outlaw staggered momentarily, then went for me, sweeping me off my feet in one powerful blow. The difference in our levels and gear was impressive. I tried to jump back to my feet but he punched me again with all the might of his mechanical enhancers, forcing my inadequate breastplate into my ribs. The agony was such that I couldn't breathe. He must have broken a few ribs for sure. My suit's split seams began to froth with the sealing foam. I think I passed out.

This had to be another respawn. I could neither

focus nor think straight. The Outlaw must have thought this was the end of me. He turned away and picked up the plasma torch. No idea what Charon was doing.

I struggled to breathe, feeling the bloody froth bubble on my lips. The metabolic implant went into overdrive, burning my own body resources, but it made me feel better. An unnatural, feverish surge of energy flooded over me barely thinning out the crimson haze before my eyes — but it was enough to allow me to breathe and move.

Charon burst into view. He and the Outlaw must have been almost equal... but I spoke too soon. A shattering blow sent the Haash flying across the floor.

Why was Jurgen still inside? Groaning, I scrambled to one knee. I'd dropped the gun but it was useless anyway against this custom-made armored suit.

The toxic haze was thinning out. The massive hatch of Jurgen's room was red-hot. The Outlaw was in a decisive mood. He didn't care about me anymore.

I want armor like his. And a new level in exchange for my broken ribs, my mind switched over to gaming mode, instinctively trying to block out the hopelessness of the situation.

I whipped out the sniper rifle from my inventory and aimed it at his head even as I realized this was nothing but a vain attempt to appease my ego. There was just no way I could bring him down.

My hands were shaking. My left hand pulsated under the glove, the Founders' neuronet reminding me of itself. But what was the point?

The gun sights kicked in, outlining the massive power unit of the plasma torch in red.

This was suicide. That thing would explode with a

vengeance.

I limped back to the relative safety of the mangled car and took aim.

A shot. A flash.

You've received a new level!
You've received a new level!

Everything went dark.

* * *

MY AWAKENING WAS SLOW and painful. It hurt me to breathe. A strange room floated before my eyes. A massive figure bent over me.

The Outlaw?

"Calm down, you," Jurgen's voice came through as a weak far-off echo. "Hold still. You're safe."

I heard the socket covers snap open on my wrist. The air reeked with something utterly foul.

"More!" Jurgen addressed someone out of my field of vision. "Pass me the exo #15. These things are useless."

I croaked, struggling to find my voice. I needed none of their exo shit!

But they didn't seem interested in my opinion.

"Now, Zander. It's gonna hurt. But you'll feel a whole lot better afterwards. There's no other way we can do it. You've got a punctured lung from your broken ribs. So brace yourself."

I screamed.

It felt as if they were pouring molten metal down my veins.

I passed out.

Darkness lasted but a moment, relieving and absolute. Then I came to again, readying myself for a new agony. But all I felt was an incredible lightness in my entire body as if I'd just been born again. I was alert and full of energy.

Two people leaned over me. Their gear was just as good as the one the Outlaw had had, albeit not black. Cargonite has this particular bluish sheen. I could see their faces behind their visors: Jurgen and a strange woman I'd never seen before.

"Charon," I still couldn't believe I wasn't hurting. My mouth was dry. It tasted foul.

"Who, the Haash?" Jurgen asked. "He's all right. His gear took a bit of flak so he has trouble moving."

"Think you can fix it?" I still couldn't think straight after our close shave.

"I'll think of something. But you, Zander, I owe you. It's been twice you've saved my butt now. Here, take a look."

The wall parted, revealing a niche. A massive armored suit strode out into the room.

"Take it," Jurgen said. " You've earned it."

My jaw dropped.

"Don't be shy," he apparently misunderstood my silence. "Take your cheap junk off. I've sealed the room with a power shield. Come on now, put it on!"

Who did he think he was, bossing me around?

I couldn't take my eyes off the brand-new armor. Even the Wiki didn't mention anything about it. This had to be one of the Technologists' custom-made designs even though in places it looked suspiciously like the one worn by the Outlaw I'd just smoked.

No wonder, actually, considering that two of the Technologists' leaders had turned coat and joined the

Outlaws.

This exo stuff was worrying me. Even though I felt good at the moment, it might just backfire later.

I removed my helmet and handed it to Jurgen. "There're two devices left in the slots. Do you think you can reinstall them in this new suit?"

He cast a quick glance at them. "Why on earth would you need this old tat?"

"Sentimental value."

He didn't argue. "If you say so."

"How long will this exo stuff work?"

"About twenty hours, I think. I've given you one hell of a dose."

"And then what?"

"Then you need to keep your metabolic implant in overdrive," he said. "We need your ribs to knit while you're still under the influence of the exo. Then all you'll get is a minor energy loss. Might keep you in bed for a day and that's it."

"I need another dose."

Jurgen's eyes filled with suspicion. "Have you taken them before?"

"I haven't but I might. Twenty hours is not enough. I need much more time than that."

"What for? Spit it out."

There was no point in me making a secret of it so I put him in the picture.

Hearing about the children, he paled. "Can you guarantee us a safe respawn point?"

"Look at me. If I managed to survive there — and I was only level 1-"

"Right," he quickly made up his mind. "Our clan doesn't exist anymore. The station is about to disintegrate. Frieda and I, we wanted to have a baby too. But-" he made a helpless gesture. His face darkened. "All I want to say is you can count on us. Here, take this," he handed me my activation code and a hefty helmet with my slave collar controller and sniper sights already installed. "Suit up. I'll go check on your Haash."

The suit's servodrives whirred. Its heavy armor plates parted, inviting me in.

How was I supposed to climb inside?

"Turn round and step back toward it," Jurgen said, noticing my confusion.

I obeyed.

The suit's interior was lined with some porous springy substance studded with sensors. Once my body came into contact with them, they activated the sealing protocol. The armor plates slid back into place. Sharp needles penetrated my skin. The mind expander hurried to report new peripherals installed.

But where were their stats?

The new interface icons were gray and unresponsive. I stretched my neck, reached for the helmet and put it on.

With a hiss, the neck ring rotated into place.

You've received a set of heavy armor!
Item class: unique. Hand-made. Custom design.
+3 to Strength, -2 to Agility, +3 to Stamina, +15 to Armor, +10 to Power Field.
Warning! Using this type of gear requires 9 pt. Strength. You won't be able to control the suit once your exo ingredient expires.

Not good. But I'd have to think about that when I came to it. At the moment, I was desperate for exactly this kind of gear. And then we'd see.

* * *

I SPENT THE NEXT TEN MINUTES getting used to my new suit. It felt funny. Agility had indeed become a problem. The muscle enhancers were too sensitive and unpredictable. I'd clattered to the ground a couple of times before I got used to it. As for the rest, the suit was a treat. It came with two integrated heavy pulse machine guns and five power units with a possibility to recharge from stationary power sources. Plus a 0.5 megawatt power shield! Add to it all sorts of sensors, analyzers and various subsystems whose new icons now flickered before my eyes.

I could even lug around almost five hundred pounds at earth's gravity, even at the cost of a further drop in agility.

Getting the hang of the suit's basic functions hadn't taken me much time. All the advanced functions would have to be tested in action. This new gear had one unquestionable plus: it offered high personal protection levels which to a degree compensated for my character's deficiency in level.

In the meantime, Jurgen had patched up Charon's suit. Unlike myself, Charon had withstood the Outlaw's assault. No critical damage, no bones broken. He cast unkind glances at Jurgen, barely suppressing his desire to whack someone to alleviate his stress.

Never mind. He might just have plenty of ass to kick soon.

I shook my head at him: *don't.* Then I walked out into the corridor to test my integrated weapons. The bodies in charred gear were still lying around the hatch.

I bent over the Outlaw and shook him out of his distorted armor. He could respawn in the nude for a change.

I studied the trophy. The cargonite was too heavy — no good for my inventory. Still, I read the stats. This kind of armor demanded 12 pt. Strength!

But the maximum you could have was 10, wasn't it? What was that supposed to mean? Were the Outlaws constantly on exo? To the best of my knowledge, it was the only thing that could drive your characteristics beyond the limit.

Or was it? How about my newly-acquired skills, then? *Friend of the Haash* gave you +1 to all characteristics. And if, say, I had Agility already maxed out?

Shame I couldn't check it. But it was something worth making a mental note of. I wouldn't be surprised if they had certain ingredients or artifacts with a perpetual bonus.

The built-in machine guns worked like a dream. I tested them on the ravaged electric car. The power unit explosion had turned the vehicle into a lump of molten steel. Now I literally pulverized it shooting with both hands.

Awesome.

My new armor came with only one major flaw. If the power went down, it would turn it into an unmanageable heap of scrap metal.

I gave it some thought and came up with a solution. I went back to my room, picked up my old gear and forced the breastplate back into its place. My old light-armor suit only weighed 50 pounds: I could carry that much. But it could save your butt in an emergency — say, if the power units went dead.

Watching my actions, Jurgen nodded his approval. "Good job. That's not stupid!"

He opened his capacious bag and produced two gear kits. He stuffed one down his own inventory like I'd just done and handed the other one to Frieda.

His wife wasn't the talkative type. Our eyes met a couple of times. She looked slightly frightened but she stayed composed. By the time Jurgen finished repairing Charon's suit, she'd packed the supplies: some life support cartridges and metabolites in disposable tube syringes, a handful of food tubes, water purification tablets and automated first-aid kits.

Finally Charon could get up. He walked around the room checking the smooth work of his suit joints. He seemed pleased with the result.

It had been an hour since we'd left to get some supplies.

Jurgen began emptying his arsenal. I contacted Liori. "Everything okay? We've been delayed here a bit because of Charon. I'm in the Technologists' sector. We haven't been to the exo yet."

"We're fine. I've found you some mercs. Pilots are hard to come by. Until now, I've only heard from three. The others can't be reached. You need to bring the suits, remember?"

"Sure. How many mercs?"

"Twenty-five in total."

"Good enough. Just keep looking for pilots, okay? How's the situation?"

"Quiet until now. Just don't be too long."

I could understand her concern. The children had

no pressurized suits.

Jurgen signaled that he was ready to leave.

"Liori, I'll speak to you later."

* * *

WHEN I TOLD JURGEN about the assault module and personal carrier, he paused, thinking, then nodded. "I think I can get you a few modules. Not the combat ones though. Only cargo."

"That's not good. We only have five fighter ships. How are we supposed to mount an assault?"

"Five fighters is plenty to storm the station," he answered. "One can carry the mercs. I'm going to fly it. The other will carry the children, the supplies and this Arbido of yours. Frieda can fly it. The ships are rather small with an autonomy of twelve hours and enough fuel for a one-way trip. So we don't have much choice, really. This is the only option I can offer."

"Can't we talk to the Pilots clan?"

"Not really. They'll dump us."

"Why?"

"Don't you understand? They've hijacked both of the Founders' frigates. I know for certain that there are safe respawn points on board. But did they offer shelter or at least the possibility of a safe respawn to anyone?"

"No."

"So you see. How can we trust them? In this scenario, laying their hands on yet another flightworthy ship might prove too much of a temptation for them. They'll dump us, get hold of the ship and mop up the Dargians all on their own."

It made sense. "How could they create new respawn points on board?" I asked, curious.

"They have this machine. Got it from the Engineers clan."

"Can you make something similar?"

He chuckled. "The Engineers clan kept it under wraps. But I know a thing or two about it. I could try to make a copy, I suppose. Provided we manage to find all the parts. Come on now, time to move it. Tell me where you want me and Frieda to bring the modules."

"Launch Bay 7."

He frowned. "Is that the RV point?"

"Exactly."

"No. No, Zander, that won't do at all," he paused, thinking. "A big gathering like this is sure to attract attention," he opened the station map and marked a route into the station's deserted area, toward the third and still unrestored hangar. "Send your men here. Not all at once! Let them come in groups of twos and threes."

"And how about our fighter pilots?"

"Tell them to head to the RV point on autopilot. Very soon all hell will break loose, trust me. You need to withdraw the ships before somebody else lays their hands on them."

"Okay. You've talked me into it. Charon and I need to get some supplies. We're going to the Market Deck now and the exo sector."

Jurgen made some mental calculations. "I'll meet you in three hours' time," he concluded. "Good enough?"

I nodded. We had to make it. Provided the station held.

CHAPTER SIX

PHANTOM SERVER
ARGUS SPACE STATION

The Personnel Deck, two hours later

N
O ONE WAS AS HAPPY to see us back as was Arbido. He looked a sight. The children had painted him every color under the sun. I still don't know where they'd managed to get the paints.

"Now! The game's over!" Liori seemed to have no problem handling the kids. "Uncle Zander has brought you some presents! Do you know what a spacesuit is?"

"Wow!" the four-year-old Alec struggled to lift a cargonite helmet. "It's a real Dargian one! Cool. Dad promised he'd get me one like this when I grow up."

His last phrase hung in midair. Silence filled the room. Someone sniffled.

"Dasha darling!" Liori rushed to wipe the girl's

tears. "Everything's going to be all right, sweetheart. No need to cry."

"I want to see my mommy!"

"Mommy's busy, sweetheart. She'll come to see us later. I promise."

Charon turned away. His eyes too glistened with tears. I didn't know what to do or say. Even Arbido fell silent.

"Come on, don't cry!" I helped the boy to suit up and checked his life support systems. "No playing with the interface, no clicking on any unfamiliar icons!" I spoke in a loud but hopefully not too rude a voice.

"Zander," Liori began suiting up the girls. "We don't have the right cartridges for these!"

"We do. We made sure we took only already-modified suits."

"How about me?" Arbido butted in.

"Sorry, man. Couldn't find anything that would fit a goblin anatomy," I meant it as a joke but it fell flat. Arbido turned pale. I hurried to reassure him, "Cool down. We all breathe the same air, after all. Here, take this one. It should fit you fine."

"How about the metabolites?"

"What are you talking about? Are you mad? With your green skin and lack of implants? Think before you open your mouth! So? Does it fit well?"

He paraded around the room. "It's all right."

"Excellent. Children, helmets on! Report!"

They didn't look as if they'd understood me. Liori came to my rescue, "Children, the indicator lights should turn green. Can you see them? Let's switch on the standard communications."

The communication system clicked on, filling the

earphones with fragile childish voices,

"My lights are all green! And I have two red ones! Uncle Zander, the air stinks! What are these letters? Can I click on them?"

One of the girls, Inge, had to be resuited. It was a good job Charon and I had taken all ten suits available. The vendor hadn't minded. In fact, he wasn't in the shop at all.

The helmet turned out to be faulty: its neck ring didn't shut properly. It took us some effort to find a suitable replacement from whatever leftover gear we still had.

Liori checked all the systems several times, opening service access ports and meticulously testing each suit. She did the same to Arbido, earning his eternal goblin gratitude.

I had other things to worry about. We had to cover quite a distance and I wasn't a hundred percent sure Jurgen would even be there waiting for us. He didn't contact us and I had no idea where he might be and what he might be doing.

"Right. Everything seems to be okay," Liori concluded. She didn't look well. Her face was drawn, her eyes pale and faded.

I offered her a pack of exo. Her eyes sharpened. "No, thanks. I don't need it."

"When did you sleep last?"

"I can't remember. Was it the day before yesterday? I can make do with normal stimulators."

"No, you can't. It's an hour's hike to the RV. After that we need to fly the ship and storm the station."

"Very well, then," she took the tube syringe and squeezed it into the socket of her metabolic implant. As she sealed the helmet, I noticed her face distorted by disgust. I wasn't a big fan of exo, either, but given the opportunity I might ask her why she was so prejudiced against it. She'd been in the game for quite a while. She had to realize the importance of such emergency measures.

Charon froze by the hatch. On our way back we'd checked Serge's arms shop. He was there, cleaning out the broken pieces of his display cabinets. He mumbled something about the shop being closed. I reminded him about the deal we'd struck earlier. As a result, Charon checked his warehouse and came out as pleased as the proverbial pig, carrying a weird long-barreled weapon whose mounting "accidentally" fitted his anatomy.

It was called a *fier*. I never quite understood how it worked even though Charon did his best to explain its functions to me. My semantic processor was still working overtime trying to digest some of the earlier concepts, depleting my brain's already challenged processing capacity.

So in the end, I thought it might be better if I simply saw it in action.

* * *

OUTSIDE IN THE CORRIDOR, blue oxygen snowflakes floated in the cosmic cold. I lined everybody up. Charon and myself were to walk in front, followed by Arbido ten paces behind armed with my trusty pulse gun.

The children would walk next, followed by Liori in the rear. My biggest concern was meeting any Outlaws. At Serge's, I'd managed to lay my hands on a couple of plasma grenades. The explosion of the

Outlaw's power unit had been impressive but considering our lineup, I'd have hated to revert to such extreme combat techniques. I just hoped that our two large-caliber pulse guns and Charon's weird weapon would get us through in case of any trouble.

We set off. I kept my communications channel switched to the local network, listening absent-mindedly to the kids' conversations. Inge — the youngest — was telling everybody about her kitten. I could actually understand what she meant: some kind of a fluffy, cuddly, purring little NPC constantly rubbing itself around your ankles.

Welcome to the enigmas of modern mentality.

Children have a different way of thinking. For them, what they see is real. This world — the distorted, disfigured reality of Phantom Server dreamt up by its sick scriptwriters — had become the only home to these tiny figures clad in alien spacesuits as they groped through the oxygen snowstorm filling the mangled deck of an ancient space station.

I was beginning to understand my life wasn't my own any more. It scared me.

The tunnel widened, the jagged stumps of its walls parting in different directions. The starry void twinkled overhead.

Arbido sniffed, nervous. Charon breathed noisily and evenly. Liori stopped. The children did so, too. She didn't say anything. My PM box icon was inactive, and still I could somehow sense her mental state. At the moment she was taut like a coiled spring, ready to act fast and without mercy. I had a funny feeling I could see ghosts crowding behind her back.

This was a *game*. Admittedly eerily realistic but a game nevertheless.

I didn't believe myself any more.

Charon was waiting. I scanned the area. Something was wrong, I could feel it in my spine, but my sensors didn't detect any signatures at all. This part of the station was well and truly dead: not a single active marker amid the ragged wreckage of its tilting decks hanging overhead.

We had to move on. Still I waited, getting used to our gloomy surroundings and listening to my instincts. Anxiety scratched harder at my heart.

"Liori, take away the children. Get them under cover."

Although blind to the danger, she obeyed. Not having received any orders, Arbido froze, looking around.

"Charon?"

"I don't feel anything," he admitted.

"Cover me."

I moved up front. Both my mind expander and metabolic implant were in overdrive. My left hand began to tingle. I was already used to it so I simply made a mental note. The very activation of the Founders' AI neuronet was already bad news.

You've received a new level!

Why on earth? I missed a step, casting suspicious glances around. Nothing.

Very well. I'd have to look into it later. There was nothing wrong with receiving a new level even though normally you had to earn it. It must have been some glitchy patch or other.

I continued walking.

The ravaged deck became narrower, curving. To my

both sides, frayed optic cables shorted out, illuminating our way.

I was already a good fifty paces in front of everyone. The scanning radius was clear. Not a single marker. It was probably time for me to stop and wait for Charon to catch up. Then we could investigate further.

I swung round, realizing this was exactly what they wanted me to do. There was no one around here, but the moment I disappeared around the bend, a fine web of screened cables and the forest of upended beams left from the ancient disaster would block my sensors' signal.

I crouched, pretending I was fixing some gear malfunction while focusing the scanners by narrowing their apertures. Got it. Three weak signatures above and behind me.

My sniper sights promptly kicked in, zooming in on a fragment of the deck's broken ceiling. Now I could clearly see three Outlaws who lay in hiding by the edge of the deck. Their levels were rather low: ten to fifteen. Further on, the scan registered a weak thermal spike. Could this be a module with a shut-down reactor?

It could and it was.

I read their signatures: not an easy skill but when you're cornered, you learn fast.

These Outlaws weren't as well equipped as my recent opponent. I didn't see the power imprints from their individual power shields. Then again, they might have switched them off in order not to attract attention.

Their module was what interested me. Under any other circumstances I'd have tried to capture it, but now I was curious: who were they ambushing here? It couldn't be us. The only person who knew about our supposed route was Jurgen.

Jurgen.

How much did I actually know about him?

The situation wasn't good. Our potential enemy was located two floors above. Climbing up there would take me some time. Should I take the risk and tell Liori to proceed while controlling the area from where I now was? And if the Outlaws opened fire, would I be able to take them out in time?

Too risky.

Suddenly I noticed two pale power imprints deep in our rear, above the demolished stump of the tunnel that we'd just cleared. Snipers. How could I have missed them?

I PM'd Liori, *Stay where you are.*

I forwarded my mental images to Charon, trying hard to visualize them clearly. He didn't let me down. Unhurriedly he headed toward me. Arbido alone stood exposed, looking around him without seeing anything. I understood his predicament. Without implants, his level 1 avatar was virtually blind.

I sent him a message, ordering him to find cover and lie low.

He was quietly panicking but the Outlaws didn't seem to be interested in him. They still seemed to be waiting for something or other.

Charon caught up with me. We exchanged a few phrases and he disappeared uphill.

I couldn't understand it. They weren't trying to attack us. And still they'd cut off our escape routes.

My PM box blinked.

"Zander, you're not taking me alive!" Liori's voice was shaking.

Was she raving mad? Her words pierced me like a stab in the back, the hostility and contempt in her voice so tangible that I too simmered with rage. "Charon, hold on a bit."

By then, he'd already disappeared out of the enemy's line of vision and begun his perilous ascent, planning to strike their rear on my command. He now froze, fading into the mangled background, awaiting further instructions.

"What's your problem, Liori? Tell me," I struggled not to yell at her. I didn't even try to divine the reason for such a change in her attitude.

"I trusted you!" her voice was a mixture of frustration, contempt and cornered courage.

Oh, great. She'd chosen excellent timing to clear the air. Naturally, I was mad at her. We were surrounded, for crissakes! We had to think and act fast, not-

Wait up. A bad premonition arose in me. What had I gotten that new level for?

I opened my char's stats.

Zander. Outlaw. Level 17. Pilot.

Now it all began to click into place. Both the enemy's indecision and Liori's behavior had found their explanation. Had she thought I'd lured the group into a trap? Then again, what else could she have thought? With snipers behind her and armed enemies in front lying in wait next to a camouflaged module? And a freshly-minted Outlaw blocking her way to freedom?

I scanned the logs, looking for the system message in question — the one informing me about the alternative plot line activation and what consequences it could have for me. I'd actually expected it to happen later — only after Eurasia's arrival — but apparently, it wasn't supposed to happen that way. By becoming the leader of the group, I must have crossed the invisible line, probably triggering some switch of no return.

I forwarded her the logs.

I didn't expect her to reply straight away. After all, it was my fault. I should have told them. But who could have known that my status change would be so unexpected?

I contacted the Outlaws. "Who's in charge?" I asked uncivilly, addressing no one in particular. My gear had to sufficiently impress them — or at least so I hoped. My current level, too, was slightly higher than theirs.

"Riedok," they replied.

"Hold your snipers, will ya?"

"Who the fuck are you?"

"These are Jyrd's prisoners," Jyrd was the name of the elite Outlaw that I'd put on my KOS list. "Why, you wanna talk to him?"

"He's out of range."

"I bet he is. And so is his respawn point," I ad libbed while estimating the distance from the station to the asteroid belt as millions of miles — way too far for instant communications.

Chars like this Jyrd would play it safe, for sure. His respawn point must have been set up in some cozy little bunker deep in the depths of one of those space boulders.

"Zander, do I know you?" Riedok kept doubting.

"You should. So are you letting us through or do

you want me to send you back to your respawn too to improve your memory?"

He paused. "Very well. You can go now. I'll ask Jyrd about you."

"Please do. He knows me well," this time I didn't lie. It would take him some time to forget his inglorious death at the station.

I PM'd Liori.

Without replying, she walked out into the open, playing the part of a prison guard. Her status as a mercenary fitted the role well enough not to raise any suspicions. The children grew quiet, scrambling along in silence. The emotional atmosphere was depressing. Arbido joined the group: yet another frail and harmless little figure.

We disappeared uphill but it was too early to relax. From their prominent position, the Outlaws could see us well. I PM'd Liori again, telling her to contact the others and instruct them to move to the RV via tunnels without hovering around in the open.

I could already see that the mercs would be a problem. They weren't going to appreciate my inopportunely timed clan affiliation.

Charon joined us. For him, I was always a Friend of the Haash, whatever my status.

We walked quickly. Liori didn't speak. I didn't force her to.

The admins' predictions seemed to be coming true. The two Founders' frigates highjacked by the Pilots suddenly gunned their engines, approached the station and opened fire.

Once again the station shuddered with explosions. My field of vision flickered with tiny bright dots that swirled around like an enormous swarm of lightning bugs. Bigger dots started joining them. I opened the combat chat and checked the predictable information.

The station was under attack from the Dargians, Wearongs and the Kamresh. They weren't exactly allies, the chat flashing with messages about clashes between them. Still, their feuds weren't going to change the developers' new scenario.

Our two fighters — Liori's and mine — had already left their docking pads and were heading for the RV on autopilot. This had been a risky decision but we didn't have much choice. We couldn't go back to fetch them across the collapsing station: far too dangerous and way too time-consuming.

The space battle was gaining a new fierce momentum. But this wasn't our war anymore.

Had the Pilots clan had some clever unhesitant leaders, they could have united the surviving players. But judging by the messages in the combat chat, the centralized control of the station was now gone. The Corporations were busy defending their sectors. The Technologists had been pulverized by the Outlaws. Both the Mechanics and the Engineers were nowhere to be seen. The network rumors claimed that they had retreated to their well-prepared shelters in the station's inaccessible depths.

The only positive person among us who didn't seem to be concerned with future unpredictability was Charon. He looked driven and determined. He had put his full trust in me which I wished I could say about the others. Basically, we were a bunch of strangers drawn together by some overwhelming circumstances.

I took the lead. Honestly, I just didn't want to speak to anyone. I continually scanned both hemispheres, searching the rampant edge of the station in front. The area was deserted, free from both mobs and humans, the weak radioactivity level being our only intrusive companion. Apparently, we were being spared for some future tribulations.

The deck was listing to one side. I could discern the outline of the third hangar in front, the one which had never been restored. My fighter ship contacted us. Liori sent me a quick message: apparently, her ship too had safely reached the RV.

Tension grew with every step we took. We were about to face thirty mercs. I was pretty sure that they'd had dealings with the Outlaws in the past so the change in my status wouldn't be that much of a problem — but I still had to check that out. Jurgen too would demand an explanation.

But this wasn't what I was worried about. Mercenaries were loners by definition. They rarely acted in large groups. In outer space, two were a team. Naturally, large raids to other stations and planets must have taught them cooperation, but as far as I'd heard, this kind of unity dissipated the moment a battle was over. Especially if the loot was good.

I looked back, checking on the kids. They were tired, slowing us down considerably. What was going to happen to them if the adults began fighting over their trophy, refusing to come to an agreement on using the Founders' ship?

Do you think I was trying to skin a tiger before it was dead? In a situation like this, you had to think several moves ahead. One other thing worried me: I didn't think the mercs would accept the Haash. The local humans despised xenomorphs, period. I didn't know yet how I was going to get around this, but one thing I did know: over the last few days, I'd suffered a serious mindset shift.

* * *

THE LOPSIDED DECK ENDED in an abrupt jagged drop. I raised a warning hand and stopped by the edge, peering down until I noticed tiny human figures below. "Jurgen?"

The few seconds of anxious waiting were akin to eternity.

"Zander, we've made it. But you owe me an explanation. Didn't I warn you about the Outlaws?"

"You might need to ask Liori about that. I don't think you'll believe me. Just don't forget I'm the only person who knows on which of the ten stations the Founders' ship is docked," I added a large-caliber argument.

It had only been three hours and I was already exhausted. This exo stuff was by no means a solution. My ribs were aching; I struggled to breathe. I hadn't felt it at first but now all the exertion began to manifest itself.

I had to suffer in silence. Alien stimulants weren't a safe option. I just hoped my body would be able to recuperate during the two-hour flight to the station.

While Liori and Jurgen set about exchanging messages, I removed Charon's and Arbido's — yes, his too — slave collars. The situation was unpredictable. You never know, we might end up having to survive on our own.

"Zander," Jurgen finally contacted me. "Forgive me if I'm wrong but I still don't understand why your status changed like this."

"Clans have been dissolved," I answered curtly. "You'll just have to trust me that I don't mean any harm. Time will tell, anyway."

"Right. I'll trust you in the meantime. Now listen-"

"Jurgen," I interrupted him without ceremony, "you need to understand. This raid could be lethal. Our entire future depends upon it. So it can only have one leader."

"Who is-?"

"Me."

"Sorry, Zander. Don't you think you're still too-"

"I am the raid leader. That's non-negotiable."

"Check out the mercs' levels," he suggested grimly. "Do you think they'll accept you?"

"Leave that to me."

"Whatever. In a minute, Frieda will take the children aboard with those two, Charon and Arbido."

"Charon's staying with me."

"You can't! The mercs will rip him to shreds."

"That's my business." I wasn't in the mood to argue with him. I'd given my situation enough thought on the way to the RV. I'd also remembered a thing or two I knew about virtual gameplay.

So you want an alternative plot line? I looked up, staring into the fathomless void of outer space. *I'll give it to you,* I promised, addressing the invisible but omnipresent force.

Two cargo modules silently hove into view above the station's ragged edge. Jesus. This was even more primitive than I'd expected: a couple of cargo containers with a jury-rigged propulsion system and something that vaguely resembled a vitrified cockpit.

This was a disaster. Would these things even make it to the station? Having said that, they should. You could fly a soapbox in outer space if necessary, provided you didn't have to enter an atmosphere. The containers were crude and comfortless: just some seats welded to the floor. Better that than nothing, I suppose.

Cautiously the children clambered inside and took their places. Liori buckled them in while instructing Arbido who was to fly with the kids.

Charon and I took our places in the other "spacecraft".

* * *

OUR BRIEF FLIGHT BROUGHT no surprises. Jurgen controlled it well. In the absence of G-force absorbers, maneuvering this rust bucket took a lot of skill. I had to review our schedule. Our journey to the station would take at least six or seven hours.

Actually, I wasn't yet sure the raid would transpire after all.

I sensed a gentle deceleration. We'd arrived. The container's unpressurized door shuddered open.

Liori, Charon and myself stepped out, finding ourselves inside an enormous hangar.

Thirty-two mercenaries and three pilots were already there, casting curious looks at us.

I joined the group's local network. Reality faded as human faces filled my mental view.

I didn't study their expressions. They all looked grim and disinterested. I met a few stares that held nothing but a disdainful promise: *just wait till you take us there, and then you're toast.*

I wasn't at all happy with their attitude. I wasn't going to watch my back for the rest of my life. "Which of you arrived with the First Colonial Fleet?"

Not a muscle twitched on their gloomy faces. Some lips curled in a smirk. The mercs were strong. They'd been in the game for at least three or four years and not a single one of them had bought into Phantom Server's authenticity.

I PM'd each of them personally, quoting the Wiki update and adding my own thoughts on the significance of neuroimplants and our own role as guinea pigs.

It didn't look as if I'd told them something new as far as AI neuronet modules were concerned. But the Wiki update was a shock for everyone. Yeah right, they were too experienced to bother to check such newb sources.

I didn't have to explain what it meant to all of us. Their expressions changed, cold confidence giving way to reserved curiosity as they eyed me with the unasked question, *So what do we do next?*

They realized that whoever stayed on Argus was doomed. What they didn't yet realize was that our escape to the neighboring station wouldn't save us from the total purge.

I forwarded them the logs of the admins' offer and my response to them.

Not all of them grasped it at once. Some eyes glazed over as if the mercs were busy checking Argus' agonizing network for confirmation of what they'd just learned.

Predictably, they found none.

Again all eyes were on me.

"I can prove it," I said. "I can do it now. One thing, though. You need to make up your minds, now. I want no hassles in the future — no grudges, no backpedaling. Agreed?"

My words still seemed to fall on deaf ears.

"I was the one who activated the alternative plot line. Whoever wants to join me, be my guest," I pointed at an old paint marker still visible on the hangar floor. "If you're with me, step over it. That will mean you accept me as your raid leader. If our mission is a success, I will take command of the ship. This is the only invitation you'll get. Conditions are non-negotiable. That applies to everyone!"

Jurgen and Frieda looked pretty lost. My arguments meant nothing to them: stripped of their real-life memory, the two couldn't even fathom their actual meaning.

Liori, however, seemed to grasp everything perfectly well.

She'd been left with no choice. She must have thought I was putting her under pressure. But still, she was the first to cross the painted line and stand next to me.

A surprised murmur ran through this disorganized bunch of seasoned warriors. Their faces dropped.

Jurgen gave me the evil eye. Suddenly he stepped forward and stood next to me, apparently wishing to call my bluff.

Frieda startled, staring at him in horror.

I knew very well what was happening. It couldn't be any other way. A single player may initiate a certain development, but it would affect the lives of many.

I turned my head to read their markers.

Liori. Outlaw. Level 51. Pilot.
Jurgen. Outlaw. Level 43. Technologist.
Charon. Outlaw. Level 23. Sentient Xenomorph.

We had become wrenches in the works of the game.

We were the Alts. The ones capable of giving this world its alternative history.

Whether that history would be long enough to recount depended on the numbers of the mercs who'd cross the line.

Their eyes were filled with some sort of superstitious fear — but they also glinted with hope. They had enough experience to know what it meant to go against the flow.

Their ranks quivered. Five more stood next to me.

I hurried to put their nicknames on a special list. I had my reasons to question the others' sincerity. They must have already realized that joining the alternative plot line would save them from immediate elimination by the developers; and still they sat on the fence, making mental calculations — which meant that their loyalty would be of the *I'll join him and then we'll see* kind.

I wasn't happy with that. My responsibility was too high as it was.

The rest of the mercs began to cross the line, singularly and in groups, taking their places next to me.

These were the only fighters we had. There wouldn't be others. The future was nebulous but at least it was in our hands now. It lay in our intentions and our actions.

CHAPTER SEVEN

PHANTOM SERVER. OUTER SPACE

O UR JOURNEY TO THE STATION took eight hours. Charon and I took turns flying our craft. Its slow speed and smooth maneuvering (these cargo modules would have disintegrated otherwise) even allowed me to take a nap. But now it was time to act.

I took the controls. Considering we only had five fighter craft, a blatant entry was way too risky. We had to act inconspicuously, collecting whatever information we could, and then try to come up with a plan of action.

The two cargo modules changed their course, moving toward the coordinates I'd ordered. While Jurgen and Frieda gingerly maneuvered their craft, they remained within our line of vision meaning we could maintain laser communication.

I killed the engines. The other pilots followed suit. We coasted on, keeping a low profile while gathering intel.

Until now, everything was quiet. No one seemed to have noticed our approach to the station. I used the local network to forward the others the screenshots I'd made three weeks ago. I tried to draw the mercs' attention to the Guides as our most mysterious and potentially dangerous opponents. I had no information about them at all, secretly hoping that the mercs might know something. But they maintained grim silence as they listened to my meager explanations.

Unexpectedly, Frieda joined in.

Apart from her other specializations, she also possessed the unique profession of exotechnologist which demanded an extremely rare combination of abilities and skills like I'd never met before.

I told everyone about the mental pressure I'd sensed in the Guides' presence when I'd encountered them during the Dargian raid.

Having listened to my explanations, Frieda published several images on the local network. You could distinctly see five living domes that shielded the ruins of a mine on some asteroid or other. By the looks of it, these domelike creatures could survive in a vacuum at freezing cosmic temperatures. The medusa-like beings emitted a subdued glow. Their translucent bodies were threaded with capillary energy channels. Protective power fields shimmered around each of them.

"Zander, why did you think that it was the Guides who controlled the Dargians?" Frieda asked.

"Dunno. That's what I thought."

"The Guides is a rather dated name for what we now call the Emgles. They are as a matter of fact a presentient exobiological life form," she began to explicate. "They live in the atmosphere of the gas giant, just like the Wearongs do. When the First Colonial Fleet had just arrived in this star system, you could see them virtually at every one of the Founders' stations. The Dargians used them as living dome shields."

I compared them to the screenshots I'd taken. Those on the pics differed considerably in a number of ways. They'd apparently been cybergized. I pointed this fact out to Frieda but you couldn't confuse her so easily.

"It must have been the Dargians who did this," she said. "The Emgles are strong and fiercely independent creatures but they can be easily tamed during the earlier stages of their development. Young Emgles develop a strong bond with their owners provided they're well treated."

I struggled to imagine anyone "taming" a gigantic medusa from outer space. Still, Frieda insisted,

"It's their empathic nature that makes Emgles so susceptible. They're naturally curious. The adult ones can be described as defenders rather than aggressors. Their bodies may look fragile but they are in fact unique biological reactors refined through evolution, complete with an integrated power field generator. You just can't survive in the gas giant's atmosphere without one."

"But how about the planet's enormous pressure?" I insisted. "And how do the Dargians even manage to domesticate them?"

"They catch the young ones during the short period when they rise to the top layers of the atmosphere to benefit from the abundant solar energy," she explained. "The implant you noticed apparently points at the Dargians' inability to establish positive mnemonic contact with them. So they use technology to enslave them, turning them into dangerous and aggressive creatures. They use surgery to remove certain body parts, replacing them with implants. Such barbaric modification has one grave side effect. It arrests their development. As a rule, those Emgles which are unlucky enough to be trapped stop growing and don't live long afterward."

"Does that mean that those I saw were... teenagers?"

"Judging by the pictures, they were," Frieda answered.

"And can you tell me how I can deal with them?"

"The most important thing is, you should never provoke them or try to attack them first."

"Yeah, right," the mercs raised their sarcastic voices. "Just sit there and wait till they send us to our respawn points?" Their indignation was quite understandable.

"The Emgles never attack anyone first," Frieda insisted. "You must understand. The Dargians have hurt them a lot. If we treat them differently, they're bound to notice it. Also, they are very sensitive to mental images," she added. "I might try and contact them mnemonically."

Somehow I had my doubts. "What if it doesn't work? How close do you need to get to them in order to make sure they can hear you?"

"I must get within their direct line of vision," she said.

I shook my head. The Dargians weren't that stupid. They must have already put the station on high alert and taken additional security measures both on the

Founders' ship and at the station's living quarters. Getting close to them wasn't going to be at all easy.

As for the mercs, their combined opinion was pretty clear: the only way to handle any Wearong creatures was by shooting to kill.

I contacted Jurgen. "What do you think?"

"We could use the Emgles at some later date, I suppose. I could look into their implant controls."

That got me thinking. "Can't we disable their implants somehow?"

"We probably could. They're only technology, after all. But it might take some time. We still don't know their power shield's frequencies. As far as I know, they may vary."

I couldn't believe my ears. "You mean each creature has its own unique frequency?"

"It does and it can also vary its parameters," Jurgen confirmed my worst suspicions. "I suggest you listen to what Frieda's saying. The Emgles are known for their powerful empathy. Her idea just might work."

"Very well. Let's wait for the recon results and then we'll decide."

THE MODULES LEFT for the location I'd pinpointed while we drifted, collecting intel in passive reception mode, studying any signatures and watching the chosen sector of the station's surface via optical multiplayer, comparing and combining the data received.

The Dargians seemed to be continuing their restoration works on the Founders' starship. This was the only advantage we currently had. The Haash were busy working there — and by liberating them, we were going to get ourselves both some loyal allies and access to the unique ancient ship's controls.

As for the rest, things weren't as rosy. Our sensors detected ten space defense units that now encircled the station, installed in the better preserved hull structures. I was pretty sure such a reinforcement to their defenses had everything to do with the developments of the last few days. About fifty combat drones patrolled all accesses to the Founders' ship. Five Emgles enveloped its carcass, covering the larger holes and controlling the main airlock.

My eyes hurt from all the tiny shapes of Dargians. There had to be at least a hundred of them.

As the raid leader, I had to come up with the correct tactic, taking every detail into consideration. In normal gameplay, mopping up a location is a rather simple and straightforward thing. Each mob has its aggro radius. When pulled correctly, they can be taken out by ones and twos or in small groups, allowing you to advance toward your goal slowly but surely.

Here and now it was all different. Only the drones could qualify as NPCs — they and also the space defense systems. The Dargians' potential reactions remained a mystery. In the worst-case scenario, they'd be able to quickly assess the danger and kill all the Haash, then barricade themselves in the ship. This was something we couldn't allow to happen.

Then there were the Emgles. These were capable of foiling any amount of the best-laid plans timed to perfection. How were they going to react to our attack? Would they join in battle to confront our fighters? Or would they continue blocking all entry to the ship?

I knew nothing about this empathy thing. I could just about grasp its meaning thanks to Frieda's explanation but I wasn't sure I would trust it as a combat technique.

I kept watching, analyzing and mulling over what I was seeing.

There were just too many Dargians there. Even though the Haash were sure to take our side, this was going to be one desperate battle.

Whoever wanted to win had to ensure control over all respawn points and delay enemy respawning when killed by a player. These two points were paramount.

I absolutely had to speak to Jurgen but the modules had already left our line of vision, making laser communications impossible.

"Zander?" Liori PM'd me via my mnemonic inbox. "We don't have enough strength to attack the station."

"So what do you suggest?"

"The station is enormous. If we find a place that's sealed and undamaged..."

I knew of course she wasn't worried about herself. Still, I insisted, "If we want to survive, we need to take the ship."

"Impossible," she obviously had no illusions about our situation. "Ten space defense units won't let you anywhere near the station."

"That we're yet to see," I replied. My plan of attack was admittedly daring bordering on insane. But this was something the Dargians definitely didn't expect.

I sent my idea to Liori.

She paused, weighing up all the pros and cons. "You know what, Zander? It might just work," I detected a spark of hope in her voice. "Who's gonna do it?"

"You and I."

"We need to think every maneuver through. Are you that sure of the Haash prisoners?" I could hear that she'd already bought into my idea, prepared to take the risk if necessary.

"I am. They've been awaiting my return."

The mercs were apparently struggling to put their trust in xenomorphs. All their experience screamed otherwise. Still, I didn't suffer from the same kind of phobia so I didn't give in to their unspoken pressure. I told the three pilots to stay put within the path of their drift, out of the Dargian scanners' range, and to watch and perform all the necessary calculations. Liori and I were going to follow the cargo modules. Charon and I still had work to do on our craft; besides, I had a few questions to ask Jurgen. His answer might decide the outcome of the upcoming combat.

"Zander."

"Yes?"

She didn't say anything. Liori and I seemed to have some heavy chemistry going on. I just couldn't help it. The feeling had swept over me, sudden and sharp.

She never answered. Averting her gaze, she switched to the common communications channel.

A TOXIC HAZE CLOUDED OUR VIEW.

The once-icy floor of the enormous hall was now covered in pools of thawing water.

I could see the xenomorphs' hunched silhouettes in the distance. Their wailing sobs echoed from afar.

The two cargo modules moved slowly in, their landing supports jolting as they touched the ancient deck, damping their vibrations.

The scanning radius was clear. I didn't count the Kickers' signatures: they couldn't scramble away from the scene fast enough.

There is was, my first respawn point. I made out the familiar green glow in the distance. The mound of radioactive ore had to lie in that direction.

The mercs disembarked, dispersing to set up a perimeter.

The melting ice on the floor was flecked with dark blood. I pointed at it, marking the respawn point.

Jurgen sprang into action and scanned the entire depth of the floor. "Got it! A stationary respawn device. Fully functional. It's all as you said it would be, Zander."

I bet it was. How could I ever forget this place.

I walked over to Jurgen. "Mind telling me how you detected it?"

He sent me a screenshot of his interface.

I studied it, comparing it with mine. Apparently, I too had a similar scanner installed in my suit. When I activated it, an inscription read,

Search of active power imprints initiated

Just below, three buttons lit up:

Scan the device's frequency
Create a bind point
Scan the frequency and reset your personal marker

I'd love to know what Jurgen thought about

respawning, considering that he believed himself to be in real life. I also wanted to know why setting up a respawn point demanded such complex equipment. Why would the game designers waste time on creating meticulous detail deep inside the deck flooring where no one was ever going to see it? They should have invested their effort in improving their interior designs.

"Jurgen? Did your clan try to study the resurrection mechanism?" I purposefully avoided calling it a *respawn*.

"We did. With little results. You need to understand, Zander: the Founders were tens of thousands of years ahead of us. They solved the molecular replication problem. But their equipment is extremely complicated; it takes a whole lot of energy and a wealth of biological supplies. Which is why functioning respawn points are very few and far between."

So that's how he understood something as simple as a respawn trigger. Never mind. Pointless trying to reason with him.

That got me thinking. Would my top-of-the-range scanners be able to detect other respawn points in the vicinity?

I started fiddling around with their options.

Several identical markings appeared at equal distances from my current location. Most of the markers were red. Only two of the detected devices glowed emerald. Both were definitely location-bound: one was set up in the prison block, the other right under my feet.

Another weak dull green light came on screen with a considerable delay in the vicinity of the Dargianoccupied area, disrupting the others' perfect symmetry. A chill ran up my spine. It didn't look good.

Things began clicking into place. I suddenly realized why Rash had managed to avoid decompression and thrown a pursuit together so quickly. He hadn't respawned in the decompressed area.

I searched through the logs looking for the record of Charon's and my escape. Just as I suspected, the Dargians too had a respawn delay of only ten minutes (when killed by a player). But worst of all was this wretched green marker whose location coincided with the position of the Founders' ship.

"Jurgen? Take a look," I forwarded him the logs.

He turned noticeably pale. "The Dargians must have a mobile respawn point device," he said bitterly. "A super rare artifact! Zander," he switched over to the encrypted communications channel, "I hope you understand that this renders our entire plan useless? The Dargians will be respawning right here on board the starship!"

"Would it be possible to block their personal markers somehow?"

He shook his head. "I don't think so. To do that, you might need to recreate Gehenna-like conditions, and even then..."

"There must be a solution, surely!"

"There is. We'll have to destroy the artifact," Jurgen said grudgingly.

What a predicament. Why did it have to get so complicated?

"Jurgen, and what if I could get you its blueprints? Do you think you could use them to recreate the artifact at a later date?"

He sat up. "I suppose I could try. I can't promise anything, though. I just don't understand how you can get them."

"Do you have a scanner I could use?"

"As a matter of fact, I do. A professional one. It's built into my gear. It can create a detailed model of any technological artifact in a matter of minutes."

"I'm afraid, you might have to part with it for a while."

"Mind telling me your plan?"

"I will, don't worry. First I'd like you to tell me what can happen if the artifact is destroyed."

"The Dargians' personal markers will no longer be tied to this particular device. So the next time they respawn, they'll be redirected to the nearest functioning respawn point."

"You mean, here?" I pointed at the prison block marker.

"Exactly."

"And if we manage, hypothetically, to block this one too?"

I could read the silent question in his eyes, *How on earth can we do that?*

I didn't say anything. He sighed and pointed below, "Then their respawn point will be relocated down here."

I removed my power belt and laid it on the floor, then turned it back on. "Have you got a signal?"

"I have but... no, wait! Zander, you're a genius! This is how we can block their signals! Wait a bit," he activated his scanner and performed some calculations, then turned to me. He looked a different man. "Back in Gehenna, you stood right in the respawn point, remember? And both of us resurrected successfully within your power shield — Arbido and myself!"

"Of course I remember. That's why I'm asking you."

His sunken cheeks flushed with red blotches. "But if you change the power field's settings, they won't let the signal through."

"But how about us then?"

"We need to change our personal marker settings accordingly. In that case we'll still be able to respawn — but not the Dargians!"

"You mean they won't be able to respawn at all?"

"Yes, of course they will!" he answered excitedly. "They will simply be redirected further on. No idea where to! You can see that all the other respawn devices are marked as out of order. I'm pretty sure they'll find one but it'll have to be miles and miles away, probably somewhere in the ransacked part of the station."

"You mean a Gehenna-type respawn purgatory?" I gave him an evil grin.

"Possible. In any case, it would take them quite some time to rejoin the battle."

Which was exactly what I wanted to hear. The rest was academic: we had to breach their defenses, seize the prison block and fight our way to the artifact.

"You can put your belt back on," Jurgen commanded, his thoughts taking the right direction. "I'm going to use our clan's generators. They're easier for me to reset. Do you understand that if it works we might not need to destroy the artifact?"

You bet I did.

A mobile respawn point in combination with the Founders' starship would allow us to take on the

Universe!

* * *

DARKNESS SWIRLED AROUND US.

An intense beam of light cut through the toxic haze and formed a dome-shaped shield around us as Jurgen switched on the power field generator. You could actually walk through it. Once we'd changed the settings, it might still be breached and would offer no protection from bullets. What it would do though, is block the Founders' frequencies.

Liori walked over to me. She too must have noticed the change in the shield's parameters. "What's going on?"

"Just a nasty surprise for the Dargians."

I clued her in about the changes suggested by Jurgen. She listened closely.

"So this is going to be our respawn point, then?" she asked.

"Hopefully, a backup one. The main one I plan to set up in the prison block. Jurgen is now updating our personal markers. Our transmitters now work in synch with the power shield which will bounce all other incoming respawn requests."

Liori looked tense and subdued. You could see something was gnawing at her. Our eyes met and I felt lost in the depths of her gaze. We were physically drawn to each other, there was no doubt about it, and still I could sense this icy estrangement in her that she'd adapted in order to hide herself from other people.

She must have been betrayed. Repeatedly so. I could feel that. Again I had this eerie feeling of ethereal figures crowding behind her back. She knew something about Phantom Server that I hadn't even begun to fathom out. That's what gnawed at her; that's what didn't allow her to breathe freely.

Liori, who are you?

She was the first to avert her gaze.

"Are you scared?" I asked.

"Sorry, Zander. Not now. Maybe later if we survive..." she trailed off and swung around to head for one of the cargo modules. I could see Arbido peering anxiously out of it.

I watched her leave. I was scared too. The Phantom Server's authenticity levels were frightening. Many of us wouldn't come back from this battle. Our respawning chances were fifty-fifty.

I forced my mind away from these depressing thoughts. We were almost done with prep work. Time to set combat objectives.

Frieda walked over to me. "The children are asleep," she said. "I've set their suits' life support to rest mode. I don't want them to see us respawn. It might not be a pretty sight."

I nodded my agreement. Good idea.

"I'd like to join the snipers," she added. "May I?"

I knew what had prompted this decision. "You can, but on one condition. You mustn't attract attention to yourself until we work out their defense systems."

"Zander, how about my mnemotech experience? I can distract the Emgles and lure them away from the ship."

"These Emgles are cybergized," I said. "They obey the Dargians and maintain permanent communication with them. Don't they?"

"Yeah," she admitted half-heartedly.

"Which is why you aren't going to do anything until we destroy their defenses."

"But I could-"

"Our mission has been choreographed to perfection. This isn't the right time to experiment. The Dargians mustn't suspect anything. This is my last word."

I wasn't going to argue with her. An order was an order. She stared at me, looking hurt, but I'd already switched over to the mercs' network making it clear that our conversation was over.

We were faced with a very difficult task. The mercs were too few. They would have to work in small groups. I couldn't be everywhere, either, which meant that I wouldn't be able to monitor a considerable part of the action.

Oh well. Being professionals, they had to understand that this was an all-or-nothing game.

Ten of them were the snipers who had to deploy immediately, taking positions on the towering structures around the Founders' starship. They would commence on my command, taking out the Dargians and depleting their numbers.

Jurgen would lead the twenty-strong assault group. Their objective was to storm the Dargian base, then either block or destroy the respawn equipment in the prison block.

The three most trustworthy mercs recommended by Liori were going to stay here, guarding the modules and administering first aid to the wounded. They would have the use of a couple of repair robots as well as access to power units and a stock of spare parts for standard gear.

Once I was done issuing orders, I asked Charon to

see me. I was busy meting out my instructions to him when Jurgen walked over to us and handed him a plain tube filled with silvery paste: respawn markers for the remaining Haash. I'm not going to bore you with its principles; let's just say the paste contained some nano-signal transmitters.

I made sure that Jurgen and Charon successfully found common ground, then contacted our guards for one last warning,

"The Haash are our allies. When they respawn, you'd better behave yourself. If any of you doesn't think he can overcome his xenophobia, he'd better say so now!"

They frowned but said nothing. I could see already that our victory might only create more problems for me.

Once again I looked over all the current objectives and checked everyone's positions, then walked back to my ship. There I removed my helmet and handed it to Jurgen. "We'll have to install your scanner and my collar controller into Charon's helmet."

"You do realize it's a risk, don't you?" he PM'd me.

"I'm pretty sure of him."

Jurgen was paranoid about anyone he didn't know. I couldn't blame him but we'd all have to adapt to the changes. If we survived, that is. "Arbido!"

Hearing his name, the goblin peeked from behind the cargo container's hatch.

"How's it going?" I asked him.

"The children, you mean? They're asleep. They must be tired. Want to have a look?"

"It's all right. Let them sleep. You sure you'll manage?"

"I've got a grandson back in real life," he admitted.

"I miss him."

Oh really? Somehow I'd always thought he had no family. Actually, I used to think that money was the only thing he loved.

* * *

THE HATCH HISSED SHUT.

I confidently took off. The ship hovered over the deck. We'd had a second pilot's seat for Charon thrown together. Now we sat back to back.

I activated a practice drone mounted on the ship's hull. Immediately the ship's recognizable outline and unique signature changed. Now both its appearance and power imprint were identical to those of a standard Condor.

Liori took off next.

The deck slowly fell away. I accelerated smoothly, steering toward the green radioactive glow of the enormous hole formed by the ancient ship's collapse onto the station.

Once at some distance from the station, I changed my ship's course and killed the engines, drifting as I entered the data to calculate the upcoming maneuver. Charon wheezed, concentrated. I didn't distract him, both our stares focused on the cockpit's only functioning holographic screen.

The Founders' starship resembled an enormous electric ray that was clinging to the station's hull, resting.

The scampering figures of the Dargians and the Haash looked tiny in comparison. They were busy cutting out chunks of cargonite and carrying its gleaming diamond-shaped pieces to and fro, using them to patch up the gaping holes in the ship's hull.

Next to them, the Emgles looked impressive — and dangerous. Somehow I couldn't see these gas planet dwellers as innocent victims worthy of our sympathy the way Frieda seemed to believe. Their job was to block access to the starship, checking everyone who dared approach it, both Dargians and the Haash.

The data transfer was completed. The countdown kicked in. The navigation computers reported their readiness.

It was our turn. Liori's and mine.

My mind expander went into overdrive, making me one with the ship.

I initiated cruise thrust, leaving the drift point first. After a pause, Liori repeated my maneuver. We were on course. I manipulated the thrusters, sending my ship into a seemingly uncontrollable spin.

Liori kept lagging behind.

Our ships' reactors were barely glowing at five percent of their power. Both the interference created by our security systems and the tails of rarefied gas trailing in our wake served to convince our enemy that they were looking at two Condors, shot down and pilotless, their crews long gone to their respawn points. Two drifting abandoned craft which presented no threat whatsoever.

The Dargians couldn't possibly ignore a tasty morsel like that. They had to view this as a minor but welcome byproduct of the still raging battle for Argus.

Their drones couldn't get close enough to us. I could imagine how we must have looked in their scanners: the occasional flickering betrayed the presence of our power fields and our laser turrets seemingly still in working order. No, the slave drivers wouldn't risk their drones: they'd wait until the two "Condors" drifted closer and rammed into the station. In that case, our ships' equipment would attempt to cushion the impact with their power shields, depleting their batteries. Then you could catch these two powerless birds with your bare hands.

Aha, I could see them rushing about! They must have worked out my course. Liori's ship lagged far behind, tempting the Dargians to focus on mine. Excellent. Their defenses remained silent while the Dargians hurried to clear a small area not far from the Founders' ship. They then lugged some generators there to create a makeshift acceleration absorber and ensure that the ships didn't sustain much damage or bounce back into outer space.

The station was rapidly growing. My ship's spin was by no means uncontrollable, even if it may have seemed so. Its trajectory was meticulously choreographed, targeting its aft as the impact surface. The Dargians scrambled away, leaving the Haash to operate the generators. Excellent. Just as we'd planned. Liori's ship was about five hundred feet above me.

I crashed.

The shield's power plummeted. The hatches of the main airlock and the cargo holds "failed" simultaneously. Charon emerged, forced out by the airflow, while I released the chemicals from the reactor's cooling system, burying the area in thick toxic fog.

All this had taken but a couple of seconds. My ship bounced off, depressurized. Any outside observer was obliged to conclude that the craft had fallen apart on impact.

I glimpsed the silhouettes of two Haash just next to the toxic cloud: they hurried to pull Charon with his easily recognizable personal marker away from danger.

He'd done it. He was with his own now. And the Dargians were none the wiser.

Time to engage.

I released the power from the reserve batteries. It surged down the circuits, charging up the shields. The reactor was quickly regaining its capabilities. The engines kicked in. Liori's Condor mirrored my maneuver with perfect timing. We sped up and charged at the nearest defense units.

The positions of plasma generators and laser batteries were located higher and were aimed at outer space. In this situation they proved utterly useless against our lightning attack. The Dargians' desire to capture our ships had backfired on them.

We fired a broadside at close range. The two nearest structures erupted in flames while Liori and I were already speeding off, maneuvering dangerously close to the hull amid the molten peaks of its technoscape.

Two heavy lasers fired after us, followed by two discharges of plasma generators. Their guidance systems locked us in their sights, following our ships, bathing them in their scanners' waves, all the while hoping to shoot them down in full maneuver.

Liori threw her Condor into a narrow ravine formed by two monolithic blocks of the station's armor. I repeated her maneuver albeit not as gracefully, barely avoiding a collision as I fell into place as her wingman. We shot out of the ravine and banked, changing course, beginning a new attack.

Now all their defense systems were upon us. The Dargians were angry — but still uncomprehending.

We kept evading their fire.

Our shields pulsated, draining the batteries, but I'd already noticed three bright dots rapidly approaching through space. This was a wing of Condors zeroing in on their highlighted targets.

They fired their first salvo at long range, sweeping away the locator modules. I watched a tall latticed tower tilt to one side and disintegrate.

Three more hull structures cascaded with molten steel.

We passed them head on, turned around and charged again.

The Dargians scattered, desperate to leave the open area. Only a few headed for the Founders' starship, the bulk of them holing up in the openings cut in the station's hull.

The surviving defense modules switched to curtain fire. They critted one of the Condors which plunged into a chaotic spin, ramming the station in a ball of fire.

Liori and I targeted the plasma generators using this already-tested scheme: she removed the shields while I fired my pulse guns.

Got him! My missiles sliced through the armored hull structure, its powerful blast tearing up the Dargians' firing position from the inside. It fell apart in a swelling cloud of red-hot fragments like a heap of crimson autumn leaves when you kick them.

Panic set in among the Dargians. Their space defenses had been destroyed. What else would these unknown invaders do?

They rushed around like headless chickens. Little

wonder: the four fighter craft hovering overhead meant their death sentence.

Suddenly we saw the Emgles leave the Founders' ship. They soared up and headed for us.

"Frieda — your turn!" Instinctively I banked, trying to avoid a collision. Too late. One of the Emgles effortlessly caught me up and rammed me. The shields self-destructed, melting the hull of my ship. I lost control. The last thing I saw were the shreds of some translucent substance veined with power channels, flying everywhere. Then a shuddering impact knocked me out.

* * *

MY HEAVY ARMORED SUIT and the secure pilot seat had saved me from respawning.

My ship rammed the station not far from the Founders' craft.

I stared at the dying screens watching two more Condors go down. Obeying the Dargians' command, the Emgles had sacrificed themselves, bringing them down.

Liori was the only one who'd managed to escape their assault. She was now busy taking her damaged Condor toward the station's deserted area, trying to shake off two more Emgles chasing her.

I tried to move. My gear's muscle enhancers were working. My ribs ached from my scuffle with the Outlaw. My lip bled from when I'd bitten it on impact.

My ship was completely deformed, its stern squashed. I had to use the emergency exit located fore. It opened easily but proved a bit too small for my new suit. I had to force my way through.

I took cover behind a massive weapons' stanchion and contacted the others. "Drake?"

The only thing I knew about the mercs were their names — not all of them even. We'd never had the chance to get to know each other.

"In position," the snipers' leader replied. "Ready for action. Zander, two Emgles are chasing Liori. There was nothing Frieda could do."

"I saw it. Wait for my orders," I switched over to the second group's combat chat. "Jurgen?"

"In position."

"Commence the assault."

Not far from where I was, the Dargians began scrambling out of a gaping hole in the station's hull, hurrying to vacate their temporary shelter. They'd already recovered from the shock and taken stock of the situation, impatient to get even with the surviving pilots. With their levels 30 to 40, excellent gear and a nearby respawn point on board the ancient starship, they had absolutely nothing to fear.

I knew it, too. "Charon?"

Silence. His dedicated channel icon blinked aimlessly. He wasn't there.

A surge of energy hit the surface nearby, spewing fragments of hull structures into outer space. This was Jurgen's group storming the slave drivers' base.

About a dozen Dargians remained within my field of view. I scanned the area — no Haash around. Which meant that not all was lost. If Charon and his people had managed to retreat within the starship, it meant another unpleasant surprise for the slave drivers. In the meantime, they wouldn't get a respawn out of me.

My gear's manipulators clenched the mauled

weapons. I aimed at the floor under the Dargians' feet and activated my integrated right-arm pulse gun.

The impacts ripped through the hull, striking up flames. The Dargians' boot soles lost grip with the surface, hurling their squat figures into outer space. They somersaulted and flailed their arms around, screaming in the chat rooms.

A few drones headed off to their rescue. I rose behind my cover and opened fire in two directions at once, tearing the nearest ones to pieces. They gave as good as they got. My shield pulsated with absorbed damage, my gear clicking incessantly with battery replacements.

Still, not all of the Dargians were enjoying a free flight. Two of them stayed put. I fired a long burst at them — with zero effect. Could they have individual gravity generators? Then again, what else could have kept them standing? They looked as if they were part of the station's surface.

One of them was already dead. The other scrambled back into his hole.

The Founders' starship was now some three hundred feet away from me. The problem was, our enemies were legion. At least fifty of them hovered within my direct line of sight.

"Snipers, keep at it!"

I activated my movement coordinator and headed for the dead Dargian in a series of dangerous leaps. His suit had been breached in several places. Its servomuscles were jammed, locking him in an awkward half-kneeling position.

Thanks to Jurgen's gift, my current Repair skill was at 30 points. Even though I only had my unique high tech gear to thank for that, now I could easily remove various devices from their slots and reinstall them.

I pulled his armor off and immediately ducked into the nearest gaping hole in one well-calculated leap.

The Dargian who'd escaped there earlier charged at me from out of the darkness. I shot at random. These pulse guns had a considerable recoil that in this near-zero gravity environment sent me flying backwards. My back hit a bulkhead.

Trying to work as fast as possible, I checked the loot. A purpose-built scanner soon located the gravity generator built into their gear among other ancient artifacts as yet unknown to me. They must have been rare and exorbitantly expensive. *Plus at least a dozen chips!* — my gaming mentality kept butting in. Using my manipulators, I stripped the suits of all the equipment, including a slim box containing some microscopic data storage devices. They must have contained ancient alien software. I threw one of the gravity generators into my inventory and clicked the other into an empty slot. My suit's connectors matched the Founders' equipment. The generator powered up. Excellent.

You couldn't overestimate the importance of this particular trophy. Even if the station's inner decks still had gravity, it was approaching zero outside. Every step could become your last, any impact could prove fatal, forcing your boots to lose grip with the surface and hurling you into the abyss.

Outer space was an extremely complex environment.

All this had flashed through my mind without hindering my work. My connecting a new device caused the suit to redistribute power, sending the battery charge deep into the yellow.

I climbed out. Trying to find my way through the maze of service channels wasn't an option. Everything depended on my speed now.

The station's hull was illuminated by the gas giant's weak brown light. The battle was in full swing. The surprise effect had already worn off. The Dargians must have realized that it wasn't wise to stay in the open so now they lay low: behind the stacks of diamond-shaped armor plates, within the numerous breaches or securing themselves with safety tethers. Few had their own gravity generators. Either the slave drivers had failed to understand their design or they had proved unable to reproduce them.

Lasers impacted from every direction. Drones were the biggest problem. They had already detected our snipers' positions and headed for them in groups of five or six, soaring up toward their hidey-holes.

"Jurgen, how's it going?" I asked while moving in bounds from one cover to the next, trying not to catch any return fire. I was losing power faster than I'd expected.

"We're stuck!" Jurgen's voice rang with the tension of the battle.

"Any casualties?"

"I've lost contact with ten men," he snapped back. "No idea where they are now."

"I want you to fight toward the respawn point whatever it takes! If you can't take it, you must destroy it!"

I didn't need to remind him. He knew this better than I did.

I darted for my next cover: a stack of diamond-shaped armor plates secured with loops of wire cable.

Drones darted overhead. I fired my pulse gun after them. Two of them exploded; the others switched immediately to their new target. The nearest Dargians had noticed me as well and opened fire, leaning out of their hideouts.

The disparity between me and them was frightening. My shield began to pulsate, then extinguished. I came under fire. My ability to move was my only forte so I ran as hard as I could. Finally, I took cover about fifty feet from the Founders' starship and tried to catch my breath.

My gear clicked again, switching to the emergency batteries. The main ones were as flat as a pancake. My armor was pockmarked with red-hot shrapnel. My left arm manipulator could barely move. The ammo feed in one of the integrated guns was damaged too. At least I gave them as good as I got. A trail of debris marked my wake, Dargian bodies floating among it.

I braced myself for one final sprint. "Ralph, I want you to cover me."

The snipers' leader didn't reply. I still had no idea what had happened to Charon, either. The Haash were nowhere to be seen.

Suddenly Frieda communicated to me. "Zander," she gasped, "there're only three of us left. The rest are awaiting respawn. We've downed the drones."

"Cover me," I watched my shield come back to life, its aura glowing weakly. "I'm going for the airlock!"

"Affirmative."

The Dargians were already creeping up on me trying to cut me off. I rose tentatively behind my cover and fired a generous burst from my right-arm gun, mercilessly wasting ammo.

Their assault attempt bogged down. The Dargians'

audacity had cost them dearly: I could see about a dozen bodies drifting away into space, followed by their trailing safety tethers. Others scrambled away, taking cover. I watched them being decimated by sniper fire from above.

We were giving it our all. And still this battle for survival and all the lives we'd lost would be for nothing if we failed to get to the starship respawn point.

My second integrated gun gave up the ghost.

I grabbed my trusty submachine gun. I had sixty feet to cover.

I ran as fast as I could, ignoring the Dargians' fire.

* * *

TEN MEN WITH MERCENARIES' INSIGNIA were climbing up the welded grating in the impact crater.

The echo of the battle reached them through the rarified air.

"Max," one of them scrambled out of the crater and began looking around, "D'you think we should have stayed?"

"What, with those nutcases?" the other sniffed. "That's pure suicide. Use your head, man. There're hundreds of Dargians there."

"And what if they do take the ship? We'll be losing out then, won't we?"

"They might," Max answered. "Then again, they might not. I don't like this Zander. He thinks too much of himself. Then there's all that xenomorph talk of his: don't touch them, he says. Had he said, *go smoke the Haash till you drop*, now that would have been the right thing. But the way things go, I don't think much of him, the bent bastard."

"Okay, okay. What about the ship?"

The remaining mercs scrambled out of the crater one after another. The abandoned deck lay around them.

"We're going to advance toward the reserve respawn point. We'll take over the equipment. Then if this Zander does take over the ship, we'll offer him a swap."

"What kind of swap?"

"We'll offer the children in exchange for the Founders' ship," Max grinned.

The others maintained a gloomy silence.

"There're our guys there at the respawn point," Vlast pointed out.

"So what? It's every man for himself now. There is no clan. So it's up to you."

"The goblin is no problem," one of the mercs said while scanning the location. "We'll make a quick job of him. But it looks as if Liori's Condor has landed there, too. Serge and Dan are busy trying to pull her out."

"Now," Max pinned everyone down with his glare. "You, you and you — you take over the respawn equipment. Smoke the goblin and hold. Leave Liori to me. As for Serge, Dyxt and Dan, shoot them on sight. We have nothing to discuss with them."

THE RESERVE RESPAWN POINT

INGE AWOKE FROM FREQUENT irregular tremors. She sat up, casting scared glances around.

A brown light seeped through a crack in the cargo container's open door. Uncle Arbido was gone. The other children were fast asleep.

Soon the girl felt bored just sitting and dangling her feet. Wherever could all the adults have gone? Uncle Arbido didn't count as an adult: he was too small and too funny.

Trying not to make any noise, the girl slid down the oversized seat, walked over to the door and took a peek outside.

How strange. They were all gone. She could only glimpse a few weird-looking shadows in the distance, surrounded by a dull green light.

The sensors of the girl's gear beeped a warning, their indicators soaring into the yellow sector. Still, this dark radiation-soaked place didn't scare Inge in the slightest. She adjusted her vision and focused, making out the outline of a Condor far ahead. A red-hot rut trailed on the floor in its wake. The ship must have made an emergency landing.

This is where all the adults must have gone, the girl reasoned. The downed ship was surrounded by flashing lights but she wasn't afraid of them one bit.

Inge looked up and saw two translucent shimmering creatures high overhead where an enormous gaping hole crossed the hangar's ceiling.

Transfixed, she watched them dance in the air. They were so beautiful. The play of light and fire was so delicate, the creatures gleaming with every shade of blue, crimson and emerald, weightless and graceful.

Delight filled her heart. She watched the fancy swirling of red-hot threads permeating their translucent bodies, their light reflecting in her eyes.

Her lips parted in a smile. "Come here!" she whispered. "Aren't you just *gorgeous!*"

The Emgles slowed their dance, then circled overhead in confusion.

The enthusiasm of combat had already left them. The aura of the dead ship had ceased to attract them. The two Emgles were suddenly bathing in a long-forgotten feeling that had stripped these predators of their gruesome past, reviving happy memories of free flight in their home planet's air stream when they used to soar higher and higher toward the warming rays of the system's sun.

"This is awesome!" the girl exclaimed, embracing their mental images. "Come here, please!"

* * *

EIGHT MINUTES INTO COMBAT.

The timer kept clocking up the seconds. Soon the Dargians would begin to respawn on board the Founders' ship.

The airlock was almost within reach. I limped toward it. My armor was glowing crimson from all the numerous impacts. My visor's inner rim was awash with subsystem damage reports.

The outer hatch was open. I sprang inside the airlock chamber and swung round, stopping the more brazen Dargians with short bursts of pulse fire.

"Charon!"

Still no reply.

Jurgen contacted me. "Zander? We've destroyed the respawn point. We've failed to seize the equipment. There're only five of us left."

"I'm nearly there!" I hurried to reload and drove the

last power batteries into their slots. "Keep at it!"

His voice was drowned out by interference.

Fifty seconds until the slave drivers' respawn.

I grabbed at the massive hatch and strained my servomuscles as hard as I could, forcing it into the "Closed" position.

I'd never been on board a Founders' ship before so I knew nothing about its layout. I only had Charon's utility blueprint to go by. According to it, I had to cover a hundred and fifty feet of the main corridor before I got to the room with the respawn artifact.

The floor shuddered underfoot. There was a battle going on here.

It was then that the last of the slave collars must have switched off. A message popped up into my mental view,

Quest completion alert: The Ties That Bind. Quest completed!
You've received a new level!

The inner hatch wasn't locked. I grabbed at it and pulled with all my might. Concealed within the bulkhead, its locking mechanism resisted my every effort. The hatch kept inching sideways until suddenly it gave way as if something had snapped inside, releasing the hatch that slid freely along its rails.

Good enough. I forced my body through the gap.

In the dim yellow light, the corridor floor was littered with Haash bodies apparently savaged by bursts of automatic fire. I glanced over them. No Charon. Deep down, the main channel was lit up by flashes of firing.

I bolted toward it.

Damaged cables sparked under the curving ceiling. Light panels flickered. The power spikes suggested someone was trying to activate some power-hungry equipment, like stationary weapons.

The corridor was decompressed. Somebody had switched the life support systems off and let the vacuum in.

My movements started to slow down. WTF? Three slave drivers ran out of the nearest door. I tried to raise my gun but my muscles seemed to weigh a hundred tons.

They froze in disbelief. I couldn't even use their hesitation. What could have been easier than to mow them down with a well-aimed burst of my gun? Only that my arms didn't obey me anymore. I still had plenty of power; my suit functioned well. What was going on?

Your exo ingredient has expired!
You're no longer able to control your suit!

Dammit! I couldn't even move, couldn't inject myself with a new helping of the metabolite. I hadn't even thought I might need it again!

The Dargians had come out of their stupor. Two of them shrank back to the walls while the third one raised his cumbersome weapon mounted on a complex support.

A shiver ran down my spine. I recognized Rash.

I felt paralyzed. The sheer weight of the suit in combination with a functional pseudo gravity generator pinned me to the ground. I hadn't even had time to look into the suit's settings. I'd activated it but now I had no idea how to switch it off!

Too late to sift through the icons looking for the option I needed. I had to change into my old gear but I couldn't do it in the vacuum.

What was Rash waiting for?

He wasn't in a hurry to shoot. He too had recognized me. He lowered his gun and motioned his henchmen to leave the two of us alone. Slowly he approached, studying me and trying to work out what might have caused my immobilization. He too wore an individual gravity generator. Last time he'd had nothing as good as that.

"Human," his sneer echoed through my mind. Little wonder: it had been he who'd implanted me with the semantic processor, after all, so he knew how to use it.

I froze in helpless fury. The one single mistake I'd made! Not a mistake even, just a fatal oversight, but now it was threatening the lives of all those who trusted me.

Arbido might survive. He might take the children to some unexplored far-flung location. He'd manage, I knew it. Still I couldn't even begin to imagine how hard it would be for them.

In moments like these, a lot can flash through your mind. I had less than a hundred feet between myself and the artifact. Three Dargians were all that stood between me and the respawn point we needed. In any other game world I'd be able to change into my spare gear — but not in Phantom Server! I'd explode from decompression within seconds.

"Rash, just do it," I said.

"Oh no, Human. Death would be too easy," his voice held the promise of a torturous agony. I didn't care. I was searching for a solution even though I knew there wasn't one. Too late, anyway. More Dargians appeared from the far end of the corridor. Only a few: those who'd been the first to die and respawn.

"The suit's a bit too heavy for you, eh?" Rash must have put two and two together so he was habitually arrogant, fearing nothing and no one. A wild beast, safe in his high tech shell. "Too late, Zander. Forget the gravity generator. You can't switch it off, pointless even trying. So you can tell the others to surrender. We need new slaves to replace all the Haash that died today."

My mind boiled in silent fury. A red haze clouded my vision. I strained every sinew, trying to lift and fire the gun.

I couldn't.

A door began to open to my side. I could sense the gelatinous flow of hatred seeping from within, directed at the Dargians.

A Haash?

I struggled in vain to establish mnemonic contact with him. All I could sense was his craving for revenge, desperate and violent.

A message popped up in my mental view,

A unique ability activated: Friend of the Haash.
Every time you fight alongside the Haash, you receive +1 to all characteristics.

The servodrives of my suit rustled softly.

The internal manipulators of my gear sprang to life, apparently happy with my current Strength level. In one swipe of my eyes, I injected myself with a bumper dose of exo.

"So what do you say, Zander?" the slave driver grinned, enjoying his power over me, savoring my immobility. "You do realize, don't you, that you stand no chance? Yes, you've managed to kill quite a few of us, but even that is only temporary, don't you understand? What did you expect, tell me?"

More and more Dargians filled the corridor. The Haash's image within my mind had taken a familiar shape.

Danezerath?

Zander?

Danny, wait up! We'll do it together! Wait for my signal!

Shaking, I forwarded him the mental image of the situation in the corridor.

My nerves were ablaze with the strain. A hundred feet. Only a hundred feet and a couple dozen Dargians.

Rash's patience must have run out. The respawned Dargians were pressing on him from behind. Slowly he raised his heavy gun: most likely a hand-held plasma generator. No amount of cover could save you from a round of one of those. You could forget respawning.

Danny — go!

The door flew aside into the bulkhead. Rash's attention was distracted by a lanky Haash shape. I charged at him, knocking him down before he could use his plasma generator.

Danezerath reached for it and jerked it out of the slave driver's hands, breaking its mountings and firing it on the swing.

Wow.

The nearest Dargians were burned to ashes — all I

noticed were a few blinding flashes followed by thin clouds of murky discharge.

Rash had survived and was struggling back to his feet. I punched him in the visor, investing all my fury into the blow.

The visor split. I'd learned the Outlaw's lesson well: those muscle enhancers were a force to be reckoned with.

Without saying a word, Danezerath tore the power units off the slave driver's belt.

I picked up my gun and we ran for the mobile respawn point.

* * *

ABOUT A HUNDRED FEET further on, the corridor widened into a hemispheric hall.

At its center, the Founders' artifact lay on a small pedestal, shaped as a rather plain-looking glowing octahedron.

It was surrounded by the silent evidence of a battle that must have raged here earlier. The floor was littered with dead bodies of both the Haash and the Dargians. Broken defense turrets and gutted drones were strewn everywhere.

"Danny, hold the entrance!"

Silently Danezerath began heaping up Dargian bodies to barricade the passage. I hurried to check the dead for Charon's body.

The Haash were a horrible sight. Most of them were still alive, their gear molten and decompressed, gaping holes filled with a mixture of sealing foam and blood. The cost-conscious Dargians hadn't finished them off knowing that the prison block respawn point had been destroyed.

I had a small stock of metabolites on me. I injected one of the survivors with some. "Where's Charon?"

He pointed weakly at the heaped Dargian bodies. I threw them this way and that and leaned helplessly over my *friend*.

Charon was still alive, the two emitters attached behind his back. He hadn't yet installed them.

"Zander," a hand touched my shoulder.

I swung round.

"Metabolites?" croaked the Haash I'd just saved, his eyes overflowing with agony, his body moving on willpower alone.

"There," I unstrapped the bags from Charon's belt. They held whatever meager supply of metabolites we'd managed to come by in the exo sector. "Make sure you inject only those who can still fight."

I was forced to make hard decisions. Still, Marogeron — that was the Haash's name — seemed to understand. He used the first dose to inject Charon, then staggered toward the others, overturning bodies in the ravaged suits and peering into faces, deciding who of them would live.

Time pressed.

I opened the bags on Charon's back and yanked out Jurgen's new improved power field generators, hurrying to set them up.

The room lit up with a respawn's emerald glow. Dammit.

The way the artifact worked was rather unusual. A few clots of emerald light clustered together next to the room's wall, letting out five Dargians. They hadn't yet realized that their respawn point had been captured.

"Come here, slave!" one of them hissed, noticing Danezerath.

I let go of the generator and whipped out my gun. My intervention wasn't necessary, though. One by one, the already-injected Haash rose from the bloodied floor — awesome and merciless in their fury.

* * *

WE CLOSED THE PERIMETER and powered up the generators. I sent a remote command, activating the modified force shield. Charges of iridescent light sparked about, morphing and acquiring the shape of a flattened dome.

My heart knocked against my chest, counting down the seconds. In the depths of my visor's screen, the fine line of the shield's graph surged with five peaks: five respawn requests.

Respawn denied. Request redirected.

It didn't say where they'd been redirected to. There wasn't a single respawn point left available to the Dargians within the scanners' effective range.

Charon was sitting on the floor, still coming to. He'd had it tough. Not a limb was untouched; his whole suit was covered with a layer of sealing foam pink with his blood.

"Zander!"

I offered him my hand, helping him to his feet. We didn't have a chance to say anything as a plasma charge flared up, casting long ragged shadows all around.

Those of the Haash who'd already armed

themselves rushed toward the barricades.

"Jurgen!" I hurried toward the hall's second exit, also barricaded.

"Zander! What have you got there?" Jurgen's voice reached me through the interference.

"We've blocked the artifact!"

"The Dargians are building up on the other side of the ship! We can't reach them from here!"

"I suppose we'll just have to hold the fort." What else could I say?

"We'll try to attack them from the rear!"

Then his voice died away, swallowed by white noise.

Charon and I took up our positions at the barricade. Three more Haash joined us. Just in time. The squat figures of the Dargians flitted within the corridor's depths. They had nothing left to lose. Five of them were dragging a stationary laser gun. It had to be at least two hundred megs.

Its very first blast made a large smoking hole in the barricade. The slavers charged.

We didn't budge. We met them with intense fire, mowing down the more eager and stupid of them and thwarting their attack. The others shrank back to the walls, seeking cover. The laser struck again, raising a swirling blizzard of ash in the vacuum. One of the Haash collapsed, sliced in two. He could forget respawning.

There was no way we'd last more than a minute under this kind of fire.

I still had the two plasma grenades in my bag, those I'd picked up in Serge's looted shop. "Charon and the others, cover me!"

I switched on the movement coordinator,

simultaneously deactivating my individual gravity generator and marking my future route with a swipe of my eyes: up the walls to the ceiling to reach the wretched laser gun.

Me, I had a lot to lose. I was scared. My reflex enhancer, mind expander and metabolic corrector were all in overdrive.

The Haash opened fire, forcing the Dargians' heads down.

Go!

* * *

RESPAWN

A TOXIC HAZE clouded my view. I was still convulsing, struggling to breathe, as sealing foam filled the holes in my suit.

Ten minutes.

I struggled in my dead suit, trying to get to my feet. Anything could have happened in those ten minutes. Several messages hung on my visor's screen,

You've destroyed the enemy's laser device!
You've received a new level!
You have new Talent and Characteristic points available!
Ability expired: Friend of the Haash.

Why was I alone? The thought jarred me to my senses. "Everybody... report!"

Silence. The angular bodies of the two cargo modules towered at a distance. The door of one of them stood ajar. Overhead, the ceiling was lit up by the Emgles' fiery aura.

I broke out in a cold sweat. Struggling with the suit, I tried to sit up. The Emgles were soaring overhead under the hangar's ceiling.

"Uncle Zander, it's all right!" a child's brittle voice broke into my mind.

"Inge? Where's... everyone? What's going on?"

"It's Emgles, they've come to see us! Everything's so beautiful! They're so nice! And all the adults are gone," the girl's voice betrayed no fear, filled only with curiosity.

"Where are they gone?"

"Over there," the girl pointed at the darkness enveloping the deck. I struggled to make out a Condor's dying glow.

"Uncle Arbido, has he been gone long?" I managed.

"He fell down and he won't get back up," the girl complained.

I forced myself to my feet. Mangled beyond repair, my suit was crippling me. I hurried to change into my old gear.

"Inge," I crouched next to the girl, "where's Uncle Arbido? Show me."

Fear filled her eyes. Immediately both Emgles began to descend. I could feel that if Inge started crying now they would simply torch me, end of story. How on earth had she managed to establish mental contact with alien creatures was yet to be determined. The fact remained, they were trying to protect her.

"Don't worry, sweetheart. I'll go look at him myself. You'd better go and join the other kids, okay?"

She pouted her lips. "It's boring. May I stay here, please?"

Well, I suppose, with guards like these she had nothing to fear. I'd just have to accept what Frieda had told me. The Emgles must have connected to the girl. If they hadn't attacked her yet, she must be safe then.

At least I hoped so.

"Very well, princess. You stay here. Just promise me not to leave this place, okay? I'll be back."

She smiled. My mind was still in combat mode, my anxiety growing. I couldn't contact the others and I had no idea why.

Every moment was precious. I gave the girl an encouraging smile even though she looked perfectly comfortable.

I checked the open module. The other kids were fast asleep.

I walked out. The floor was spotted with green blood. I followed its trail to the landing site.

Arbido lay there on the icy floor, clutching the pulse gun.

At a short distance lay the bodies of three mercs peppered with pulse rounds. I checked their markers, then bent over Arbido and carefully turned him onto his back. The gun's magazine blinked with a red light: empty. His Dargian suit was all dented. I could see at least two breach holes.

Arbido had bled to death, fighting to the last.

Why would these traitors have attempted to take control of the reserve respawn point? It had been available to them all along!

The answer was soberingly evident.

They had wanted to take the children hostage to blackmail me into surrendering the Founders' starship.

Bunch of lowlifes.

But I could only see three bodies there. Whatever had happened to the rest?

I carried Arbido's body to the other cargo module, hoping against all hope that he'd respawn, desperately praying that the agony of dying hadn't scorched his mind.

One of the Emgles glided over me anxiously, listening in to my thoughts, but I didn't sense any emotional reaction coming from it.

I looked around.

The second Emgle had descended, levitating about seven feet off the floor. It then took the shape of a dome, two of its deadly bioenergetic tentacles hanging down like two thick luminous cables clutching a scrap of metal plate. What was that supposed to mean?

I stood there in bewilderment while Inge shrieked with delight on seeing the weird shape. She ran toward it and climbed onto the makeshift seat, grabbing the radiant cables, then started swinging, dangling her legs in the air.

I broke out in a cold sweat. This was a swing! A child's swing!

"Uncle Zander, look! This is so nice!"

I stopped shaking. Could the Emgle dip into the girl's mind? Apparently so, otherwise how else would have it been able to create something as alien to it as a swing?

I felt completely lost. Still, time was an issue. The children were safe now, that little was clear. The mind-reading Emgles wouldn't let any scheming bastard anywhere near the kids, be he human or Dargian. It was a good job I hadn't shown any express fear or aggression.

I just couldn't stay there in suspended animation without contact with anyone. I had to put my trust in these creatures from Wearong. Somehow I didn't think there were any Dargians left in the vicinity capable of controlling them, but even if there were, the intuitive Emgles would just ignore them. Could it be that their mental vibes were already affecting my thoughts?

Go, a silent alien whisper nudged me toward the downed Condor.

* * *

THE RESERVE RESPAWN POINT dissolved in the toxic haze as I ran toward the Condor's dying signature.

A few xenomorphs shrank out of my way. Whatever had attracted them to the ship?

I stopped, catching my breath.

The icy floor was littered with mercs' bodies, each and every one of them awaiting respawning. Killed by a player.

Further away I made out the ship's outline — and four motionless figures next to it, clad in combat gear. Liori and the three guards. The girl sat leaning against her Condor's broken undercarriage. The long trail of an emergency landing stretched across the deck.

I rushed toward her.

She sat in a pool of molten slush and blood littered with empty pulse clips. The three guards I'd left to control the reserve respawn point had fought to the last.

Liori was unconscious but still alive. She'd lost a lot of blood. Her face was ashen.

"Hold on," I injected her with the emergency metabolite supply.

She flinched weakly but didn't regain consciousness. My suit's diagnostic system scanned her biorhythms. Her pulse was weak and uneven, her breathing labored. Her injuries were fatal.

Would she respawn?

No one knew that.

My communication system repeatedly scanned the empty frequencies. Their crackling was doing me in. Where were all the rest?

Liori's eyelids quivered. "Zander," her whisper burned through my mind.

"I'm here," I supported her head, helping her to shift into a more comfortable position.

"The children..."

"They're fine. They're safe. Don't speak. The injection will work in a minute."

"Zander, you must... erase... their respawn marks," she pointed at the mercs' bodies. "They're traitors..." she drifted off.

I still had the reserve device that Jurgen had issued me. I darted back and pulled the gear off the mercs' bodies, destroying their respawn marks. This was the least I could do to these sharks who had tried to use the children as bargaining chips for the ship. If any of them respawned now, they'd share the same fate as the Dargians. I put their nicknames on my personal KOS list. Sooner or later, I was going to find them wherever they respawned.

I hurried back to Liori.

She had momentarily come to. She clenched my hand, her eyes awash with pain and frustration. "Zander. There was so much... I wanted to tell you..."

I sensed that she was trying to send me a mnemonic PM. Why? That would absolutely drain her!

"So much I wanted to... sorry... I was afraid..."

Our mind expanders connected.

Don't speak! Just don't! You need to spare yourself!

She didn't answer. An agonizing haze shifted before my eyes, revealing strange, unknown shapes. I focused. The mental image grew clearer. I recognized the outlines of some machines that looked rather like the in-mode devices. Thousands of them. A low ceiling hung overhead, strewn with cables and pipes that ran to each and every one of the devices.

A bunker? Was it my imagination or had I seen a Haash patrolling the machines?

The image faded, distorting. I didn't have time to take in the details.

"Phantom Server..." I could barely hear her whisper. "You still don't know anything... do you..."

"You can tell me later! Later, when you respawn! Everything is going to be fi-"

"Zander... it does exist..."

Our thoughts were entwined.

"What does?" the question came out before I could stop myself.

"The Server..."

Her fingers clenched in a spasm. "There's no respawn... for me... sorry..."

I stared at her wrist in disbelief. A gun burst had ripped her suit open, destroying the silver mark.

"Wait!" I whipped out the tube I'd received from Jurgen. Too late. Her avatar began to fade.

"Liori!"

"Sorry," her fingers clutched my hand, the unfulfilled life within her eyes.

She was fading, slipping away from me. The yellowed skin of her arm began to glow, outlining the web of veins beneath. I knew this glow. Her skin glistened with a silvery substance that seeped through it, trying to take the shape of a ring and failing. It reached for my fingers and bled onto them, flashing and seeping under my skin.

The back of my head went numb. Liori's shape began to dematerialize.

Then it disappeared, dissolved by the toxic haze.

* * *

I COULDN'T BREATHE.

My heart was exploding.

"I'll find you! I'll come and get you wherever you respawn!"

The same toxic gaze swallowed my outcry.

Both my hands were aglow. I gnashed my teeth, choking on my own tears. The mercs' bodies were fading too now. Two artifacts — two of the Founders' ancient neuronet modules — reached inside me, reshaping me irreversibly. I could see green flashes coming from the respawn point; I could hear the radio spring to life with Arbido's and Frieda's voices and the growling of the respawned Haash. I couldn't speak back. I was paralyzed, my mind plunging into some new dimension.

"Zander," Liori's soft voice reached my mind through the gelatinous silence.

Where was I now?

The pain was gone.

I turned slowly but saw nothing. Gray mist enveloped me, spongy and tangible. It was everywhere, denying direction, harboring something scaringly alien.

"Zander."

I could hear her voice, trying to work out where it was coming from. The gray mist began to seep away, gaining substance, forming objects and facts. My mind kept expanding until I stood on a hard curved surface staring at the close horizon of an artificial celestial body.

A Founders' station?

The hull was dominated by a group of tall structures, their spire-like silhouettes reaching out into space. An unusual design. I'd never seen anything like it. Together they formed a graceful group stretching out to the stars.

"Zander."

I studied the area around me in search of Liori. The station looked undamaged. The surface was of familiar bluish steel, its cargonite blurred and rippled.

This couldn't be happening. My mind was awash with an icy feeling of danger, blurring again until the stars stretched into straight lines — and then disappeared.

The gray mist quivered around me, thickening into rough stone walls.

Once again I stood on a hard surface. My heart beat slowly, the pain in my chest melting slowly.

The air here was cold and thin. Where was my suit? I stepped forward, feeling the roughly chiseled wall. A weak echo reached me. I noticed a dull light ahead.

I walked toward it.

Gradually the walls parted, the light growing brighter. Now I understood. I was inside an asteroid riddled with mine shafts and galleries.

The short tunnel took me outside to a small opening. In the past, it had been used as a landing pad for cargo ships. A few remaining parts of docking mechanisms were broken and powdered with dust.

The landing ended in the ragged edge of an abyss. The cosmos lay beyond.

Where was I? Where was the Founders' station?

"Liori!"

My voice echoed back to me.

No answer. Then the asteroid's rotation brought an enormous technogenic structure into view.

This wasn't a station. This was something much more than that. Its size defied imagination. I could observe a multitude of spired structures pointing into space, their configuration mirroring the outline of the sky's unfamiliar constellations.

This incredible space creation was filled with a silvery mist as if it was wrapped in a gauze of the finest dust.

The mind expander automatically zoomed in on the structure. It focused on one of the specks of silvery dust, bringing its familiar outline into view.

A Phantom Raider?

Billions of them, their serried ranks surrounding the mammoth structure.

Some of the towering structures oscillated with charges of lightning, pulsating each in its own rhythm.

"Server..."

Barely audible, Liori's voice was a mere whisper coming from the depths of the Universe.

Once again the stars blurred to fiery lines and disappeared.

* * *

I SHUDDERED BACK TO LIFE, feeling my body pumped with metabolites.

The place was almost dark. A squat figure clad in a Dargian suit with no helmet nervously shifted from one foot to the other next to me. Further on I could just make out the figures of the Haash hunched up in the small space between the rows of seats haphazardly welded to the cargo container's floor.

My throat was dry, my muscles taut to the point of cramping. My mind expander was in overdrive.

"Arbido," my voice sounded like a croak.

With a startle, he turned to me.

"Can I have a drink?"

He fussed about, ripping open our emergency supply and bringing a plastic flask to my lips.

I struggled to take a couple of gulps. It felt better. "Tell me. How long has it been?"

"Just over an hour. Zander, I thought you'd never come round."

Judging by the smooth acceleration, we must have been in outer space. "Cut the crap, just tell me."

"The Haash have kept the ship," he looked me in the eye as if not daring to ask some important question. "We found you lying next to Liori's ship. You were flat out. We tried to bring you round with some metabolites but they didn't work. Frieda scanned your brain and said you might not get back at all. Zander... is that true about your second neuronet?"

"Yes," I saw no point in keeping it from him. The images still crowded my mind, defying explanation. "Have you found Liori?"

He frowned, shaking his head. "She's gone. No idea

where her respawn point is."

"Give me a hand."

He helped me to my feet. My bulky suit crowded out the small space between the seats, its surface twinkling with electric charges. The built-in repair systems squeaked to life, their thin manipulators snaking around the suit, the breaches gradually filling with a hardening purple substance.

My mind expander kicked in, activating its interface icons. The darkness dispersed. I could see clearly now.

Hanging onto the backs of the seats, I made my way forward to the cockpit. Danezerath hunched himself up in the crowded space, forced to lean forward in a pilot's seat too small for a Haash. Still, you could see he knew how to fly a ship. The makeshift observation window offered a panoramic view of outer space, including the corner of the station with the Founders' starship clinging to it.

The second cargo module was on a parallel course with our own, closely followed by the Emgles.

I could see some strange dots moving amid the station's molten hull structures. Mechanically I zoomed in. The Haash! They were busy towing four of their ships by hand — those that the Dargians had kept on the launch pads. Two of the Condors — one burned and deformed, the other virtually intact — already waited next to the ancient starship's docking pods. Next to them I made out the figures of the surviving mercs.

"Jurgen," I sent him a mnemonic PM.

He didn't sound too happy to hear from me. He was his usual paranoid self. "We need to talk."

"Why, what's the problem?"

"Frieda scanned your brain and she says that the scans showed nothing but the Founders' network activity for at least an hour."

"So what do you suggest? Spit it out."

A flat latticed surface came into my metal view.

"What's this?"

"This is your neurogram," Jurgen answered. "As you can see, not a single spike the whole time. And this," a 3D image replaced it, covered with peaks of activity, "this is the scan of your two neuronet modules. I'm very sorry, but I can't be a hundred percent sure I'm speaking to you and not to some ancient AI."

"I'm fine. It's you who is paranoid."

"That remains to be seen."

"We have no time for all this. Didn't you say that two artifacts weren't enough to form a proper-"

"In this case would you be so kind to explain where your mind has been for the last hour? Frieda is an expert mnemotech. She needs to know what's going on."

"She's very welcome. But not now."

I had a funny feeling I knew where my mind had traveled to. This was something you might find hard to accept but I knew I'd seen those pointy structures in some database or other. They were supposed to be the hyperspace communication devices that the Founders used to transmit their identity matrices from one star system to the other.

And what if everything I'd seen in my unconscious state was more than just a hallucination?

Did that mean I'd seen the Phantom Server? The central juncture of the Founders' network? Or was it the second AI that had uploaded the images to my mind?

My heart twanged with frustration. Liori. I refused to believe she was dead.

The cargo module's landing gear touched down on the station's hull.

* * *

WE DISEMBARKED. The two Condors were already sitting in the docking pods. The surviving Haash stubbornly towed their four craft toward the Founders' starship.

The children looked around in amazement. Then they filed on board the starship, shepherded by Arbido. Judging by the few reports I'd received, they'd already managed to seal several living modules and restored their life support systems.

The ship's reactor functioned at 20%. The power system was intact. As for the rest, the entire scope of the repair works wasn't yet clear.

Four mercs and twelve Haash. That's all the survivors. Those of the Haash who hadn't had their personal marks changed must have respawned too, but we had no idea where.

The ship's corridors were empty. Everything here screamed of a desperate battle. The walls were dented and molten, covered in blood. Many of the cables and much of the pipework had been damaged in the shootout.

I finally found Jurgen in one of the modules of the radar center.

We did need to talk. We needed to set the record straight. This ship could only have one commander. I could understand his suspicions about me being the host to an alien neuronet but so far I didn't feel any intrusion into my personality and I was quite prepared to stand by my conviction.

Restored by the Dargians, the location equipment took up a large hall in its entirety — decompressed but functional. An enormous holographic screen domed overhead, receiving data from the sensors.

Jurgen turned round. "Perfect timing!"

He seemed to have forgotten about our argument, at least for the time being. Whatever had happened now?

Noticing the anxiety in my stare, he pointed at a cluster of dots.

I frowned, unable to read the data. "What's that?"

Jurgen paused. The device nearest to us was blinking with a plethora of multicolored lights, its screens filling with the scrolling lines of the Founders' fancy script.

I peered at them. They formed messages that became perfectly clear to me,

Unidentified signatures detected
Intense radio traffic detected
Decoding in process. Decryption equipment activated

"Number one to flagship. Scanning and orbiting completed. Initial data confirmed. Argus is being controlled by xenomorphs."

"Flagship to number one. Withdraw. We are initiating an attack."

My blood ran cold. I looked up, zooming in on Argus, watching the cluster of sparks heading toward it.

The Eurasia fleet had entered the space of the Darg

system.

We kept scanning and listening in.

"Number seven to flagship. I'm within range. Have completed my approach. The station is abandoned. An unidentified signature detected."

My skin began to crawl: a familiar sensation.

"Penetration scanning completed. Unidentified spacecraft detected. It's docked on the station. Signs of organic life on board detected."

"Who are they?"

"I'm not sure, Sir. The signals are mixed. It looks like the ship's crew is made of both humans and xenomorphs."

"They have to be Outlaws. They did warn us about them back on Earth, didn't they? Number seven, forward their coordinates to the assault group."

They meant us.

Should we contact them, should we try to explain? Pointless. They thought this was a game. For us, this was life.

I wasn't quite prepared to drop to my knees and plead for mercy, sacrificing the Haash in the hope of saving our bacon.

Jurgen was pale. He looked lost.

"Remove the engines' governors!" I barked. "Increase reactor power!"

"Zander, you can't-" his voice was rife with emotion. He knew what I was going to do.

"I can and I will."

No time to ponder the alternatives. Once again we'd been thrown into the thick of it. We were under attack — so basically, we had no choice. It was either do or die.

* * *

THE ENTRANCE TO THE FOUNDERS' cockpit was blocked by the iridescent shimmer of a power field. As I approached, it disappeared.

The room was small, with only three antigravity pilot's seats installed. But then... that was funny. The seats actually fit human anatomy. Now why would the Dargians have installed them if they were so apparently big for them?

Later. I had no time for it now.

I took the first pilot's seat. Triggered by the seat sensors' signals, holographic screens sprang to life. Astronavigational control columns hung with assorted devices softly rose out of the deck.

The Founders' starships used to be controlled by AIs: a big problem which the Dargians had failed to solve. I connected to the ship's network and its external sensors, scanning both hemispheres. All I did so, it made me realize that although I had access to all of the ship's subsystems, together they created an incredibly complex web that lacked a nucleus.

Their controls were like nothing I'd seen before. I reached for the spongy joysticks. My mind expander was working flat out. I saw the two Emgles that hastened to come down, covering two large holes in the ship's hull with their bodies.

My breathing sped up. Hundreds of devices were trying to connect to my mind, mistaking me for the system's brain.

Steady, Zander.

I disconnected from everything I didn't need, leaving only the engine control, navigation, weapons and shields.

The palms of my hands became sweaty in the gloves, my fingers somehow sensing the thrust triggers. My mind plunged into digispace.

Please don't let me down, I addressed the two ancient neuronet modules within me. The tingling sensation turned to intense heat as both artifacts took control over from me. My mind blurred, then came back with amazing clarity.

Data began streaming through my mind. Now I could feel all of the ship's subsystems as part of my own body. No idea how long it was going to last though.

"Zander, the engines are ungoverned. Charon and I are coming."

"No. Stay where you are. Distribute the subsystems between yourselves and control them from the reserve positions."

* * *

THE EURASIAN FIGHTERS were getting closer. Their pilots had switched to encrypted channels, but the Founders' deciphering module decoded their messages in no time.

"Number seven to flagship. The enemy craft has changed its signature and is preparing to launch."

"Attack it. Disable its shields. Destroy its engines. Do whatever it takes but don't let it escape. The assault group is one light minute away."

The swarm of bright dots split up. Twenty of them — the new improved versions of Condors — came for us.

Our reactors were at 50%. Plasma-forming had commenced in their working zone. My docking pylons

— yes, *mine*, that's exactly how I felt it — grappled the station's hull.

It shuddered from impacts.

"We're under attack!"

"All posts be prepared!"

The ship's shields were throbbing. I activated the space defense systems. The upper hemisphere weapons opened up with automatic fire. The assault group was heading straight for us, trying an attacking pass but unable to break through our barrage fire. We shot down three of the Condors; the others turned back and resumed scanning, seeking for gaps in our defense.

The ship shuddered again. The station didn't want to let us go. Some of the millennia-old docking pylons had jammed.

I activated the lower thrusters. The unyielding docking pylons crunched under pressure. A few of them ripped out of the station's hull together with some of its superstructure. The starship listed to one side as it took off followed by a trail of debris, but its body was intact, its shields still absorbing the impacts, the upper hemisphere turrets chattering away.

The station's surface dipped sharply downwards.

I maneuvered slowly. Stars drifted by the observation window. My stare, supported by the location sensors, focused on the asteroid belt.

I became engulfed in the throbbing aura of power fields. Deep space was my natural environment.

I was millions of years old.

The cruise thrusters kicked in. It felt like a miraculous liberation from an age-long captivity.

My mind kept changing, remolding. No idea what

kind of creature I'd be once this was over.

The Founders' station opened up to my mental eye, dull and static apart from one particular location signaling an anomaly.

I concentrated. My heart missed a beat. About seventy miles away from the launch pad, the ship's sensors detected a familiar power imprint.

An active respawn point.

The engines throbbed powerfully and monotonously, continuing to accelerate. The remaining five enemy ships dared not pursue us.

The scanning sphere was pockmarked with pale dots, but the assault group was unlikely to catch up with us. Our star pilgrim was way out of their league.

I made out thick clusters of rocks up ahead. Beyond them lay the Universe — the untraveled void of outer space.

I accelerated. The G-force absorbers kept the crew safe as the ship covered millions of miles within minutes. The sheer power of this mammoth was beyond anything I could have ever imagined.

I carefully decelerated as the ship immersed into the asteroid belt — the domain of the Outlaws.

It calculated its course while I maneuvered amid clumps of enormous boulders that closed back up behind me, shield-like.

My temples were throbbing. There was no one pursuing us anymore.

My strength was dwindling quickly. These past few minutes felt like a whole new life. I directed the ship toward a family of asteroids and synchronized my speed with their orbital parameters.

I killed the engines. We were coasting through a thick mass of space boulders.

My mind felt as if it had been re-fused. The ship's sensors focused my stare, searching for the barely discernible glint of the Founders' station.

My caked lips whispered, "Liori, hold on. I'm coming."

* * *

JURGEN, ARBIDO AND CHARON were waiting for me next to the docking module.

Jurgen tried to step in my way. "Where d'you think you're going?"

I shoved him aside. "I'm taking a Condor. I'm going to get Liori."

"You can't take it anywhere without the activation code!"

I didn't answer. I opened the hatch. The Founders' neuronet modules in my body were sure to override any code.

"Zander, wait! You can't do it!"

Why did he need to interfere? Didn't he understand that every second was precious?

I swung round, clenching my teeth. "You seem to have forgotten all about Gehenna."

"No," he locked my eyes with his angry, determined stare. "Zander, please. Keep your hair on. Ralph has the code. It's his Condor. It'll only take seconds. In fact, I might go instead. I can do it just as well as you, trust me."

"This is nothing to do with you. This is about me."

"But Zander, what if you don't come back? Do you expect us to keep drifting? Waiting for the Outlaws to arrive? You're the only person who can fly this thing, don't forget!"

His words barely reached me through a fog of raging emotion. My mind was still metamorphing. On one hand, I sensed myself being the nucleus of this enormous starship but on the other, this sensation faded under the pressure of all the reviving human emotions.

Arbido pulled my hand. "He's right."

I glared back at him. "So do you suggest I should stay here and leave her there to die?"

"Jurgen's right," Arbido insisted. "You're our commander. If you hack the Condor, the mercs are sure to misinterpret it. You might just as well fit them with slaves' collars. This doesn't give you the right to do whatever you want. You need to do it properly."

"Right. Where's Ralph?"

"He's right over there, fixing some pipes," Jurgen said. "But please, Zander, think about it. Liori must be dead, otherwise her implant wouldn't have changed its host. It transferred part of her identity to you and is now trying to nudge you into action!"

His arguments ripped my heart apart. If anything, they forced my hand. "Liori might have given it to me of her own free will," I paused and added sharply, "Jurgen, your job is to restore the ship's systems. So that's what you should be doing. I'll be back. Don't ever doubt that."

"Charon, you tell him!"

The Haash cast Jurgen a grim look. "He's going," he growled. "I'm going with him, too."

"You're both nuts!"

I was about to explode. The memory of Liori put my mind in meltdown. Her desperate eyes full of longing for an unfulfilled life were burning though my brain.

I turned to Charon. "You're staying with them.

There isn't enough room for the two of us in the Condor's cockpit."

"I can go in the cargo module."

"No, you don't." The plan was ready in my mind. I was pretty sure that the respawn point I'd seen on the screen was used not only by the Dargians and the treacherous mercs, but also by those of the Haash who hadn't received their personal markers. The Condor's cargo hold was their only chance of survival.

I had no time to argue with him so I PM'd him some mental images. He might grasp their significance faster than words.

Jurgen shook his head as he watched me leave.

I found Ralph almost straight away, directed by the flashes of his plasma torch and the acrid smoke filling the corridor.

The life support pipework, damaged during the ancient battle, now gleamed with fresh patches. I touched the man's shoulder, attracting his attention.

"I need your ship."

"You gonna bring it back?"

I knew what he must have been thinking. His ship was his most treasured possession. I was pretty sure he'd maxed it out to the limit, making it truly unique, otherwise the ship would never have survived its encounter with the Emgles. A merc's Condor was a guarantee of his or her freedom — survival even. But this was the only functional one left. Besides, after our successful escape attempt the Dargians had removed all of the reactor controls from the Haash' ships and we had no idea how long it might take us to restore them.

Without saying a word, I offered him the slim box still lined with the same spongy substance and containing all of the Founders' unexplored software I'd looted in Gehenna and whatever cyber devices I'd ripped out of the drones there.

I threw in a dozen neurochips I'd seized during the recent fight with the Dargians. Both of us knew that the Phantom Server's economy had collapsed, but at least this kind of currency was still acceptable.

Ralph scanned the box's contents, considered all the alternatives and gave a reluctant nod, appreciating my gesture. "Here," he handed me the code. "It's yours for the time being. I might buy it back off you if I get the chance."

* * *

I SOON LOST THE FOUNDERS' starship from view. To find it among all the clusters of asteroids without knowing its exact coordinates would be totally unrealistic.

I began an approach maneuver on the station. My pilot's instincts uploaded with the reflex enhancer had allowed me to master the Condor's controls in no time. This ship was well and truly unique. With its beefed-up engines, enlarged holds, powerful shields and a well-conceived weapon configuration, it was nothing like the standard factory-issue Condor.

All this flashed through my focused, strung-out mind as it continued scanning the area.

A thick group of bright dots was moving through space: the Eurasia fleet. Argus was surrounded by a shimmering cloud: there, the battle was raging, the Second Colonial Fleet's avant-garde confronting the Dargians within the station's orbit. They seemed to be losing at the time: if you maxed out the zoom you could see the station's defense systems working, preventing the attackers from launching any assault groups.

The abandoned Founders' station seemed quiet. I scanned the frequencies, listening in on the Eurasia's conversations. All their attention was on the battle for Argus which would decide the fate of this world.

I was too tired to look into everything that had happened in less than twenty-four hours of gaming time. My nerves were burning out. The station loomed rapidly into view. The respawn point I'd discovered earlier continued flashing its bright round marker.

The only thing I wanted now was to snatch Liori and the remaining Haash from the never-ending circle of inhuman torture. If I could just look her in the eye and see the pain dissipate, I wouldn't want for anything else.

I initiated the maneuver with the station. At first, the numerous hull structures seemed to blur into endless lines on the screens; then their rapid rotation slowed down, breaking them up into separate groups of ruins. I kept descending, passing through their ragged summits until the ship's docking pylons caressed the hull.

The target respawn point was 450 feet away. It must have been located in one of the burned-out modules of the primary hull. My suit's sensors registered its signature. The navigation system busied itself plotting the route.

I had a couple of repair robots in my inventory as well as some spare parts for the suit, batteries and life support cartridges. I got out and activated the movement coordinator in order to reach the nearest hole in the station's hull. Below it lay the opening of an ancient tunnel.

Far ahead, I could make out some weak flashes of green light. Mechanically I quickened my pace, grateful for the individual gravity generator which allowed me to move freely.

The flashes grew brighter and closer but I couldn't see their source yet from behind the deformed bulkheads. To add to it, the collapsed hull with its spars and depleted armor hung down overhead. Vacuum reigned here.

I headed for the light, making my way through the destroyed rooms. Then I froze on the spot. My heart missed a beat.

The respawn point.

A new green flash materialized a Dargian in a decompressed suit. Immediately he dropped to the ground, his avatar fading. Two Haash followed. They managed to run a few paces more, with identical results. The vacuum and the cosmic cold left them no chance.

New flashes kept coming. I kept the power shield at the ready.

Liori, where the hell are you?

Suddenly the brief succession of reincarnations stopped, submerging the crumbling deck into darkness.

What was that now? I switched over to the sensors, my stare searching for the already-familiar icon and activating it.

Scan the respawn point equipment.

The deck's floor revealed the outlines of cables and pipework. As far as I knew, everything was in perfect working order.

The movement detector pinged anxiously.

Several figures clad in high tech suits similar to mine stepped out of the darkness. Outlaws. About twenty of them, closing in on me.

I still could fight my way through.

"Not so fast, Zander," the voice definitely sounded familiar. "You've got nowhere to run."

I recognized him, of course. "Jyrd? What's up?" I turned round slowly, playing for time while trying to decide on which direction was best to fight through. "Why has the respawning stopped? Is it you controlling it?" I invested all my sarcasm and disbelief into the last phrase.

He stepped toward me. "You can't control the Founders' machines," he answered calmly, ignoring my quip. "You can use the Founders' neuronet implants though to switch them on or off. Like when you need to attract someone's attention," he grinned.

"You're lying. I've just seen some Dargians and Haash resurrect here."

'Holographic artwork," he replied nonchalantly. "Let's get to the point. I'm sorry but you've stolen my ship, man. You'll have to give it back."

"I didn't steal it. We won it in battle."

"The Dargians worked for *me*!" he snapped, losing his patience. "I was surprised, I have to admit, when you managed to fly it. I want its coordinates. Where is it?"

They hadn't managed to trace its course, great.

My friends were waiting for me there. There was no way I was going to hand them over to the Outlaws.

Jyrd seemed to realize that. "If you don't tell us now, your neural AIs will," his voice was rife with menace. "You know very well what happens when someone dies without a respawn point available. Their bodies reject the artifacts. All I'll do, I'll pick them up from your dead body and absorb them."

I threw my both arms up in the air, pointing the integrated guns at him. They didn't work. The servomotors were dead.

"Good try," he walked over to me, fearing nothing anymore. "For future reference: I was the founder of the Technologists' Clan. I developed much of its equipment personally. Jurgen doesn't know everything," he added confidentially. "Every armored suit has a secret remote control module. Here, look."

My helmet's visor lit up with a system message,

Maintenance mode initiated. Time until decompression: 60 seconds.

The message blinked and went out.

"I have to admit, Zander, you're a bit of a dark horse. You have potential. Apparently you can fly the Founders' ship and this is a very valuable skill. Also, neural AIs have their own fragmented personalities, so to speak. They're very choosy who they work with. It's funny how your worst enemy can become a friend sometimes," he added. "But Jurgen painted us in a very bad light and you believed him, didn't you?"

"Why, was he wrong?"

"It all depends on your point of view. Jurgen is a wuss. He bought into this world's authenticity forgetting who he used to be. We haven't."

"So what do you want?" I asked. "To bring the Logout button back? You want to escape? Then why would you need the ship or the artifacts? What's the point using the Founders' stuff? Go cap in hand to the Admins and see if they succumb to your pleas."

He smirked. "Do you really think they can do it? What if you're mistaken and they're but pawns in somebody else's game? Has Liori told you anything at all about the Founders' network?"

"Is she alive?"

"You bet she is," he said with disdain. "Once you give me the ship's coordinates, you can have everything you want."

"No. Sorry."

"Whatever," he shrugged. "I might be back after the first thirty respawns or so. To give you a moment to think. Trust me, that's plenty of time to reconsider."

He swung round and walked away. The others followed. My suit was still dead.

I was enveloped by darkness, my heavy breathing the only sound in the cosmic silence.

Images from the neural AIs flooded my mind, blending.

I could see the Haash resting in life support capsules not unlike our in-mode ones.

I could see the Phantom Server. Still, I didn't believe Jyrd. This was a game, a familiar world that followed a well-programmed set of gaming rules.

He'd been trying to deceive and confuse me. You couldn't create a game using a real-world hyperspatial network.

He'd been lying — trying to trick me into betraying the ship's location. As simple as that.

Once again the visor lit up with the spiteful warning,

Maintenance mode initiated. Time until

decompression: 60 seconds.

Jyrd knew what he was doing. The events of the last few days flashed through my mind. Both neural AIs sprang back to life.

Time until decompression: 60 seconds
                              59 seconds
                              58 seconds
                              57 seconds...

— End of Book One —

ANNEX

The MC's stats as of the first book's end:

Zander. Outlaw. Level 20. Pilot.

Intellect, 7pt. (+1 bonus from the Semantic Processor)

Strength, 7 pt.

Willpower, 7 pt. (mind expander installation conditions met)

Agility, 5 pt.

Perception, 5 pt (+2 bonus from the semantic processor)

Stamina, 5pt.

Learning Skills, 7pt. (mind expander installation conditions met)

Skills:

Piloting of Small Spacecraft
Piloting of Medium and Large Spacecraft
Combat Maneuvering
Repairs

Alien Technologies
Combat Skills
Navigation
Unique abilities:

Friend of the Haash.
+1 to all characteristics every time the character fights alongside the Haash.

Berserk
Whenever Zander fights unarmed with less than 5% Health, he is able to ignore the enemy's defenses, dealing only critical damage.

The sight of him terrifies all creatures under level 20. They flee, unable to attack him.

Robot Technician
+10% to damage dealt to all machines.

Implants installed:

Semantic processor (Dargian configuration)
Mind expander SynapsZ Universal (by Neurus Corporation)
Reflex enhancer (a one-of-a-kind working model developed by the Technologists Clan)
Metabolic corrector: Xenus Universal (by Xenus Corporation)
The Founders' AI neuronet: two modules

Quests yet to be completed:

Phantom Server 1. The Mystery of Hyperspace

Immortal Hardware
Alien Mind

ALSO BY ANDREI LIVADNY:

The Outlaw (Phantom Server Book #2)

The Eurasia fleet has entered the Darg star system. The unsuspecting players look forward to the adventure of their lifetimes. Zander alone is now facing a harsh and unpredictable "alternative storyline".

The girl he loved is gone. His nervous system is impregnated with artificial neurons that contain fragments of ancient AIs and their identities. Zander's body is implanted with alien artifacts that allow him to survive in the deadly cyberspace of Phantom Server. But his unique development branch pushes him toward the edge of the precipice where his every step may become his last; where future itself is vague and uncertain.

Black Sun (Phantom Server Book #3)

Zander and his gamer friends used to face danger without fear, finding strength in the promise of a safe respawn. Nothing could harm or destroy them. This was only a game... or was it?

A game, played in an ancient hyperspace network. A game involving dozens of real-life alien civilizations.Earth is deserted. The fate of humanity is unknown.

The few human survivors are now stuck in the Darg star system. All they can do is fight to the last. They must find the Phantom Server - the nucleus of the interstellar network created by the ancient civilization of the Founders. In order to live, they must solve its mystery or die trying.

The Island of Hope

An intergalactic war has scorched dozens of planets and destroyed millions of lives, leaving in its wake dead carcasses of drifting spacecraft where desperate battles used to unfold. These are perilous places unfit for habitation... or are they?

About the Author

Andrei Livadny is a popular Russian science fiction author. Born on May 27 1969 in the city of Pskov, he was an avid reader from an early age. But it was the Russian translation of Robert A. Heinlein's *The Orphans of the Sky* that decided his choice of future occupation. The story has become a pivotal moment in the boy's life, leaving a lasting impression on him.

Andrei wrote his first book at the age of eight. Since then, he's never stopped working on new books. His passion for science fiction has gradually become his career.

In 1998, Andrei debuted in Russia's leading publishing house EKSMO with his novella *The Island of Hope*. Since then, he has penned over 90 books that have enjoyed a total of 153 editions.

Andrei has created several unique worlds, each unlike the previous. He wrote *A History of Our Galaxy* with humanity itself as a protagonist. This sixty-book series creates a history of our future civilization and its contacts with alien races, forming a convincing and logical picture of humanity's development for two millennia from now.

Besides hard science fiction, Andrei Livadny also works in cyberpunk genres which allow him to focus on human relationships and raise questions about artificial intelligence and identity uploading, describing cyberspace as humanity's future environment.

The English translation of *A History of Our Galaxy* will be available shortly.

Want to be the first to know about our latest LitRPG, sci fi and fantasy titles from your favorite authors?

Subscribe to our **NEW RELEASES** newsletter:
http://eepurl.com/b7niIL

Thank you for reading *Edge of Reality!*
If you like what you've read, check out other LitRPG
novels published by Magic Dome Books:

Dark Paladin LitRPG series by Vasily Mahanenko:
The Beginning
The Quest

**The Dark Herbalist LitRPG series
by Michael Atamanov:**
Video Game Plotline Tester
Stay on the Wing

The Neuro LitRPG series by Andrei Livadny:
The Crystal Sphere
The Curse of Rion Castle

**The Way of the Shaman LitRPG series
by Vasily Mahanenko:**
Survival Quest
The Kartoss Gambit
The Secret of the Dark Forest
The Phantom Castle
The Karmadont Chess Set
The Hour of Pain (a bonus short story)

Galactogon LitRPG series by Vasily Mahanenko:
Start the Game!

Phantom Server LitRPG series by Andrei Livadny:
Edge of Reality
The Outlaw
Black Sun

**Perimeter Defense LitRPG series by Michael
Atamanov:**
Sector Eight
Beyond Death
New Contract

In order to have new books of the series translated faster, we need your help and support! Please consider leaving a review or spread the word by recommending *Edge of Reality* to your friends and posting the link on social media. The more people buy the book, the sooner we'll be able to make new translations available.

Thank you!

Till next time!

www.ingramcontent.com/pod-product-compliance
Lightning Source LLC
Chambersburg PA
CBHW071647260626
47170CB00001B/269